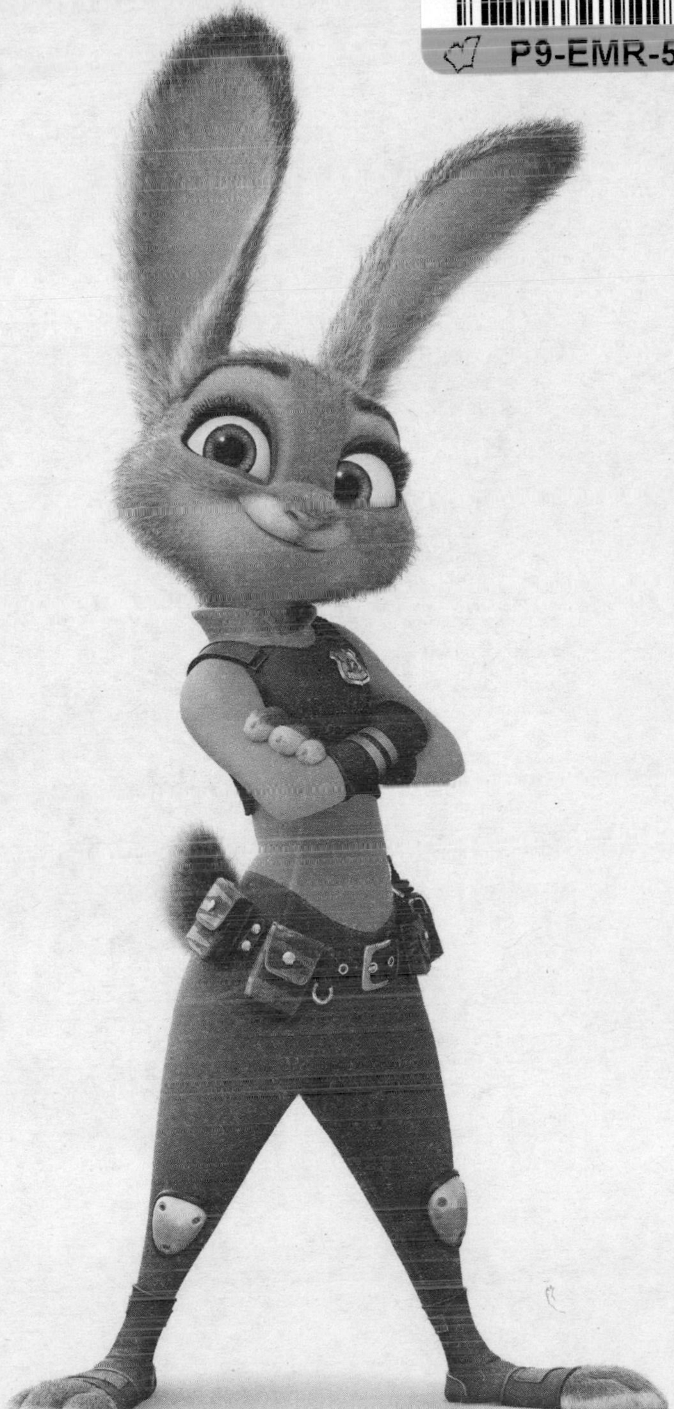

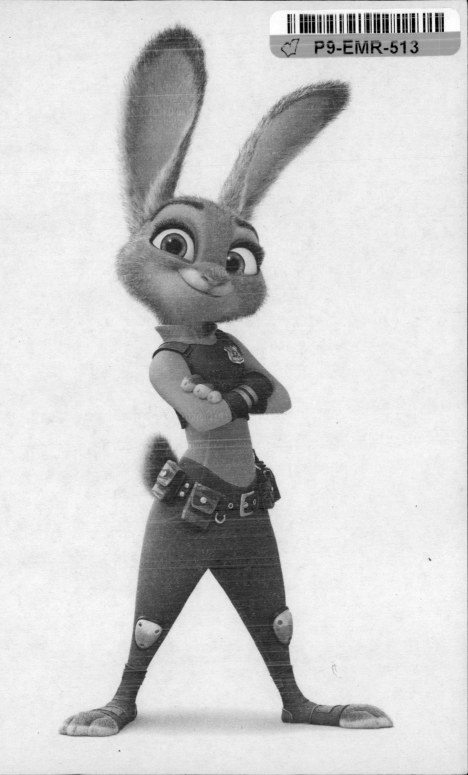

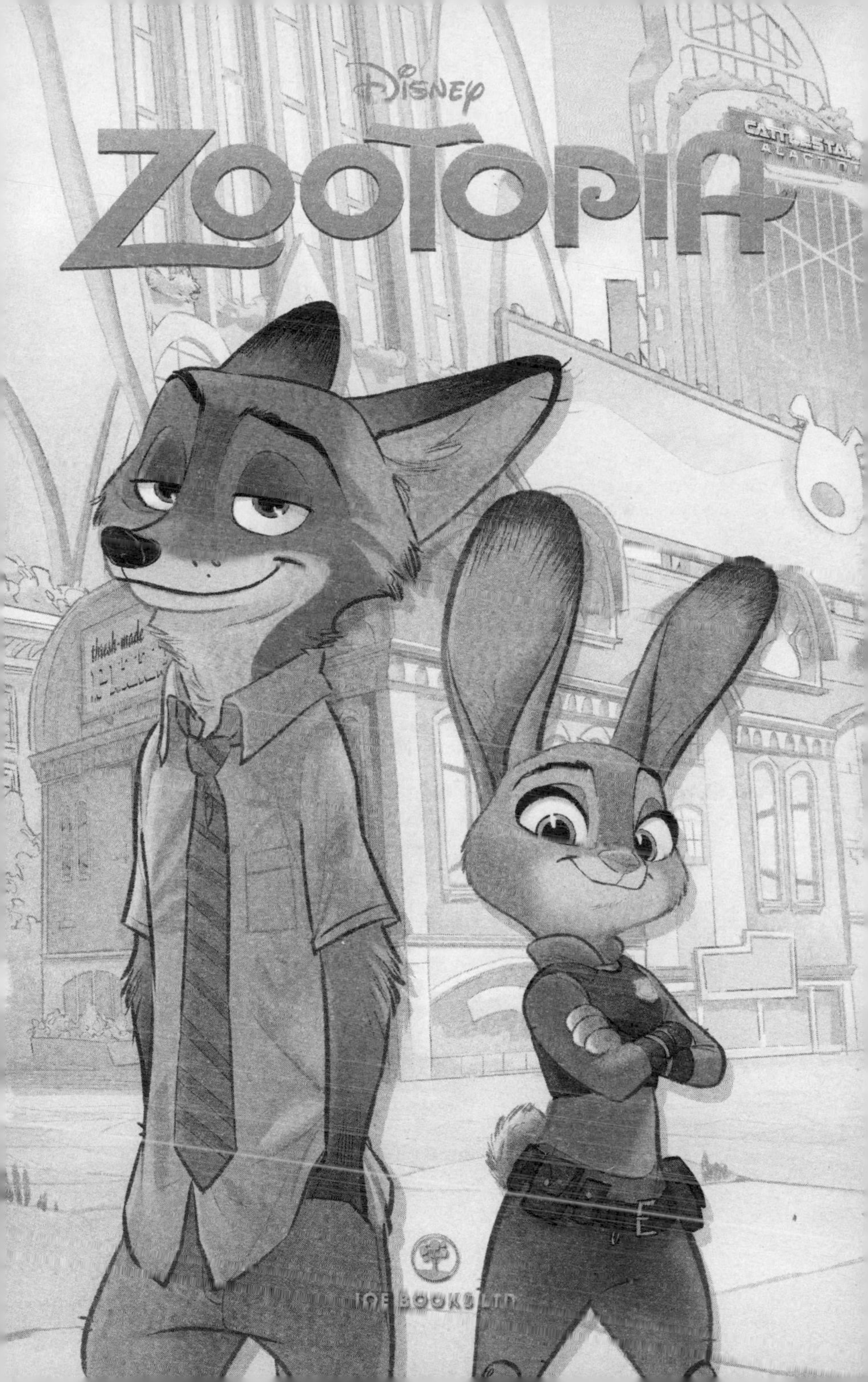
Disney
Zootopia
JOE BOOKS LTD

Published simultaneously in the United States and Canada by Joe Books Ltd,
489 College Street, Suite 203, Toronto, Ontario, M6G 1A5

www.joebooks.com

First Joe Books Edition: September 2016

print ISBN: 978-1-77275-177-2
eISBN: 978-1-77275-293-9

Library and Archives Canada Cataloguing in Publication
information is available upon request

Printed and bound in the United States
1 3 5 7 9 10 8 6 4 2

Disney Publishing Worldwide Global Magazines, Comics and Partworks

VICE PRESIDENT,
GLOBAL MAGAZINES AND NEW IP
Gianfranco Cordara

EXECUTIVE EDITOR
Carlotta Quattrocolo

EDITORIAL TEAM
Bianca Coletti (Director, Magazines),
Guido Frazzini (Director, Comics),
Stefano Ambrosio (Executive Editor, New IP),
Camilla Vedove (Senior Manager, Editorial Development),
Behnoosh Khalili (Senior Editor),
Julie Dorris (Senior Editor - Project Lead),
Megan Adams (Associate Editor),
Manny Mederos (Comics and Magazines Creative Manager)

DESIGN
Enrico Soave (Senior Design)

ART
Ken Shue (VP, Global Art),
Roberto Santillo (Creative Director),
Marco Ghiglione (Creative Manager),
Stefano Attardi (Computer Art Designer)

PORTFOLIO MANAGEMENT
Olivia Ciancarelli (Director)

BUSINESS & MARKETING
Mariantonietta Galla (Marketing Manager), Virpi Korhonen (Editorial Manager),
Kristen Ginter (Publishing Coordinator)

GRAPHIC DESIGN & EDITORIAL
co·d S.r.l. – Milano

SPECIAL THANKS
Jessica Julius, Laura Hitchcock,
Cory Loftis, Matthias Lechner,
Dave Goetz, Albert Ramirez, Stevi Carter,
Jeff Clark, Shiho Tilley, Renato Lattanzi,
Chris Troise, Heather Knowles,
Jared Bush, Clark Spencer

FOR JOE BOOKS
Adam Fortier (Editor)
Rachel Gluckstern (Editorial Content Writer)

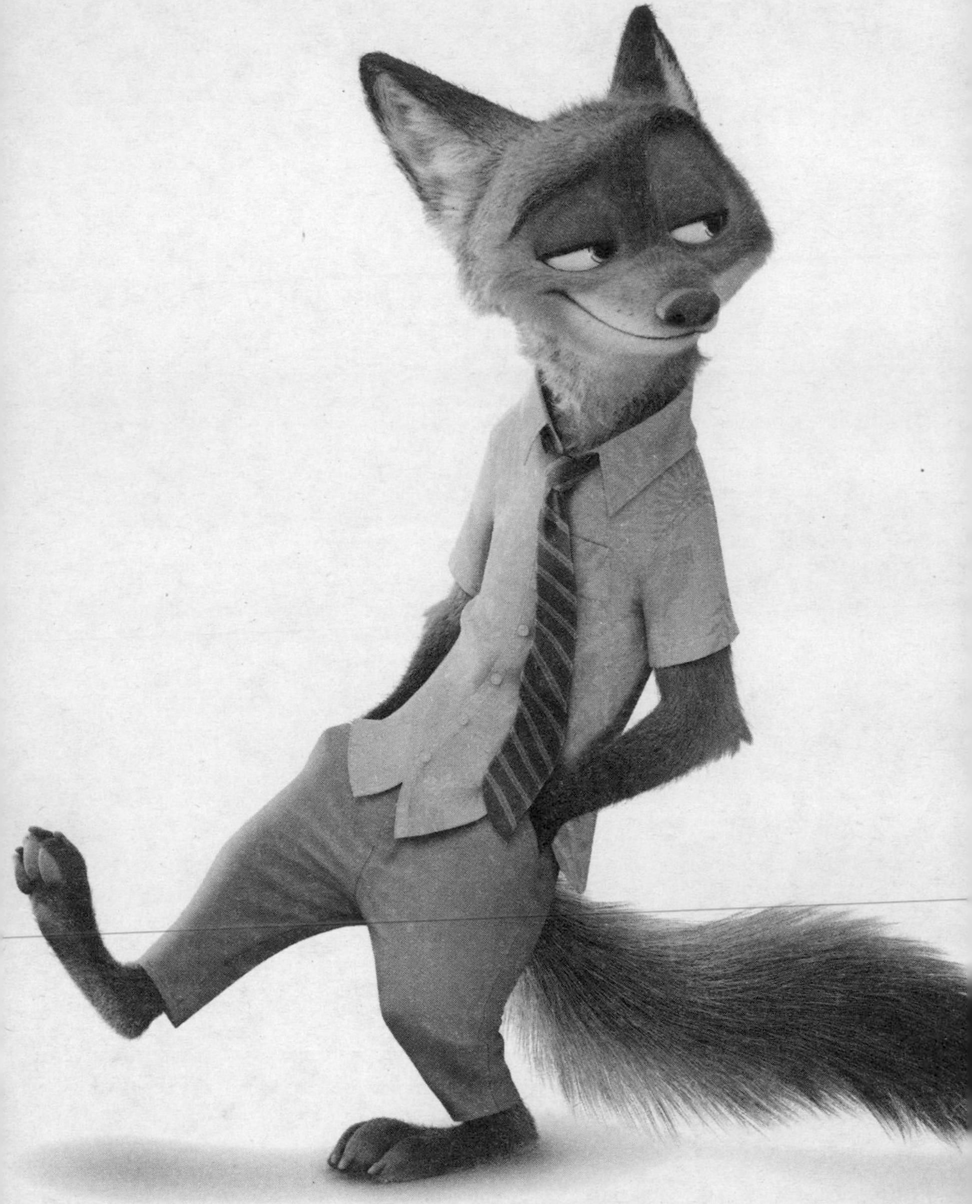

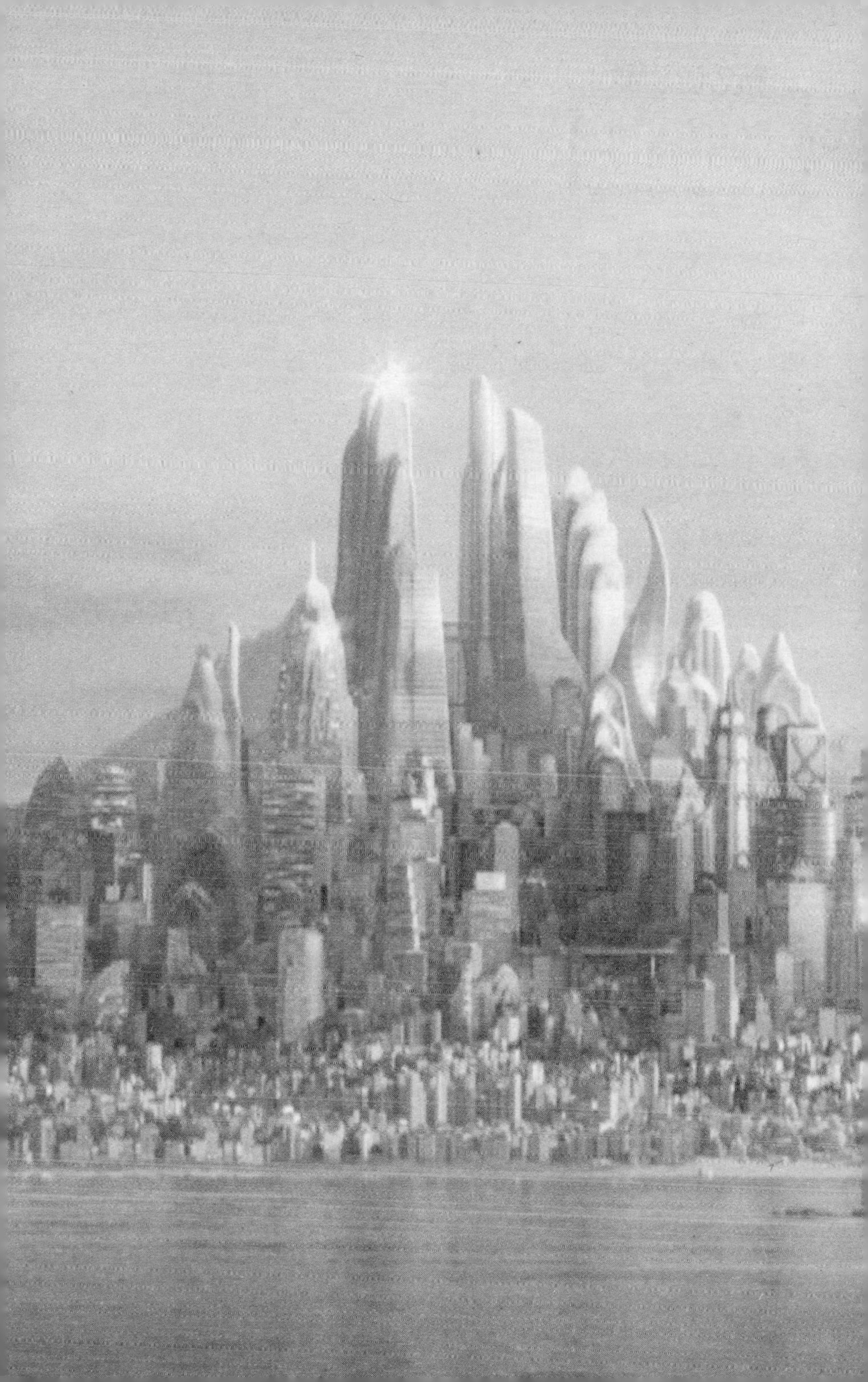

ZOOTOPIA

CONTENTS

COMICS

CINESTORY COMICS

MEET THE CHARACTERS

EXPLORE THE CITY

OFFICIAL ZPD BUSINESS

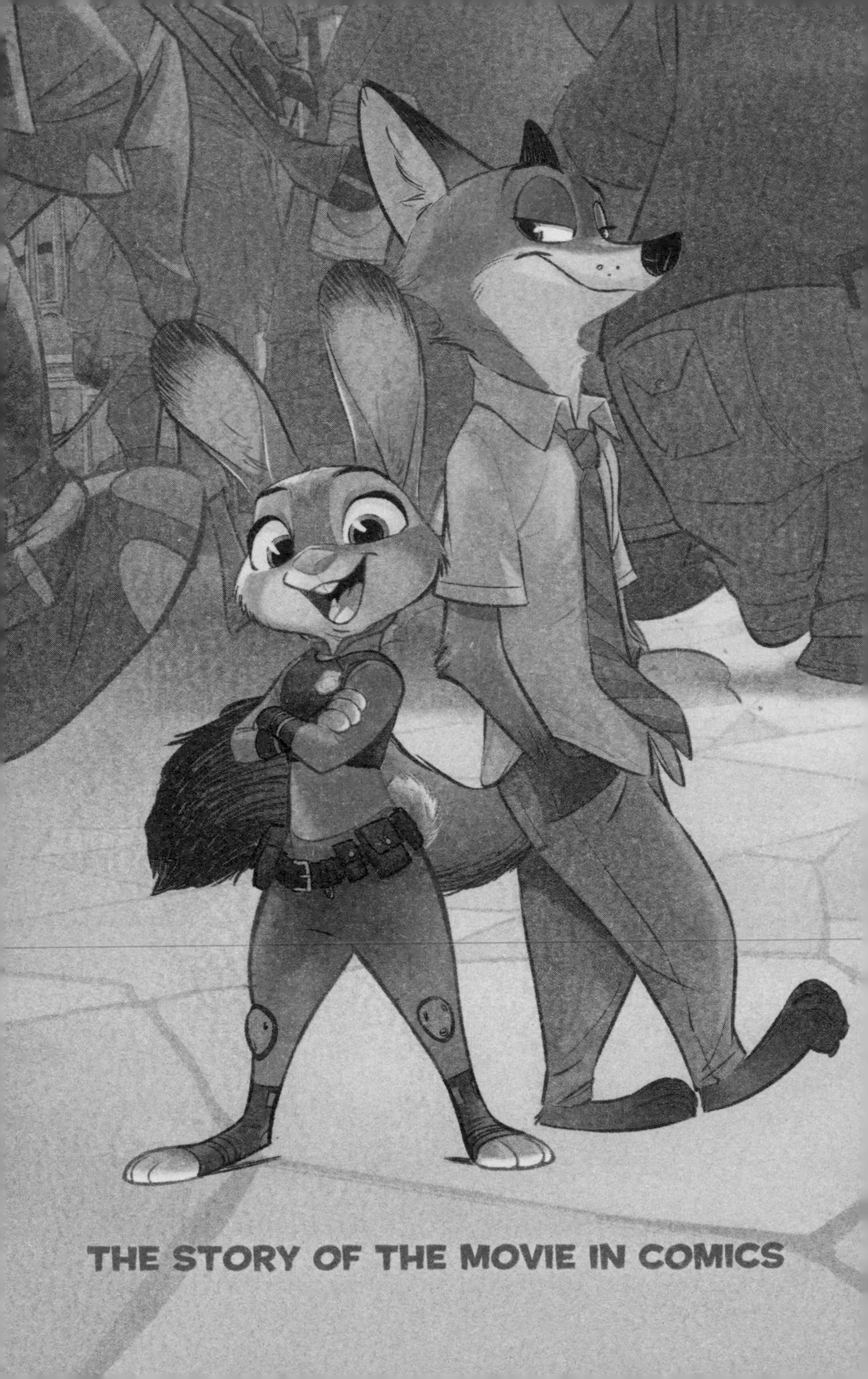

THE STORY OF THE MOVIE IN COMICS

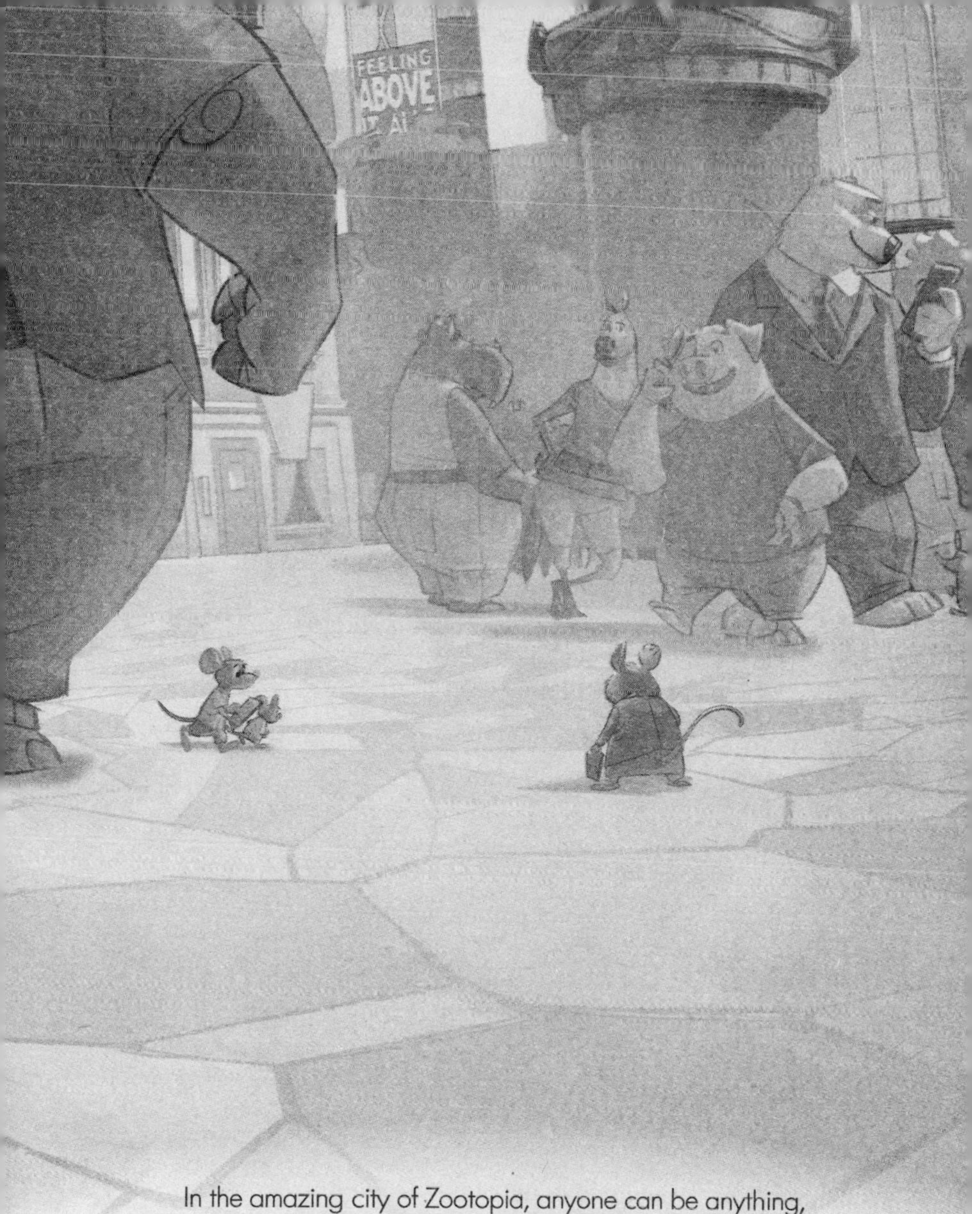
FEELING
ABOVE

In the amazing city of Zootopia, anyone can be anything, though it's not always easy. Judy Hopps accomplishes her dream of becoming a cop, but she ends up on a police force with buffalo, lions, rhinos, polar bears and elephants. When she gets the chance to work on a real case, she knows she has to prove herself. The problem is, she needs the help of a fast-talking, scam-artist fox called Nick Wilde. But can a rabbit really trust a fox?

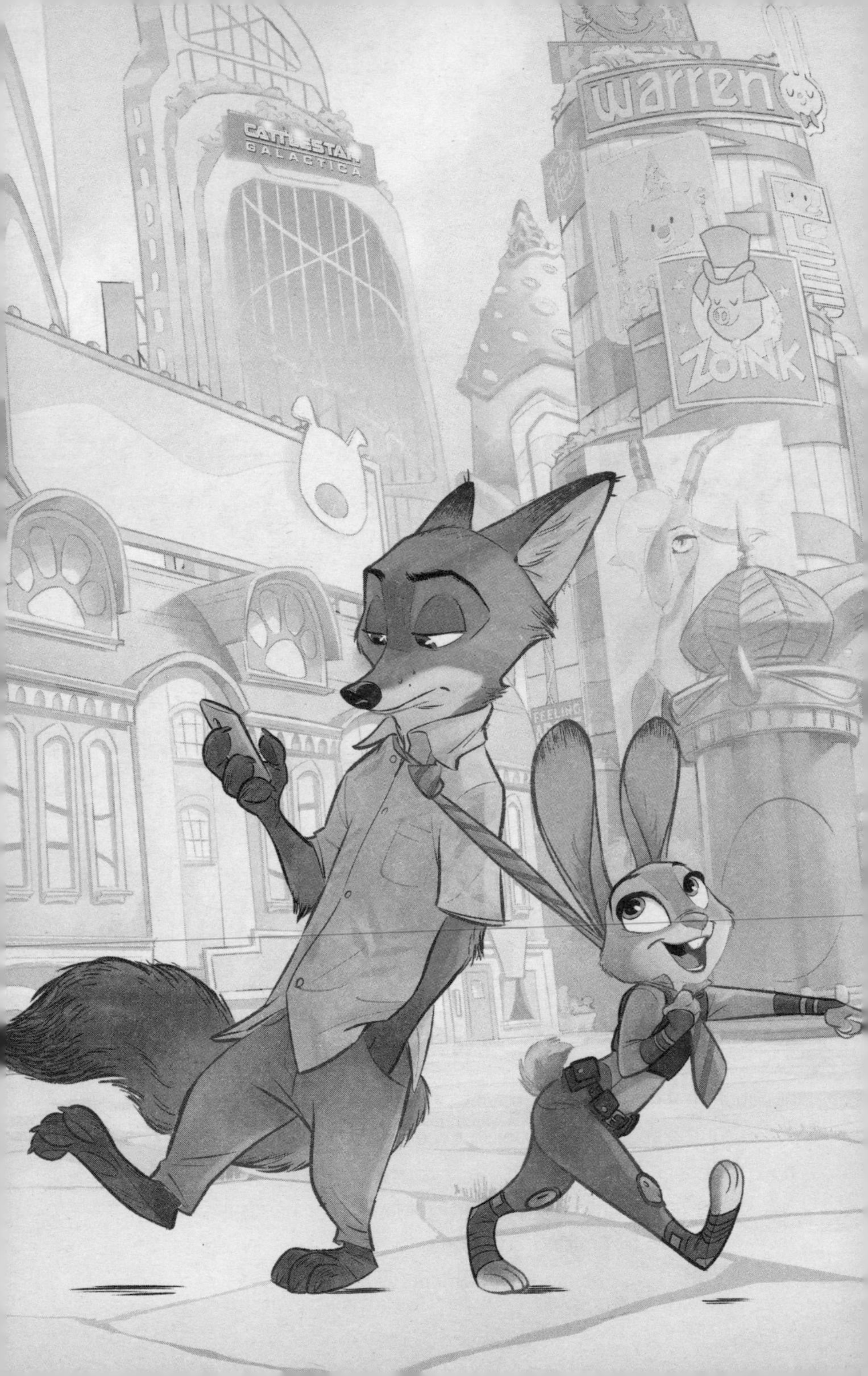
CATTLESTAR GALACTICA
warren
ZOINK
FEELING

JUDY HOPPS

It's me! An idealistic, optimistic and extremely resolute bunny! There are three things you must know about me: never call me cute, never call me dumb bunny, never underestimate me.

My dream? I've come to Zootopia to become a ZPD officer. There's never been a rabbit cop before, so I know it won't be easy. But I will persist in pursuing my dream, because in Zootopia anyone can be anything, right? Right!

Read on to know all about my fellow Zootopians...

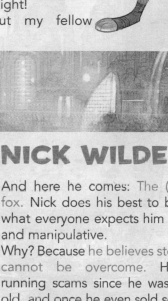

NICK WILDE

And here he comes: The (in)famous fox. Nick does his best to be exactly what everyone expects him to be: Sly and manipulative.

Why? Because he believes stereotypes cannot be overcome. He's been running scams since he was 12 years old, and once he even sold someone a very expensive wool rug made from the fur of a skunk's butt!

To him I'm just a dumb bunny and he thinks I will never become a real cop. Don't tell him, but I'm pretty sure he's wrong.

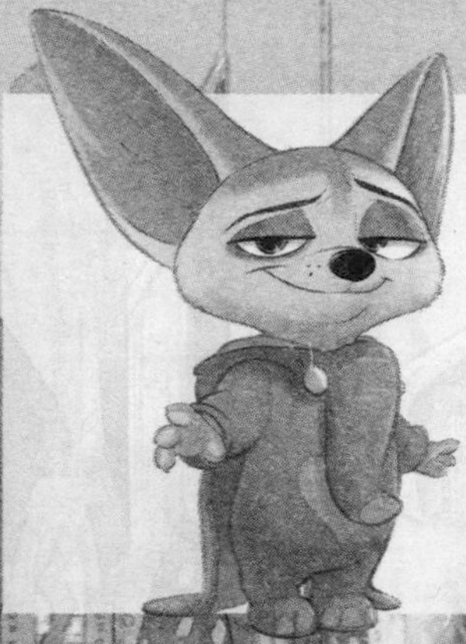

FINNICK

Finnick is a three-pound fennec fox and Nick's partner in crime. Thanks to his small size he can easily pass for a small, sweet toddler… As long as he doesn't use his super-deep voice!

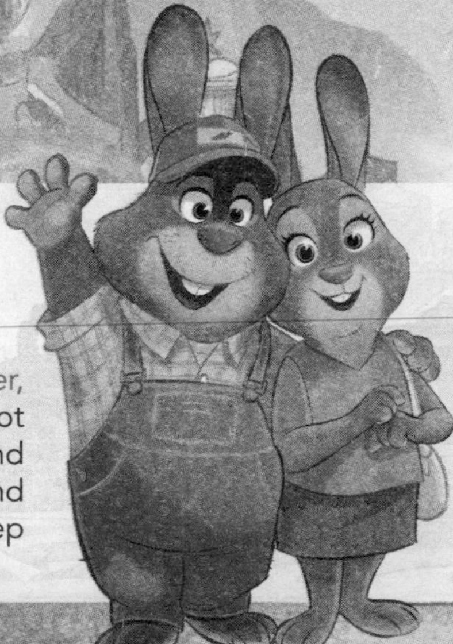

BONNIE & STU HOPPS

Bonnie and Stu, my mother and father, would prefer for me to be a carrot farmer, just like my 275 brothers and sisters. Even so, they believe in me and that I can change the world if I keep trying.

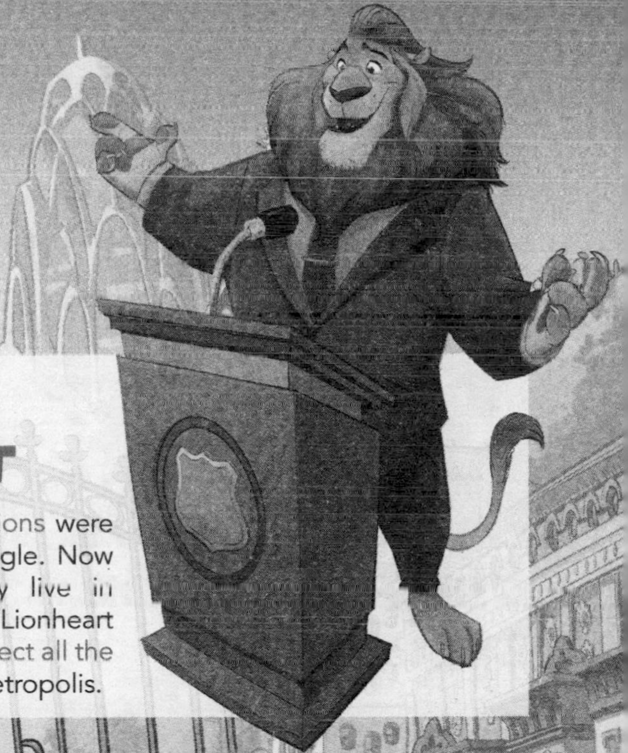

MAYOR LIONHEART

Thousands of years ago lions were the cruel kings of the jungle. Now that predators and prey live in harmony, Mayor Leodore Lionheart would do anything to protect all the citizens of our beloved metropolis.

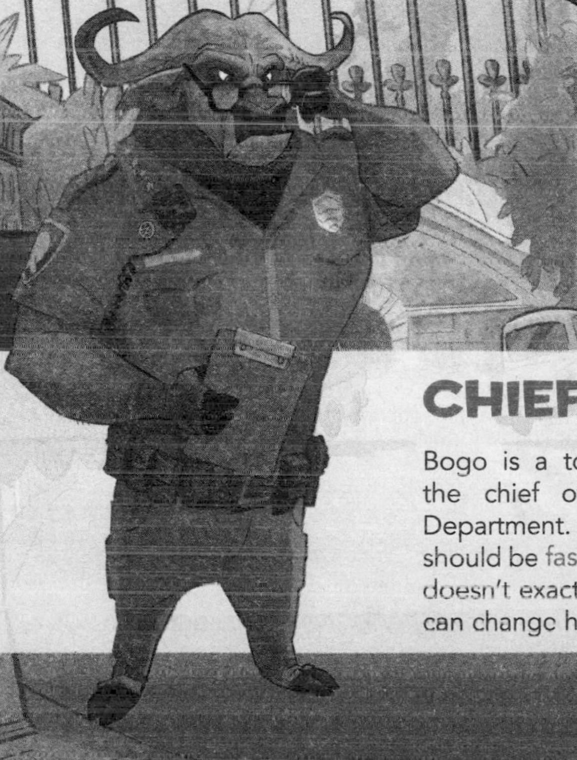

CHIEF BOGO

Bogo is a tough Cape buffalo and the chief of the Zootopia Police Department. He believes a good cop should be fast, strong and big... so he doesn't exactly like me. But I'm sure I can change his mind!

BENJAMIN CLAWHAUSER

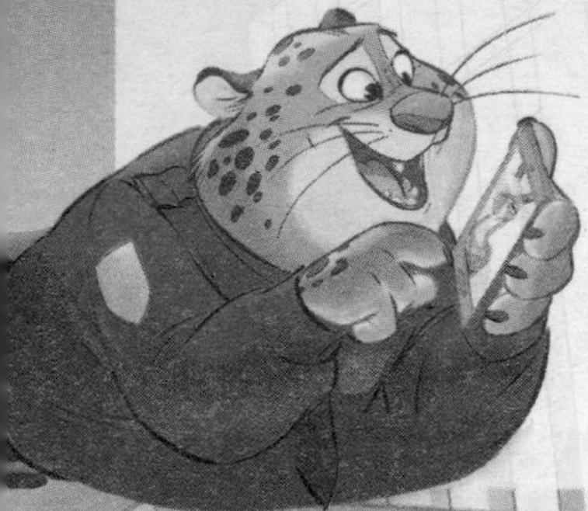

Everyone thinks he is just a flabby, donut-loving cop, and officer Benjamin Clawhauser is... exactly like that!
But he is also a gentle, honest cheetah and the first friend I made at ZPD.

DEPUTY MAYOR BELLWETHER

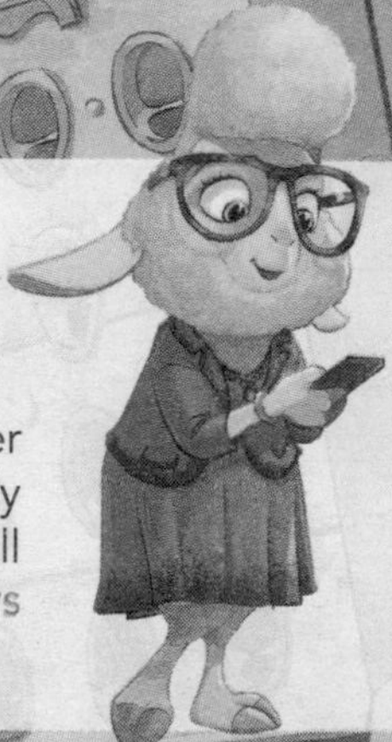

Quiet, loyal and gentle, Deputy Mayor Bellwether is a hardworking sheep: Mayor Lionheart really depends on her for help. Bellwether believes all the little guys need to stick together and is always ready to help a prey in need.

MR. BIG

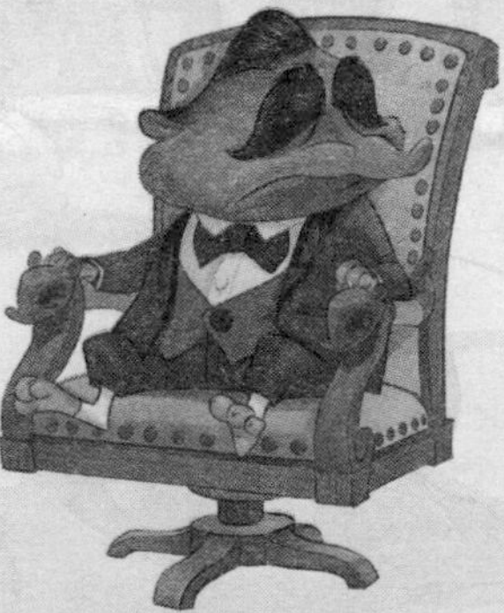

Mr. Big is a small Arctic shrew who lives in Tundratown. He is a really dangerous crime boss–protected by a gang of enormous polar bears. Mr. Big does not like Nick at all, but he values kindness more than anyone could think, so... there's hope for him yet!

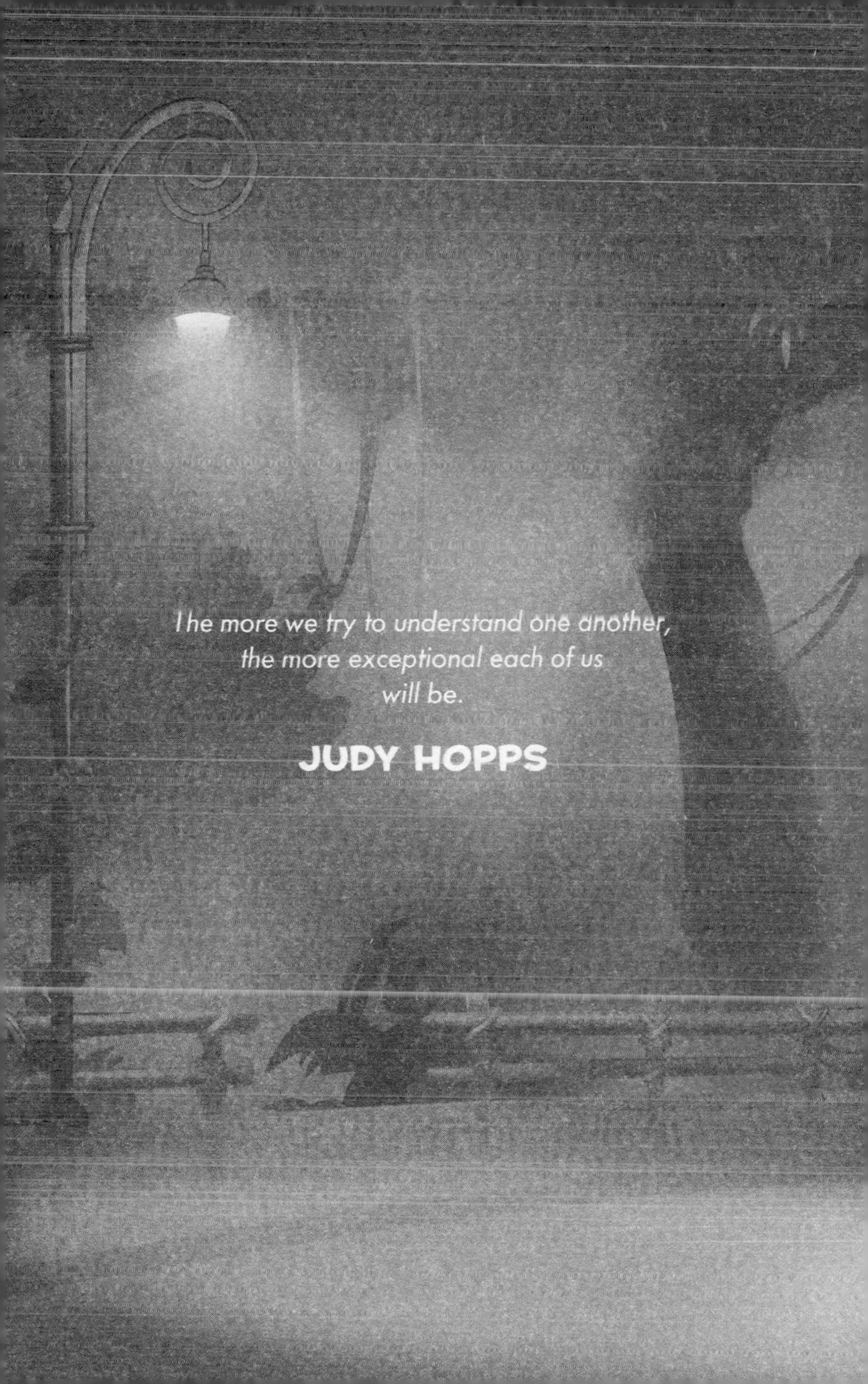

The more we try to understand one another,
the more exceptional each of us
will be.

JUDY HOPPS

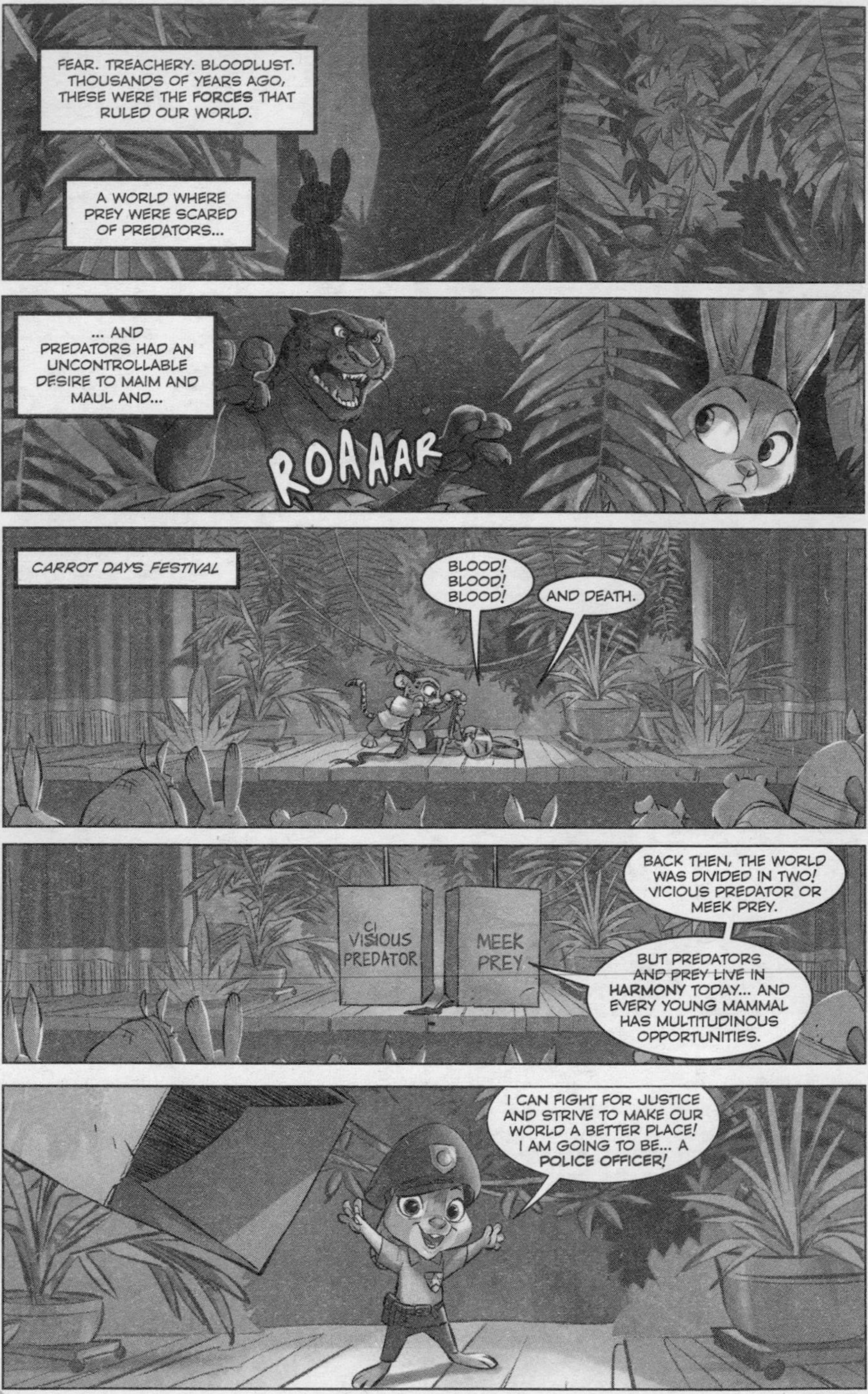
FEAR. TREACHERY. BLOODLUST. THOUSANDS OF YEARS AGO, THESE WERE THE FORCES THAT RULED OUR WORLD.
A WORLD WHERE PREY WERE SCARED OF PREDATORS...
... AND PREDATORS HAD AN UNCONTROLLABLE DESIRE TO MAIM AND MAUL AND...
ROAAAR
CARROT DAYS FESTIVAL
BLOOD! BLOOD! BLOOD!
AND DEATH.
BACK THEN, THE WORLD WAS DIVIDED IN TWO! VICIOUS PREDATOR OR MEEK PREY.
CI VISIOUS PREDATOR
MEEK PREY
BUT PREDATORS AND PREY LIVE IN HARMONY TODAY... AND EVERY YOUNG MAMMAL HAS MULTITUDINOUS OPPORTUNITIES.
I CAN FIGHT FOR JUSTICE AND STRIVE TO MAKE OUR WORLD A BETTER PLACE! I AM GOING TO BE... A POLICE OFFICER!

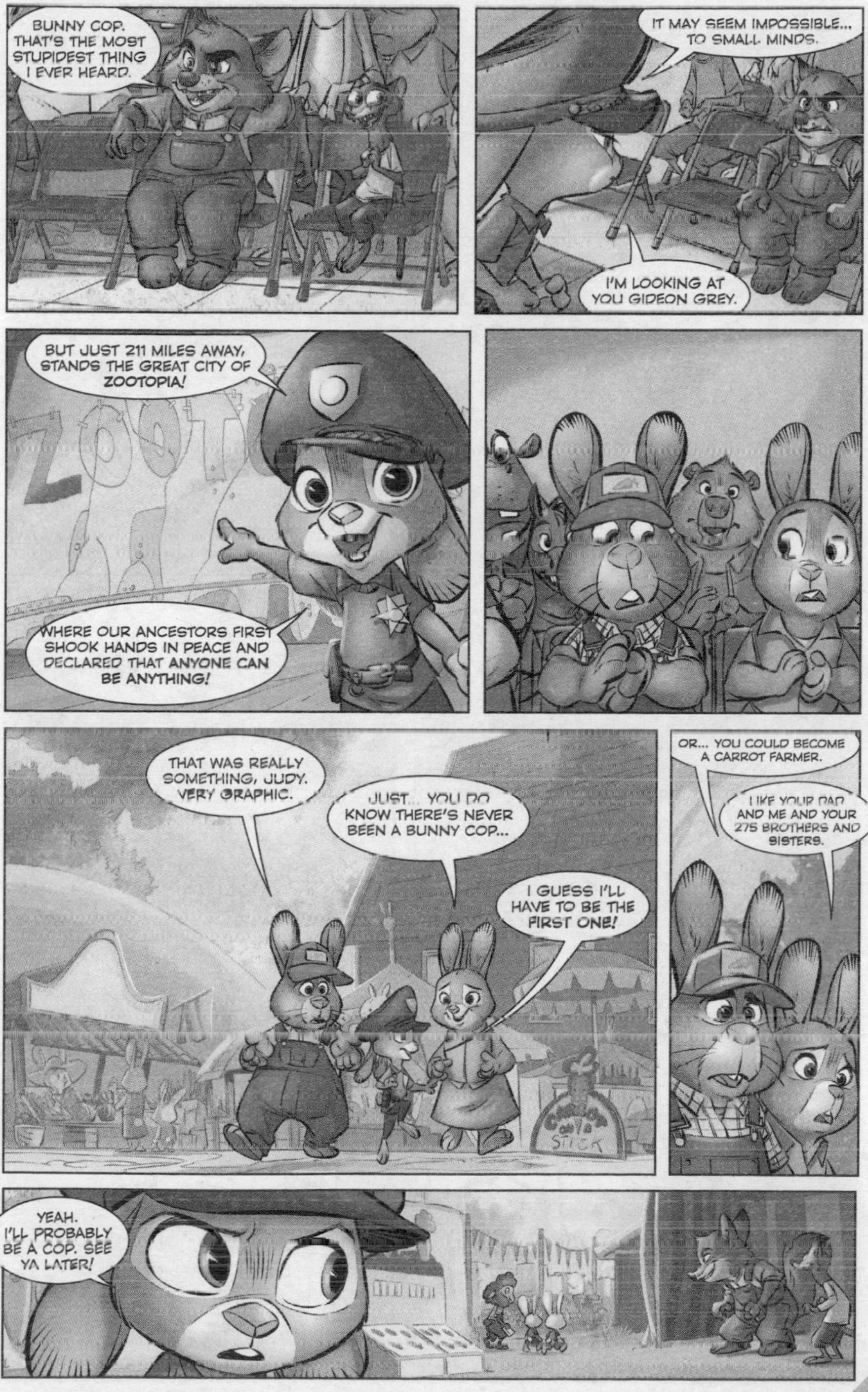
BUNNY COP. THAT'S THE MOST STUPIDEST THING I EVER HEARD.
IT MAY SEEM IMPOSSIBLE... TO SMALL MINDS.
I'M LOOKING AT YOU GIDEON GREY.
BUT JUST 211 MILES AWAY, STANDS THE GREAT CITY OF ZOOTOPIA!
WHERE OUR ANCESTORS FIRST SHOOK HANDS IN PEACE AND DECLARED THAT ANYONE CAN BE ANYTHING!
THAT WAS REALLY SOMETHING, JUDY. VERY GRAPHIC.
JUST... YOU DO KNOW THERE'S NEVER BEEN A BUNNY COP...
I GUESS I'LL HAVE TO BE THE FIRST ONE!
OR... YOU COULD BECOME A CARROT FARMER.
LIKE YOUR DAD AND ME AND YOUR 275 BROTHERS AND SISTERS.
YEAH. I'LL PROBABLY BE A COP. SEE YA LATER!

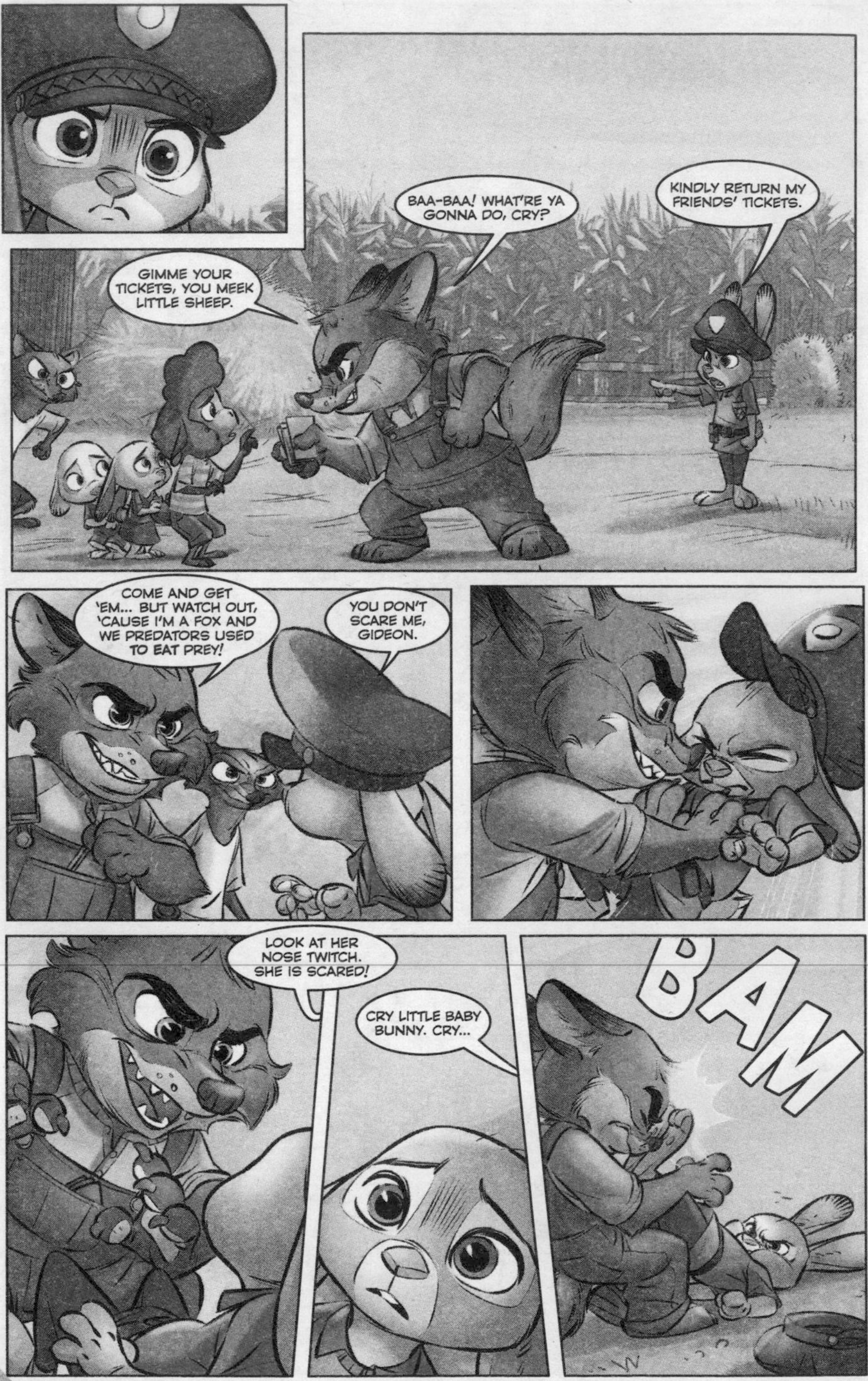
GIMME YOUR TICKETS, YOU MEEK LITTLE SHEEP.
BAA-BAA! WHAT'RE YA GONNA DO, CRY?
KINDLY RETURN MY FRIENDS' TICKETS.
COME AND GET 'EM... BUT WATCH OUT, 'CAUSE I'M A FOX AND WE PREDATORS USED TO EAT PREY!
YOU DON'T SCARE ME, GIDEON.
LOOK AT HER NOSE TWITCH. SHE IS SCARED!
CRY LITTLE BABY BUNNY. CRY...
BAM

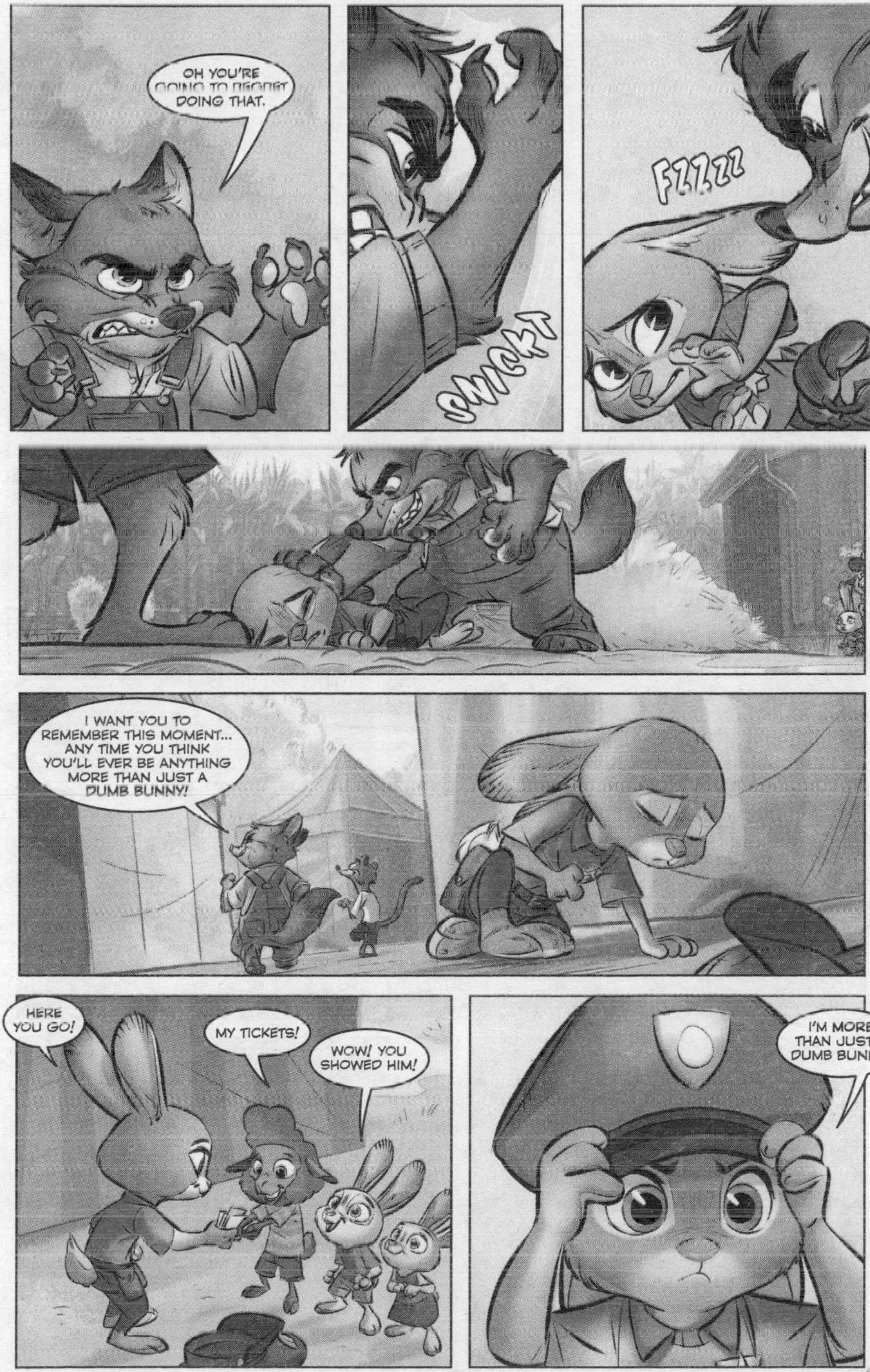

OH YOU'RE GOING TO REGRET DOING THAT.
SNICKT
FZZZZ
I WANT YOU TO REMEMBER THIS MOMENT... ANY TIME YOU THINK YOU'LL EVER BE ANYTHING MORE THAN JUST A DUMB BUNNY!
HERE YOU GO!
MY TICKETS!
WOW! YOU SHOWED HIM!
I'M MORE THAN JUST A DUMB BUNNY!

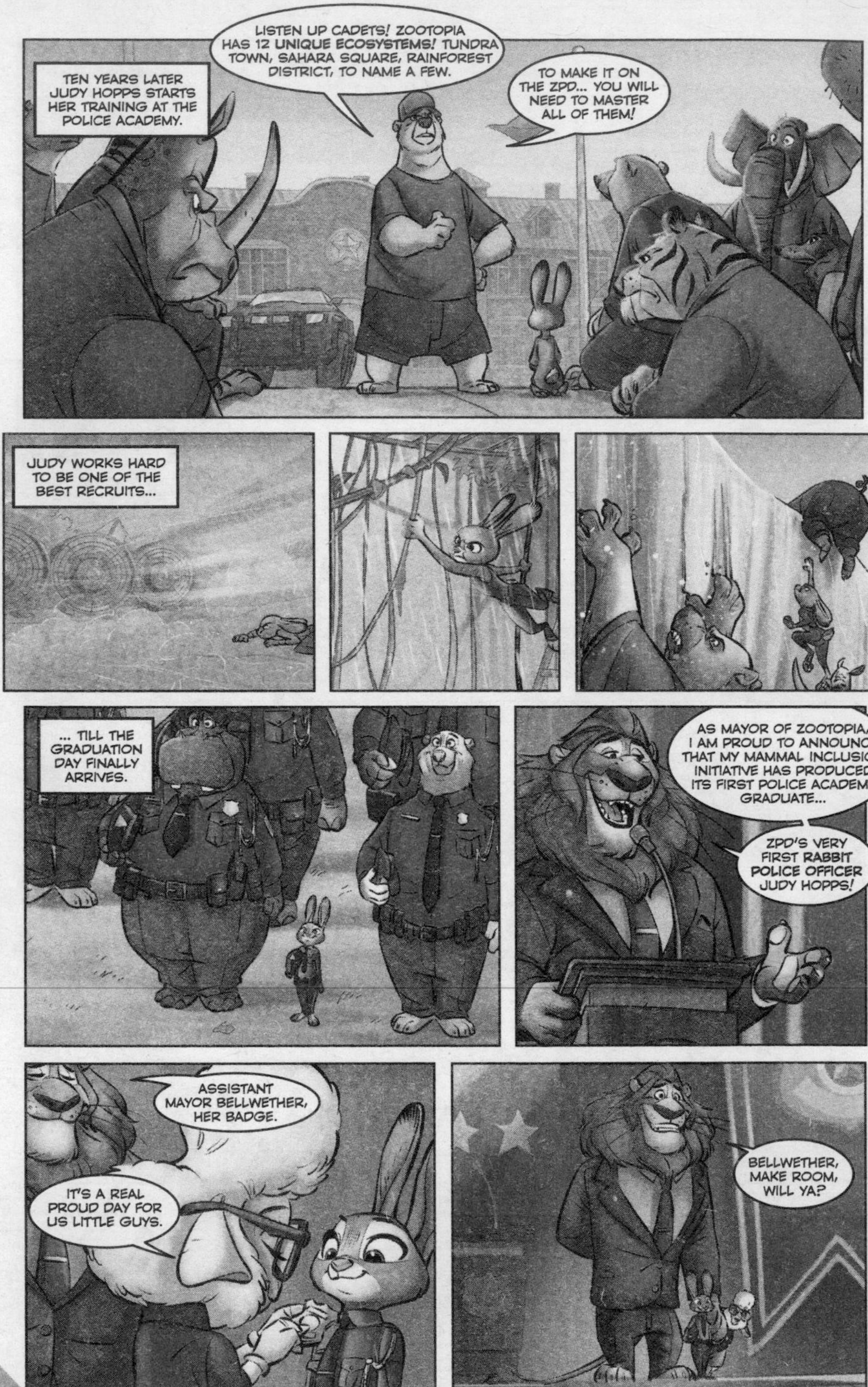
TEN YEARS LATER JUDY HOPPS STARTS HER TRAINING AT THE POLICE ACADEMY.
LISTEN UP CADETS! ZOOTOPIA HAS 12 UNIQUE ECOSYSTEMS! TUNDRA TOWN, SAHARA SQUARE, RAINFOREST DISTRICT, TO NAME A FEW.
TO MAKE IT ON THE ZPD... YOU WILL NEED TO MASTER ALL OF THEM!
JUDY WORKS HARD TO BE ONE OF THE BEST RECRUITS...
... TILL THE GRADUATION DAY FINALLY ARRIVES.
AS MAYOR OF ZOOTOPIA, I AM PROUD TO ANNOUNCE THAT MY MAMMAL INCLUSION INITIATIVE HAS PRODUCED ITS FIRST POLICE ACADEMY GRADUATE...
ZPD'S VERY FIRST RABBIT POLICE OFFICER JUDY HOPPS!
ASSISTANT MAYOR BELLWETHER, HER BADGE.
IT'S A REAL PROUD DAY FOR US LITTLE GUYS.
BELLWETHER, MAKE ROOM, WILL YA?

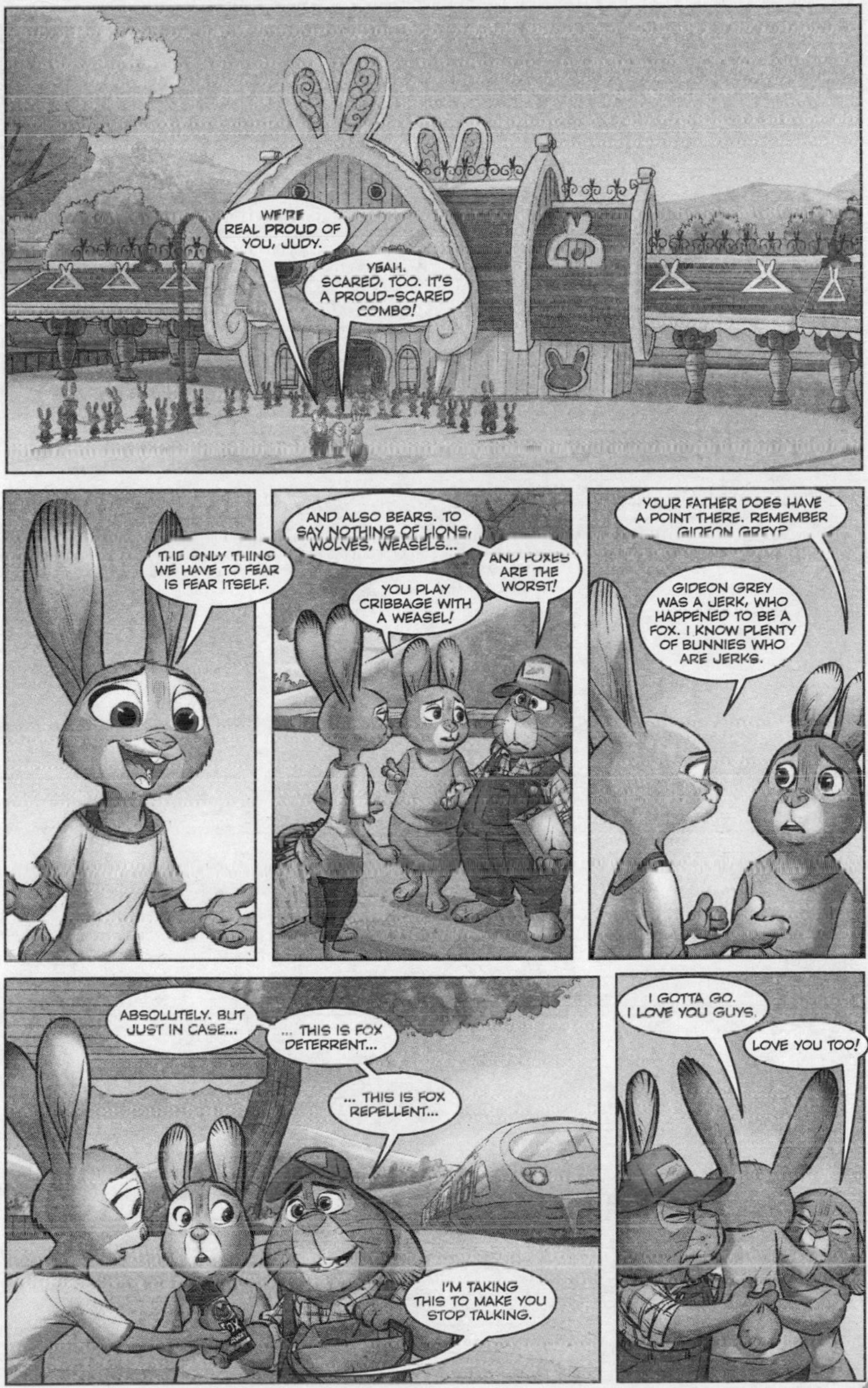
WE'RE REAL PROUD OF YOU, JUDY.
YEAH. SCARED, TOO. IT'S A PROUD-SCARED COMBO!
THE ONLY THING WE HAVE TO FEAR IS FEAR ITSELF.
AND ALSO BEARS. TO SAY NOTHING OF LIONS, WOLVES, WEASELS...
YOU PLAY CRIBBAGE WITH A WEASEL!
AND FOXES ARE THE WORST!
YOUR FATHER DOES HAVE A POINT THERE. REMEMBER GIDEON GREY?
GIDEON GREY WAS A JERK, WHO HAPPENED TO BE A FOX. I KNOW PLENTY OF BUNNIES WHO ARE JERKS.
ABSOLUTELY. BUT JUST IN CASE...
... THIS IS FOX DETERRENT...
... THIS IS FOX REPELLENT...
I'M TAKING THIS TO MAKE YOU STOP TALKING.
I GOTTA GO. I LOVE YOU GUYS.
LOVE YOU TOO!

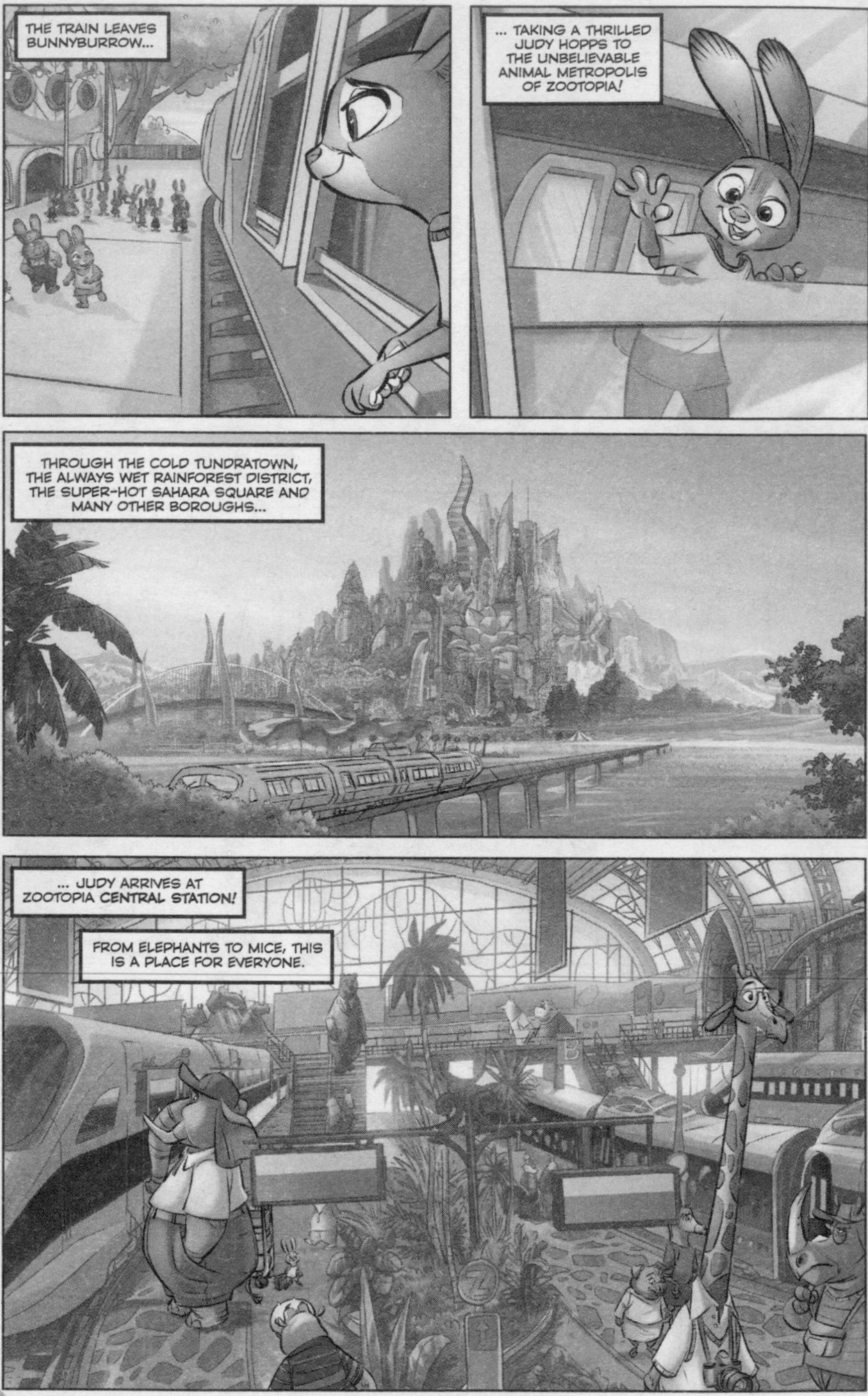
THE TRAIN LEAVES BUNNYBURROW...
... TAKING A THRILLED JUDY HOPPS TO THE UNBELIEVABLE ANIMAL METROPOLIS OF ZOOTOPIA!
THROUGH THE COLD TUNDRATOWN, THE ALWAYS WET RAINFOREST DISTRICT, THE SUPER-HOT SAHARA SQUARE AND MANY OTHER BOROUGHS...
... JUDY ARRIVES AT ZOOTOPIA CENTRAL STATION!
FROM ELEPHANTS TO MICE, THIS IS A PLACE FOR EVERYONE.

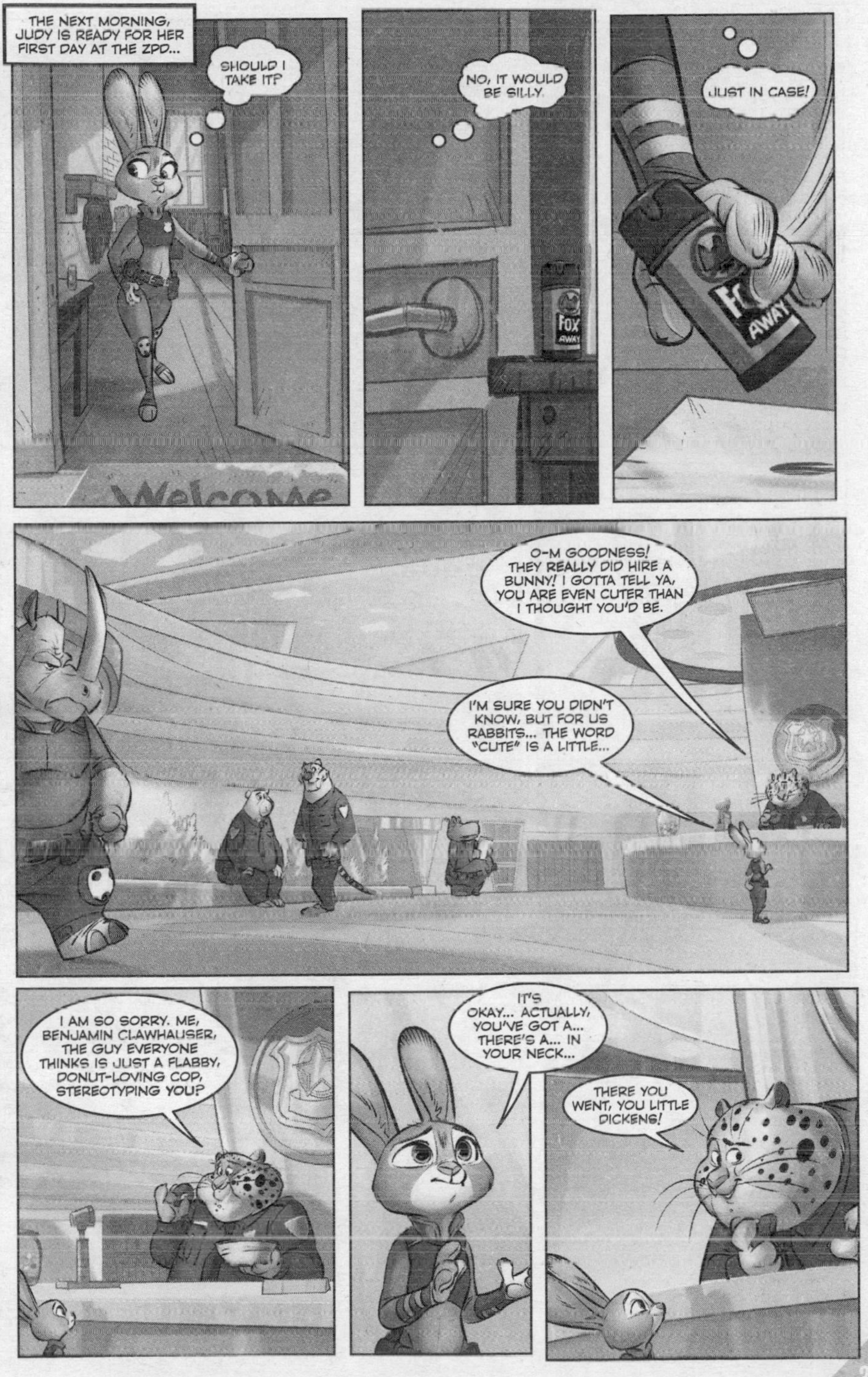
THE NEXT MORNING, JUDY IS READY FOR HER FIRST DAY AT THE ZPD...
SHOULD I TAKE IT?
Welcome
NO, IT WOULD BE SILLY.
FOX AWAY
JUST IN CASE!
FOX AWAY
O-M GOODNESS! THEY REALLY DID HIRE A BUNNY! I GOTTA TELL YA, YOU ARE EVEN CUTER THAN I THOUGHT YOU'D BE.
I'M SURE YOU DIDN'T KNOW, BUT FOR US RABBITS... THE WORD "CUTE" IS A LITTLE...
I AM SO SORRY. ME, BENJAMIN CLAWHAUSER, THE GUY EVERYONE THINKS IS JUST A FLABBY, DONUT-LOVING COP, STEREOTYPING YOU?
IT'S OKAY... ACTUALLY, YOU'VE GOT A... THERE'S A... IN YOUR NECK...
THERE YOU WENT, YOU LITTLE DICKENS!

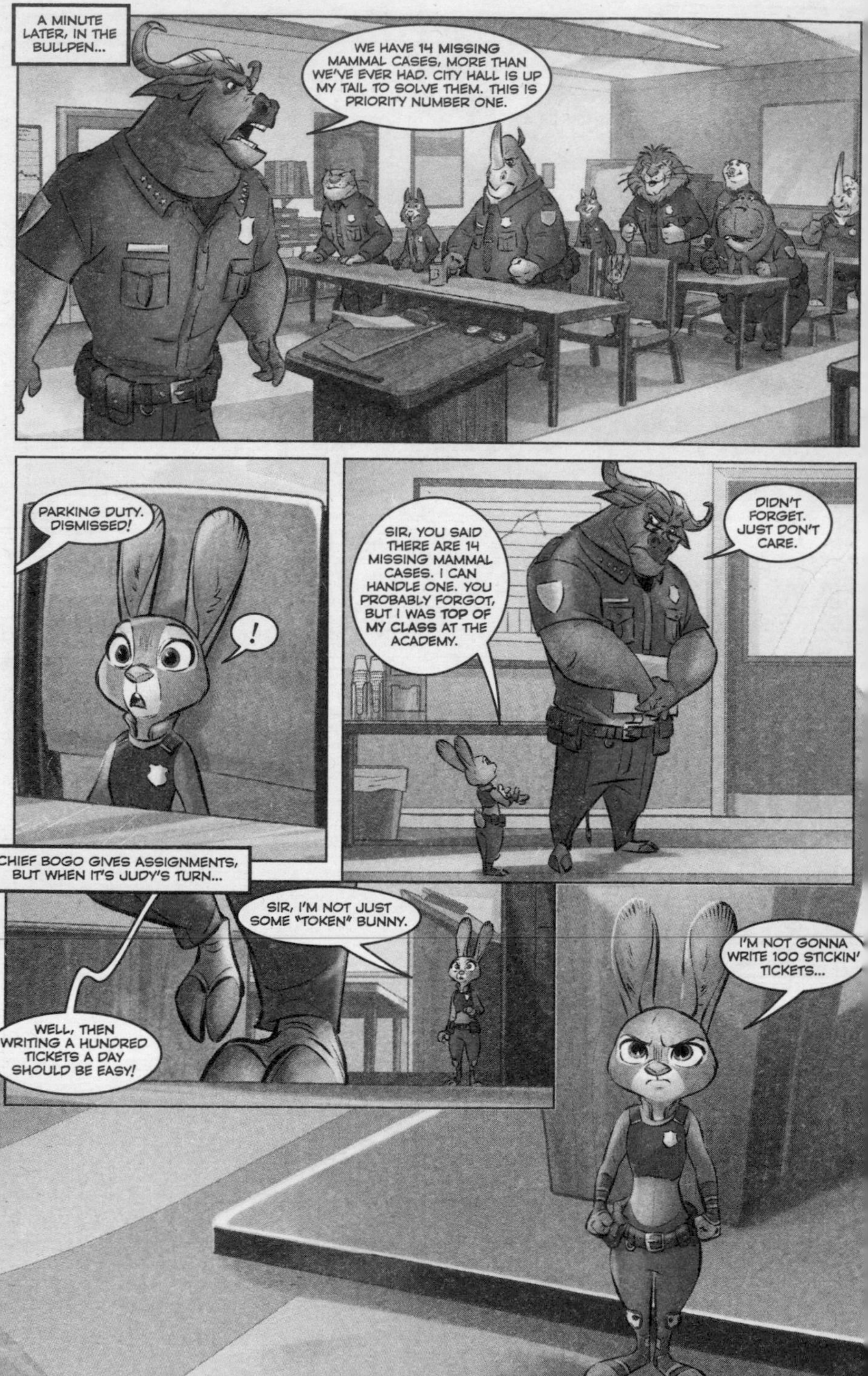
A MINUTE LATER, IN THE BULLPEN...
WE HAVE 14 MISSING MAMMAL CASES, MORE THAN WE'VE EVER HAD. CITY HALL IS UP MY TAIL TO SOLVE THEM. THIS IS PRIORITY NUMBER ONE.
CHIEF BOGO GIVES ASSIGNMENTS, BUT WHEN IT'S JUDY'S TURN...
PARKING DUTY. DISMISSED!
!
SIR, YOU SAID THERE ARE 14 MISSING MAMMAL CASES. I CAN HANDLE ONE. YOU PROBABLY FORGOT, BUT I WAS TOP OF MY CLASS AT THE ACADEMY.
DIDN'T FORGET. JUST DON'T CARE.
SIR, I'M NOT JUST SOME "TOKEN" BUNNY.
WELL, THEN WRITING A HUNDRED TICKETS A DAY SHOULD BE EASY!
I'M NOT GONNA WRITE 100 STICKIN' TICKETS...

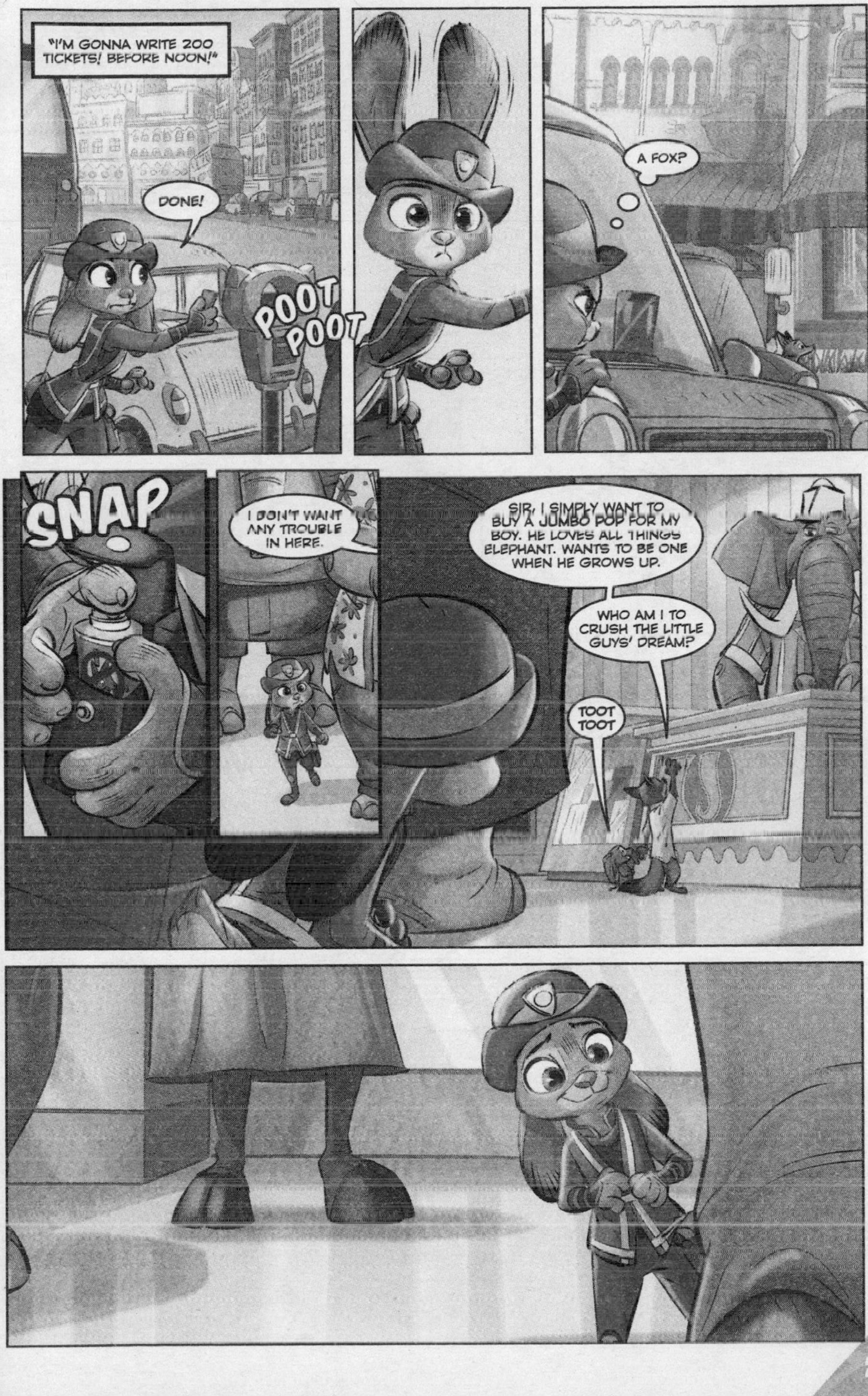

"I'M GONNA WRITE 200 TICKETS! BEFORE NOON!"
DONE!
POOT POOT
A FOX?
SNAP
I DON'T WANT ANY TROUBLE IN HERE.
SIR, I SIMPLY WANT TO BUY A JUMBO POP FOR MY BOY. HE LOVES ALL THINGS ELEPHANT. WANTS TO BE ONE WHEN HE GROWS UP.
WHO AM I TO CRUSH THE LITTLE GUYS' DREAM?
TOOT TOOT

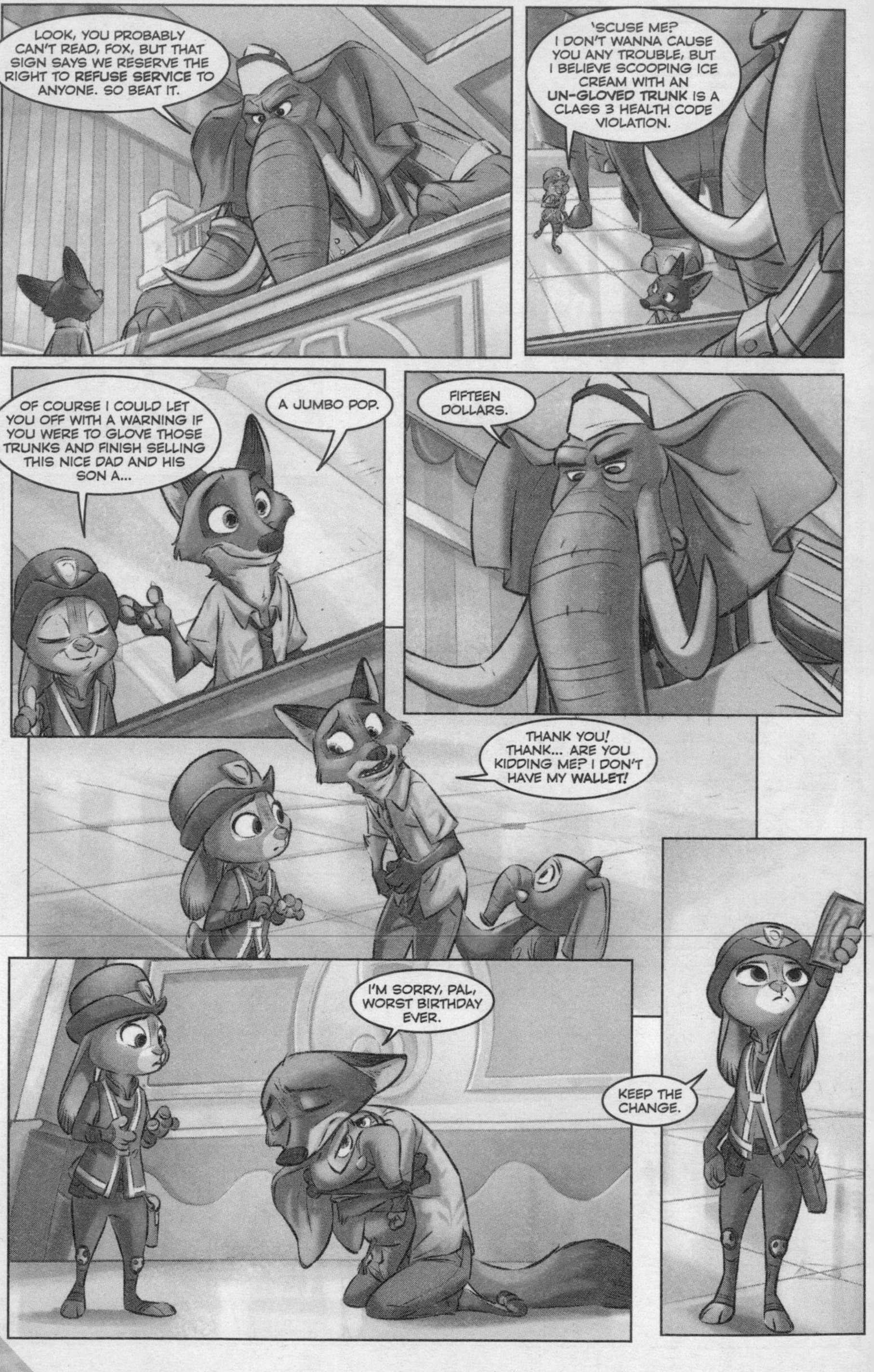
LOOK, YOU PROBABLY CAN'T READ, FOX, BUT THAT SIGN SAYS WE RESERVE THE RIGHT TO **REFUSE SERVICE** TO ANYONE. SO BEAT IT.
'SCUSE ME? I DON'T WANNA CAUSE YOU ANY TROUBLE, BUT I BELIEVE SCOOPING ICE CREAM WITH AN **UN-GLOVED TRUNK** IS A CLASS 3 HEALTH CODE VIOLATION.
OF COURSE I COULD LET YOU OFF WITH A WARNING IF YOU WERE TO GLOVE THOSE TRUNKS AND FINISH SELLING THIS NICE DAD AND HIS SON A...
A JUMBO POP.
FIFTEEN DOLLARS.
THANK YOU! THANK... ARE YOU KIDDING ME? I DON'T HAVE MY **WALLET!**
I'M SORRY, PAL, WORST BIRTHDAY EVER.
KEEP THE CHANGE.

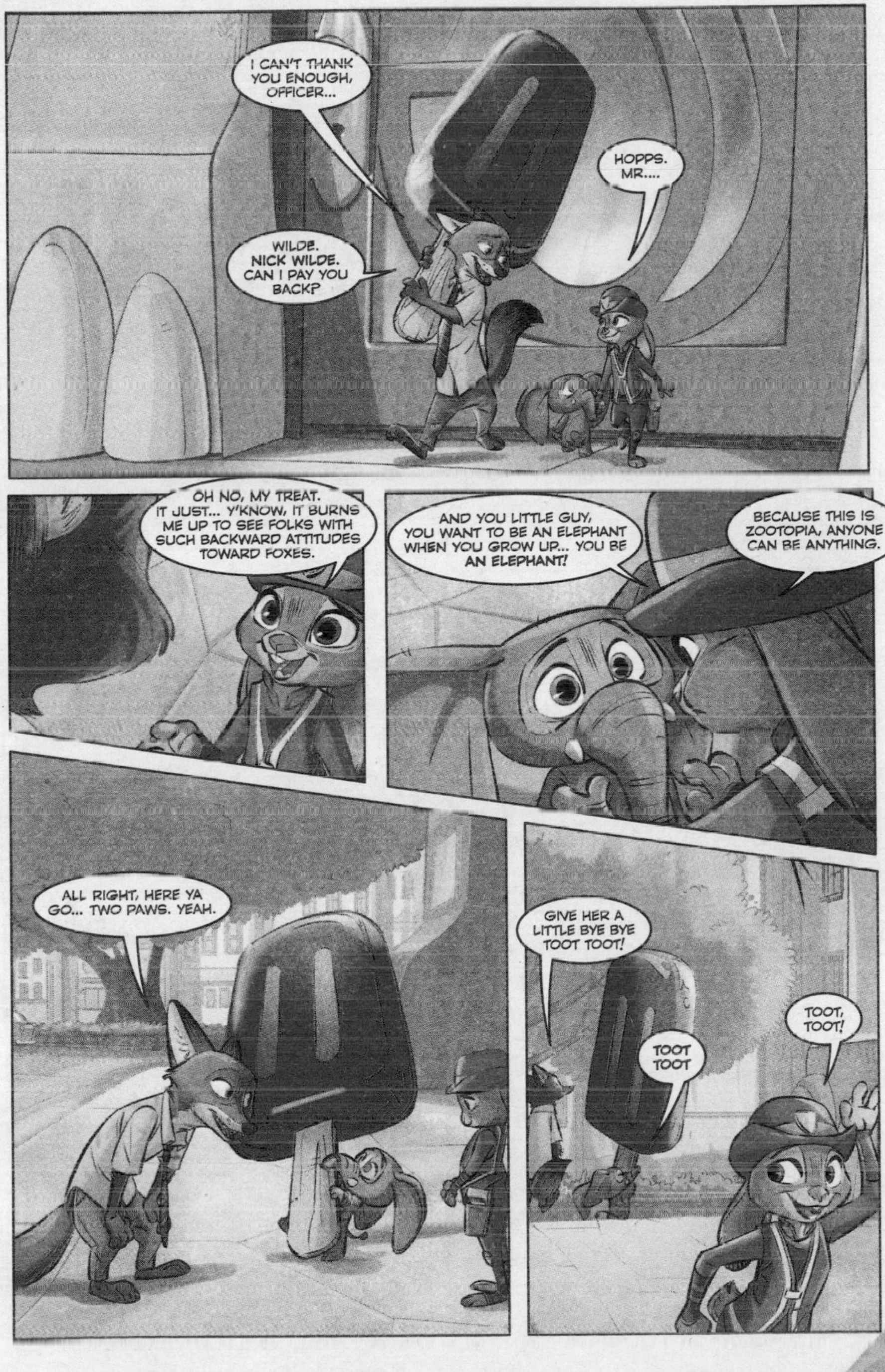
I CAN'T THANK YOU ENOUGH, OFFICER...
HOPPS. MR....
WILDE. NICK WILDE. CAN I PAY YOU BACK?
OH NO, MY TREAT. IT JUST... Y'KNOW, IT BURNS ME UP TO SEE FOLKS WITH SUCH BACKWARD ATTITUDES TOWARD FOXES.
AND YOU LITTLE GUY, YOU WANT TO BE AN ELEPHANT WHEN YOU GROW UP... YOU BE AN ELEPHANT!
BECAUSE THIS IS ZOOTOPIA, ANYONE CAN BE ANYTHING.
ALL RIGHT, HERE YA GO... TWO PAWS. YEAH.
GIVE HER A LITTLE BYE BYE TOOT TOOT!
TOOT TOOT
TOOT, TOOT!

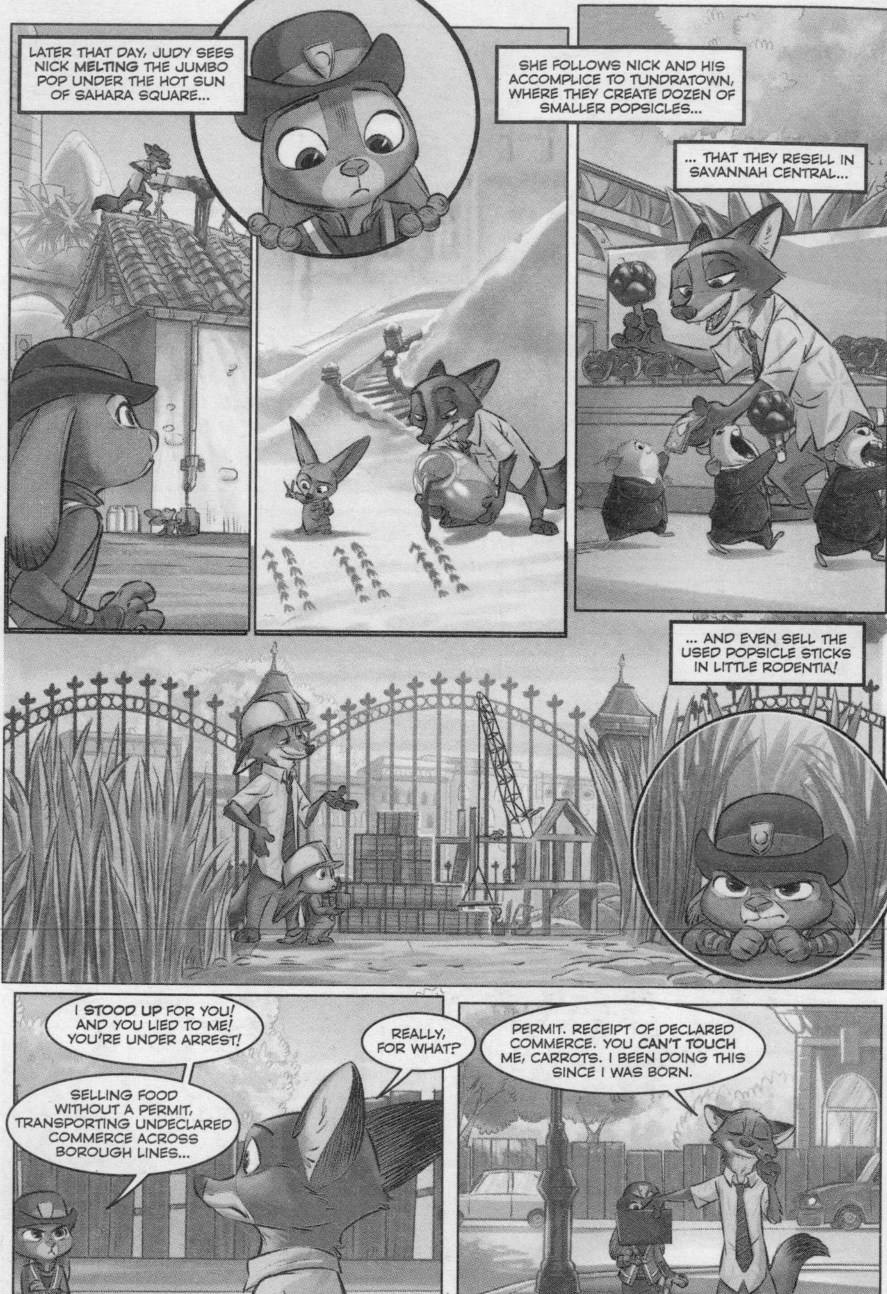

LATER THAT DAY, JUDY SEES NICK MELTING THE JUMBO POP UNDER THE HOT SUN OF SAHARA SQUARE...
SHE FOLLOWS NICK AND HIS ACCOMPLICE TO TUNDRATOWN, WHERE THEY CREATE DOZEN OF SMALLER POPSICLES...
... THAT THEY RESELL IN SAVANNAH CENTRAL...
... AND EVEN SELL THE USED POPSICLE STICKS IN LITTLE RODENTIA!
I STOOD UP FOR YOU! AND YOU LIED TO ME! YOU'RE UNDER ARREST!
REALLY, FOR WHAT?
SELLING FOOD WITHOUT A PERMIT, TRANSPORTING UNDECLARED COMMERCE ACROSS BOROUGH LINES...
PERMIT. RECEIPT OF DECLARED COMMERCE. YOU CAN'T TOUCH ME, CARROTS. I BEEN DOING THIS SINCE I WAS BORN.

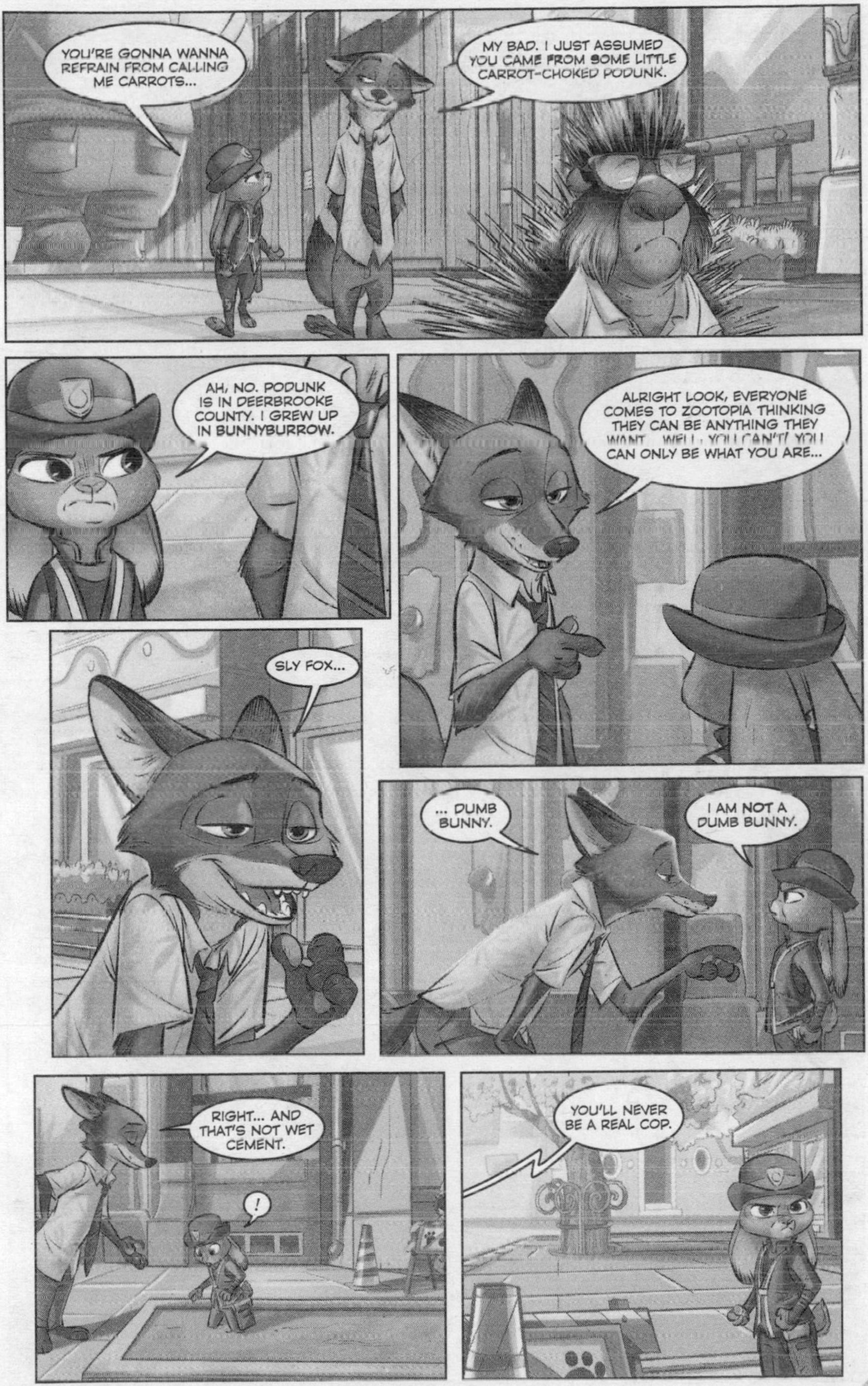

YOU'RE GONNA WANNA REFRAIN FROM CALLING ME CARROTS...
MY BAD. I JUST ASSUMED YOU CAME FROM SOME LITTLE CARROT-CHOKED PODUNK.
AH, NO. PODUNK IS IN DEERBROOKE COUNTY. I GREW UP IN BUNNYBURROW.
ALRIGHT LOOK, EVERYONE COMES TO ZOOTOPIA THINKING THEY CAN BE ANYTHING THEY WANT... WELL, YOU CAN'T! YOU CAN ONLY BE WHAT YOU ARE...
SLY FOX...
... DUMB BUNNY.
I AM NOT A DUMB BUNNY.
RIGHT... AND THAT'S NOT WET CEMENT.
!
YOU'LL NEVER BE A REAL COP.

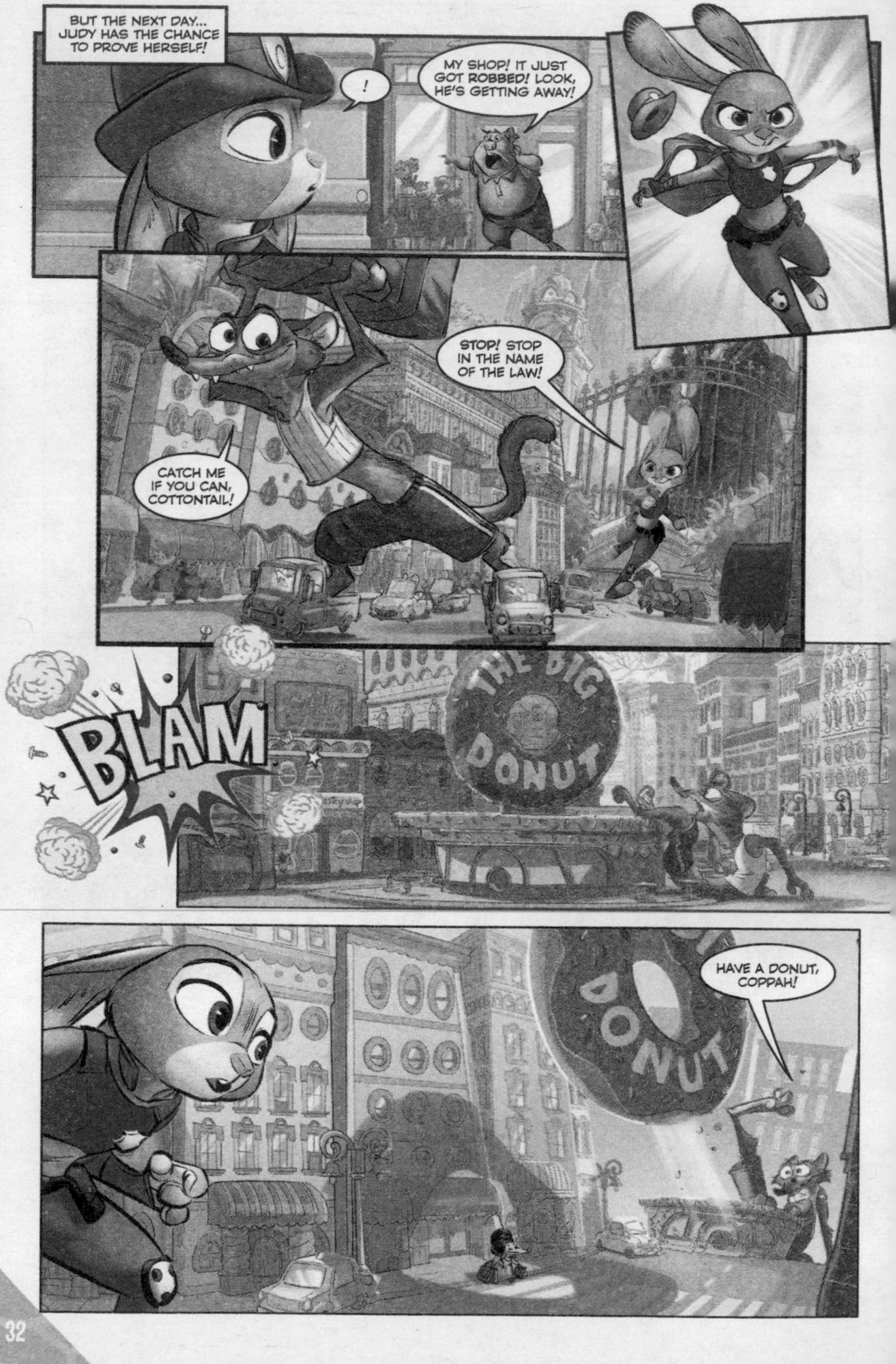
BUT THE NEXT DAY... JUDY HAS THE CHANCE TO PROVE HERSELF!
!
MY SHOP! IT JUST GOT ROBBED! LOOK, HE'S GETTING AWAY!
STOP! STOP IN THE NAME OF THE LAW!
CATCH ME IF YOU CAN, COTTONTAIL!
BLAM
THE BIG DONUT
HAVE A DONUT, COPPAH!
DONUT

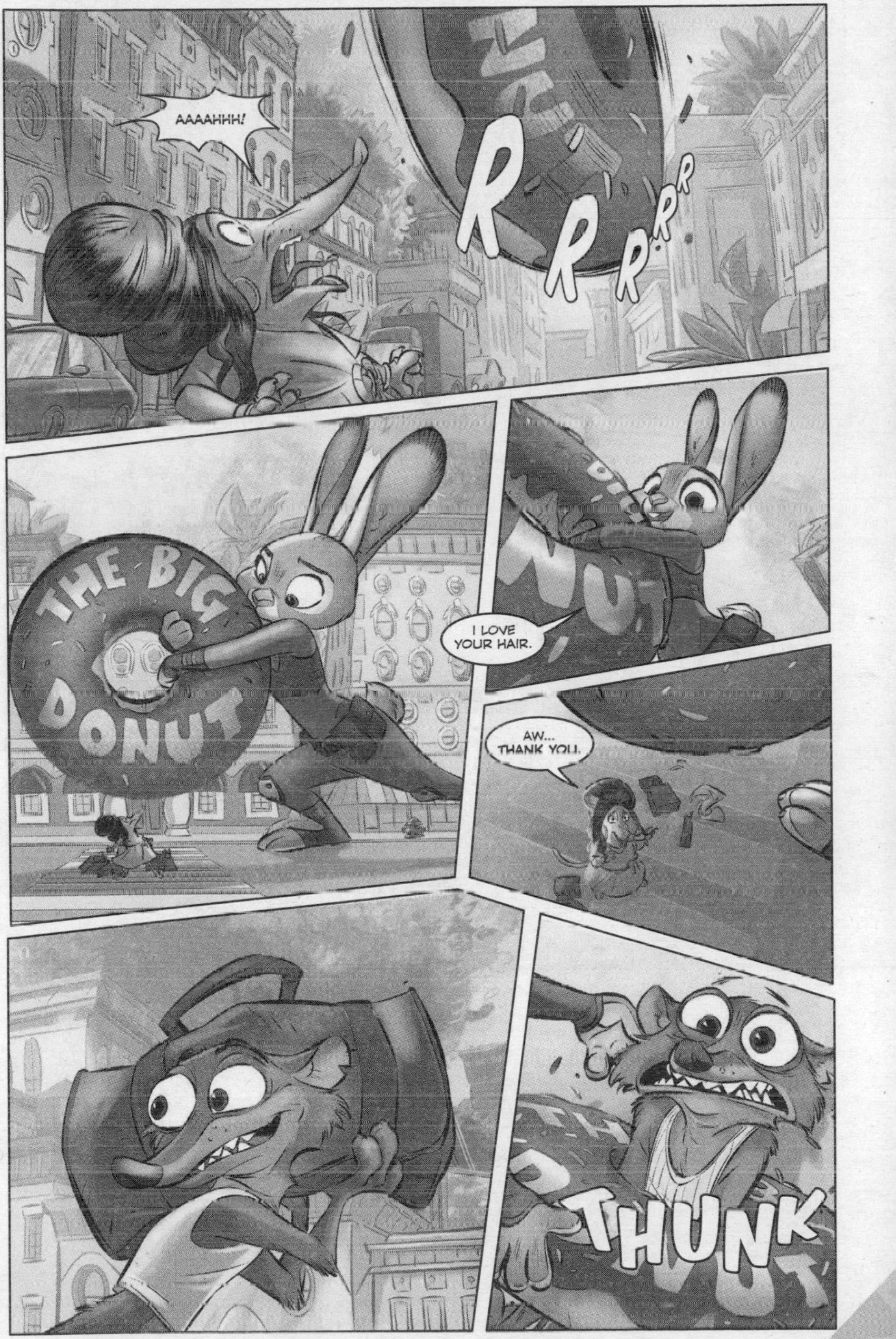
AAAAHHH!
RRRRRR
THE BIG DONUT
I LOVE YOUR HAIR.
AW... THANK YOU.
THUNK

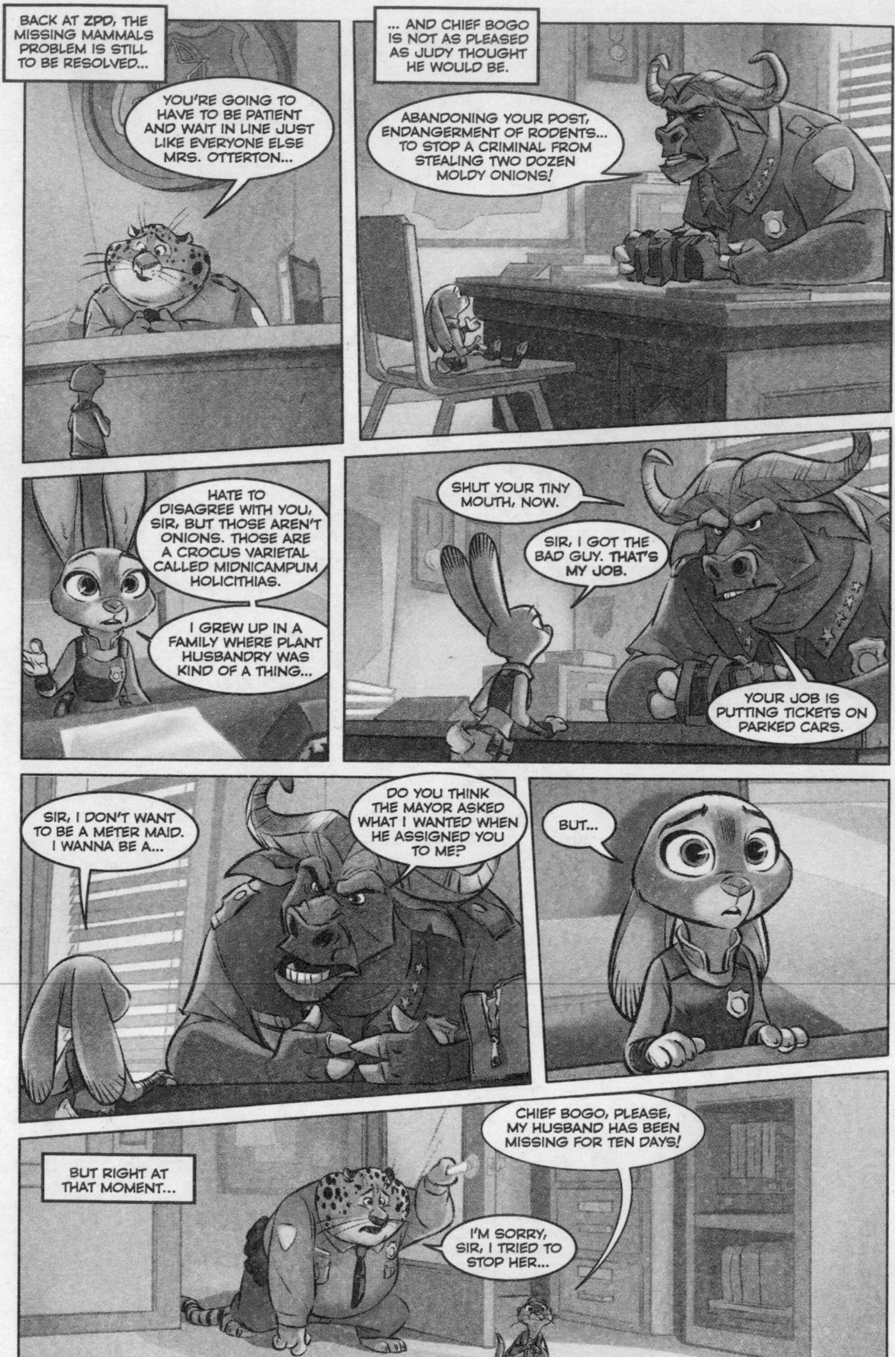
BACK AT ZPD, THE MISSING MAMMALS PROBLEM IS STILL TO BE RESOLVED...
YOU'RE GOING TO HAVE TO BE PATIENT AND WAIT IN LINE JUST LIKE EVERYONE ELSE MRS. OTTERTON...
... AND CHIEF BOGO IS NOT AS PLEASED AS JUDY THOUGHT HE WOULD BE.
ABANDONING YOUR POST, ENDANGERMENT OF RODENTS... TO STOP A CRIMINAL FROM STEALING TWO DOZEN MOLDY ONIONS!
HATE TO DISAGREE WITH YOU, SIR, BUT THOSE AREN'T ONIONS. THOSE ARE A CROCUS VARIETAL CALLED MIDNICAMPUM HOLICITHIAS.
I GREW UP IN A FAMILY WHERE PLANT HUSBANDRY WAS KIND OF A THING...
SHUT YOUR TINY MOUTH, NOW.
SIR, I GOT THE BAD GUY. THAT'S MY JOB.
YOUR JOB IS PUTTING TICKETS ON PARKED CARS.
SIR, I DON'T WANT TO BE A METER MAID. I WANNA BE A...
DO YOU THINK THE MAYOR ASKED WHAT I WANTED WHEN HE ASSIGNED YOU TO ME?
BUT...
BUT RIGHT AT THAT MOMENT...
CHIEF BOGO, PLEASE, MY HUSBAND HAS BEEN MISSING FOR TEN DAYS!
I'M SORRY, SIR, I TRIED TO STOP HER...

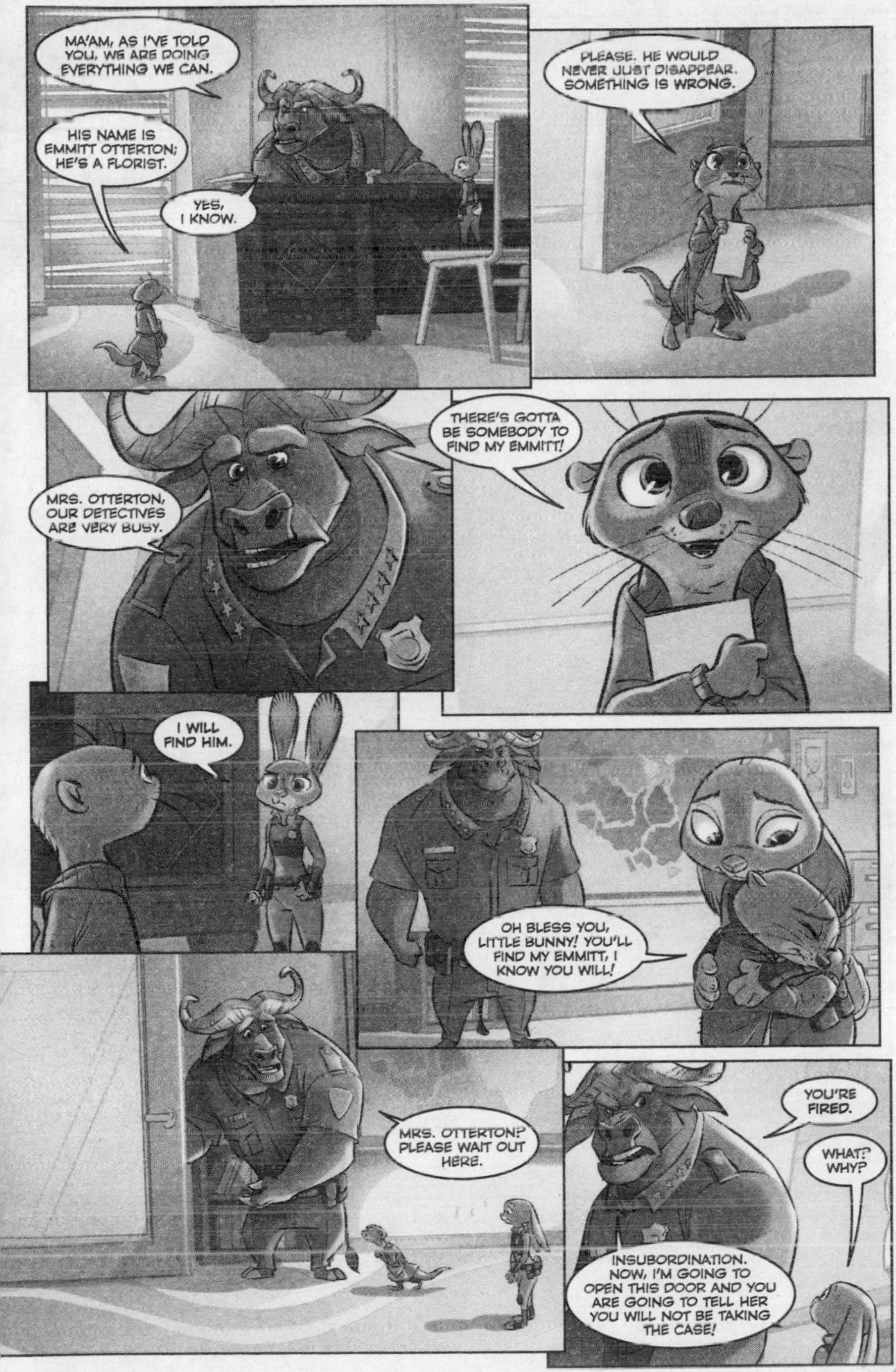
MA'AM, AS I'VE TOLD YOU, WE ARE DOING EVERYTHING WE CAN.
HIS NAME IS EMMITT OTTERTON; HE'S A FLORIST.
YES, I KNOW.
PLEASE. HE WOULD NEVER JUST DISAPPEAR. SOMETHING IS WRONG.
MRS. OTTERTON, OUR DETECTIVES ARE VERY BUSY.
THERE'S GOTTA BE SOMEBODY TO FIND MY EMMITT!
I WILL FIND HIM.
OH BLESS YOU, LITTLE BUNNY! YOU'LL FIND MY EMMITT, I KNOW YOU WILL!
MRS. OTTERTON? PLEASE WAIT OUT HERE.
YOU'RE FIRED.
WHAT? WHY?
INSUBORDINATION. NOW, I'M GOING TO OPEN THIS DOOR AND YOU ARE GOING TO TELL HER YOU WILL NOT BE TAKING THE CASE!

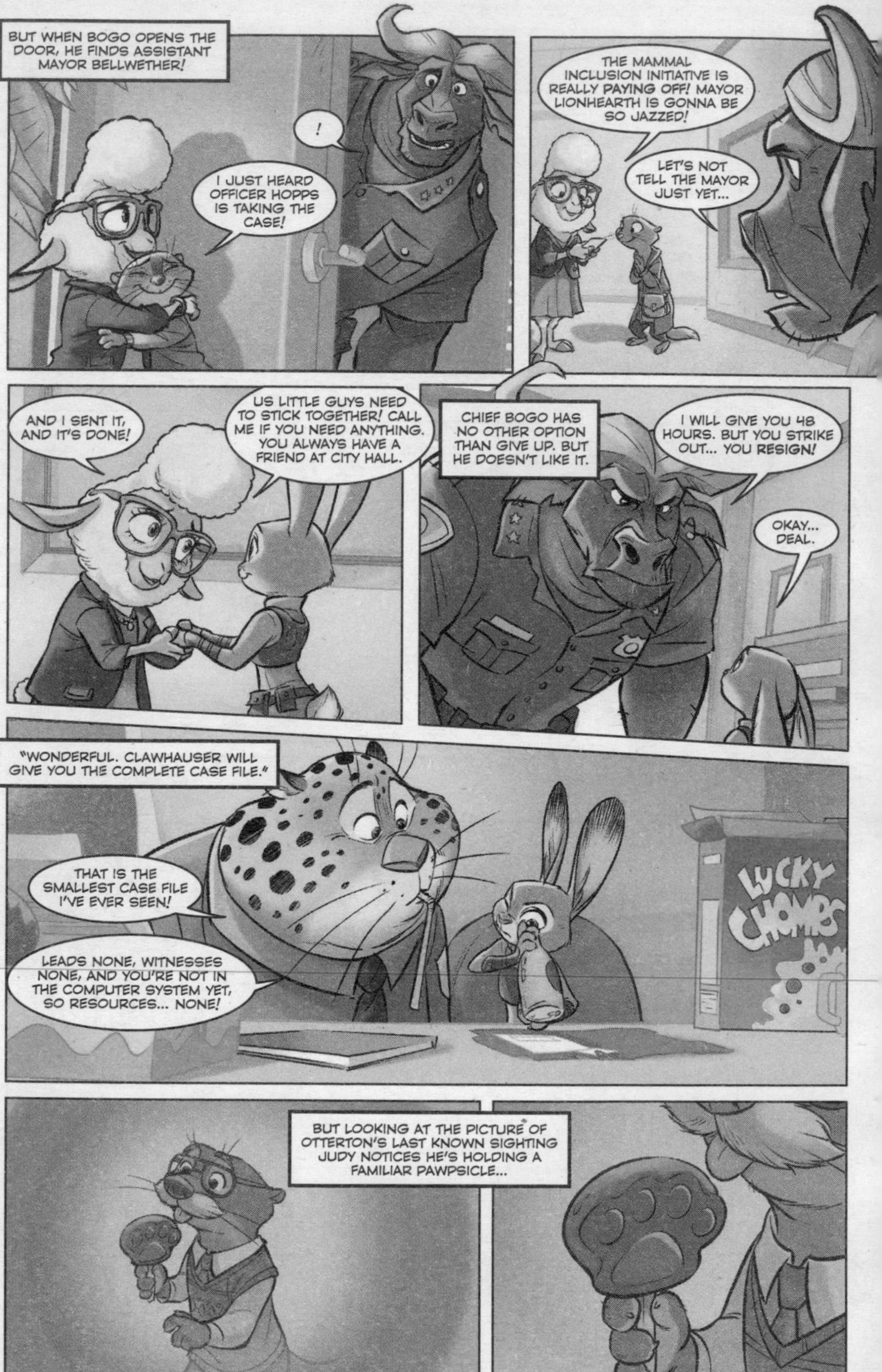
BUT WHEN BOGO OPENS THE DOOR, HE FINDS ASSISTANT MAYOR BELLWETHER!
!
I JUST HEARD OFFICER HOPPS IS TAKING THE CASE!
THE MAMMAL INCLUSION INITIATIVE IS REALLY PAYING OFF! MAYOR LIONHEARTH IS GONNA BE SO JAZZED!
LET'S NOT TELL THE MAYOR JUST YET...
AND I SENT IT, AND IT'S DONE!
US LITTLE GUYS NEED TO STICK TOGETHER! CALL ME IF YOU NEED ANYTHING. YOU ALWAYS HAVE A FRIEND AT CITY HALL.
CHIEF BOGO HAS NO OTHER OPTION THAN GIVE UP. BUT HE DOESN'T LIKE IT.
I WILL GIVE YOU 48 HOURS. BUT YOU STRIKE OUT... YOU RESIGN!
OKAY... DEAL.
"WONDERFUL. CLAWHAUSER WILL GIVE YOU THE COMPLETE CASE FILE."
THAT IS THE SMALLEST CASE FILE I'VE EVER SEEN!
LEADS NONE, WITNESSES NONE, AND YOU'RE NOT IN THE COMPUTER SYSTEM YET, SO RESOURCES... NONE!
LUCKY CHOMPS
BUT LOOKING AT THE PICTURE OF OTTERTON'S LAST KNOWN SIGHTING JUDY NOTICES HE'S HOLDING A FAMILIAR PAWPSICLE...

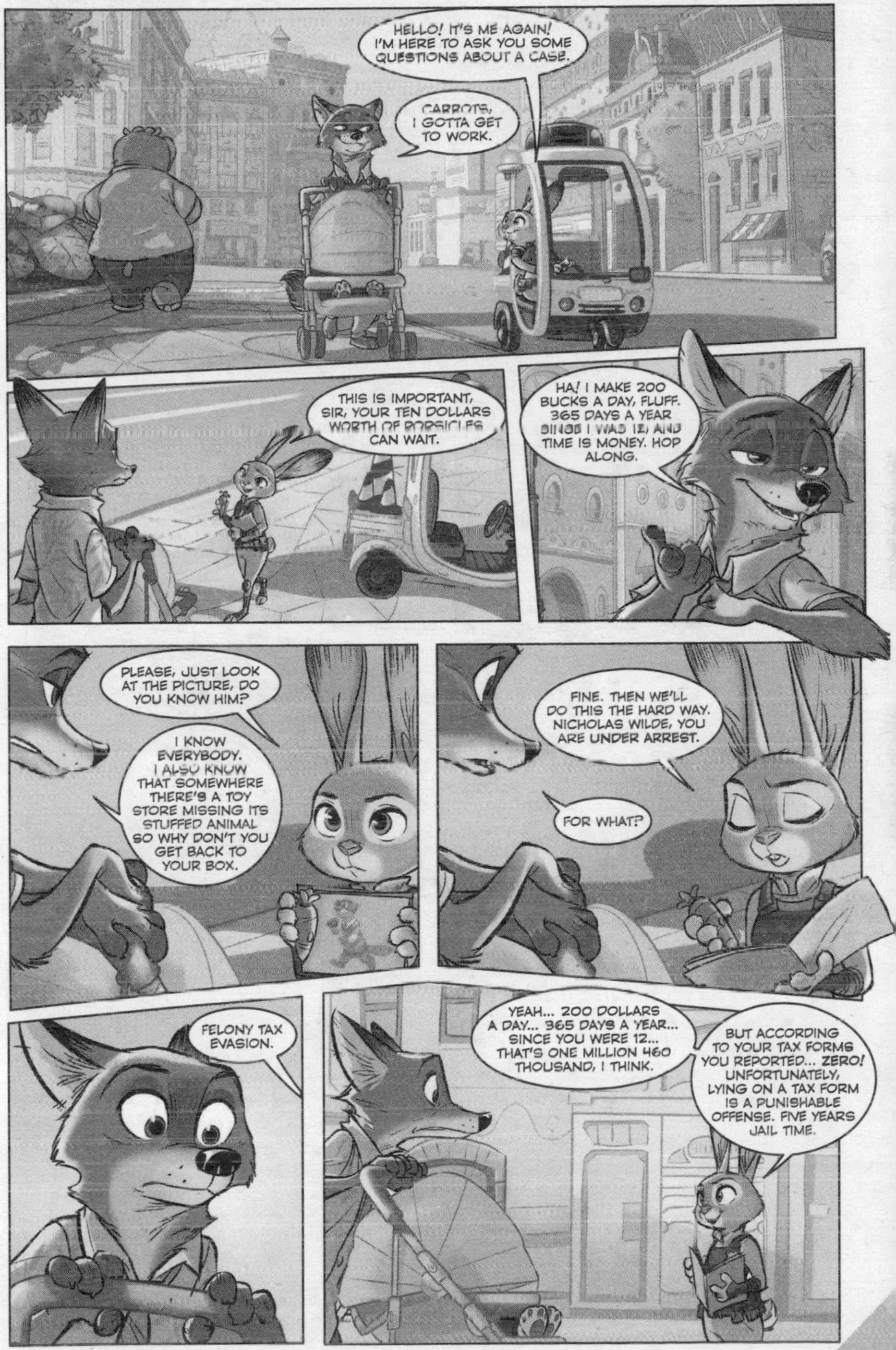
HELLO! IT'S ME AGAIN! I'M HERE TO ASK YOU SOME QUESTIONS ABOUT A CASE.
CARROTS, I GOTTA GET TO WORK.
THIS IS IMPORTANT, SIR, YOUR TEN DOLLARS WORTH OF POPSICLES CAN WAIT.
HA! I MAKE 200 BUCKS A DAY, FLUFF. 365 DAYS A YEAR SINCE I WAS 12, AND TIME IS MONEY. HOP ALONG.
PLEASE, JUST LOOK AT THE PICTURE, DO YOU KNOW HIM?
I KNOW EVERYBODY. I ALSO KNOW THAT SOMEWHERE THERE'S A TOY STORE MISSING ITS STUFFED ANIMAL SO WHY DON'T YOU GET BACK TO YOUR BOX.
FINE. THEN WE'LL DO THIS THE HARD WAY. NICHOLAS WILDE, YOU ARE UNDER ARREST.
FOR WHAT?
FELONY TAX EVASION.
YEAH... 200 DOLLARS A DAY... 365 DAYS A YEAR... SINCE YOU WERE 12... THAT'S ONE MILLION 460 THOUSAND, I THINK.
BUT ACCORDING TO YOUR TAX FORMS YOU REPORTED... ZERO! UNFORTUNATELY, LYING ON A TAX FORM IS A PUNISHABLE OFFENSE. FIVE YEARS JAIL TIME.

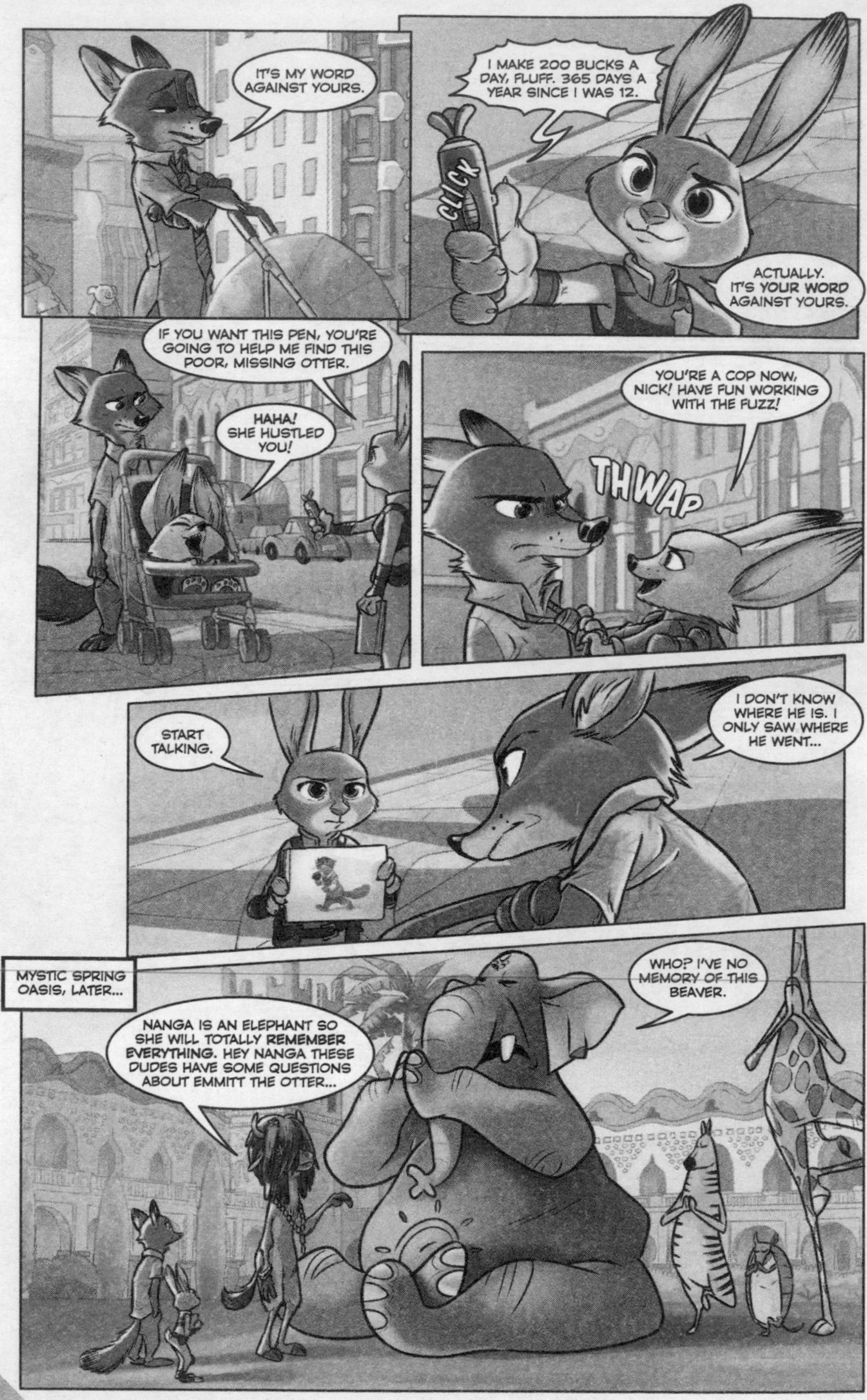

IT'S MY WORD AGAINST YOURS.
I MAKE 200 BUCKS A DAY, FLUFF. 365 DAYS A YEAR SINCE I WAS 12.
CLICK
ACTUALLY. IT'S YOUR WORD AGAINST YOURS.
IF YOU WANT THIS PEN, YOU'RE GOING TO HELP ME FIND THIS POOR, MISSING OTTER.
HAHA! SHE HUSTLED YOU!
YOU'RE A COP NOW, NICK! HAVE FUN WORKING WITH THE FUZZ!
THWAP
START TALKING.
I DON'T KNOW WHERE HE IS. I ONLY SAW WHERE HE WENT...
MYSTIC SPRING OASIS, LATER...
NANGA IS AN ELEPHANT SO SHE WILL TOTALLY REMEMBER EVERYTHING. HEY NANGA THESE DUDES HAVE SOME QUESTIONS ABOUT EMMITT THE OTTER...
WHO? I'VE NO MEMORY OF THIS BEAVER.

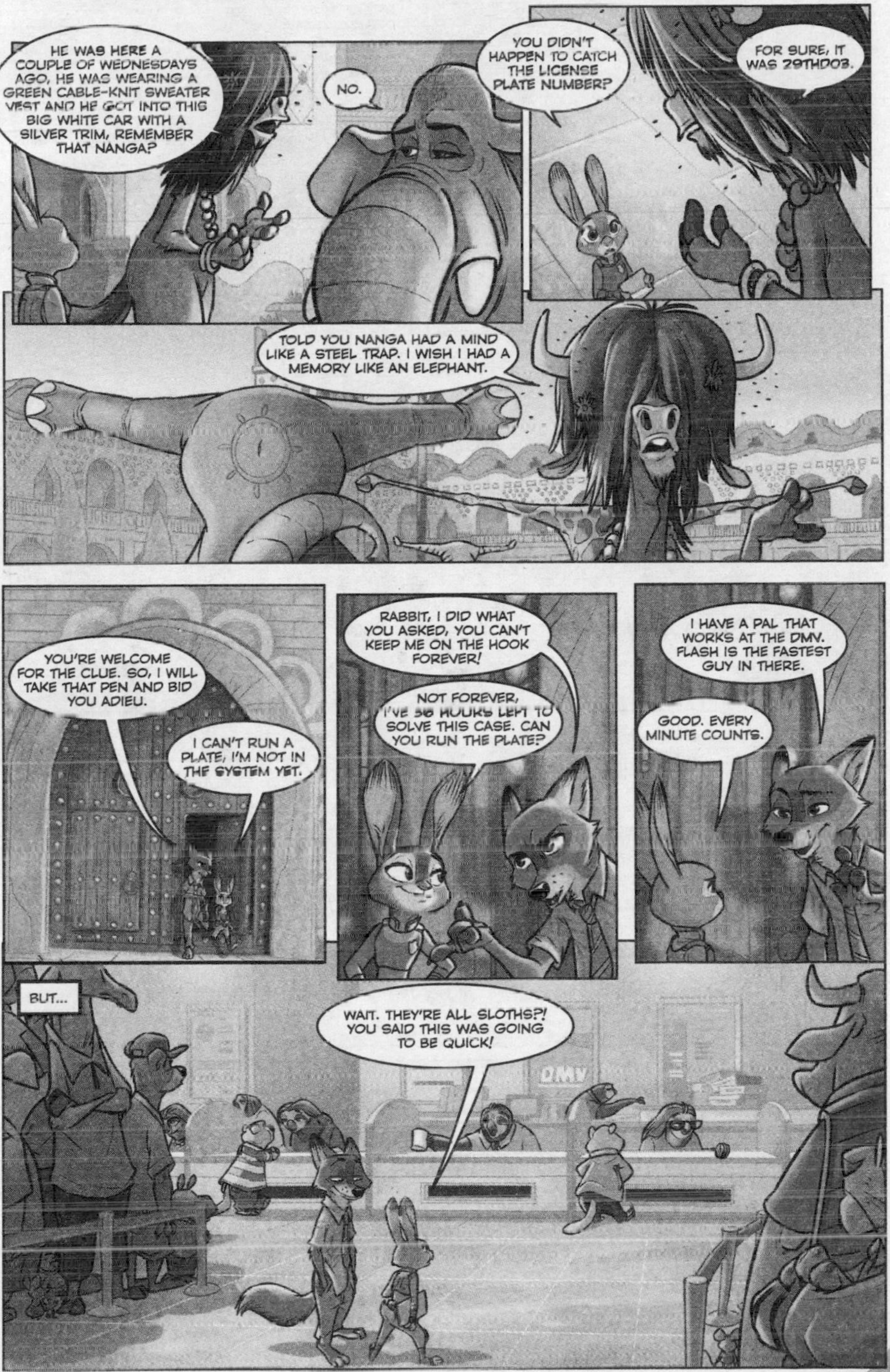

HE WAS HERE A COUPLE OF WEDNESDAYS AGO, HE WAS WEARING A GREEN CABLE-KNIT SWEATER VEST AND HE GOT INTO THIS BIG WHITE CAR WITH A SILVER TRIM, REMEMBER THAT NANGA?
NO.
YOU DIDN'T HAPPEN TO CATCH THE LICENSE PLATE NUMBER?
FOR SURE, IT WAS 29THD03.
TOLD YOU NANGA HAD A MIND LIKE A STEEL TRAP. I WISH I HAD A MEMORY LIKE AN ELEPHANT.
YOU'RE WELCOME FOR THE CLUE. SO, I WILL TAKE THAT PEN AND BID YOU ADIEU.
I CAN'T RUN A PLATE, I'M NOT IN THE SYSTEM YET.
RABBIT, I DID WHAT YOU ASKED, YOU CAN'T KEEP ME ON THE HOOK FOREVER!
NOT FOREVER, I'VE 36 HOURS LEFT TO SOLVE THIS CASE. CAN YOU RUN THE PLATE?
I HAVE A PAL THAT WORKS AT THE DMV. FLASH IS THE FASTEST GUY IN THERE.
GOOD. EVERY MINUTE COUNTS.
BUT...
WAIT. THEY'RE ALL SLOTHS?! YOU SAID THIS WAS GOING TO BE QUICK!
DMV

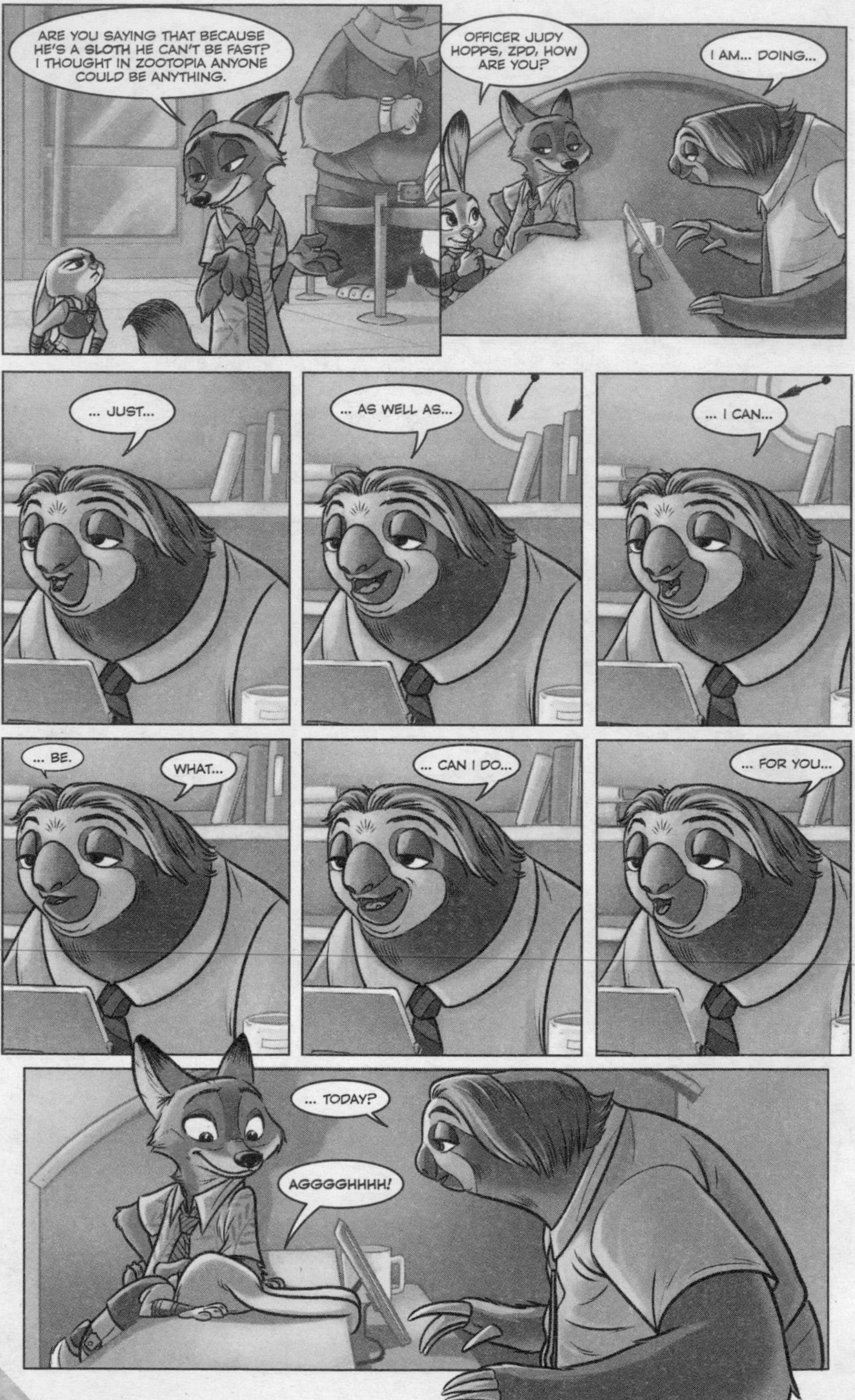
ARE YOU SAYING THAT BECAUSE HE'S A SLOTH HE CAN'T BE FAST? I THOUGHT IN ZOOTOPIA ANYONE COULD BE ANYTHING.
OFFICER JUDY HOPPS, ZPD, HOW ARE YOU?
I AM... DOING...
... JUST...
... AS WELL AS...
... I CAN...
... BE.
WHAT...
... CAN I DO...
... FOR YOU...
... TODAY?
AGGGGHHHH!

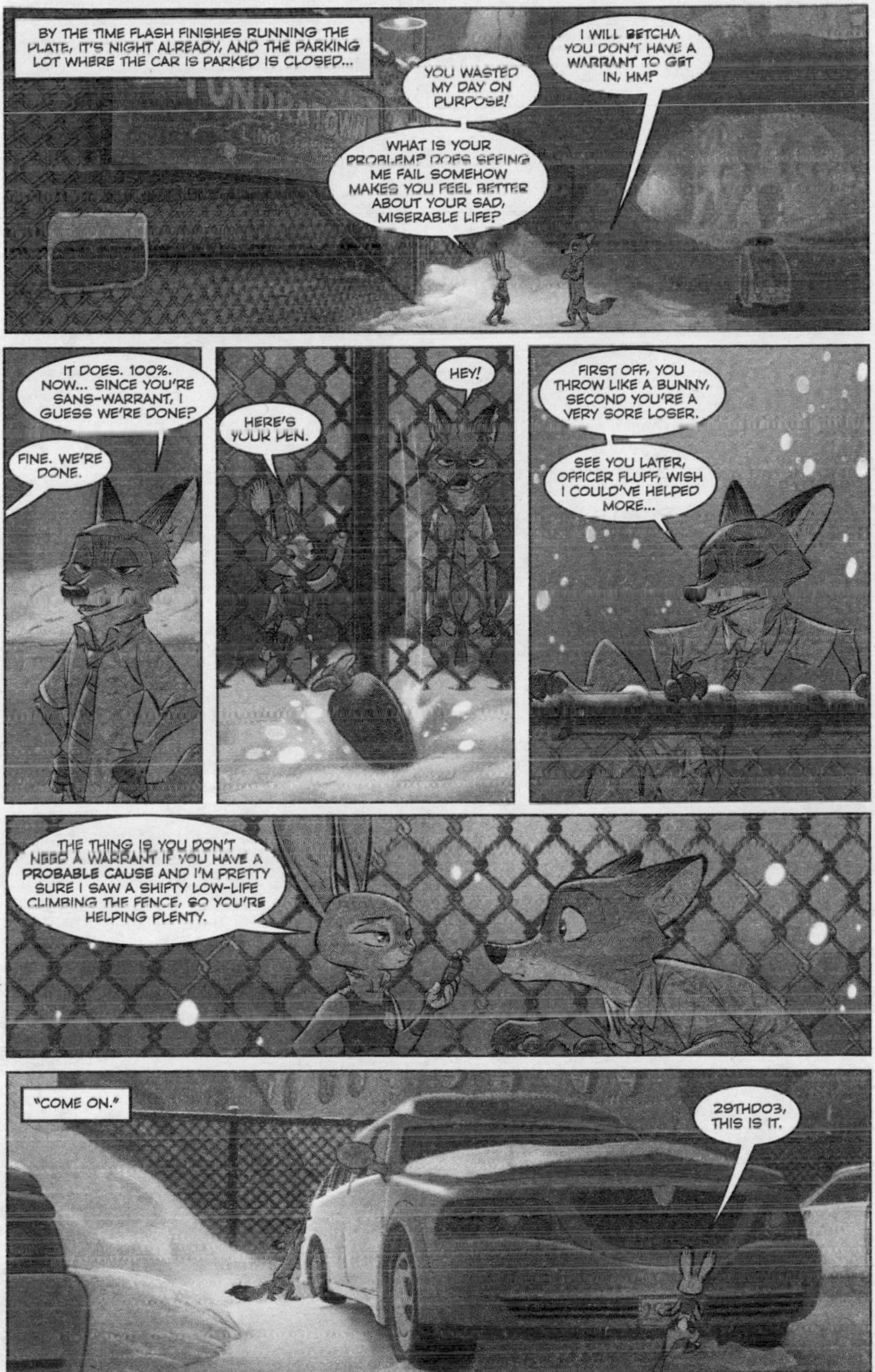
BY THE TIME FLASH FINISHES RUNNING THE PLATE, IT'S NIGHT ALREADY, AND THE PARKING LOT WHERE THE CAR IS PARKED IS CLOSED...
YOU WASTED MY DAY ON PURPOSE!
WHAT IS YOUR PROBLEM? DOES SEEING ME FAIL SOMEHOW MAKES YOU FEEL BETTER ABOUT YOUR SAD, MISERABLE LIFE?
I WILL BETCHA YOU DON'T HAVE A WARRANT TO GET IN, HM?
IT DOES. 100%. NOW... SINCE YOU'RE SANS-WARRANT, I GUESS WE'RE DONE?
FINE. WE'RE DONE.
HEY!
HERE'S YOUR PEN.
FIRST OFF, YOU THROW LIKE A BUNNY, SECOND YOU'RE A VERY SORE LOSER.
SEE YOU LATER, OFFICER FLUFF, WISH I COULD'VE HELPED MORE...
THE THING IS YOU DON'T NEED A WARRANT IF YOU HAVE A PROBABLE CAUSE AND I'M PRETTY SURE I SAW A SHIFTY LOW-LIFE CLIMBING THE FENCE, SO YOU'RE HELPING PLENTY.
"COME ON."
29THD03, THIS IS IT.

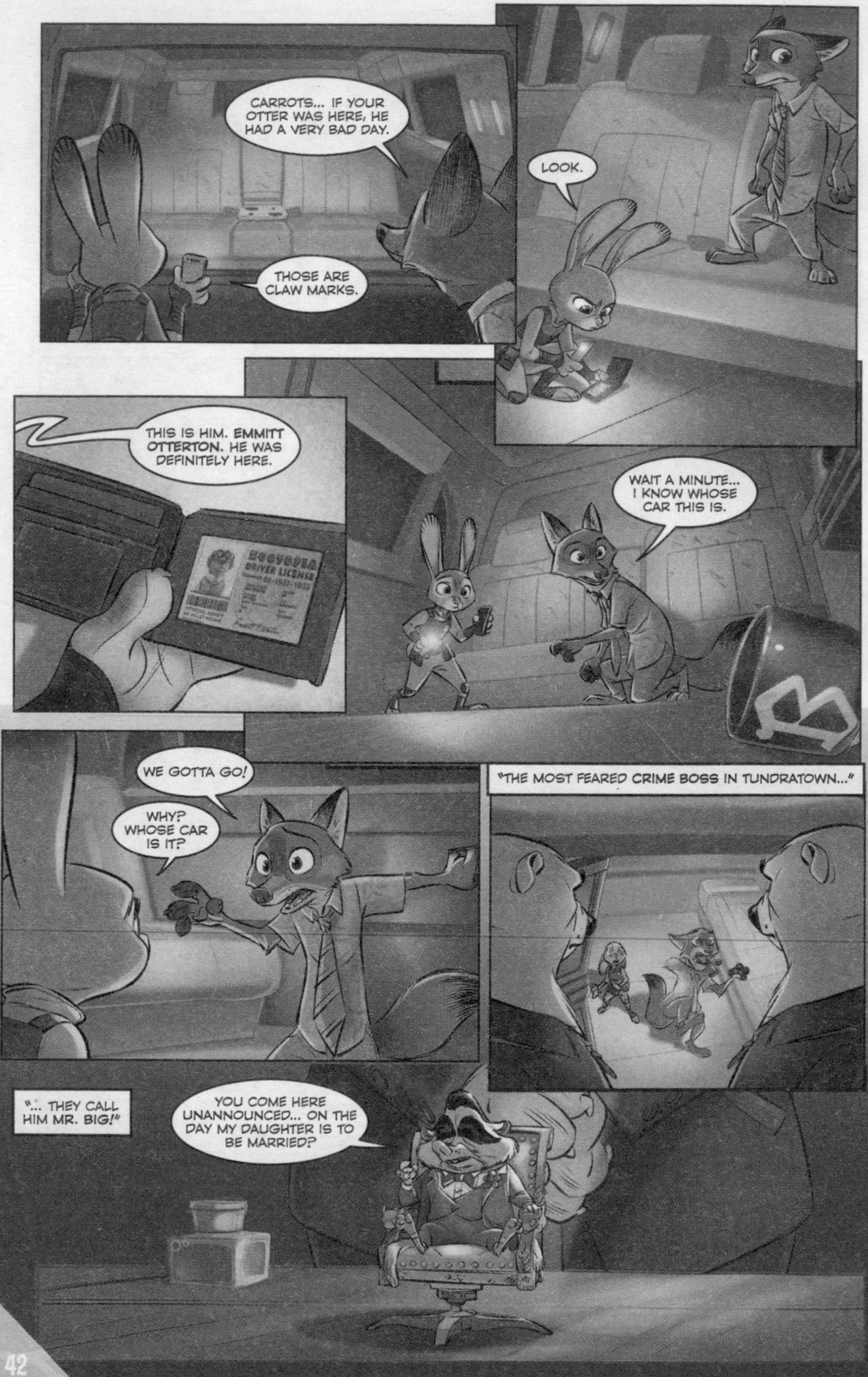
CARROTS... IF YOUR OTTER WAS HERE, HE HAD A VERY BAD DAY.
THOSE ARE CLAW MARKS.
LOOK.
THIS IS HIM. EMMITT OTTERTON. HE WAS DEFINITELY HERE.
DRIVER LICENSE
WAIT A MINUTE... I KNOW WHOSE CAR THIS IS.
WE GOTTA GO!
WHY? WHOSE CAR IS IT?
"THE MOST FEARED CRIME BOSS IN TUNDRATOWN..."
"... THEY CALL HIM MR. BIG!"
YOU COME HERE UNANNOUNCED... ON THE DAY MY DAUGHTER IS TO BE MARRIED?

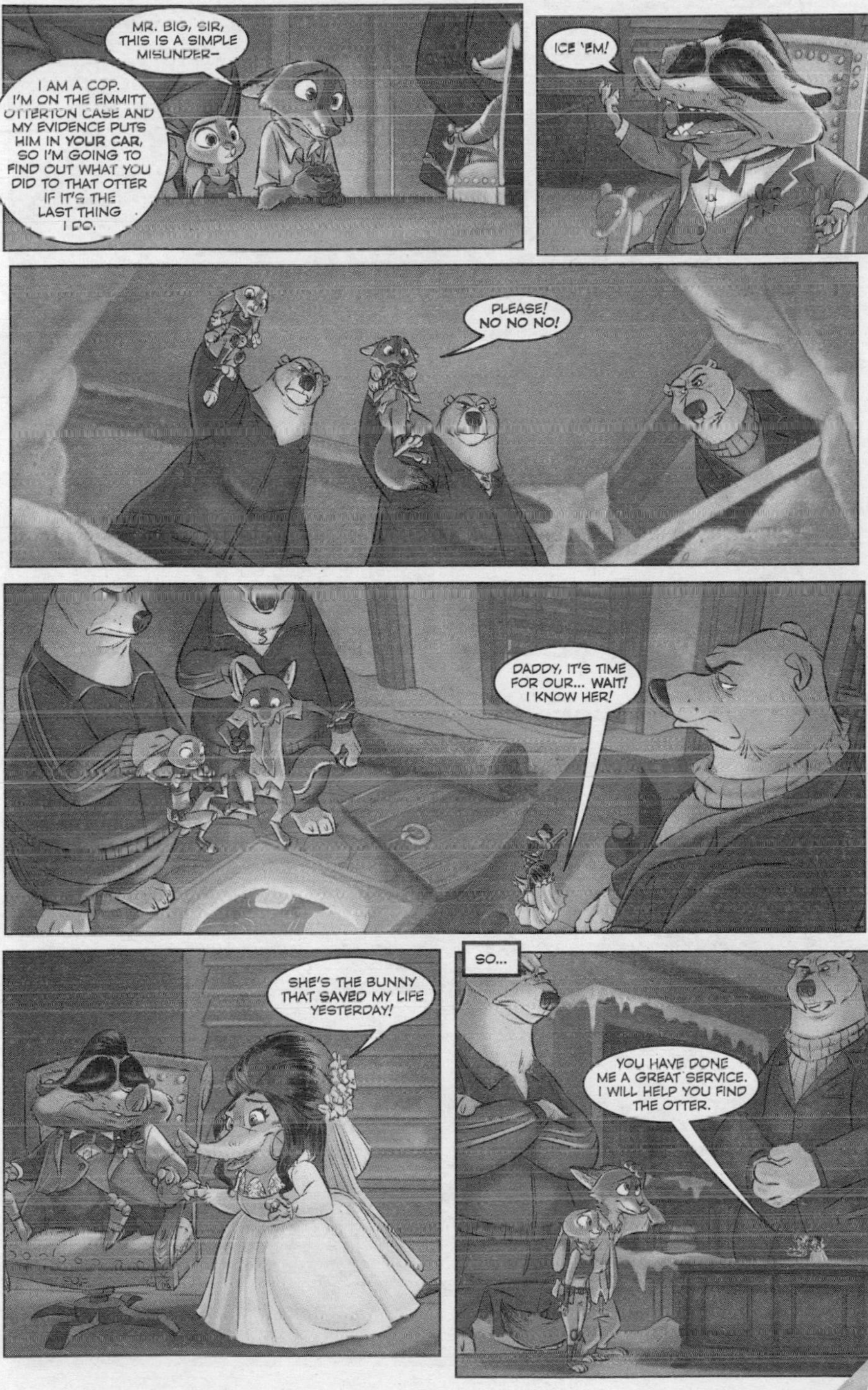
MR. BIG, SIR, THIS IS A SIMPLE MISUNDER–
I AM A COP. I'M ON THE EMMITT OTTERTON CASE AND MY EVIDENCE PUTS HIM IN YOUR CAR, SO I'M GOING TO FIND OUT WHAT YOU DID TO THAT OTTER IF IT'S THE LAST THING I DO.
ICE 'EM!
PLEASE! NO NO NO!
DADDY, IT'S TIME FOR OUR... WAIT! I KNOW HER!
SHE'S THE BUNNY THAT SAVED MY LIFE YESTERDAY!
SO...
YOU HAVE DONE ME A GREAT SERVICE. I WILL HELP YOU FIND THE OTTER.

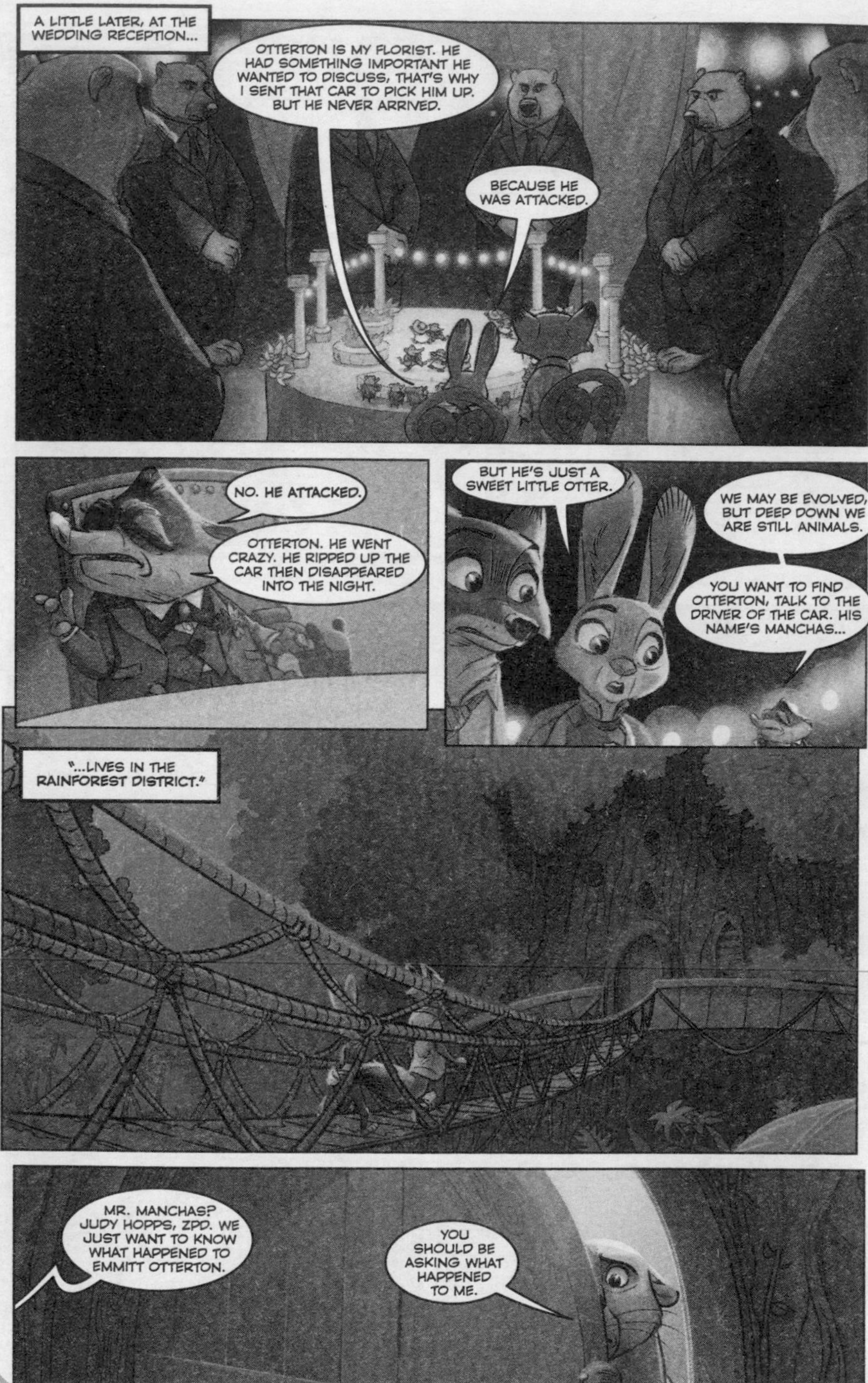

A LITTLE LATER, AT THE WEDDING RECEPTION...
OTTERTON IS MY FLORIST. HE HAD SOMETHING IMPORTANT HE WANTED TO DISCUSS, THAT'S WHY I SENT THAT CAR TO PICK HIM UP. BUT HE NEVER ARRIVED.
BECAUSE HE WAS ATTACKED.
NO. HE ATTACKED.
OTTERTON. HE WENT CRAZY. HE RIPPED UP THE CAR THEN DISAPPEARED INTO THE NIGHT.
BUT HE'S JUST A SWEET LITTLE OTTER.
WE MAY BE EVOLVED, BUT DEEP DOWN WE ARE STILL ANIMALS.
YOU WANT TO FIND OTTERTON, TALK TO THE DRIVER OF THE CAR. HIS NAME'S MANCHAS...
"...LIVES IN THE RAINFOREST DISTRICT."
MR. MANCHAS? JUDY HOPPS, ZPD. WE JUST WANT TO KNOW WHAT HAPPENED TO EMMITT OTTERTON.
YOU SHOULD BE ASKING WHAT HAPPENED TO ME.

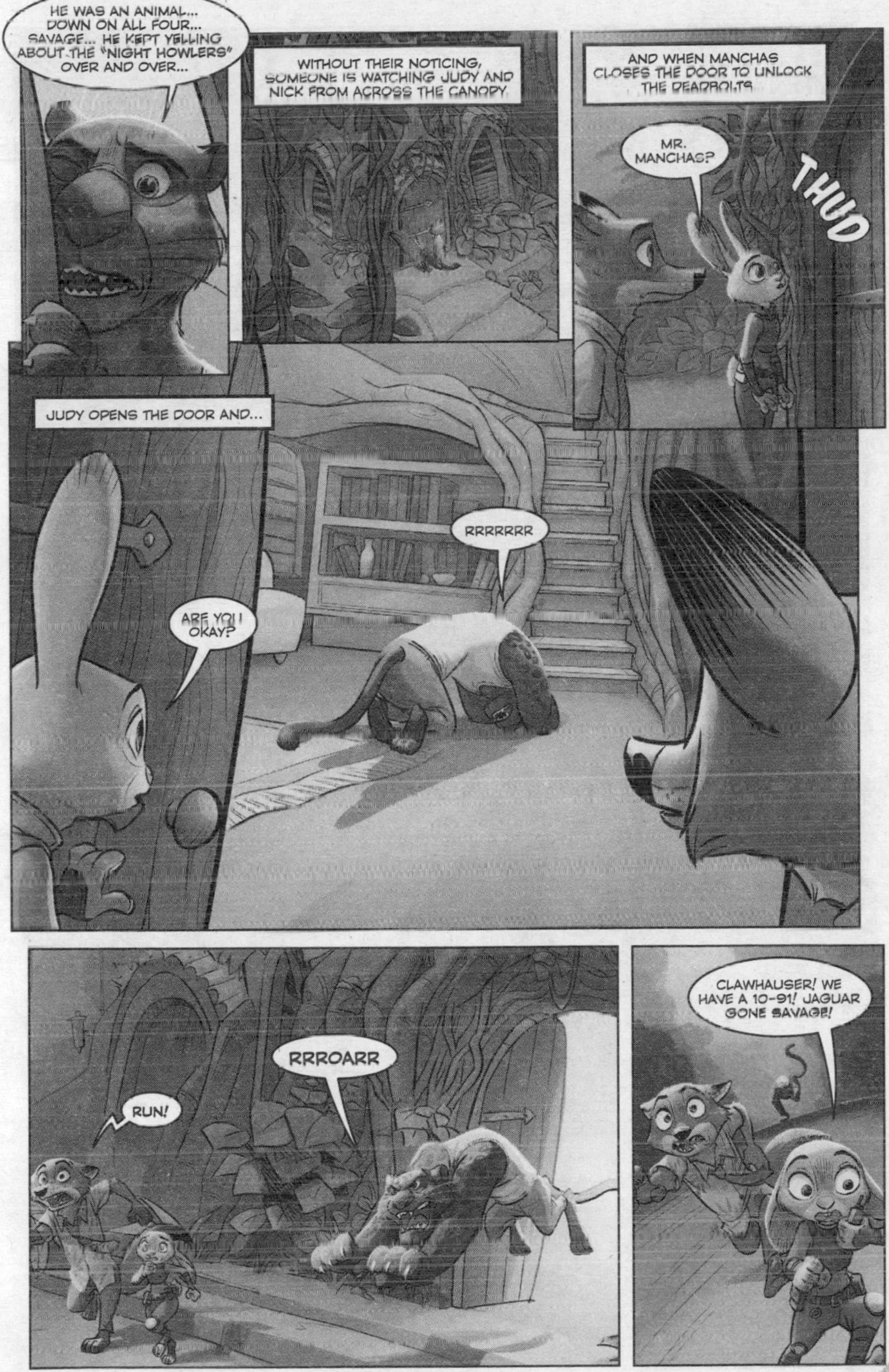
HE WAS AN ANIMAL... DOWN ON ALL FOUR... SAVAGE... HE KEPT YELLING ABOUT THE "NIGHT HOWLERS" OVER AND OVER...
WITHOUT THEIR NOTICING, SOMEONE IS WATCHING JUDY AND NICK FROM ACROSS THE CANOPY.
AND WHEN MANCHAS CLOSES THE DOOR TO UNLOCK THE DEADBOLTS
MR. MANCHAS?
THUD
JUDY OPENS THE DOOR AND...
RRRRRRR
ARE YOU OKAY?
RUN!
RRROARR
CLAWHAUSER! WE HAVE A 10-91! JAGUAR GONE SAVAGE!

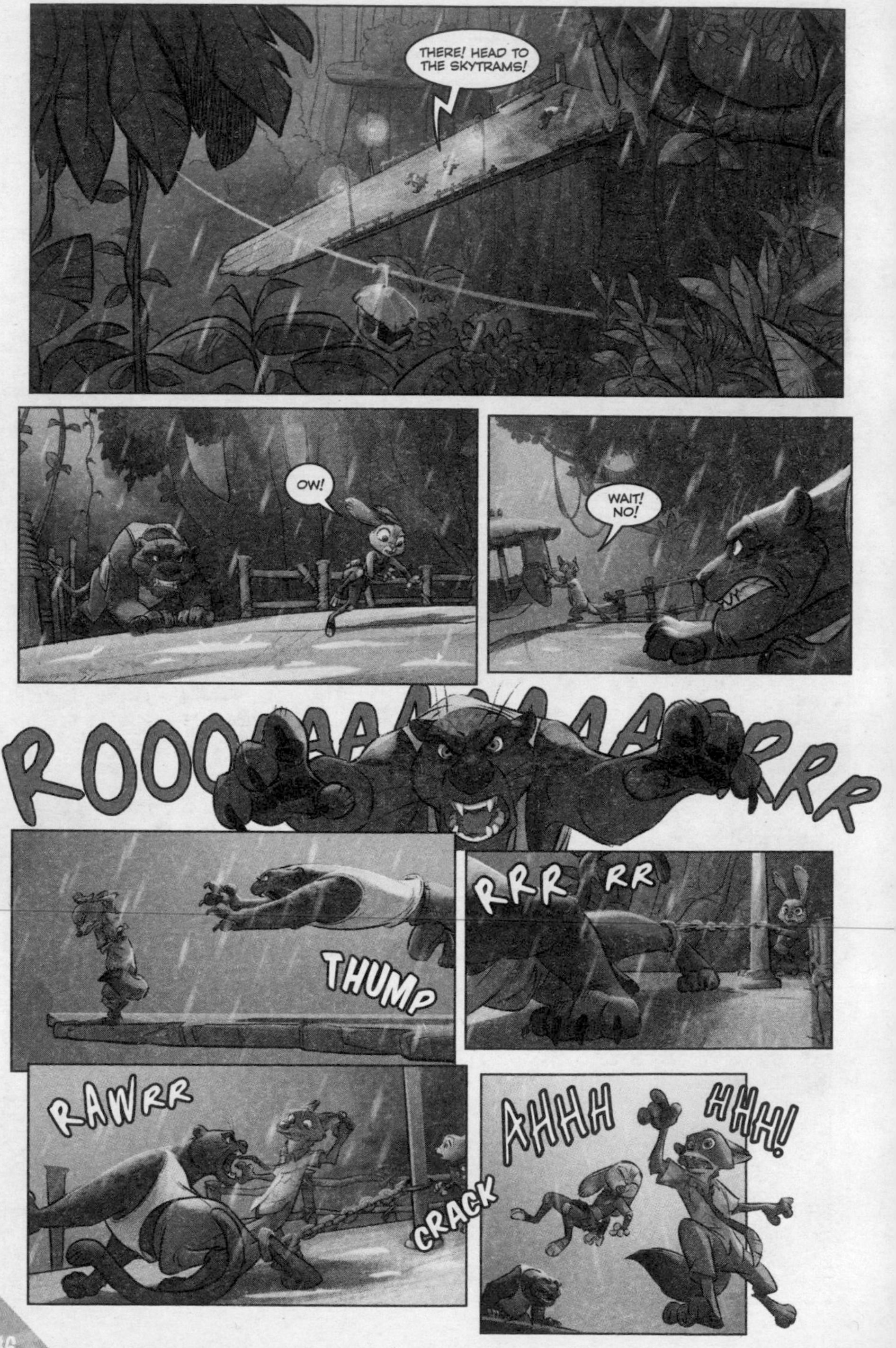
THERE! HEAD TO THE SKYTRAMS!
OW!
WAIT! NO!
ROOOAAAAAAAARRRR
RRR RR
THUMP
RAWRR
CRACK
AHHHHHH!

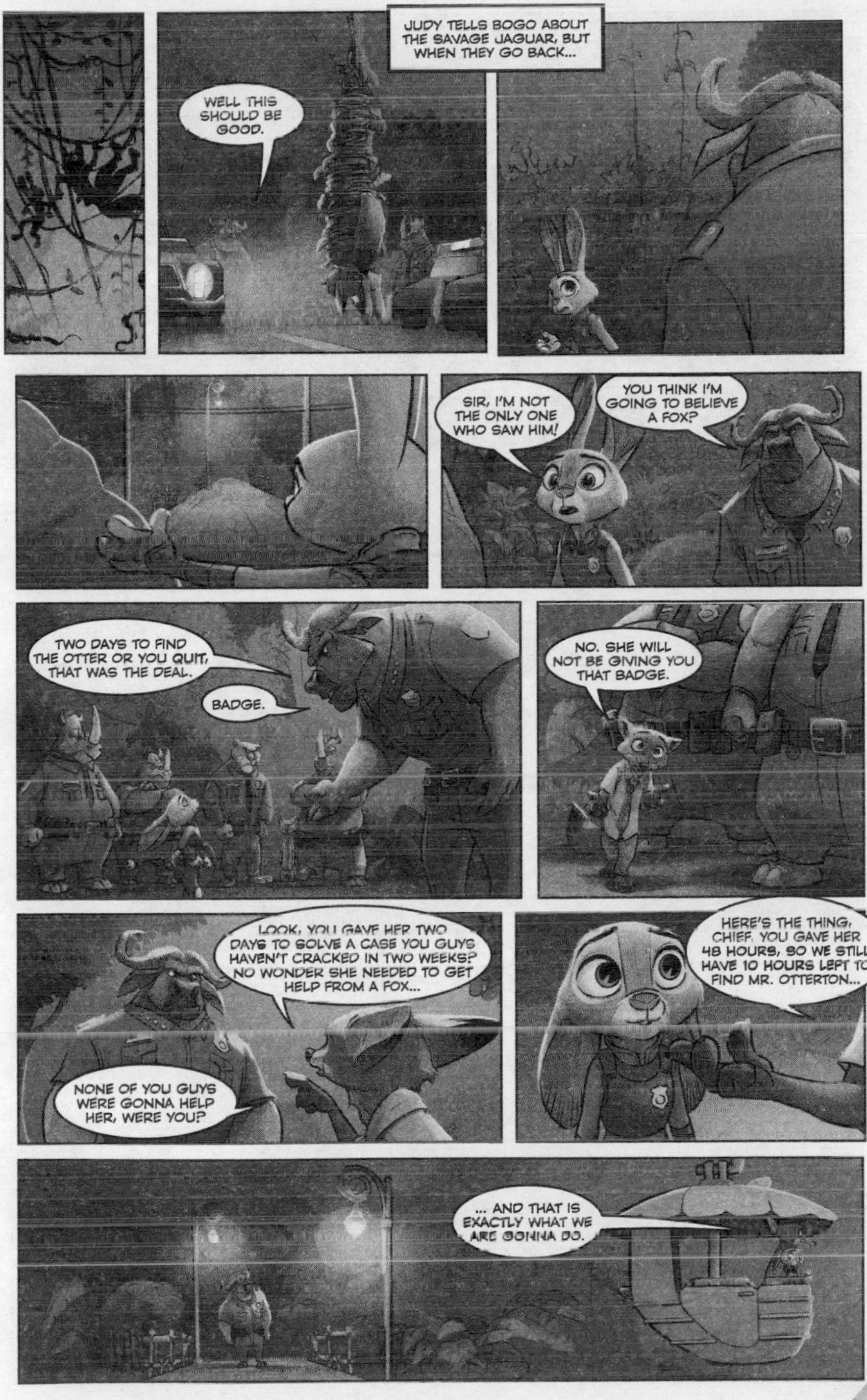
WELL THIS SHOULD BE GOOD.
JUDY TELLS BOGO ABOUT THE SAVAGE JAGUAR, BUT WHEN THEY GO BACK...
SIR, I'M NOT THE ONLY ONE WHO SAW HIM!
YOU THINK I'M GOING TO BELIEVE A FOX?
TWO DAYS TO FIND THE OTTER OR YOU QUIT, THAT WAS THE DEAL.
BADGE.
NO. SHE WILL NOT BE GIVING YOU THAT BADGE.
LOOK, YOU GAVE HER TWO DAYS TO SOLVE A CASE YOU GUYS HAVEN'T CRACKED IN TWO WEEKS? NO WONDER SHE NEEDED TO GET HELP FROM A FOX...
NONE OF YOU GUYS WERE GONNA HELP HER, WERE YOU?
HERE'S THE THING, CHIEF. YOU GAVE HER 48 HOURS, SO WE STILL HAVE 10 HOURS LEFT TO FIND MR. OTTERTON...
... AND THAT IS EXACTLY WHAT WE ARE GONNA DO.

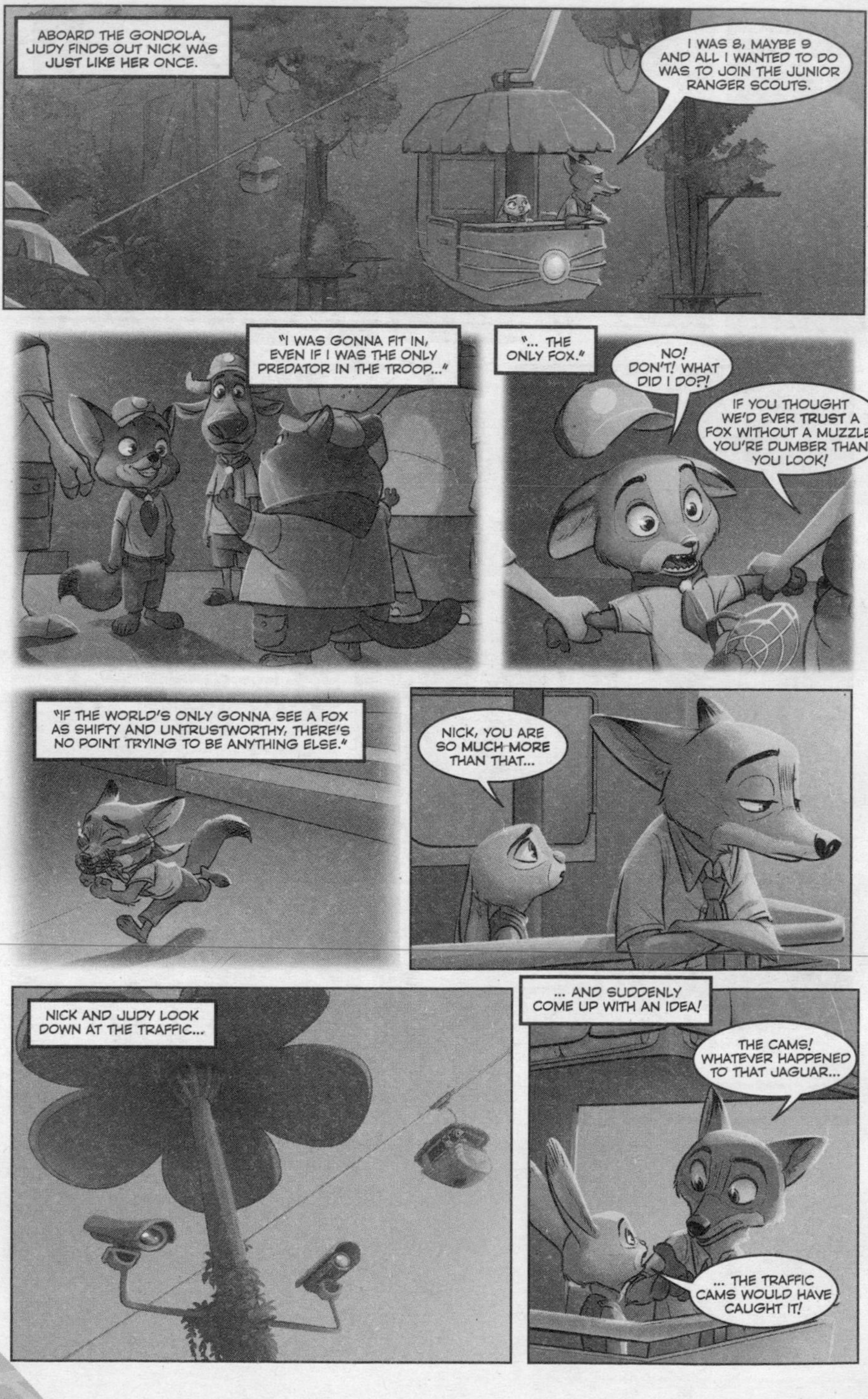
ABOARD THE GONDOLA, JUDY FINDS OUT NICK WAS JUST LIKE HER ONCE.
I WAS 8, MAYBE 9 AND ALL I WANTED TO DO WAS TO JOIN THE JUNIOR RANGER SCOUTS.
"I WAS GONNA FIT IN, EVEN IF I WAS THE ONLY PREDATOR IN THE TROOP..."
"... THE ONLY FOX."
NO! DON'T! WHAT DID I DO?!
IF YOU THOUGHT WE'D EVER **TRUST** A FOX WITHOUT A MUZZLE, YOU'RE DUMBER THAN YOU LOOK!
"IF THE WORLD'S ONLY GONNA SEE A FOX AS SHIFTY AND UNTRUSTWORTHY, THERE'S NO POINT TRYING TO BE ANYTHING ELSE."
NICK, YOU ARE SO MUCH MORE THAN THAT...
NICK AND JUDY LOOK DOWN AT THE TRAFFIC...
... AND SUDDENLY COME UP WITH AN IDEA!
THE CAMS! WHATEVER HAPPENED TO THAT JAGUAR...
... THE TRAFFIC CAMS WOULD HAVE CAUGHT IT!

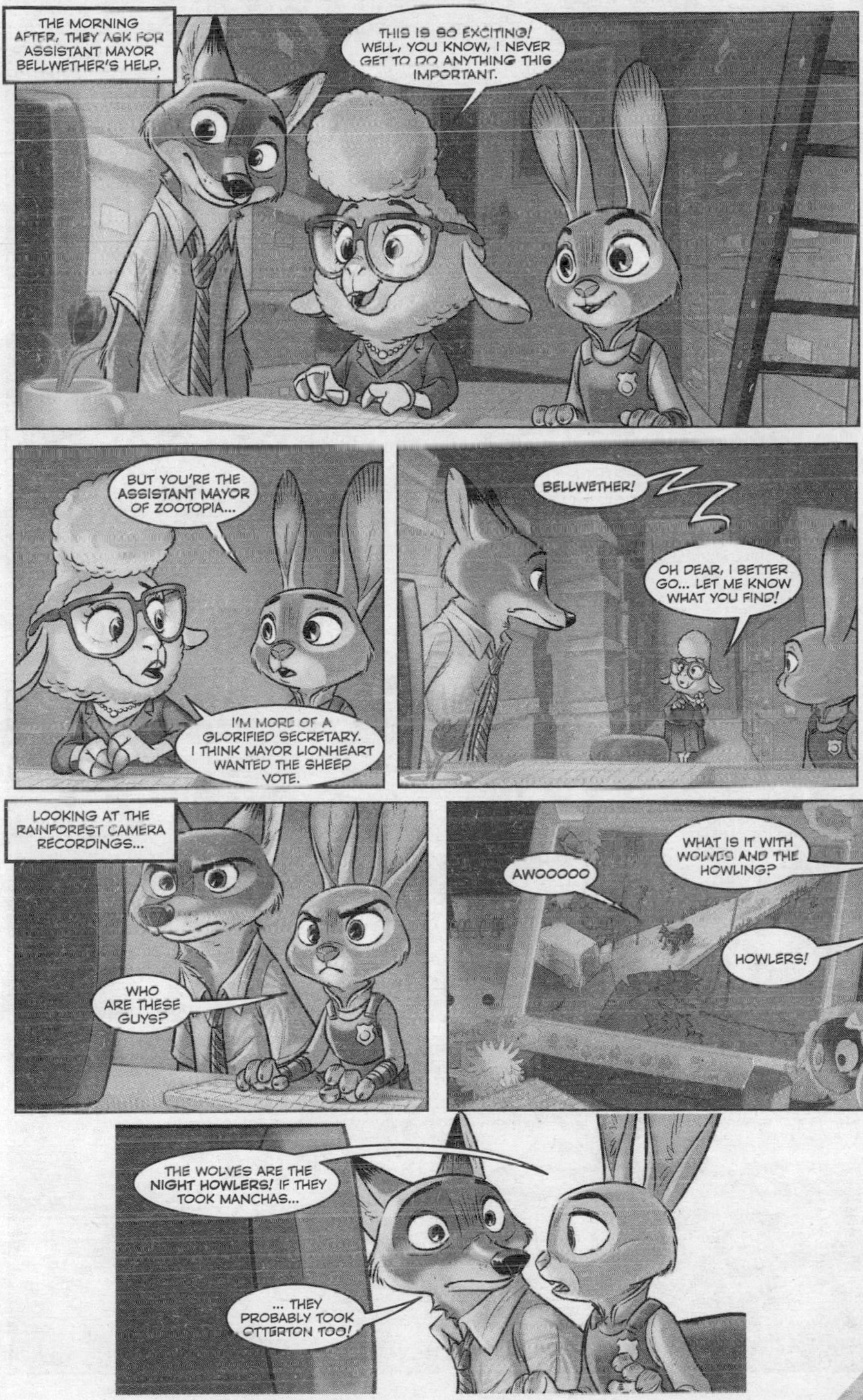

THE MORNING AFTER, THEY ASK FOR ASSISTANT MAYOR BELLWETHER'S HELP.
THIS IS SO EXCITING! WELL, YOU KNOW, I NEVER GET TO DO ANYTHING THIS IMPORTANT.
BUT YOU'RE THE ASSISTANT MAYOR OF ZOOTOPIA...
I'M MORE OF A GLORIFIED SECRETARY. I THINK MAYOR LIONHEART WANTED THE SHEEP VOTE.
BELLWETHER!
OH DEAR, I BETTER GO... LET ME KNOW WHAT YOU FIND!
LOOKING AT THE RAINFOREST CAMERA RECORDINGS...
WHO ARE THESE GUYS?
AWOOOOO
WHAT IS IT WITH WOLVES AND THE HOWLING?
HOWLERS!
THE WOLVES ARE THE NIGHT HOWLERS! IF THEY TOOK MANCHAS...
... THEY PROBABLY TOOK OTTERTON TOO!

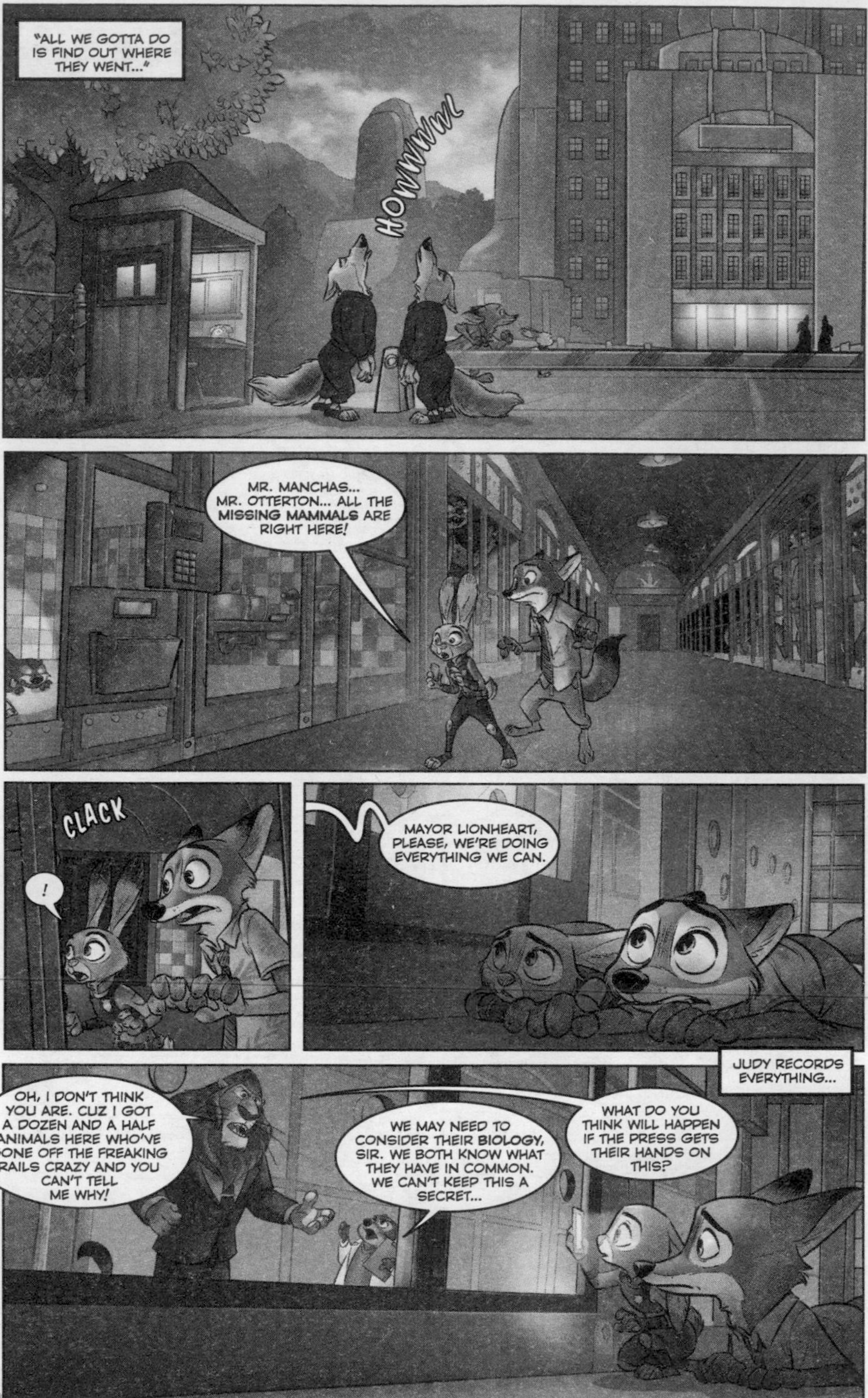

"ALL WE GOTTA DO IS FIND OUT WHERE THEY WENT..."
HOWWWWL
MR. MANCHAS... MR. OTTERTON... ALL THE MISSING MAMMALS ARE RIGHT HERE!
CLACK
!
MAYOR LIONHEART, PLEASE, WE'RE DOING EVERYTHING WE CAN.
JUDY RECORDS EVERYTHING...
OH, I DON'T THINK YOU ARE. CUZ I GOT A DOZEN AND A HALF ANIMALS HERE WHO'VE GONE OFF THE FREAKING RAILS CRAZY AND YOU CAN'T TELL ME WHY!
WE MAY NEED TO CONSIDER THEIR BIOLOGY, SIR. WE BOTH KNOW WHAT THEY HAVE IN COMMON. WE CAN'T KEEP THIS A SECRET...
WHAT DO YOU THINK WILL HAPPEN IF THE PRESS GETS THEIR HANDS ON THIS?

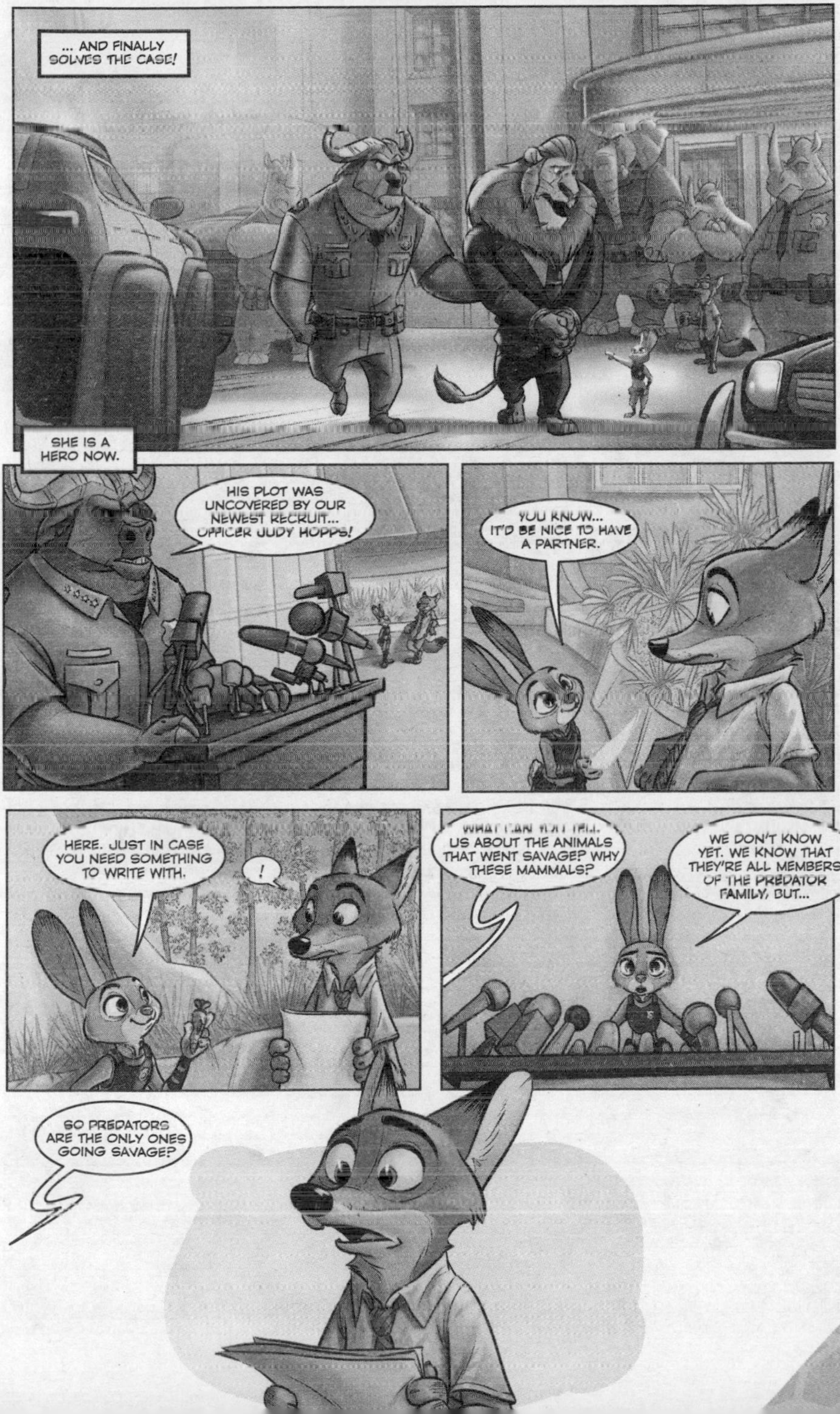
... AND FINALLY SOLVES THE CASE!
SHE IS A HERO NOW.
HIS PLOT WAS UNCOVERED BY OUR NEWEST RECRUIT... OFFICER JUDY HOPPS!
YOU KNOW... IT'D BE NICE TO HAVE A PARTNER.
HERE. JUST IN CASE YOU NEED SOMETHING TO WRITE WITH.
!
WHAT CAN YOU TELL US ABOUT THE ANIMALS THAT WENT SAVAGE? WHY THESE MAMMALS?
WE DON'T KNOW YET. WE KNOW THAT THEY'RE ALL MEMBERS OF THE PREDATOR FAMILY, BUT...
SO PREDATORS ARE THE ONLY ONES GOING SAVAGE?

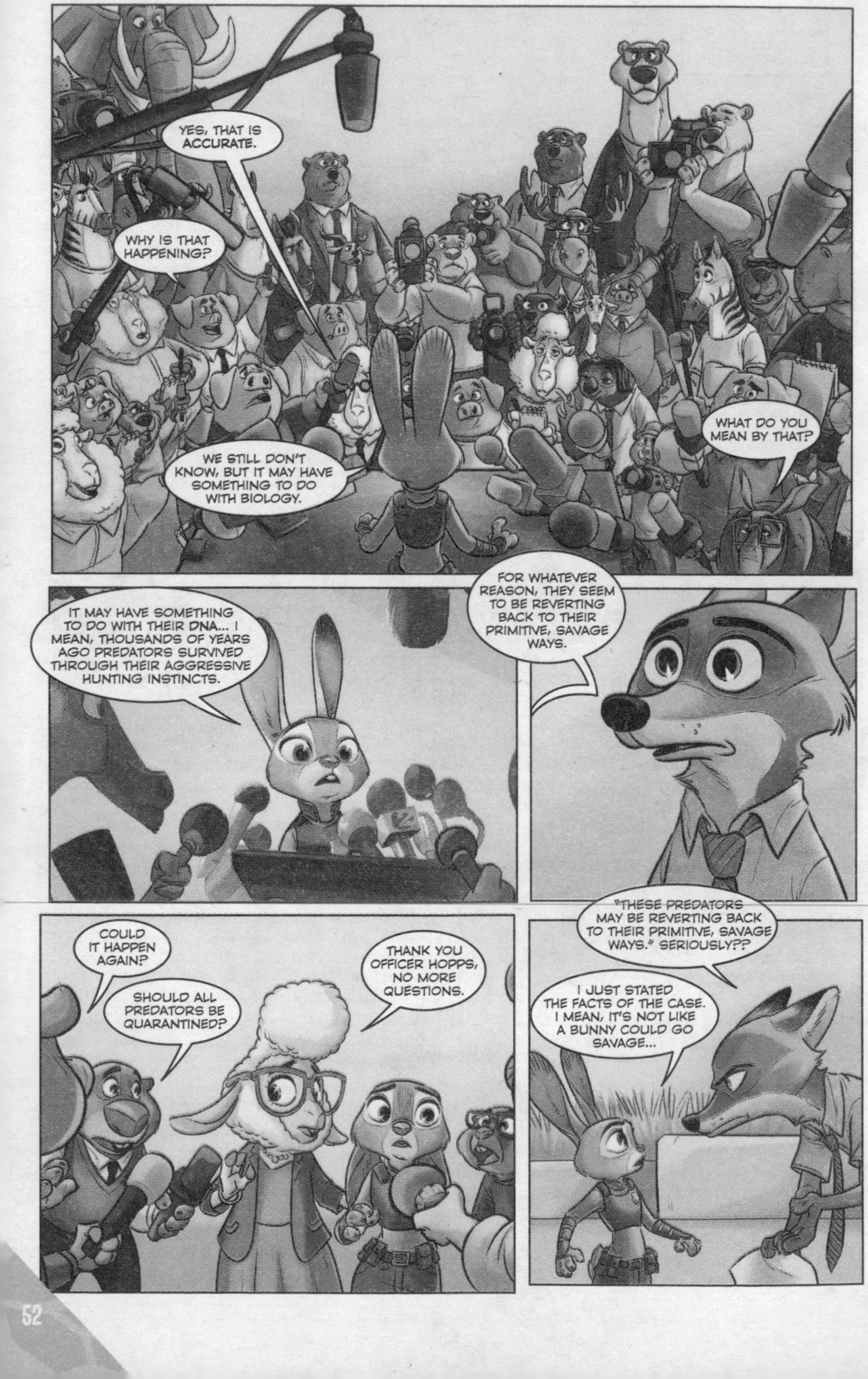
YES, THAT IS ACCURATE.
WHY IS THAT HAPPENING?
WE STILL DON'T KNOW, BUT IT MAY HAVE SOMETHING TO DO WITH BIOLOGY.
WHAT DO YOU MEAN BY THAT?
IT MAY HAVE SOMETHING TO DO WITH THEIR DNA... I MEAN, THOUSANDS OF YEARS AGO PREDATORS SURVIVED THROUGH THEIR AGGRESSIVE HUNTING INSTINCTS.
FOR WHATEVER REASON, THEY SEEM TO BE REVERTING BACK TO THEIR PRIMITIVE, SAVAGE WAYS.
COULD IT HAPPEN AGAIN?
SHOULD ALL PREDATORS BE QUARANTINED?
THANK YOU OFFICER HOPPS, NO MORE QUESTIONS.
"THESE PREDATORS MAY BE REVERTING BACK TO THEIR PRIMITIVE, SAVAGE WAYS." SERIOUSLY??
I JUST STATED THE FACTS OF THE CASE. I MEAN, IT'S NOT LIKE A BUNNY COULD GO SAVAGE...

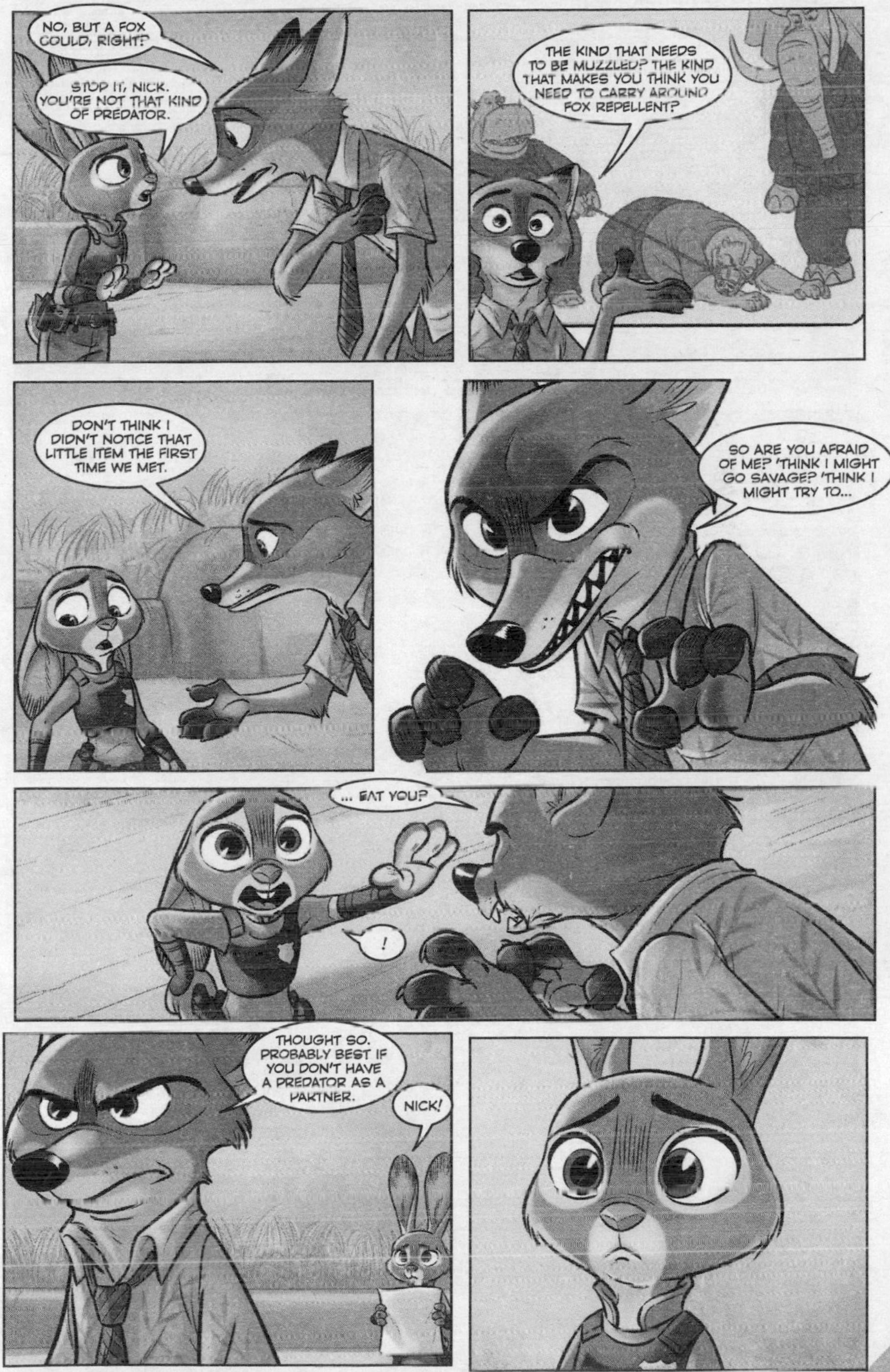
NO, BUT A FOX COULD, RIGHT?
STOP IT, NICK. YOU'RE NOT THAT KIND OF PREDATOR.
THE KIND THAT NEEDS TO BE MUZZLED? THE KIND THAT MAKES YOU THINK YOU NEED TO CARRY AROUND FOX REPELLENT?
DON'T THINK I DIDN'T NOTICE THAT LITTLE ITEM THE FIRST TIME WE MET.
SO ARE YOU AFRAID OF ME? 'THINK I MIGHT GO SAVAGE? 'THINK I MIGHT TRY TO...
... EAT YOU?
!
THOUGHT SO. PROBABLY BEST IF YOU DON'T HAVE A PREDATOR AS A PARTNER.
NICK!

IN THE FOLLOWING DAYS, TENSIONS CONTINUE TO RISE IN THE CITY...

STICK TO YOUR OWN KIND!

PRED PRIDE!

CLAWHAUSER? WHAT'RE YOU DOING?

THEY THOUGHT IT WOULD BE BETTER IF A PREDATOR WASN'T THE FIRST FACE YOU SEE WHEN YOU WALK INTO THE ZPD...

SO, THEY'RE MOVING ME TO RECORDS DOWNSTAIRS. BY THE BOILER.

MAYOR BELLWETHER TELLS JUDY SHE IS GOING TO BE THE PUBLIC FACE OF THE ZPD...

OUR CITY IS 90% PREY, JUDY, AND RIGHT NOW THEY'RE JUST REALLY SCARED. YOU'RE A HERO TO THEM. THEY TRUST YOU.

... BUT JUDY DOESN'T FEEL LIKE A HERO.

I CAME HERE TO MAKE THE WORLD A BETTER PLACE BUT... I THINK I BROKE IT. A GOOD COP IS SUPPOSED TO HELP THE CITY, NOT TEAR IT APART.

I DON'T DESERVE THIS BADGE.

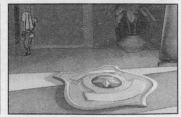

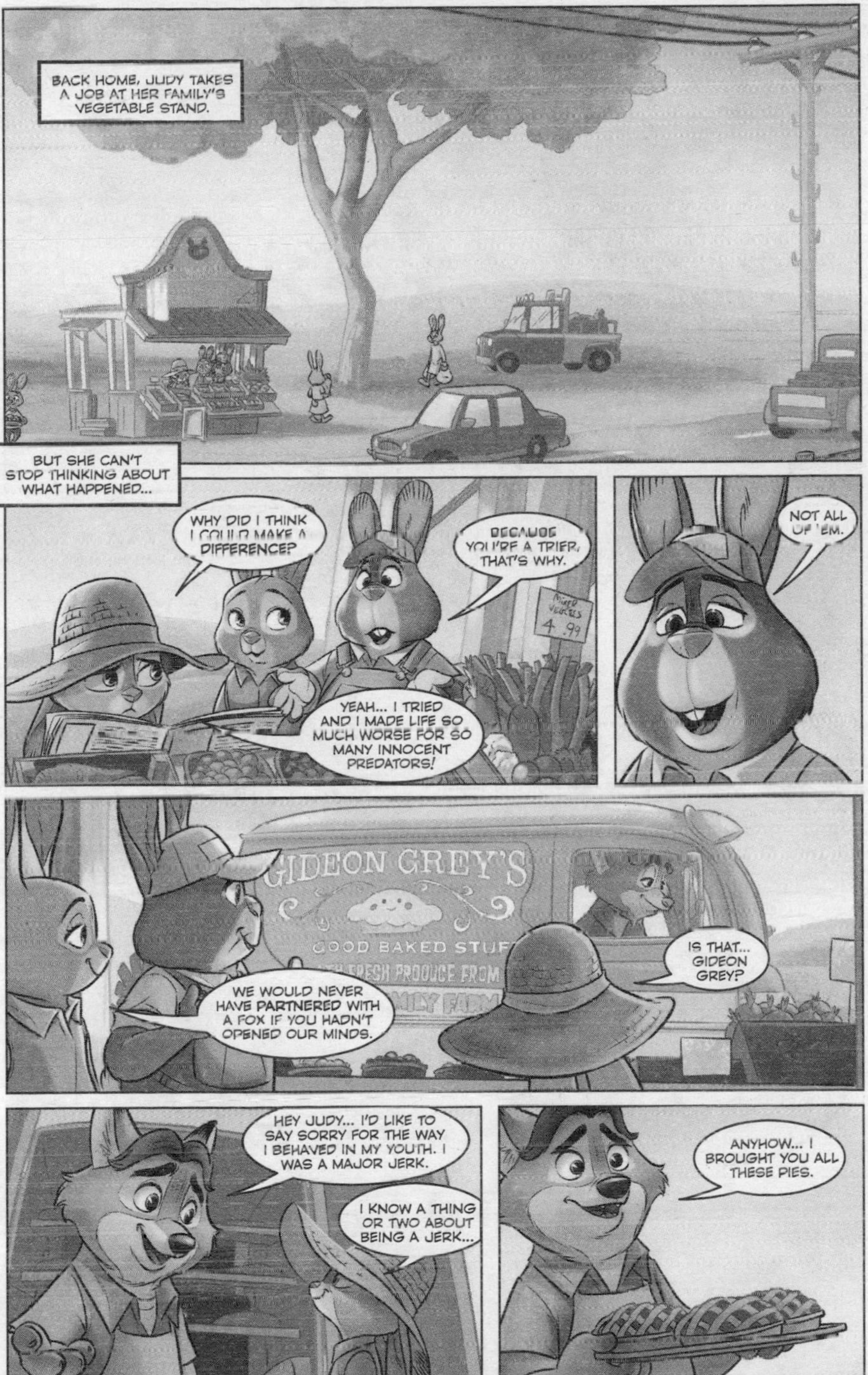
BACK HOME, JUDY TAKES A JOB AT HER FAMILY'S VEGETABLE STAND.
BUT SHE CAN'T STOP THINKING ABOUT WHAT HAPPENED...
WHY DID I THINK I COULD MAKE A DIFFERENCE?
BECAUSE YOU'RE A TRIER, THAT'S WHY.
YEAH... I TRIED AND I MADE LIFE SO MUCH WORSE FOR SO MANY INNOCENT PREDATORS!
NOT ALL OF 'EM.
GIDEON GREY'S
GOOD BAKED STUFF
IS THAT... GIDEON GREY?
WE WOULD NEVER HAVE PARTNERED WITH A FOX IF YOU HADN'T OPENED OUR MINDS.
HEY JUDY... I'D LIKE TO SAY SORRY FOR THE WAY I BEHAVED IN MY YOUTH. I WAS A MAJOR JERK.
I KNOW A THING OR TWO ABOUT BEING A JERK...
ANYHOW... I BROUGHT YOU ALL THESE PIES.

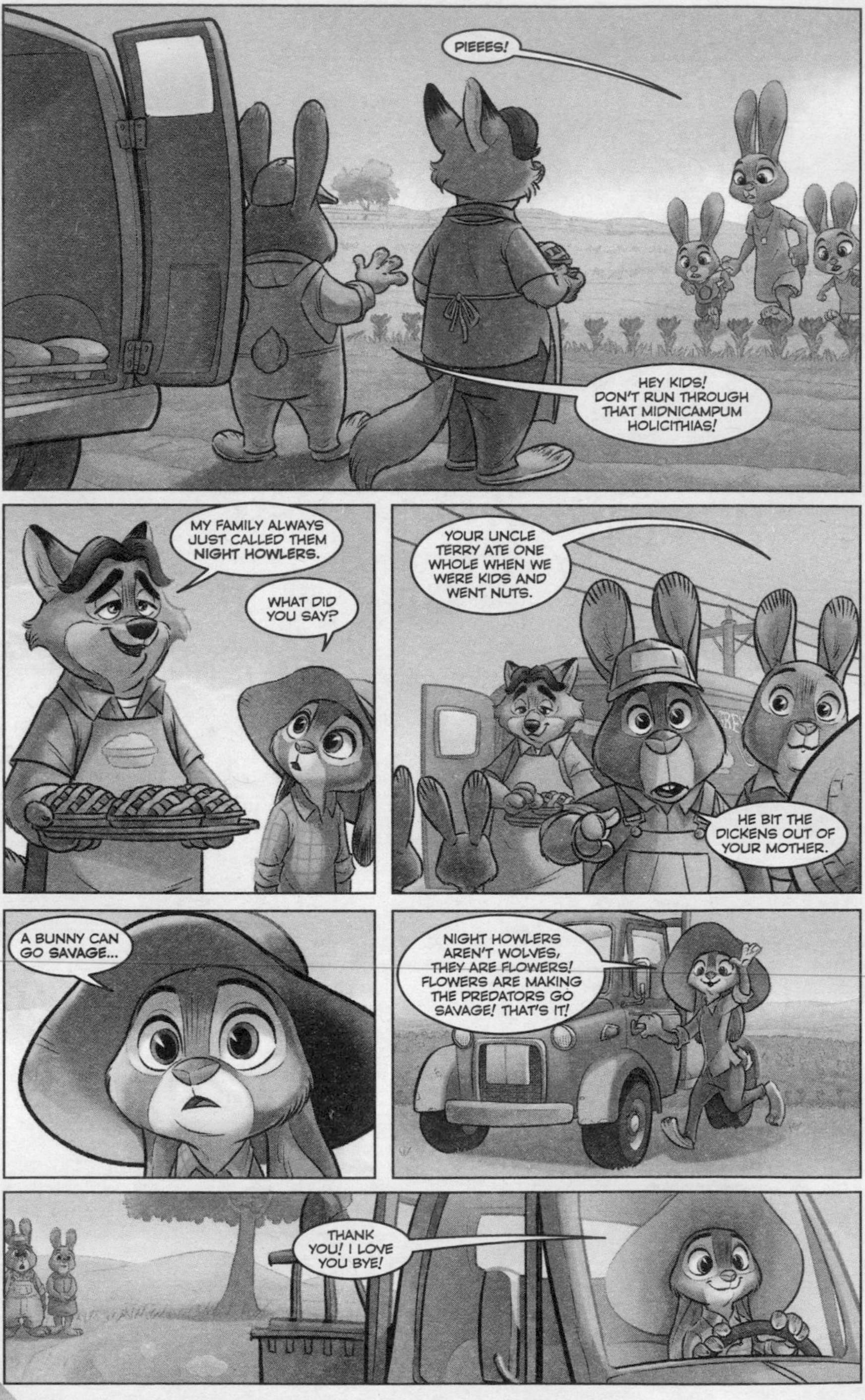
PIEEES!
HEY KIDS! DON'T RUN THROUGH THAT MIDNICAMPUM HOLICITHIAS!
MY FAMILY ALWAYS JUST CALLED THEM NIGHT HOWLERS.
WHAT DID YOU SAY?
YOUR UNCLE TERRY ATE ONE WHOLE WHEN WE WERE KIDS AND WENT NUTS.
HE BIT THE DICKENS OUT OF YOUR MOTHER.
A BUNNY CAN GO SAVAGE...
NIGHT HOWLERS AREN'T WOLVES, THEY ARE FLOWERS! FLOWERS ARE MAKING THE PREDATORS GO SAVAGE! THAT'S IT!
THANK YOU! I LOVE YOU BYE!

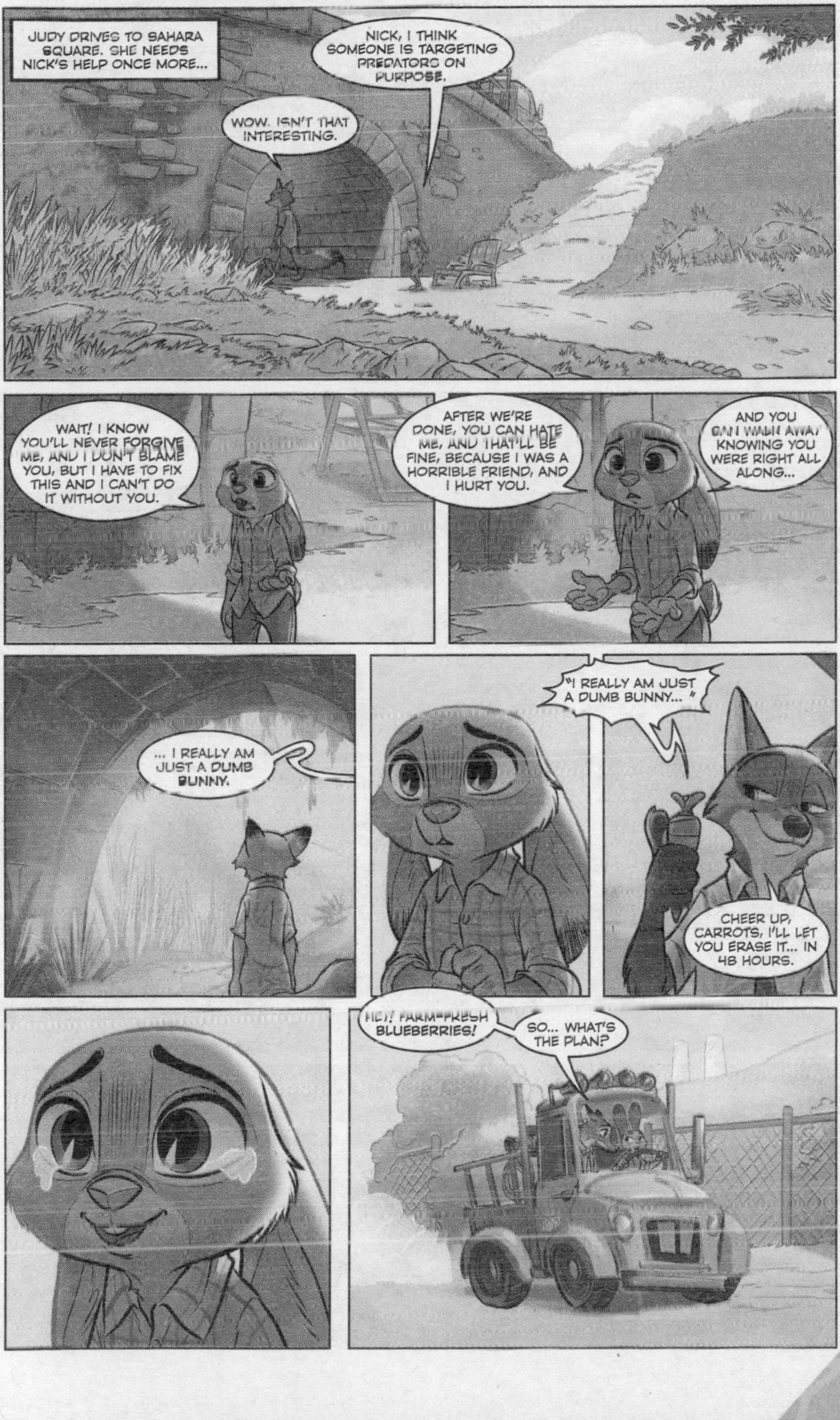
JUDY DRIVES TO SAHARA SQUARE. SHE NEEDS NICK'S HELP ONCE MORE...
NICK, I THINK SOMEONE IS TARGETING PREDATORS ON PURPOSE.
WOW. ISN'T THAT INTERESTING.
WAIT! I KNOW YOU'LL NEVER FORGIVE ME, AND I DON'T BLAME YOU, BUT I HAVE TO FIX THIS AND I CAN'T DO IT WITHOUT YOU.
AFTER WE'RE DONE, YOU CAN HATE ME, AND THAT'LL BE FINE, BECAUSE I WAS A HORRIBLE FRIEND, AND I HURT YOU.
AND YOU CAN WALK AWAY KNOWING YOU WERE RIGHT ALL ALONG...
... I REALLY AM JUST A DUMB BUNNY.
"I REALLY AM JUST A DUMB BUNNY... "
CHEER UP, CARROTS, I'LL LET YOU ERASE IT... IN 48 HOURS.
HEY! FARM-FRESH BLUEBERRIES!
SO... WHAT'S THE PLAN?

USING MR. BIG'S HELP, JUDY AND NICK QUESTION THE WEASEL WHO STOLE THE NIGHT HOWLERS...

THE WEASEL LEADS THEM TO AN ABANDONED SUBWAY STATION...

WAIT! STOP! I'LL TALK, I'LL TALK!

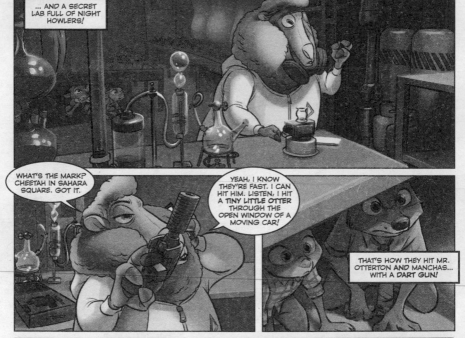

... AND A SECRET LAB FULL OF NIGHT HOWLERS!

WHAT'S THE MARK? CHEETAH IN SAHARA SQUARE. GOT IT.

YEAH, I KNOW THEY'RE FAST. I CAN HIT HIM. LISTEN, I HIT A TINY LITTLE OTTER THROUGH THE OPEN WINDOW OF A MOVING CAR!

THAT'S HOW THEY HIT MR. OTTERTON AND MANCHAS... WITH A DART GUN!

HEY, DOUG!

I'M COMING.

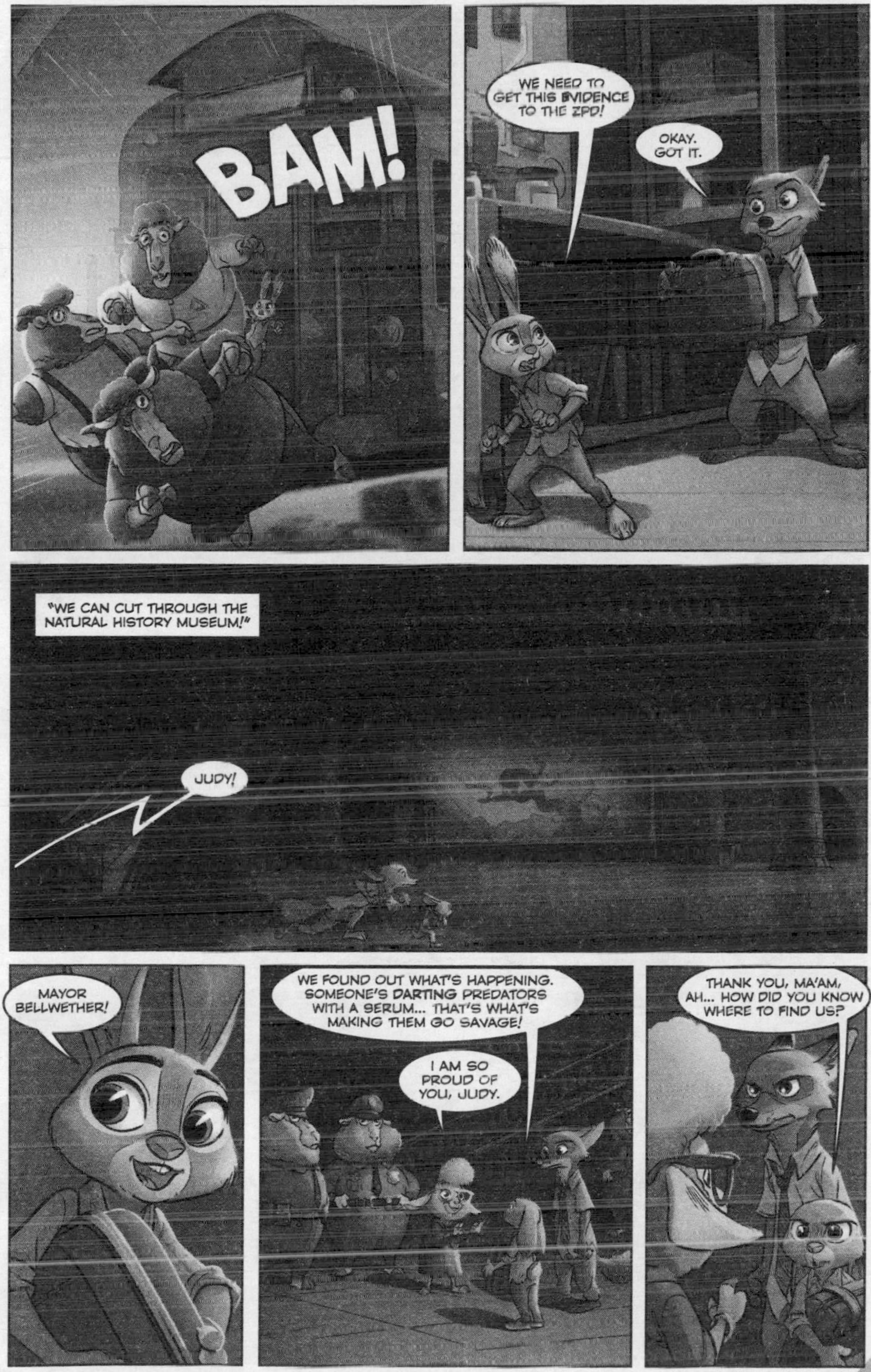
BAM!
WE NEED TO GET THIS EVIDENCE TO THE ZPD!
OKAY. GOT IT.
"WE CAN CUT THROUGH THE NATURAL HISTORY MUSEUM!"
JUDY!
MAYOR BELLWETHER!
WE FOUND OUT WHAT'S HAPPENING. SOMEONE'S DARTING PREDATORS WITH A SERUM... THAT'S WHAT'S MAKING THEM GO SAVAGE!
I AM SO PROUD OF YOU, JUDY.
THANK YOU, MA'AM, AH... HOW DID YOU KNOW WHERE TO FIND US?

RUN!

ACH!

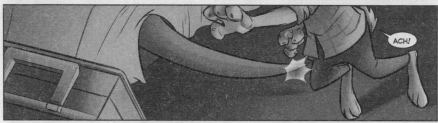

I GOT YA, COME HERE.

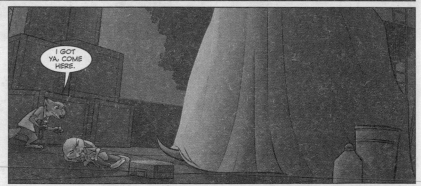

UH? BLUEBERRIES?

PASS.

I CAN'T WALK.

WE'LL THINK OF SOMETHING.

WE'RE ON THE SAME TEAM, JUDY!

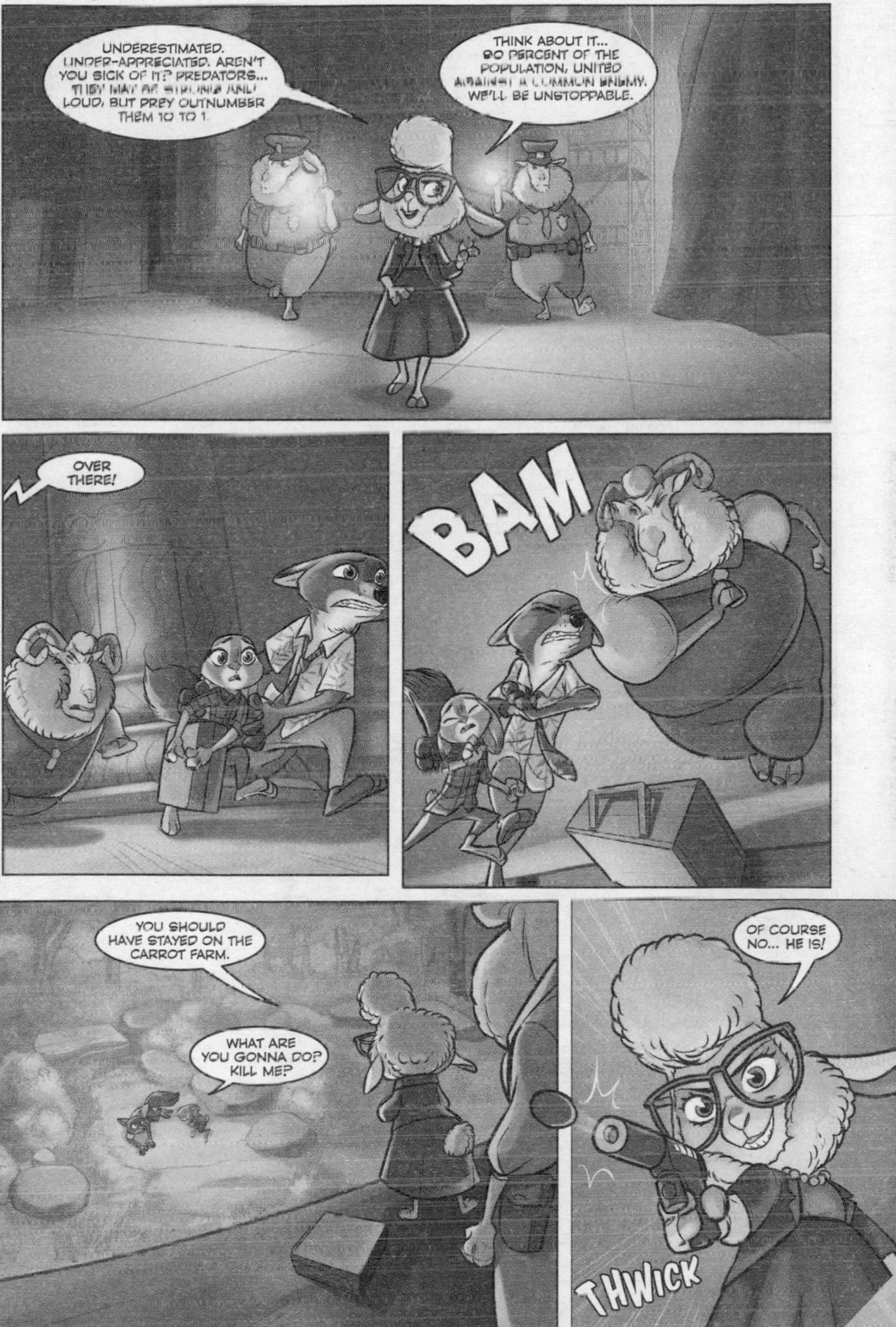
UNDERESTIMATED. UNDER-APPRECIATED. AREN'T YOU SICK OF IT? PREDATORS... THEY MAY BE STRONG AND LOUD, BUT PREY OUTNUMBER THEM 10 TO 1.
THINK ABOUT IT... 90 PERCENT OF THE POPULATION, UNITED AGAINST A COMMON ENEMY. WE'LL BE UNSTOPPABLE.
OVER THERE!
BAM
YOU SHOULD HAVE STAYED ON THE CARROT FARM.
WHAT ARE YOU GONNA DO? KILL ME?
OF COURSE NO... HE IS!
THWICK

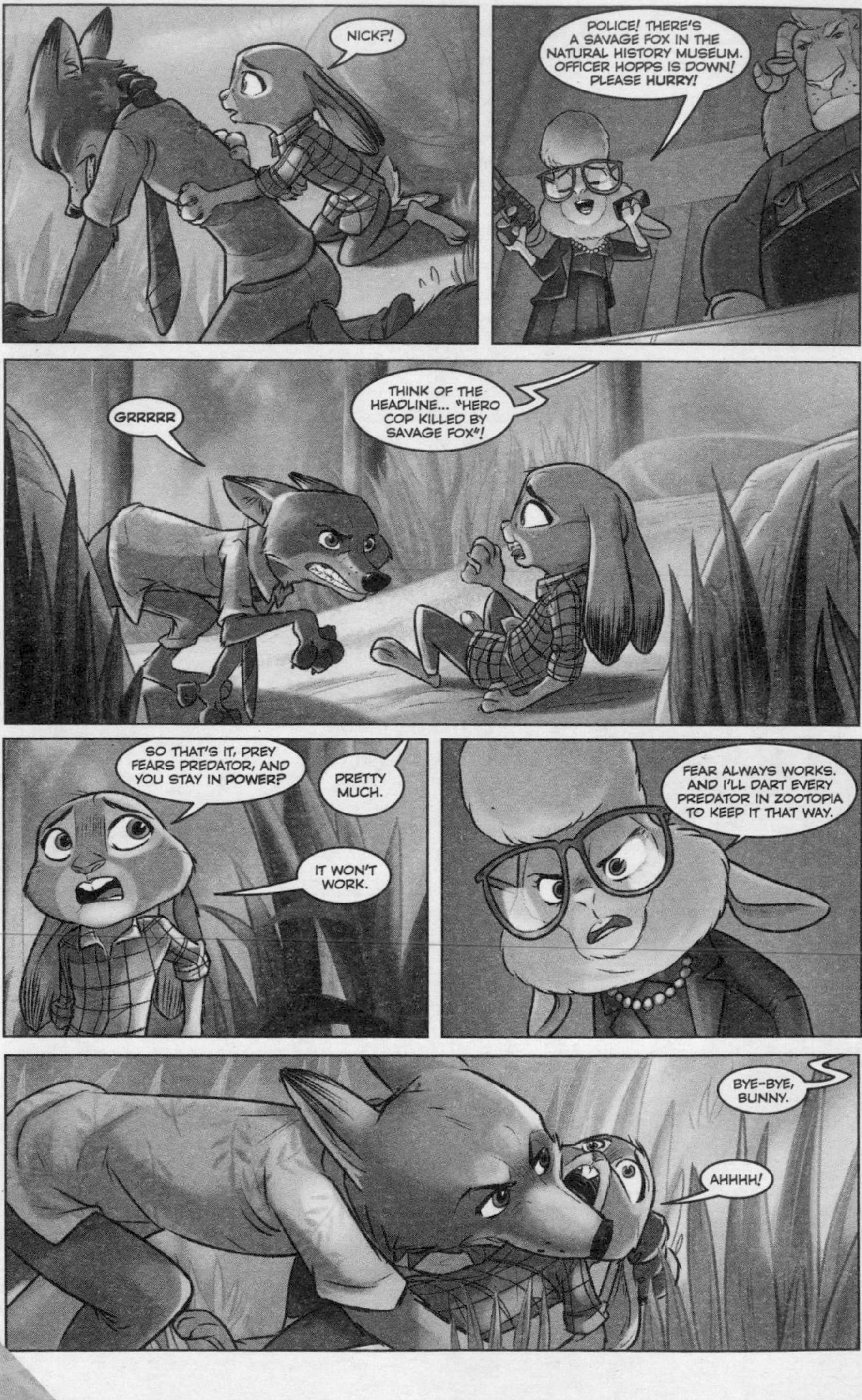
NICK?!
POLICE! THERE'S A SAVAGE FOX IN THE NATURAL HISTORY MUSEUM. OFFICER HOPPS IS DOWN! PLEASE HURRY!
GRRRRR
THINK OF THE HEADLINE... "HERO COP KILLED BY SAVAGE FOX"!
SO THAT'S IT, PREY FEARS PREDATOR, AND YOU STAY IN POWER?
PRETTY MUCH.
IT WON'T WORK.
FEAR ALWAYS WORKS. AND I'LL DART EVERY PREDATOR IN ZOOTOPIA TO KEEP IT THAT WAY.
BYE-BYE, BUNNY.
AHHHH!

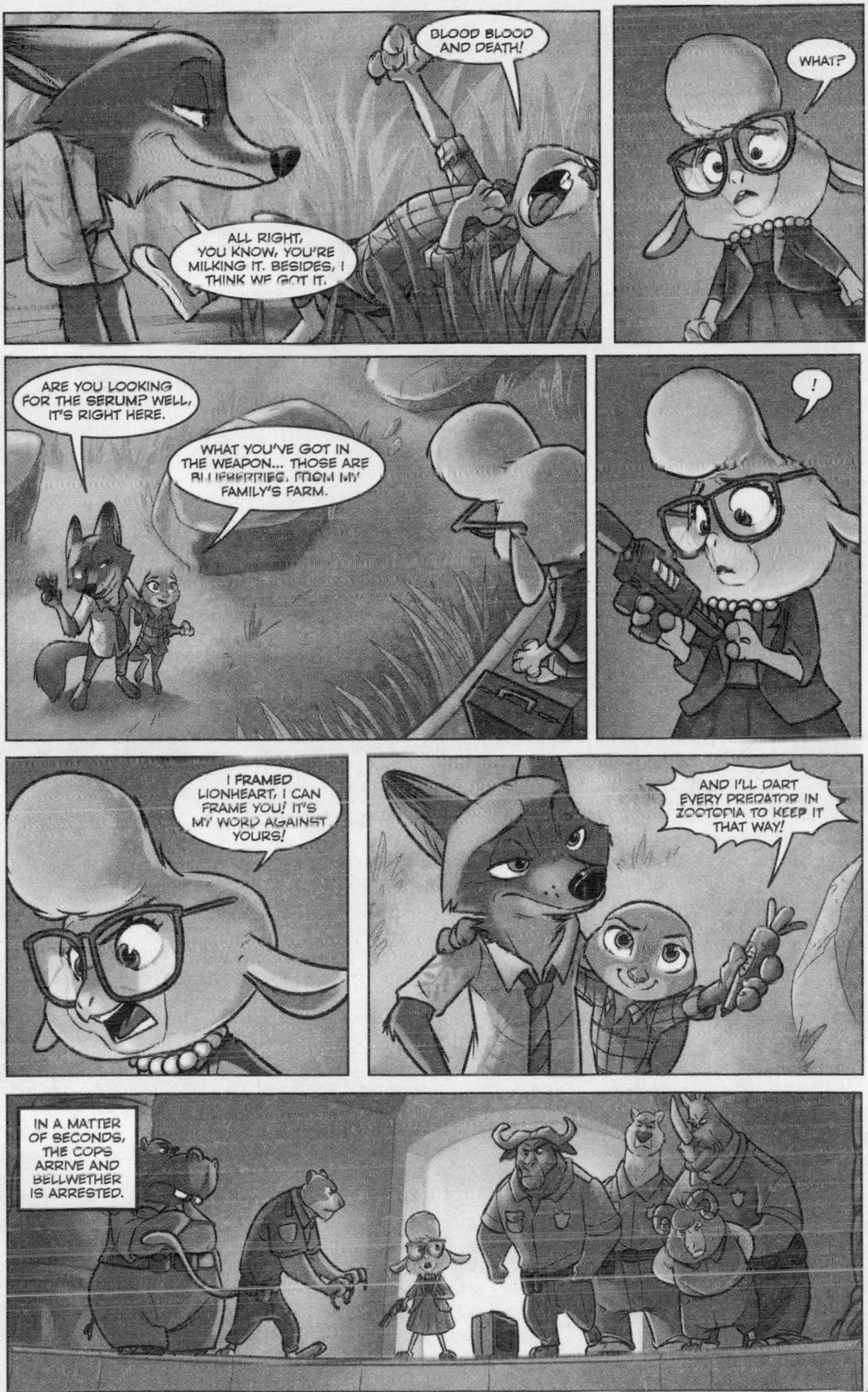
BLOOD BLOOD AND DEATH!
ALL RIGHT, YOU KNOW, YOU'RE MILKING IT. BESIDES, I THINK WE GOT IT.
WHAT?
ARE YOU LOOKING FOR THE SERUM? WELL, IT'S RIGHT HERE.
WHAT YOU'VE GOT IN THE WEAPON... THOSE ARE BLUEBERRIES. FROM MY FAMILY'S FARM.
!
I FRAMED LIONHEART, I CAN FRAME YOU! IT'S MY WORD AGAINST YOURS!
AND I'LL DART EVERY PREDATOR IN ZOOTOPIA TO KEEP IT THAT WAY!
IN A MATTER OF SECONDS, THE COPS ARRIVE AND BELLWETHER IS ARRESTED.

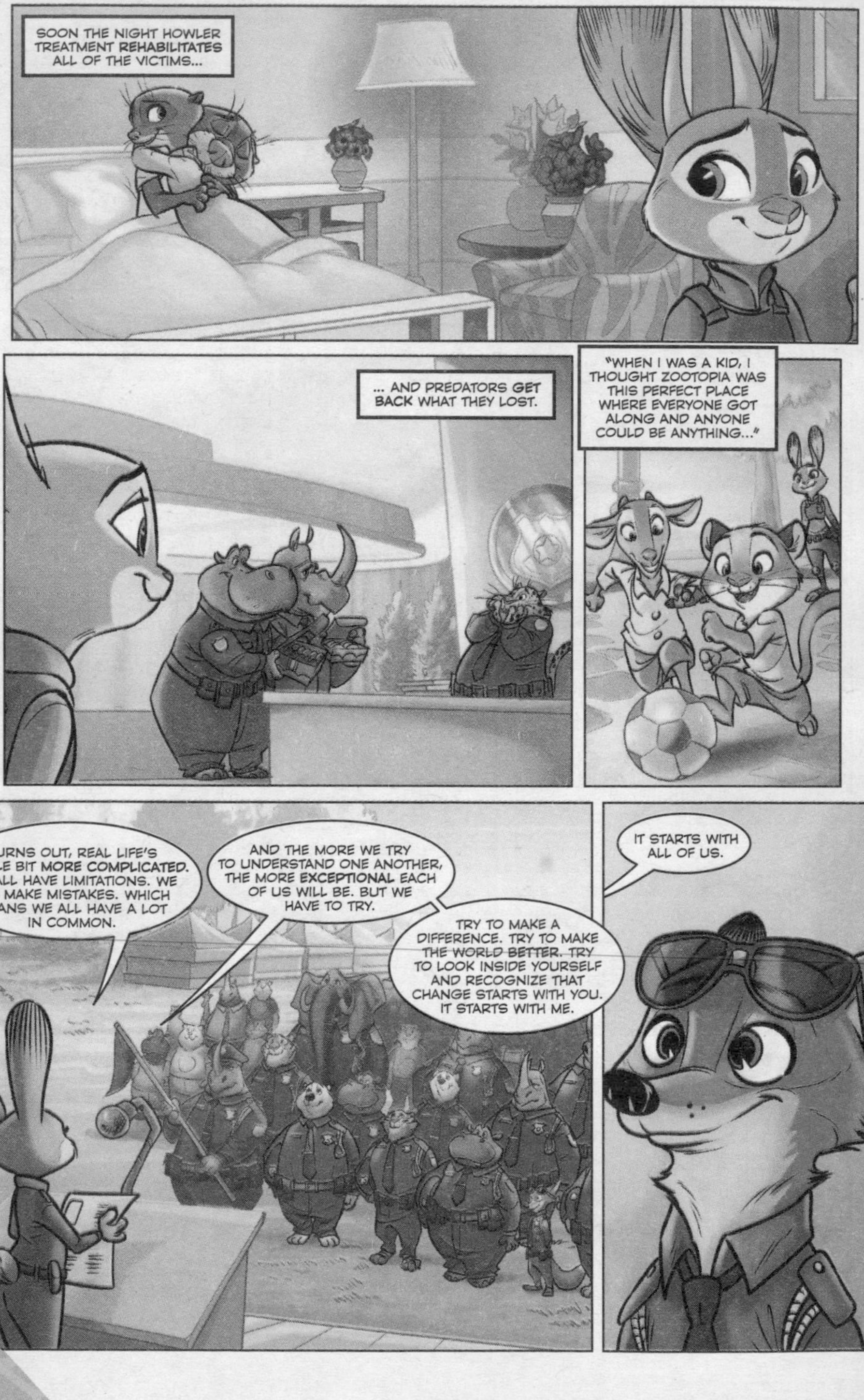

SOON THE NIGHT HOWLER TREATMENT REHABILITATES ALL OF THE VICTIMS...
... AND PREDATORS GET BACK WHAT THEY LOST.
"WHEN I WAS A KID, I THOUGHT ZOOTOPIA WAS THIS PERFECT PLACE WHERE EVERYONE GOT ALONG AND ANYONE COULD BE ANYTHING..."
TURNS OUT, REAL LIFE'S A LITTLE BIT MORE COMPLICATED. WE ALL HAVE LIMITATIONS. WE ALL MAKE MISTAKES. WHICH MEANS WE ALL HAVE A LOT IN COMMON.
AND THE MORE WE TRY TO UNDERSTAND ONE ANOTHER, THE MORE EXCEPTIONAL EACH OF US WILL BE. BUT WE HAVE TO TRY.
TRY TO MAKE A DIFFERENCE. TRY TO MAKE THE WORLD BETTER. TRY TO LOOK INSIDE YOURSELF AND RECOGNIZE THAT CHANGE STARTS WITH YOU. IT STARTS WITH ME.
IT STARTS WITH ALL OF US.

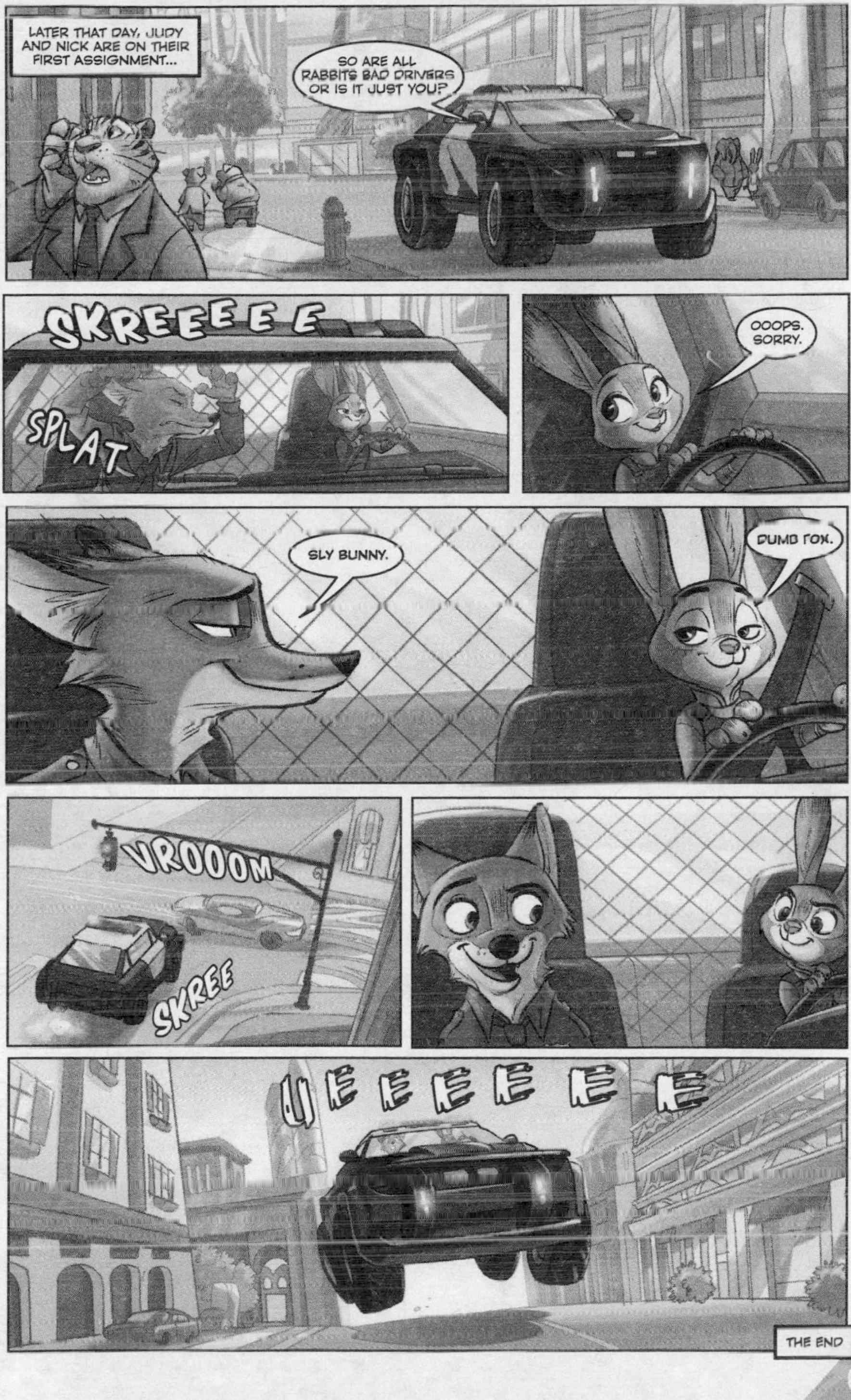
LATER THAT DAY, JUDY AND NICK ARE ON THEIR FIRST ASSIGNMENT...
SO ARE ALL RABBITS BAD DRIVERS OR IS IT JUST YOU?
SKREEEEE
SPLAT
OOOPS. SORRY.
SLY BUNNY.
DUMB FOX.
VROOOM
SKREE
WEEEEEEE
THE END

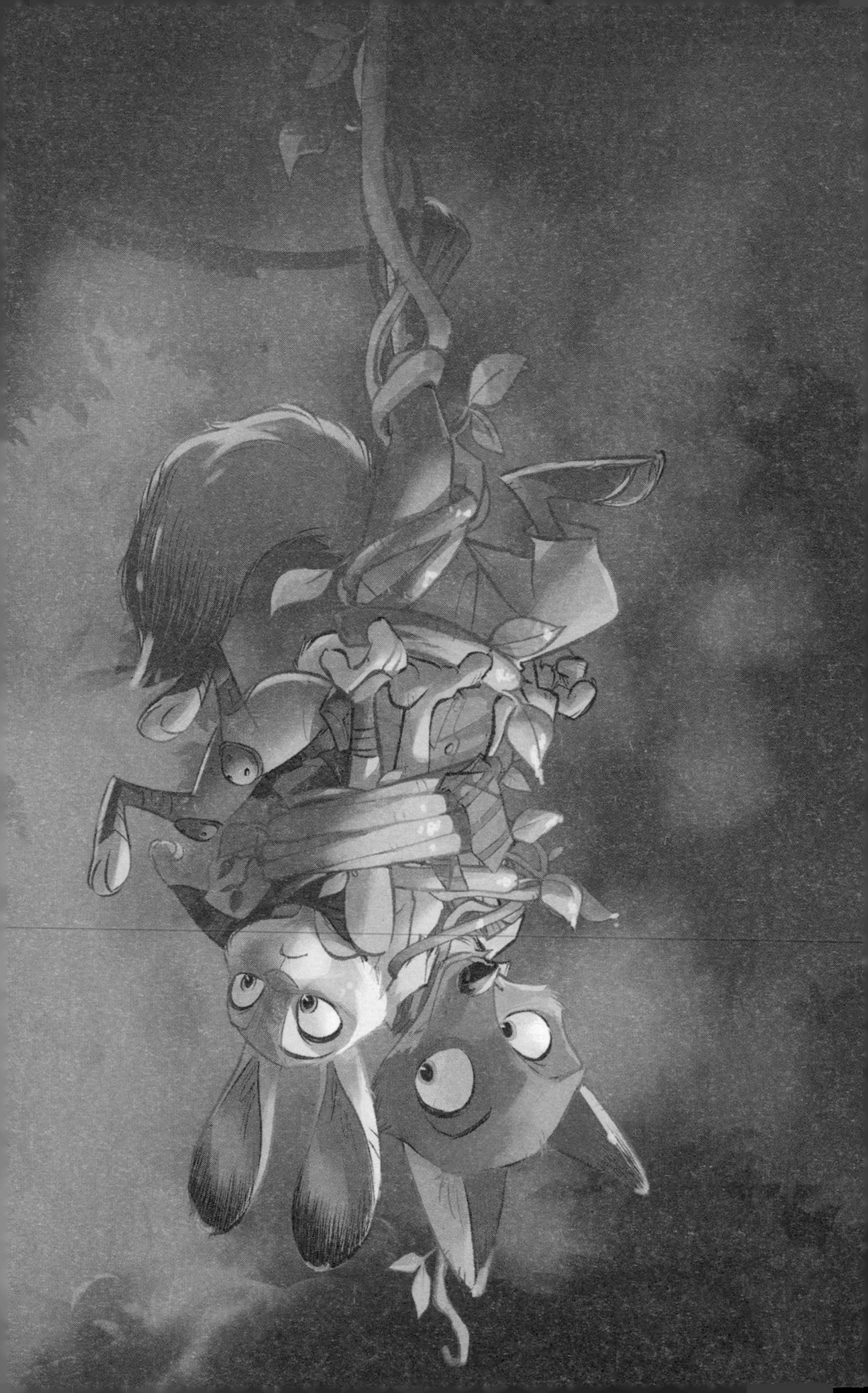

ZOOTOPIA
GRAPHIC NOVEL

MANUSCRIPT ADAPTATION
Alessandro Ferrari

LAYOUT
Antonello Dalena

CLEANUP
Roberto Di Salvo, Diogo Saito, Luca Bertelé, Simone di Meo,
Paco Desiato, Andrea Scoppetta, Salvo di Marco

PAINT
Maria Claudia Di Genova, Kawaii Studio, Alesya Barsukova,
Ludmilla Steblianko, Manuela Nerolini

EDITORIAL PAGES
Litomilano S.r.l.

PRE-PRESS
Edizioni BD S.r.l., Litomilano S.r.l.

SPECIAL THANKS TO
Cory Loftis, Dave Goetz, Matthias Lechner, Albert Ramirez,
Stevi Carter, Jeffrey Clark, Grace Lee, Heather Knowles,
Fabio Pochet, Carlo Resca

DISNEY PUBLISHING WORLDWIDE
Global Magazines, Comics and Partworks

PUBLISHER
Gianfranco Cordara

EDITORIAL DIRECTOR
Bianca Coletti

EDITORIAL TEAM
Guido Frazzini (Director, Comics), Stefano Ambrosio
(Executive Editor, New IP), Carlotta Quattrocolo (Executive
Editor, Franchise), Camilla Vedove (Senior Manager, Editorial
Development), Behnoosh Khalili (Senior Editor), Julie Dorris
(Senior Editor), Megan Adams (Associate Editor)

DESIGN
Enrico Soave (Senior Designer)

ART
Ken Shue (VP, Global Art), Roberto Santillo (Creative Director),
Marco Ghiglione (Creative Manager), Stefano Attardi
(Computer Art Designer)

PORTFOLIO MANAGEMENT
Olivia Ciancarelli (Director)

BUSINESS & MARKETING
Mariantonietta Galla (Marketing Manager), Virpi Korhonen
(Editorial Manager), Kristen Ginter (Publishing Coordinator)

WELCOME TO Z

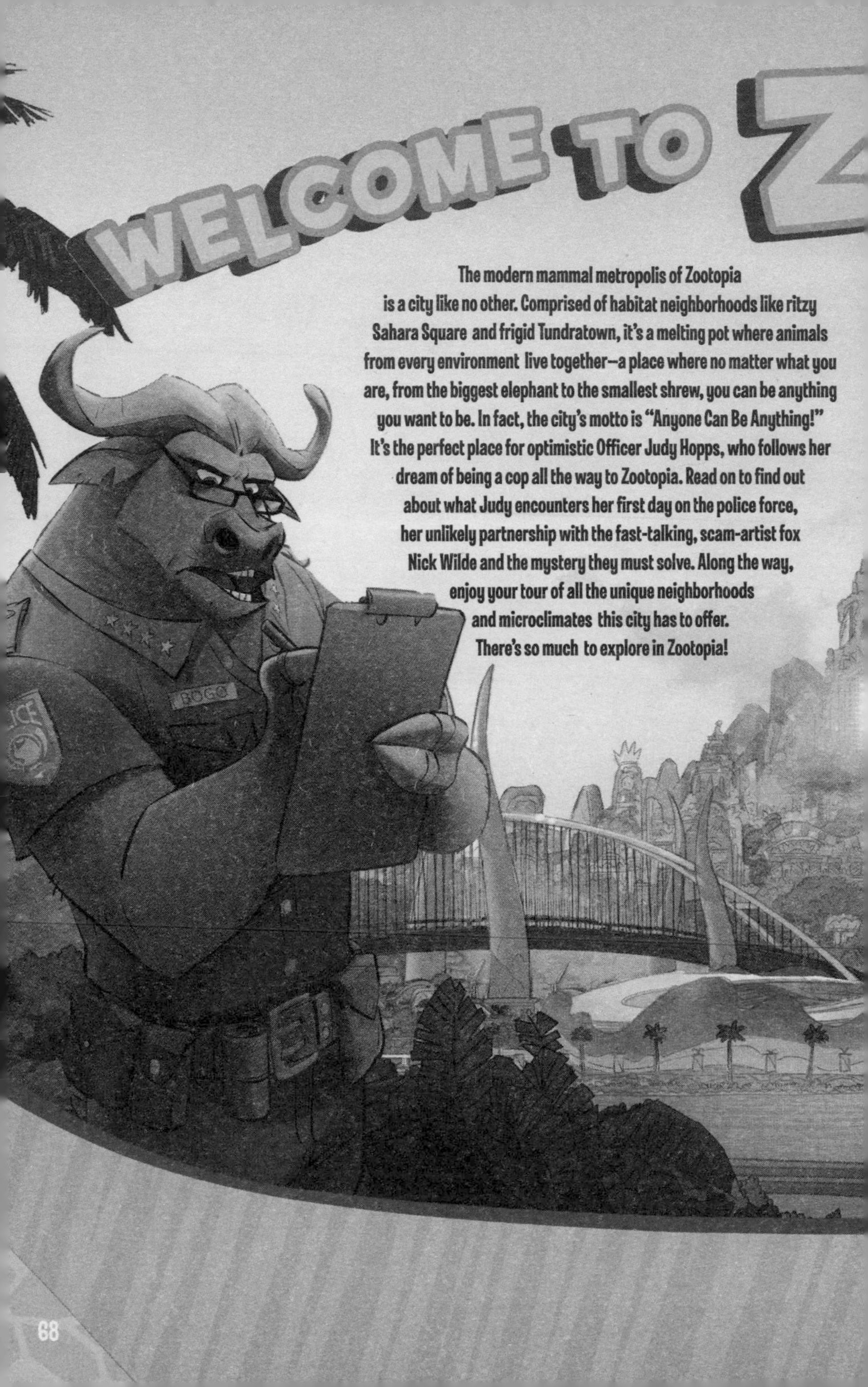

BOGO

The modern mammal metropolis of Zootopia is a city like no other. Comprised of habitat neighborhoods like ritzy Sahara Square and frigid Tundratown, it's a melting pot where animals from every environment live together—a place where no matter what you are, from the biggest elephant to the smallest shrew, you can be anything you want to be. In fact, the city's motto is "Anyone Can Be Anything!" It's the perfect place for optimistic Officer Judy Hopps, who follows her dream of being a cop all the way to Zootopia. Read on to find out about what Judy encounters her first day on the police force, her unlikely partnership with the fast-talking, scam-artist fox Nick Wilde and the mystery they must solve. Along the way, enjoy your tour of all the unique neighborhoods and microclimates this city has to offer. There's so much to explore in Zootopia!

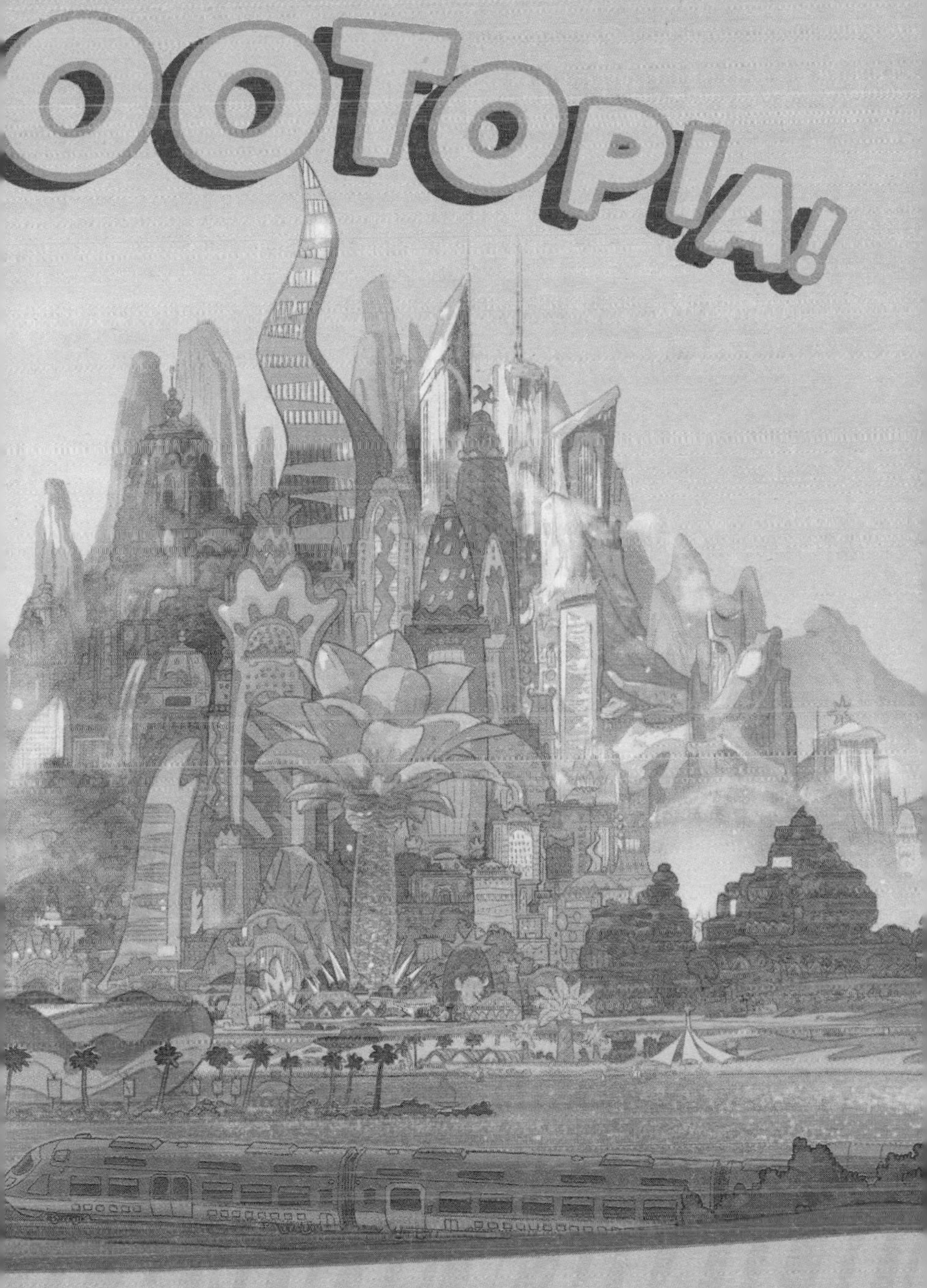
OOTOPIA!

MEET THE CHARACTERS

Judy Hopps

NOT YOUR AVERAGE BUNNY!

AS A CHILD, JUDY DREAMED OF BECOMING A POLICE OFFICER. THERE HAD NEVER BEEN A BUNNY COP BEFORE, BUT THAT DIDN'T STOP JUDY FROM PURSUING HER DREAM.

SHE ATTENDED THE POLICE ACADEMY AND GRADUATED AT THE TOP OF HER CLASS. SHE BECAME THE FIRST BUNNY OFFICER AT THE ZOOTOPIA POLICE DEPARTMENT (ZPD).

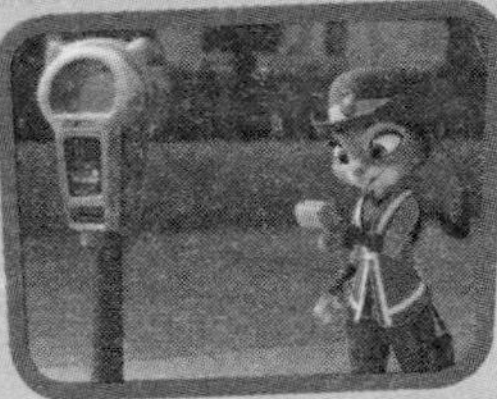

Judy's first assignment wasn't as challenging as she had hoped. Parking duty?! When ZPD Chief tells her to write 100 parking tickets on her first day, she sets the goal of 200 tickets... before noon! Her keen rabbit hearing comes in handy. She can hear each parking meter ding when it expires!

Judy never gives up! She just waits for the opportunity to show everybody that she can do something better than writing tickets! And her chance is... right around the corner! A shop owner cries that he's been robbed, so Judy chases a weasel thief through Little Rodentia.

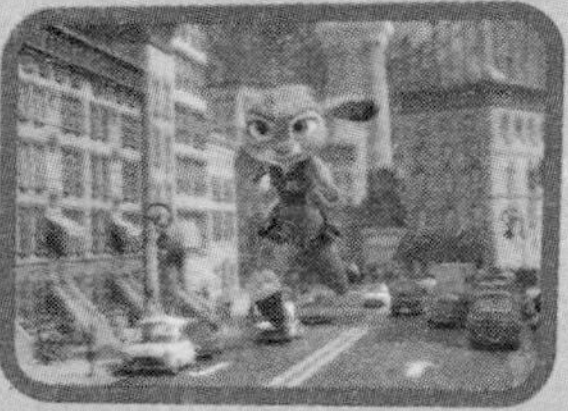

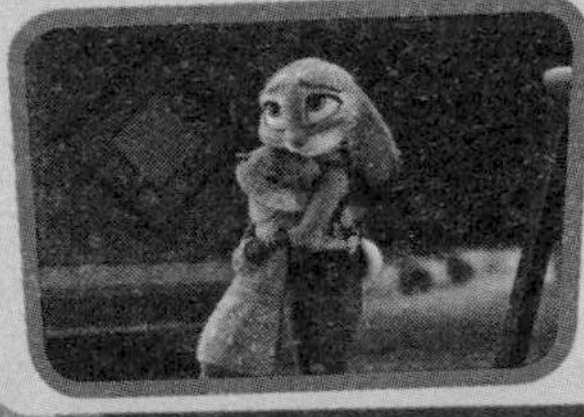

Judy is ambitious, and more than anything she wants to make the world a better place. Judy finally gets her chance to work on a missing mammal case, but she only has 48 hours to prove herself!

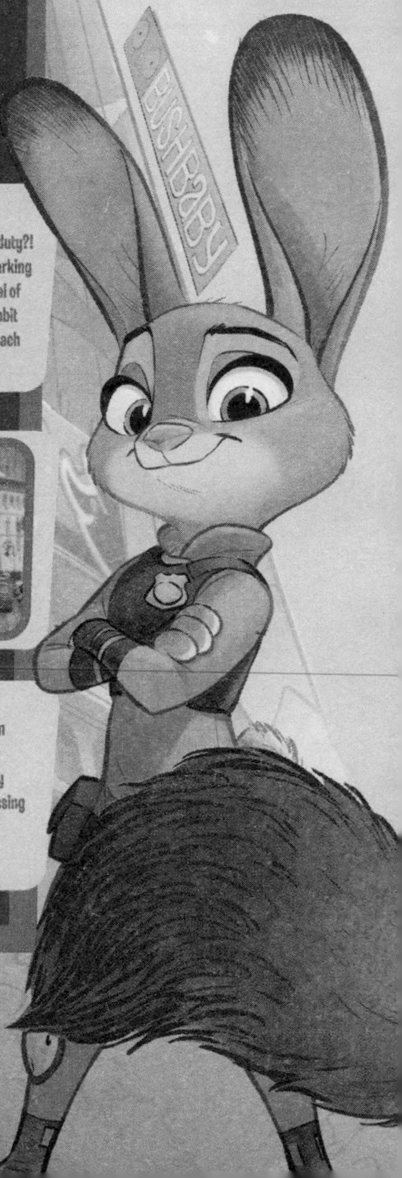
BUSHBABY

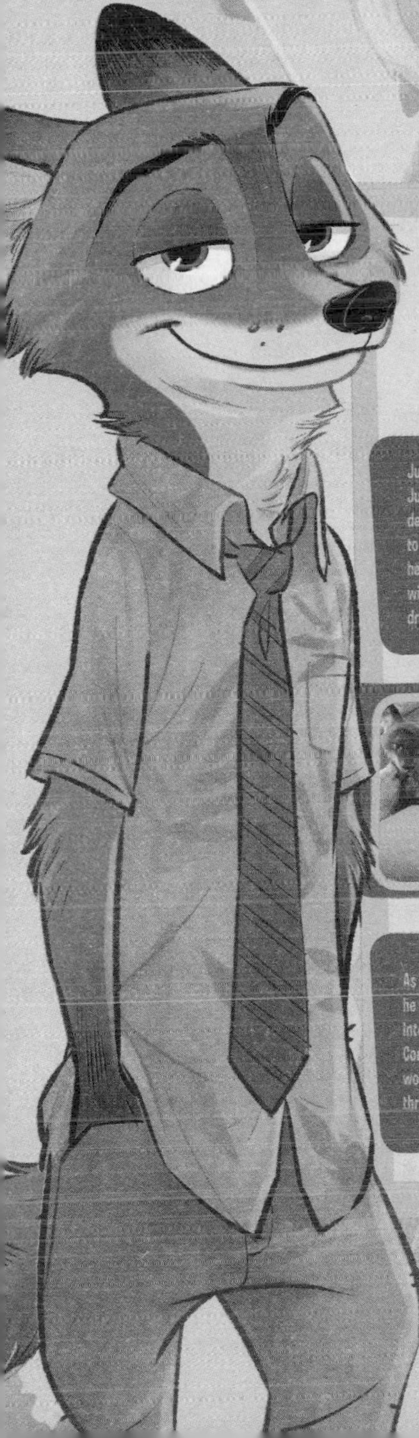

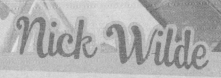

Nick Wilde

SLY GUY

NICK WILDE IS A SLICK HUSTLER WHO USES A COMBINATION OF CHARM, WIT AND CUNNINGNESS IN HIS WORK AS A CON ARTIST.

THIS SLY FOX IS ALWAYS ON THE MOVE AND CLAIMS TO KNOW EVERYONE IN ZOOTOPIA, WHICH MAKES HIM A VALUABLE ASSET TO JUDY IN HER SEARCH FOR A MISSING MAMMAL.

Judy follows Nick into Jumbeaux's Café. When he's denied service, Judy steps in to help. Little does she know he's running an elaborate scam with his partner Finnick who's dressed in an elephant costume.

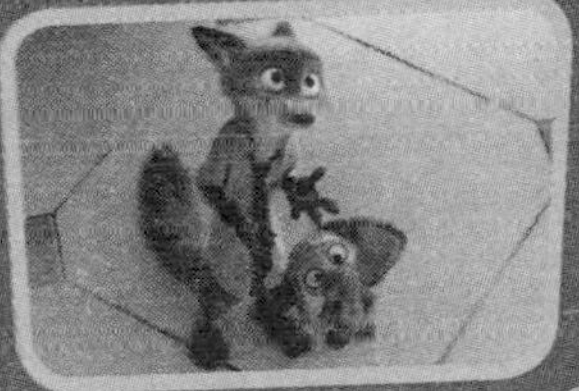

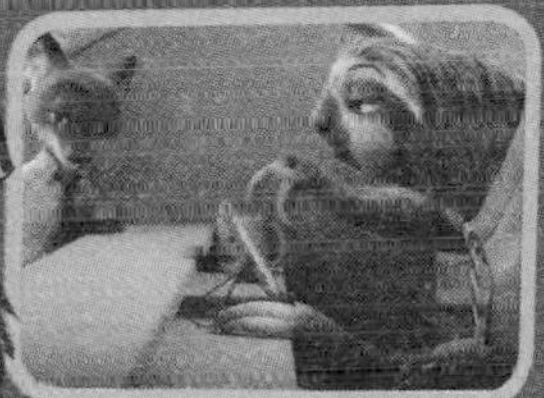

Nick thinks Judy is just a "dumb bunny" cop. But when she outsmarts him, he has no choice but to help her with the missing mammal case. Luckily, Nick has some very helpful friends, such as Flash at the DMV (Department of Mammal Vehicles).

As Nick continues to help Judy, he finds himself sinking deeper into the mystery of the case. Could a bunny and a fox actually work together to find out what's threatening the city of Zootopia?

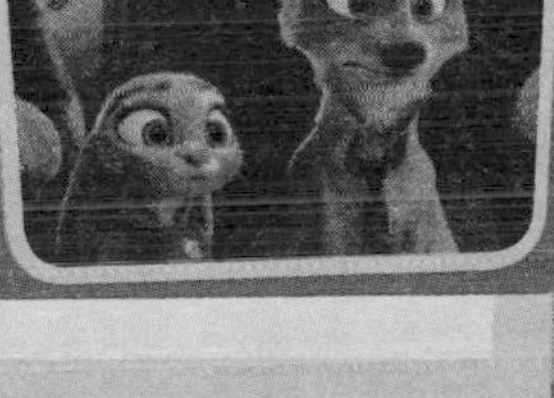

MEET THE CHARACTERS

LIFE IN
(ACCORDING TO

Street-smart Nick Wilde and eternal optimist Judy Hopps see Zootopia from very different points of view. But it's their unique experiences that make them such an awesome team.

Are you new in town? Good luck! Get ready to hustle. Don't get me wrong, I love this city: it's full of opportunities. But only the toughest and smartest mammals can survive here. Take it from me...
I LEARNED EVERYTHING I KNOW FROM LIVING IN ZOOTOPIA.

IT'S CALLED A HUSTLE!
They say in Zootopia anyone can be anything. From cop to limo driver, unlimited opportunities are available. Me? I'm a business-fox. It allows me to meet many animals and sell them what they need.

In Zootopia, it's difficult to know who you can trust. I live alone. I prefer a more, outdoorsy, natural setting!

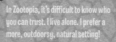

JUMBO-POPS ARE NOT FOR THE LITTLE ONES!
If you like ice cream, there's no better place than Jumbeaux's Café. The Jumbo-pops are the best. Do you want to try one? Well, if you're not an elephant, get ready to work a little harder! But me and my pal Finnick, we have our ways...

FOXES AND BUNNIES WORKING TOGETHER?
I was a firm believer that you are what you are, no matter how hard you try to be something else. Bunnies are dumb, foxes are sly, right? Guess what... I was wrong!

ZOOTOPIA
(NICK WILDE AND JUDY HOPPS)

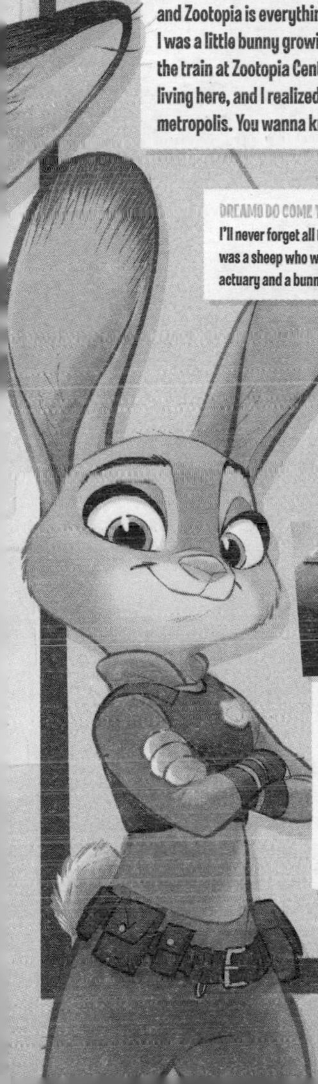

Welcome to the incredible city of Zootopia! I'M OFFICER JUDY HOPPS and Zootopia is everything I always dreamed it could be, ever since I was a little bunny growing up in Bunnyburrow. The moment I got off the train at Zootopia Central Station, I felt the energy of every animal living here, and I realized I was already in love with this amazing metropolis. You wanna know why? I can give you tons of answers!

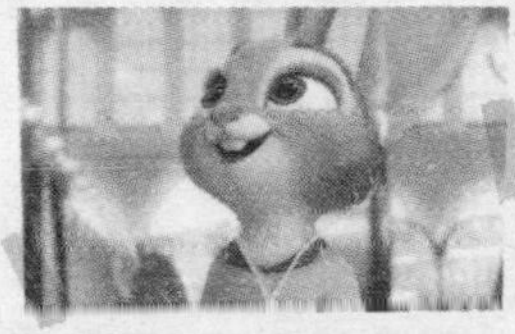

DREAMS DO COME TRUE!
I'll never forget all the big dreams we had growing up in Bunnyburrow: there was a sheep who wanted to be an astronaut, a jaguar who wanted to be an actuary and a bunny who wanted to be a police officer (me!).

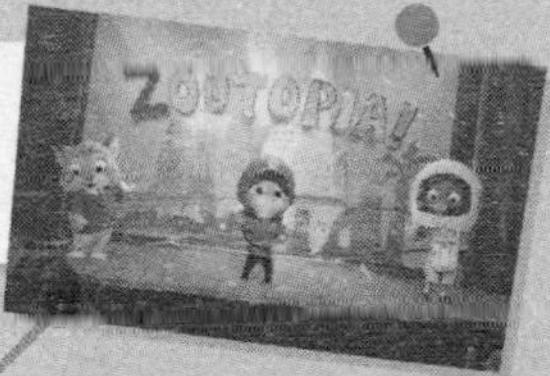
ZOOTOPIA!

I'M A COP!
Can you believe it? Sometimes I pinch myself, just to make sure it's real!

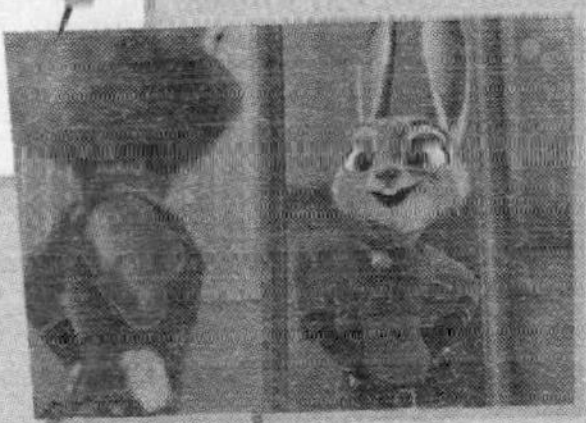

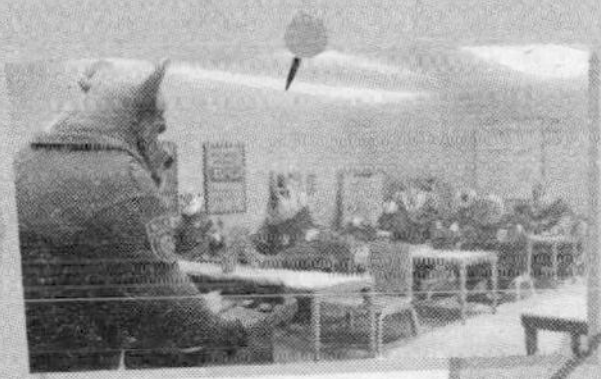

ANYONE CAN BE YOUR FRIEND!
There's no room for fear or mistrust in Zootopia. Look at me: I'm a bunny and I work side-by-side with leopards, rhinos, lions and a fox! Yes, I'm talking about you, Nick Wilde! ;)

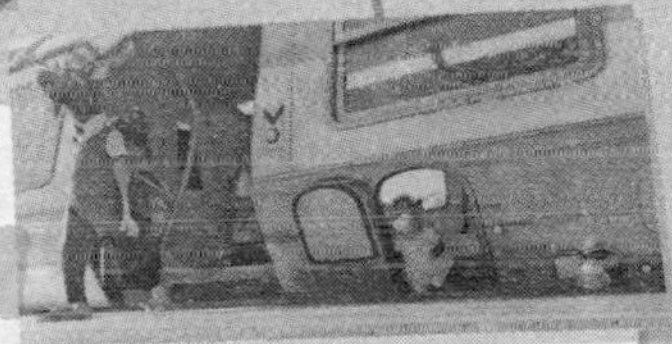

THERE'S A SIZE FOR ANY SIZE! It does not matter if you are as tall as a giraffe or as short as a shrew: from transportation to juice bars, everything is designed to suit animals of all sizes.

I don't know when to quit.

JUDY HOPPS

Welcome to ZOOTOPIA

SEE THEM DOWN THERE?

SOMEDAY YOU WILL BE DOWN THERE WITH THEM, HUSTLING AND BUSTLING, HELPING TO MAKE THE CITY WORK, FOLLOWING YOUR DREAMS.

THERE IS A GREAT, BIG BEAUTIFUL WORLD OUT THERE FOR YOU TO EXPLORE, FULL OF POSSIBILITIES. BUT FIRST...

...A NAP!

SLAM!

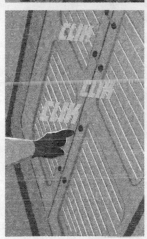

CLIK CLIK CLIK

THERE WILL BE PLENTY OF TIME TO EXPLORE THE WORLD WHEN YOU'RE A LITTLE BIT OLDER.

SLEEP TIGHT!

JOE CARAMAGNA WRITER & LETTERER - **GURIHIRU** ART

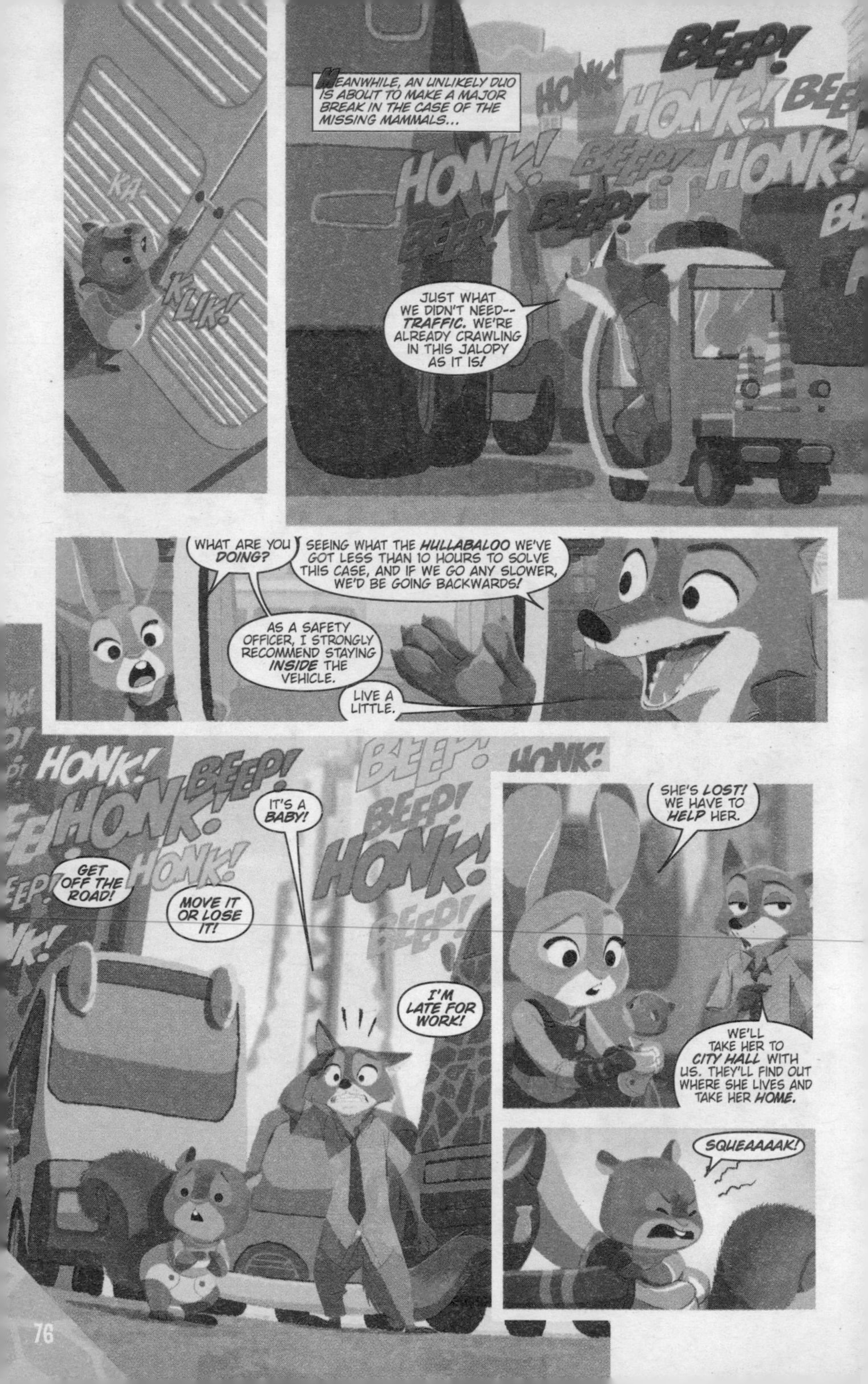
KA-
KLIK!
MEANWHILE, AN UNLIKELY DUO IS ABOUT TO MAKE A MAJOR BREAK IN THE CASE OF THE MISSING MAMMALS...
BEEP! HONK! HONK! BEE HONK! BEEP! HONK! BEEP! BEEP! BE
JUST WHAT WE DIDN'T NEED-- TRAFFIC. WE'RE ALREADY CRAWLING IN THIS JALOPY AS IT IS!
WHAT ARE YOU DOING?
SEEING WHAT THE HULLABALOO WE'VE GOT LESS THAN 10 HOURS TO SOLVE THIS CASE, AND IF WE GO ANY SLOWER, WE'D BE GOING BACKWARDS!
AS A SAFETY OFFICER, I STRONGLY RECOMMEND STAYING INSIDE THE VEHICLE.
LIVE A LITTLE.
HONK! HONK! BEEP! BEEP! HONK! HONK! BEEP! HONK! BEEP!
IT'S A BABY!
GET OFF THE ROAD!
MOVE IT OR LOSE IT!
I'M LATE FOR WORK!
SHE'S LOST! WE HAVE TO HELP HER.
WE'LL TAKE HER TO CITY HALL WITH US. THEY'LL FIND OUT WHERE SHE LIVES AND TAKE HER HOME.
SQUEAAAAK!

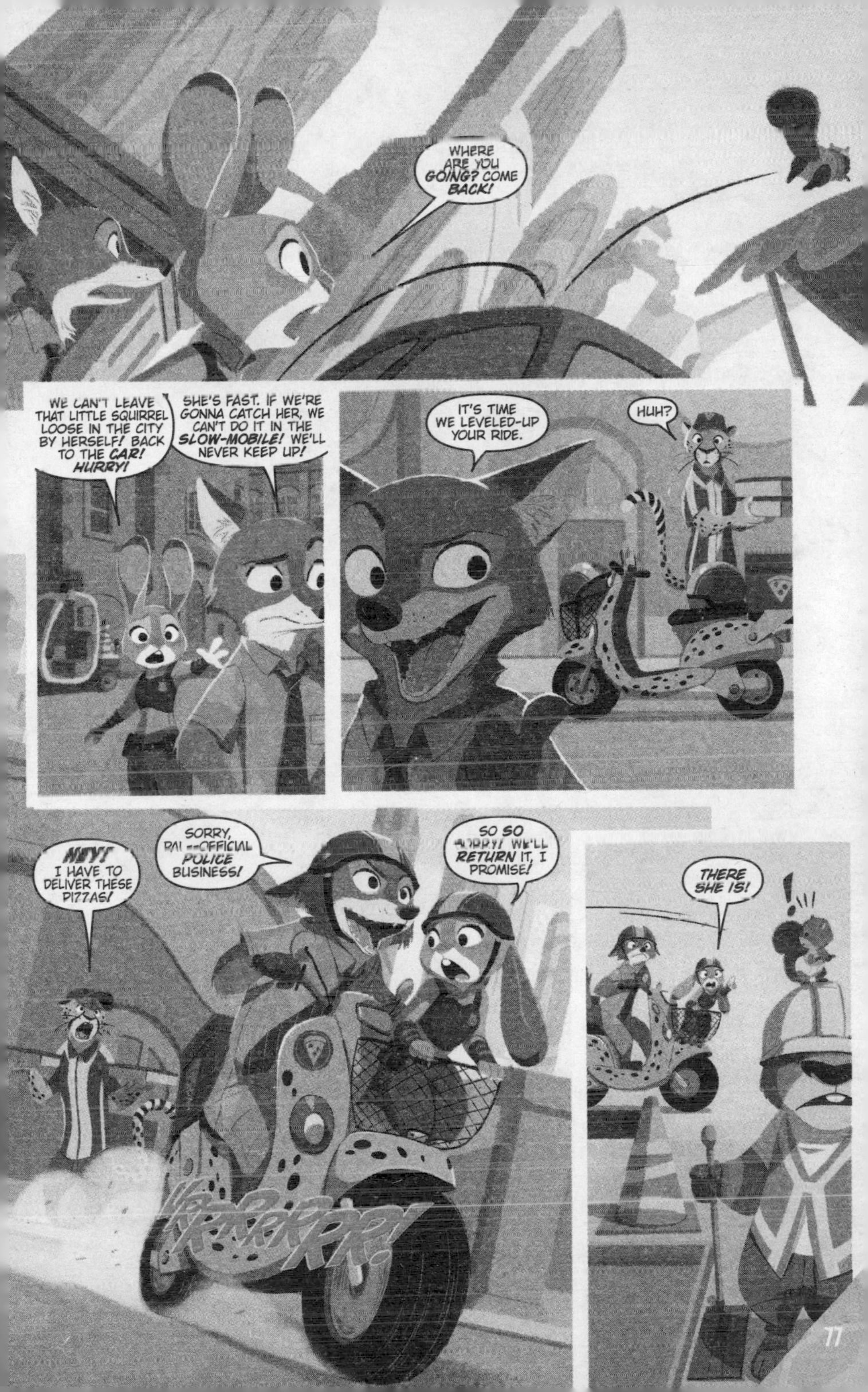
WHERE ARE YOU *GOING?* COME *BACK!*
WE CAN'T LEAVE THAT LITTLE SQUIRREL LOOSE IN THE CITY BY HERSELF! BACK TO THE *CAR! HURRY!*
SHE'S FAST. IF WE'RE GONNA CATCH HER, WE CAN'T DO IT IN THE *SLOW-MOBILE!* WE'LL NEVER KEEP UP!
IT'S TIME WE LEVELED-UP YOUR RIDE.
HUH?
HEY! I HAVE TO DELIVER THESE PIZZAS!
SORRY, PAL--OFFICIAL *POLICE* BUSINESS!
SO *SO* SORRY! WE'LL *RETURN* IT, I PROMISE!
THERE SHE IS!
!

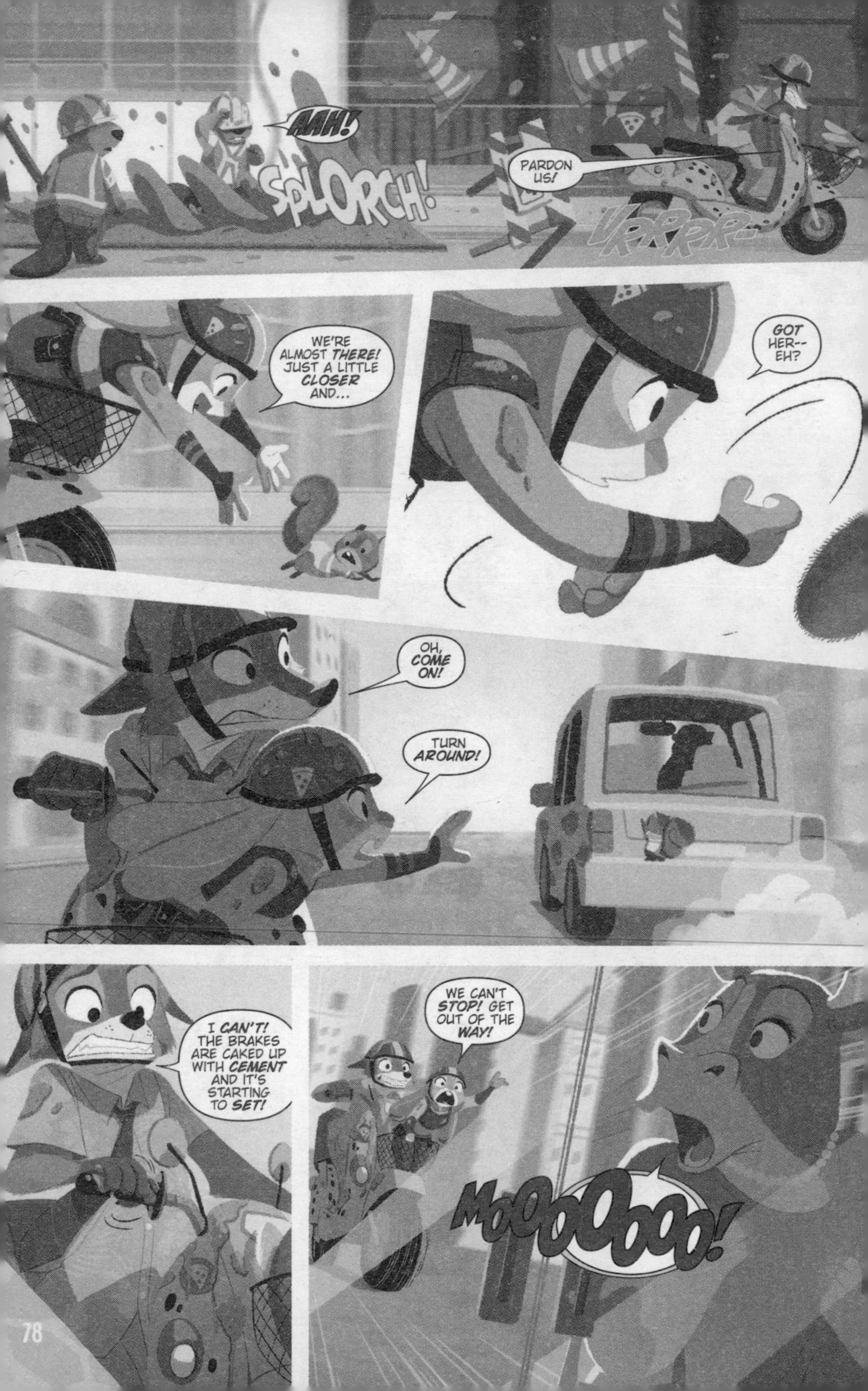
AAH!
SPLORCH!
PARDON US!
VRRRR-
WE'RE ALMOST THERE! JUST A LITTLE CLOSER AND...
GOT HER--EH?
OH, COME ON!
TURN AROUND!
I CAN'T! THE BRAKES ARE CAKED UP WITH CEMENT AND IT'S STARTING TO SET!
WE CAN'T STOP! GET OUT OF THE WAY!
MOOOOOOO!

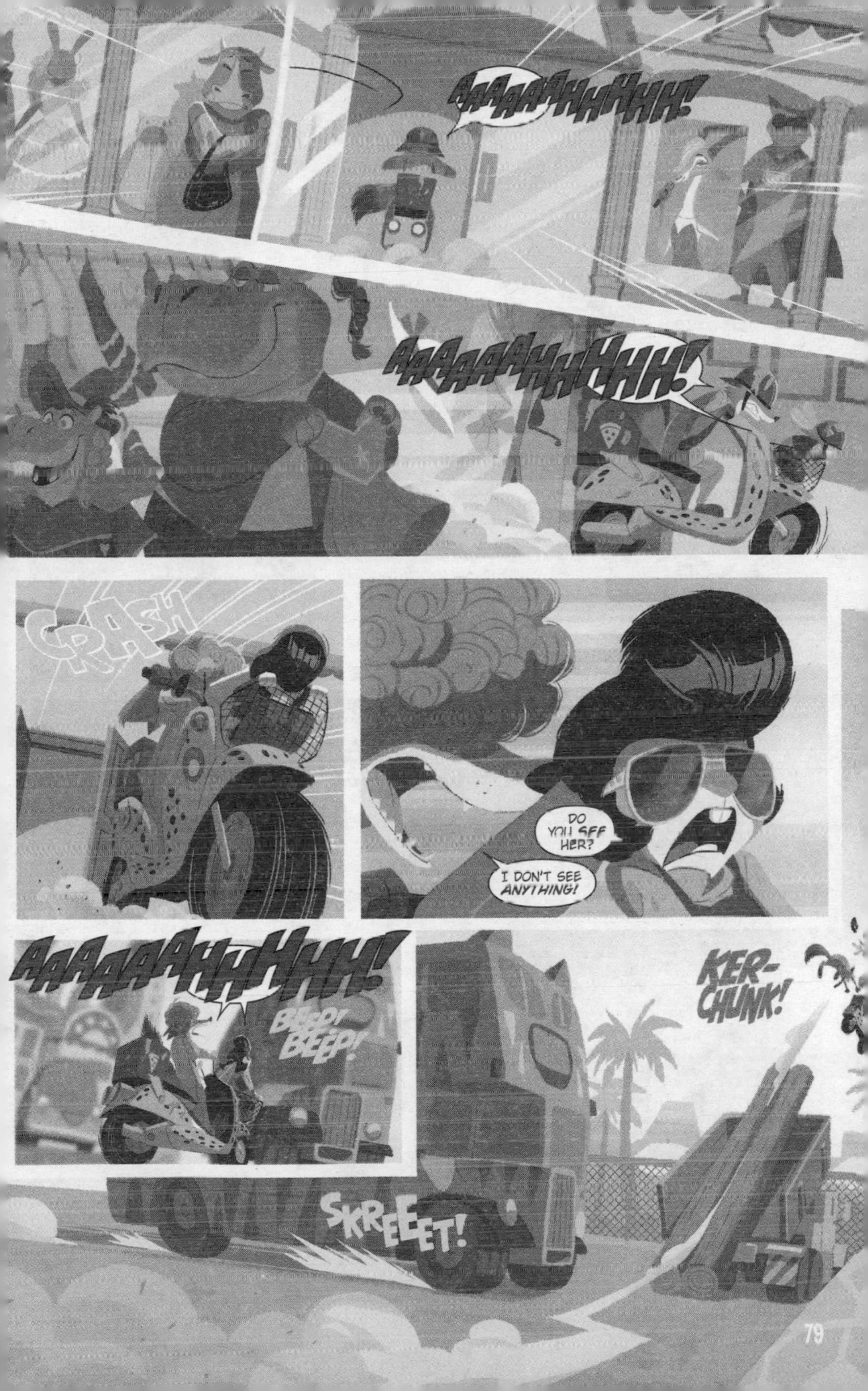
AAAAAAHHHHHH!
AAAAAAHHHHHH!
CRASH
DO YOU SEE HER?
I DON'T SEE ANYTHING!
AAAAAAHHHHHH!
BEEP! BEEP!
KER-CHUNK!
SKREEEET!

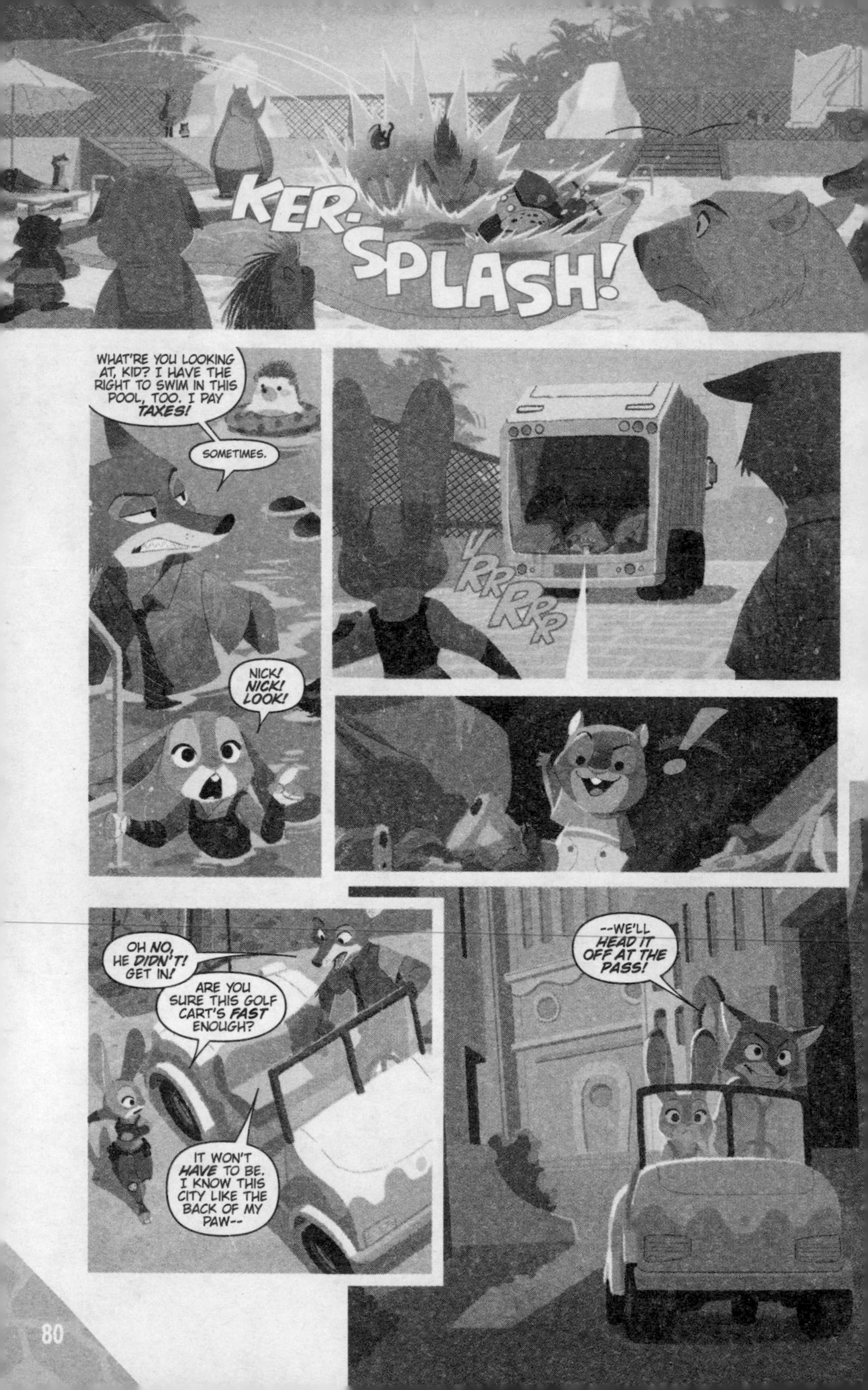
KER-SPLASH!
WHAT'RE YOU LOOKING AT, KID? I HAVE THE RIGHT TO SWIM IN THIS POOL, TOO. I PAY TAXES!
SOMETIMES.
VRRRRRR
NICK! NICK! LOOK!
OH NO, HE DIDN'T! GET IN!
ARE YOU SURE THIS GOLF CART'S FAST ENOUGH?
IT WON'T HAVE TO BE. I KNOW THIS CITY LIKE THE BACK OF MY PAW--
--WE'LL HEAD IT OFF AT THE PASS!

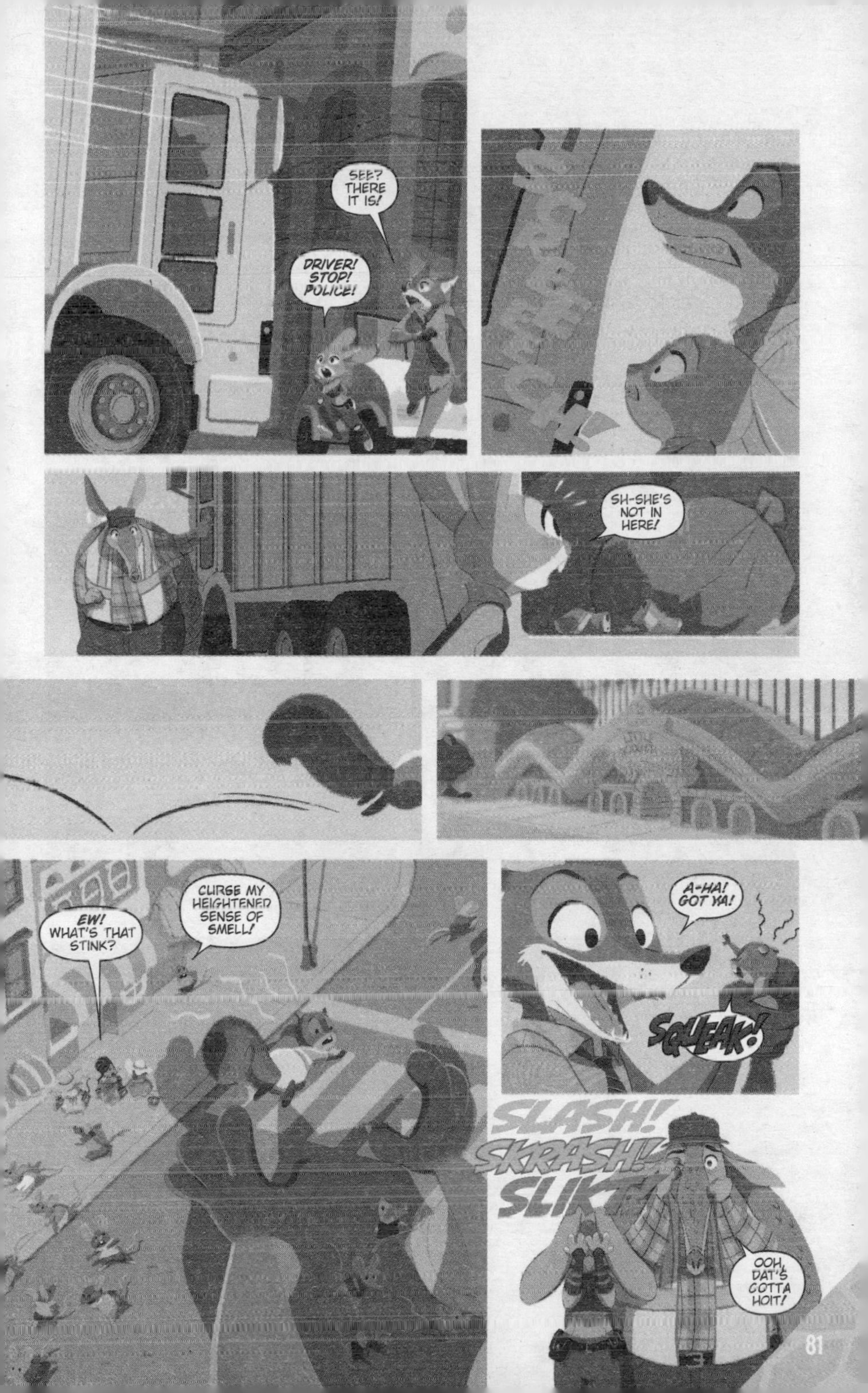
SEE? THERE IT IS!
DRIVER! STOP! POLICE!
SH-SHE'S NOT IN HERE!
EW! WHAT'S THAT STINK?
CURSE MY HEIGHTENED SENSE OF SMELL!
A-HA! GOT YA!
SQUEAK!
SLASH!
SKRASH!
SLIK!
OOH, DAT'S GOTTA HOIT!

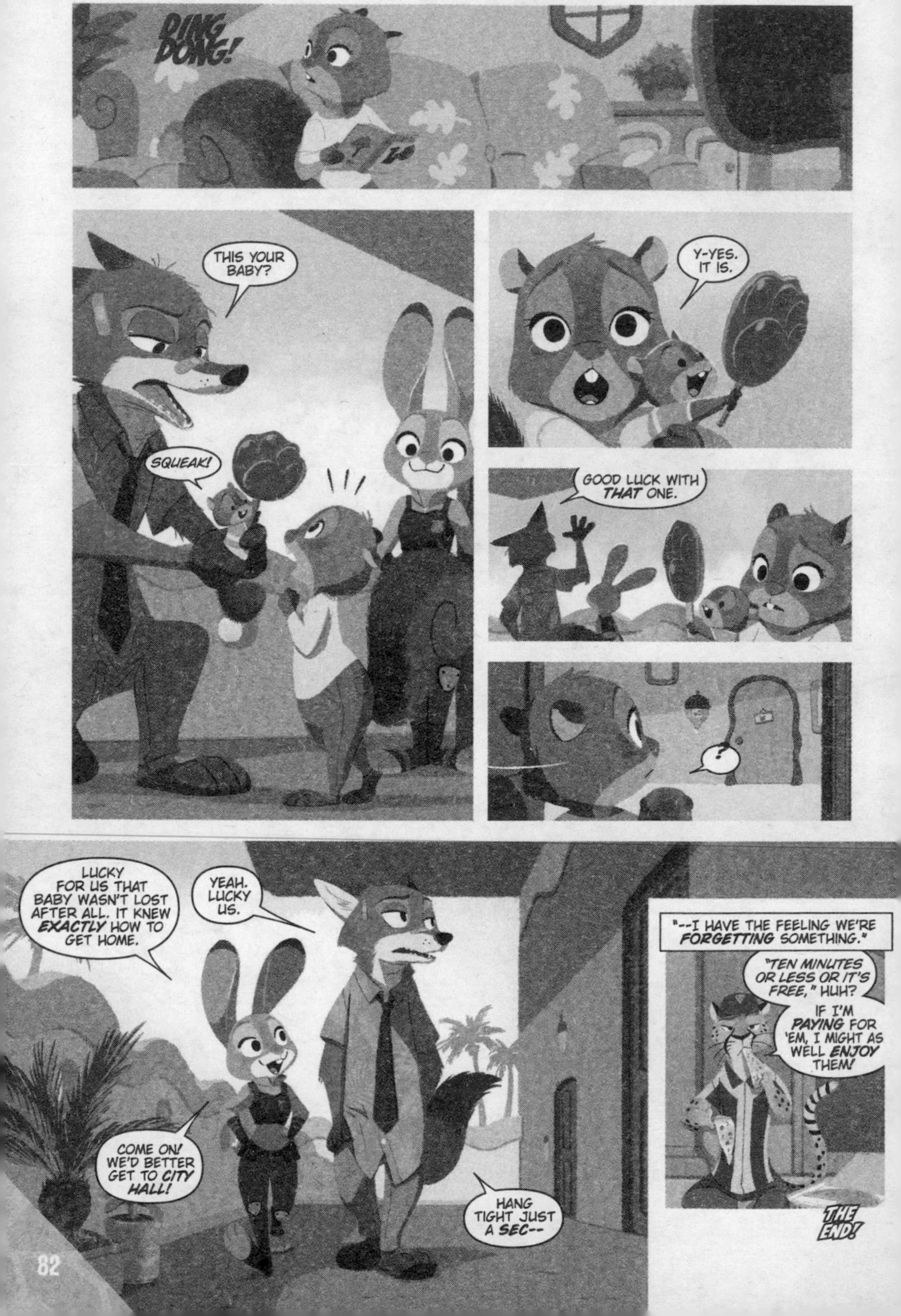
DING DONG!
THIS YOUR BABY?
SQUEAK!
Y-YES. IT IS.
GOOD LUCK WITH THAT ONE.
?
LUCKY FOR US THAT BABY WASN'T LOST AFTER ALL. IT KNEW EXACTLY HOW TO GET HOME.
YEAH. LUCKY US.
COME ON! WE'D BETTER GET TO CITY HALL!
HANG TIGHT JUST A SEC--
"--I HAVE THE FEELING WE'RE FORGETTING SOMETHING."
"TEN MINUTES OR LESS OR IT'S FREE," HUH?
IF I'M PAYING FOR 'EM, I MIGHT AS WELL ENJOY THEM!
THE END!

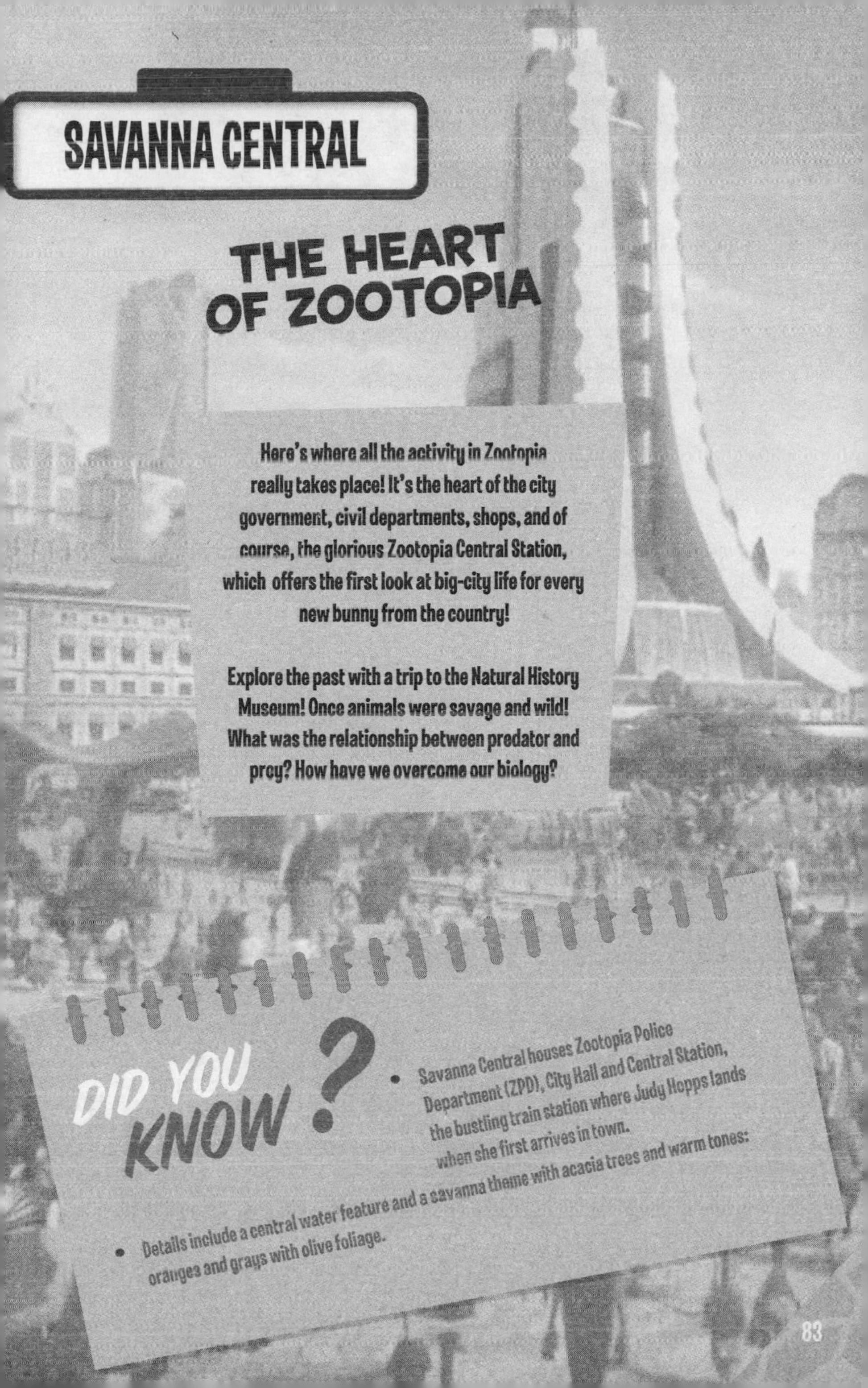

SAVANNA CENTRAL

THE HEART OF ZOOTOPIA

Here's where all the activity in Zootopia really takes place! It's the heart of the city government, civil departments, shops, and of course, the glorious Zootopia Central Station, which offers the first look at big-city life for every new bunny from the country!

Explore the past with a trip to the Natural History Museum! Once animals were savage and wild! What was the relationship between predator and prey? How have we overcome our biology?

DID YOU KNOW?

- Savanna Central houses Zootopia Police Department (ZPD), City Hall and Central Station, the bustling train station where Judy Hopps lands when she first arrives in town.
- Details include a central water feature and a savanna theme with acacia trees and warm tones: oranges and grays with olive foliage.

MEET THE CHARACTERS

The Zootopia Police Department (ZPD) and City Hall are located in Savanna Central, in Downtown Zootopia. The city's leaders work hard to keep Zootopia a safe place to live, where predator and prey live and work in harmony.

It takes a lot of work to keep a large city like Zootopia safe and running smoothly. A great city like Zootopia needs strong leaders!

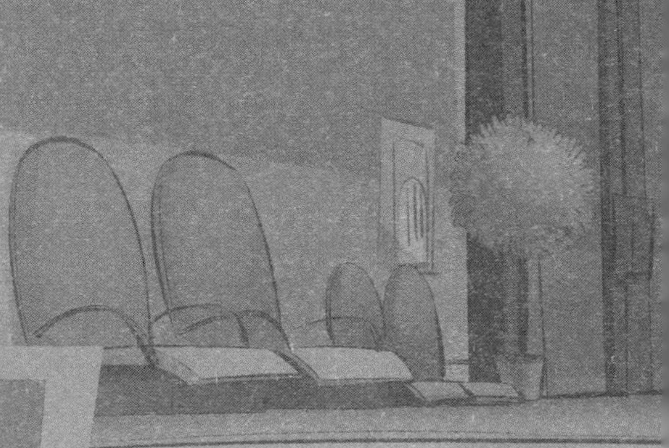

CAMERA MONITORING

One way the ZPD can keep an eye on the city is through the traffic cameras. Thanks to Assistant Mayor Bellwether, Judy and Nick check the footage for clues to their case.

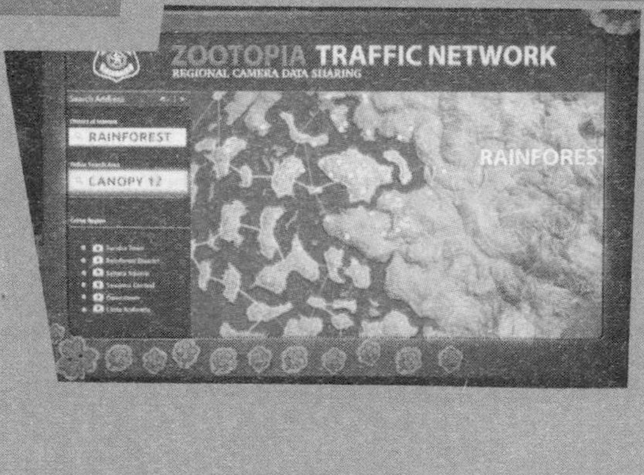
ZOOTOPIA TRAFFIC NETWORK
REGIONAL CAMERA DATA SHARING
RAINFOREST
CANOPY 12
RAINFOREST

CHIEF BOGO

This Cape buffalo is the chief of police at the ZPD. He's a huge, gruff, unwavering leader who is reluctant to give Judy the chance to show she's got what it takes.

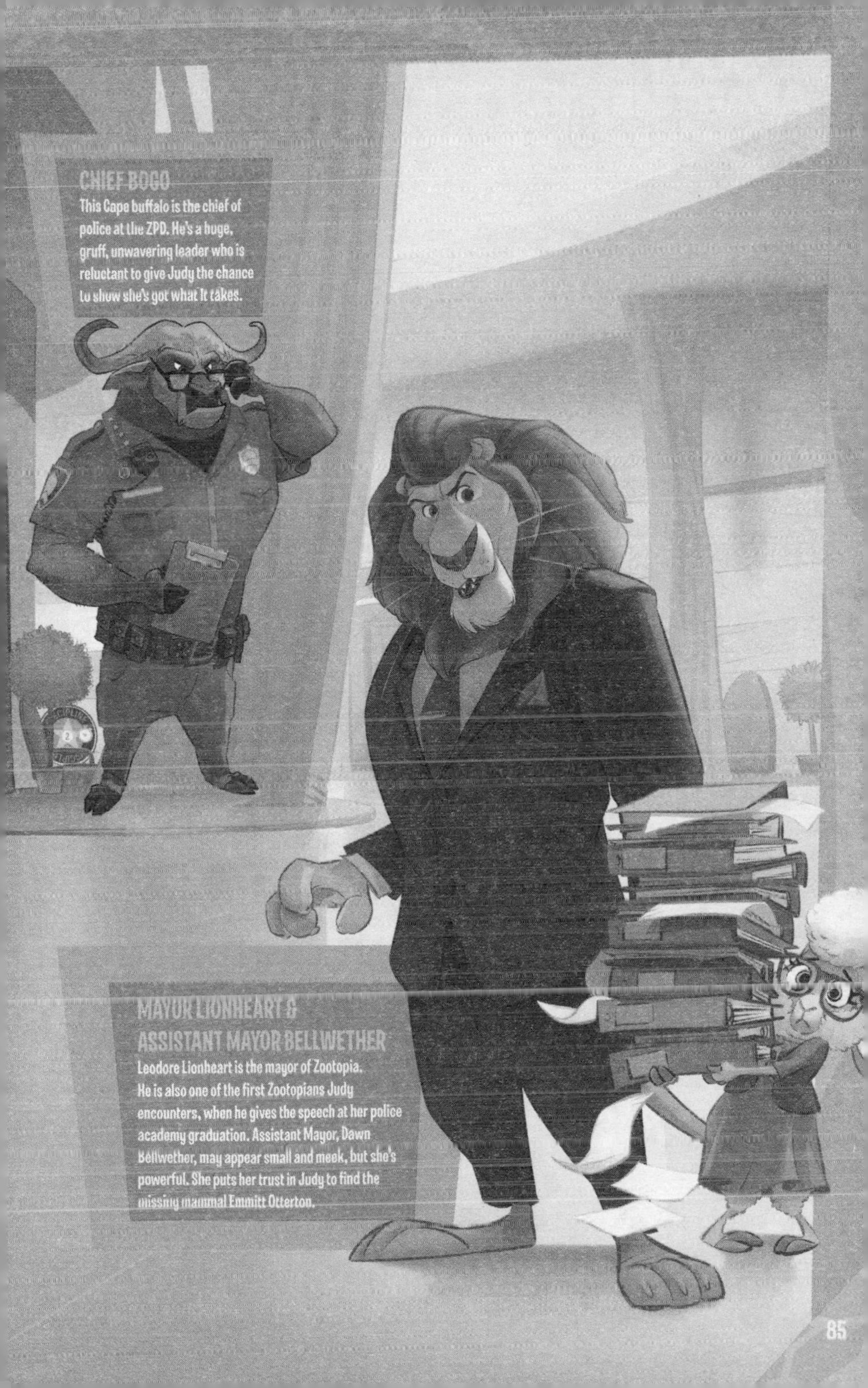

MAYOR LIONHEART & ASSISTANT MAYOR BELLWETHER

Leodore Lionheart is the mayor of Zootopia. He is also one of the first Zootopians Judy encounters, when he gives the speech at her police academy graduation. Assistant Mayor, Dawn Bellwether, may appear small and meek, but she's powerful. She puts her trust in Judy to find the missing mammal Emmitt Otterton.

JUDY'S APARTMENT

JOE CARAMAGNA & MANNY MEDEROS STORYTELLERS & LAYOUT

ANDREA SCOPPETTA CLEAN-UPS & PAINTS

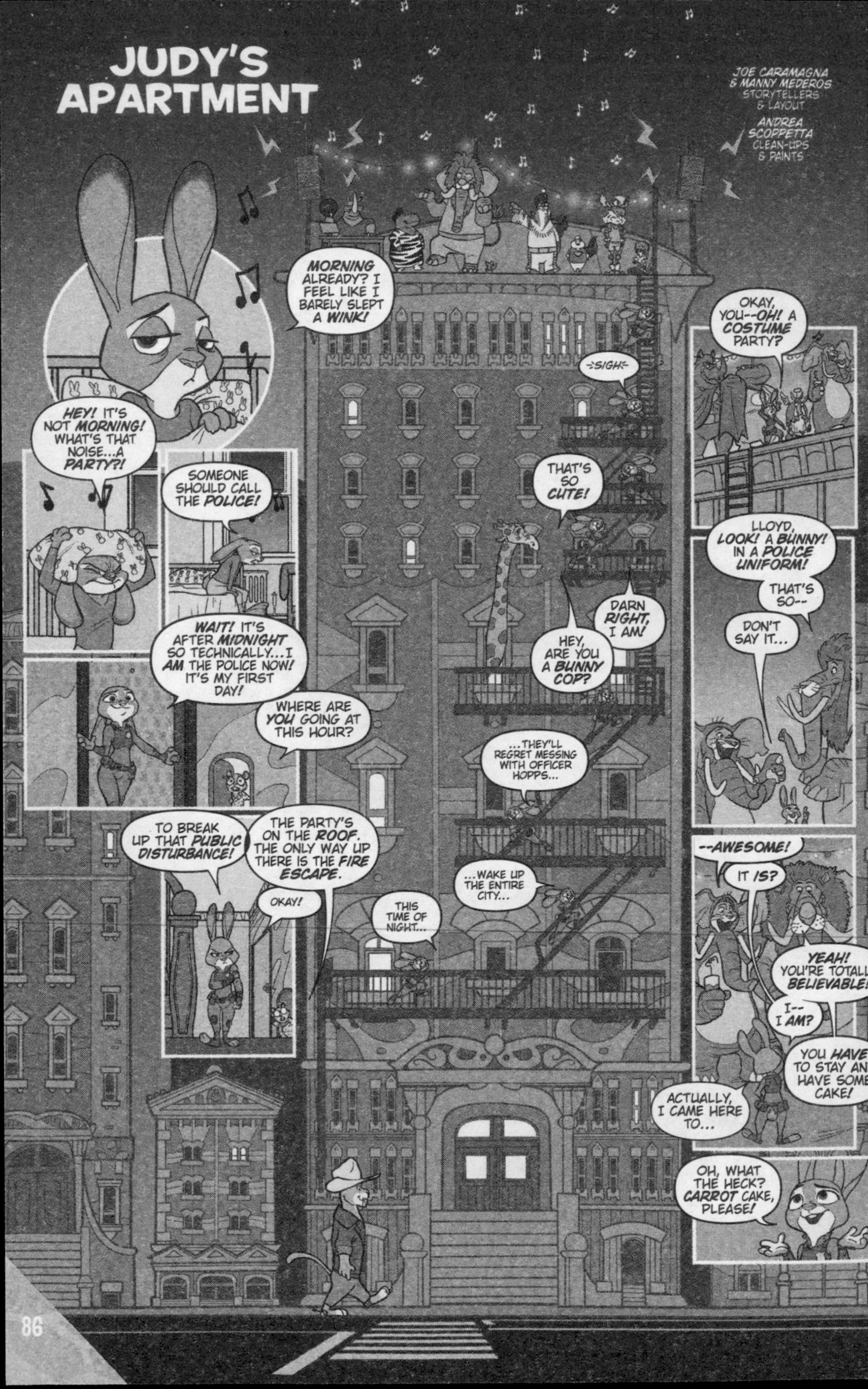
MORNING ALREADY? I FEEL LIKE I BARELY SLEPT A WINK!
HEY! IT'S NOT MORNING! WHAT'S THAT NOISE...A PARTY?!
SOMEONE SHOULD CALL THE POLICE!
WAIT! IT'S AFTER MIDNIGHT SO TECHNICALLY...I AM THE POLICE NOW! IT'S MY FIRST DAY!
WHERE ARE YOU GOING AT THIS HOUR?
TO BREAK UP THAT PUBLIC DISTURBANCE!
THE PARTY'S ON THE ROOF. THE ONLY WAY UP THERE IS THE FIRE ESCAPE.
OKAY!
THIS TIME OF NIGHT...
...WAKE UP THE ENTIRE CITY...
...THEY'LL REGRET MESSING WITH OFFICER HOPPS...
HEY, ARE YOU A BUNNY COP?
DARN RIGHT, I AM!
THAT'S SO CUTE!
SIGH
OKAY, YOU--OH! A COSTUME PARTY?
LLOYD, LOOK! A BUNNY! IN A POLICE UNIFORM!
THAT'S SO--
DON'T SAY IT...
--AWESOME!
IT IS?
YEAH! YOU'RE TOTALL BELIEVABLE!
I-- I AM?
YOU HAVE TO STAY AN HAVE SOME CAKE!
ACTUALLY, I CAME HERE TO...
OH, WHAT THE HECK? CARROT CAKE, PLEASE!

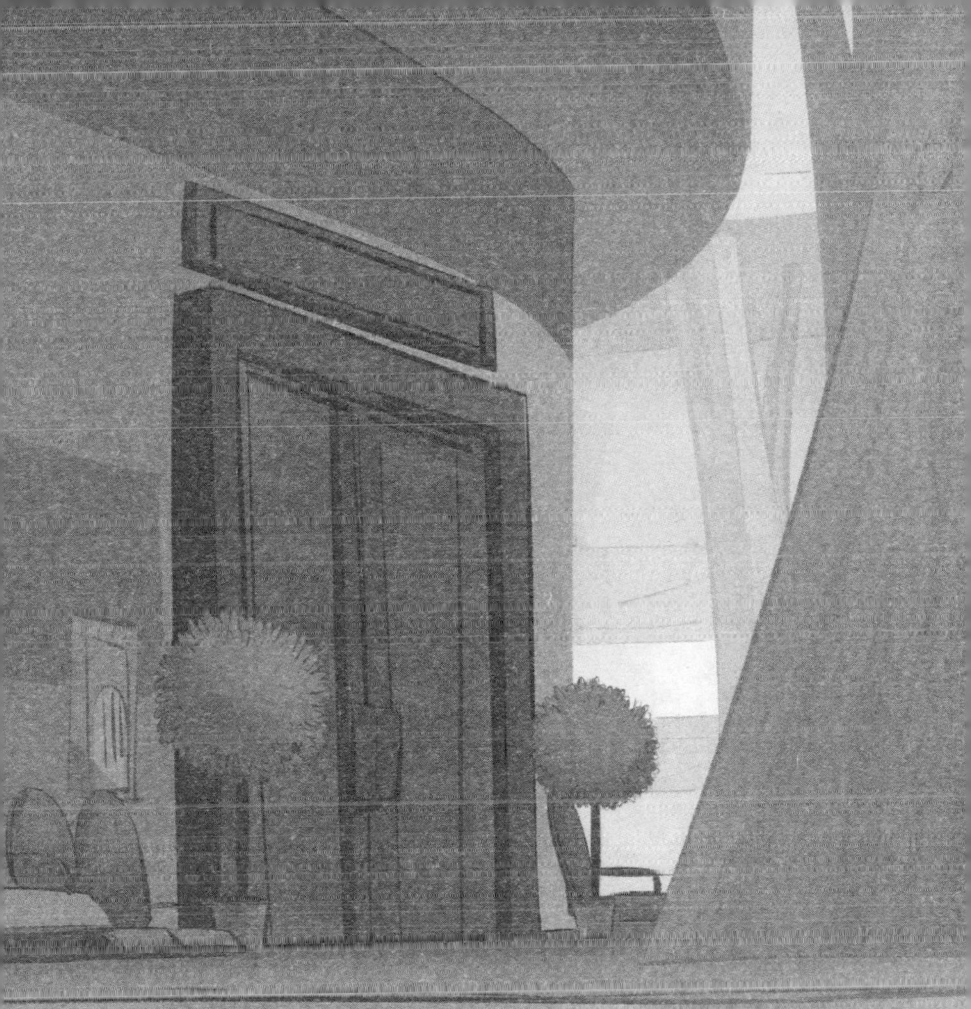

It's a real proud day for us little guys.

ASSISTANT MAYOR BELLWETHER

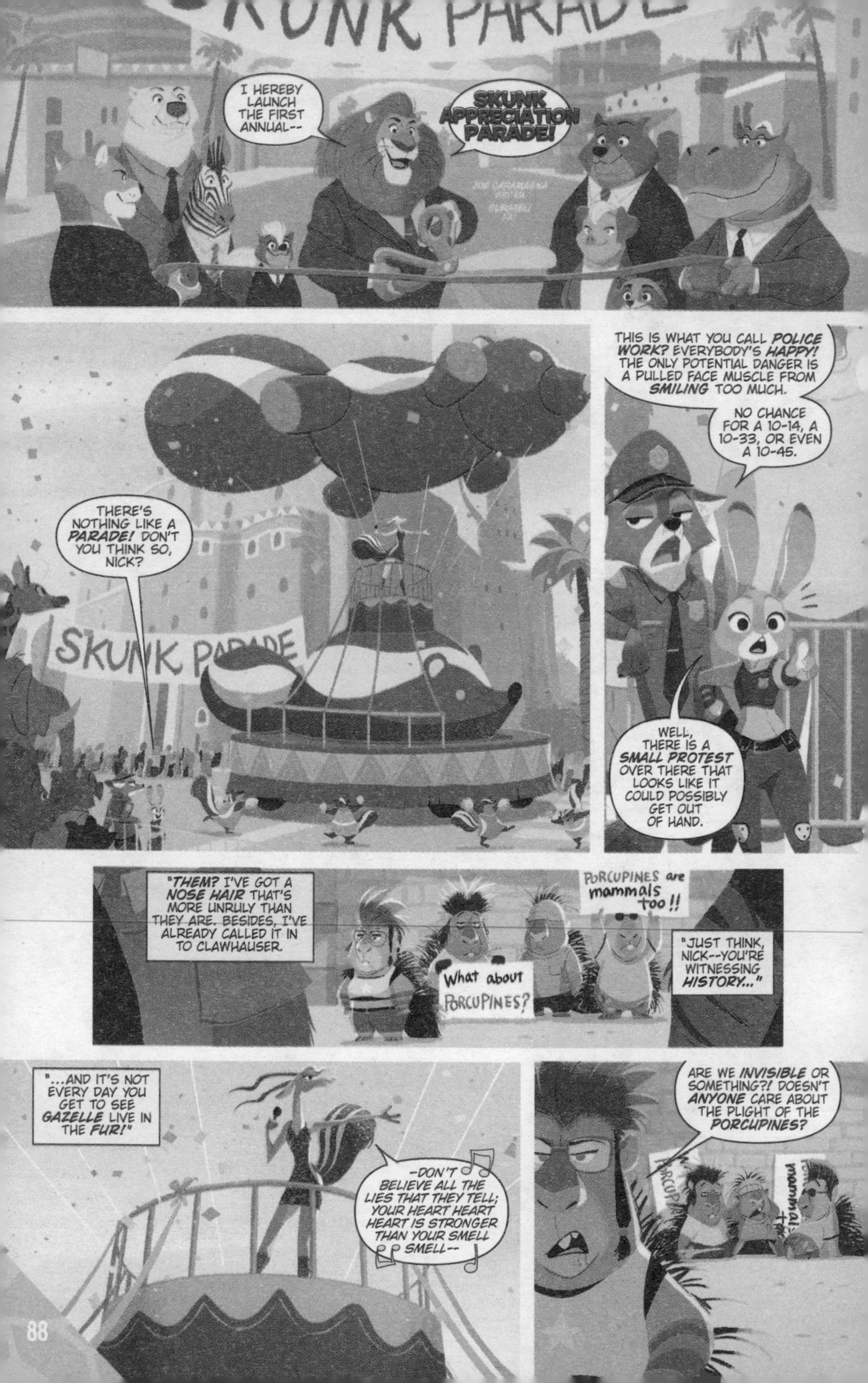
SKUNK PARADE
I HEREBY LAUNCH THE FIRST ANNUAL--
SKUNK APPRECIATION PARADE!
THERE'S NOTHING LIKE A PARADE! DON'T YOU THINK SO, NICK?
SKUNK PARADE
THIS IS WHAT YOU CALL POLICE WORK? EVERYBODY'S HAPPY! THE ONLY POTENTIAL DANGER IS A PULLED FACE MUSCLE FROM SMILING TOO MUCH.
NO CHANCE FOR A 10-14, A 10-33, OR EVEN A 10-45.
WELL, THERE IS A SMALL PROTEST OVER THERE THAT LOOKS LIKE IT COULD POSSIBLY GET OUT OF HAND.
"THEM? I'VE GOT A NOSE HAIR THAT'S MORE UNRULY THAN THEY ARE. BESIDES, I'VE ALREADY CALLED IT IN TO CLAWHAUSER.
PORCUPINES are mammals too!!
What about PORCUPINES?
"JUST THINK, NICK--YOU'RE WITNESSING HISTORY..."
"...AND IT'S NOT EVERY DAY YOU GET TO SEE GAZELLE LIVE IN THE FUR!"
-DON'T BELIEVE ALL THE LIES THAT THEY TELL; YOUR HEART HEART HEART IS STRONGER THAN YOUR SMELL SMELL--
ARE WE INVISIBLE OR SOMETHING?! DOESN'T ANYONE CARE ABOUT THE PLIGHT OF THE PORCUPINES?

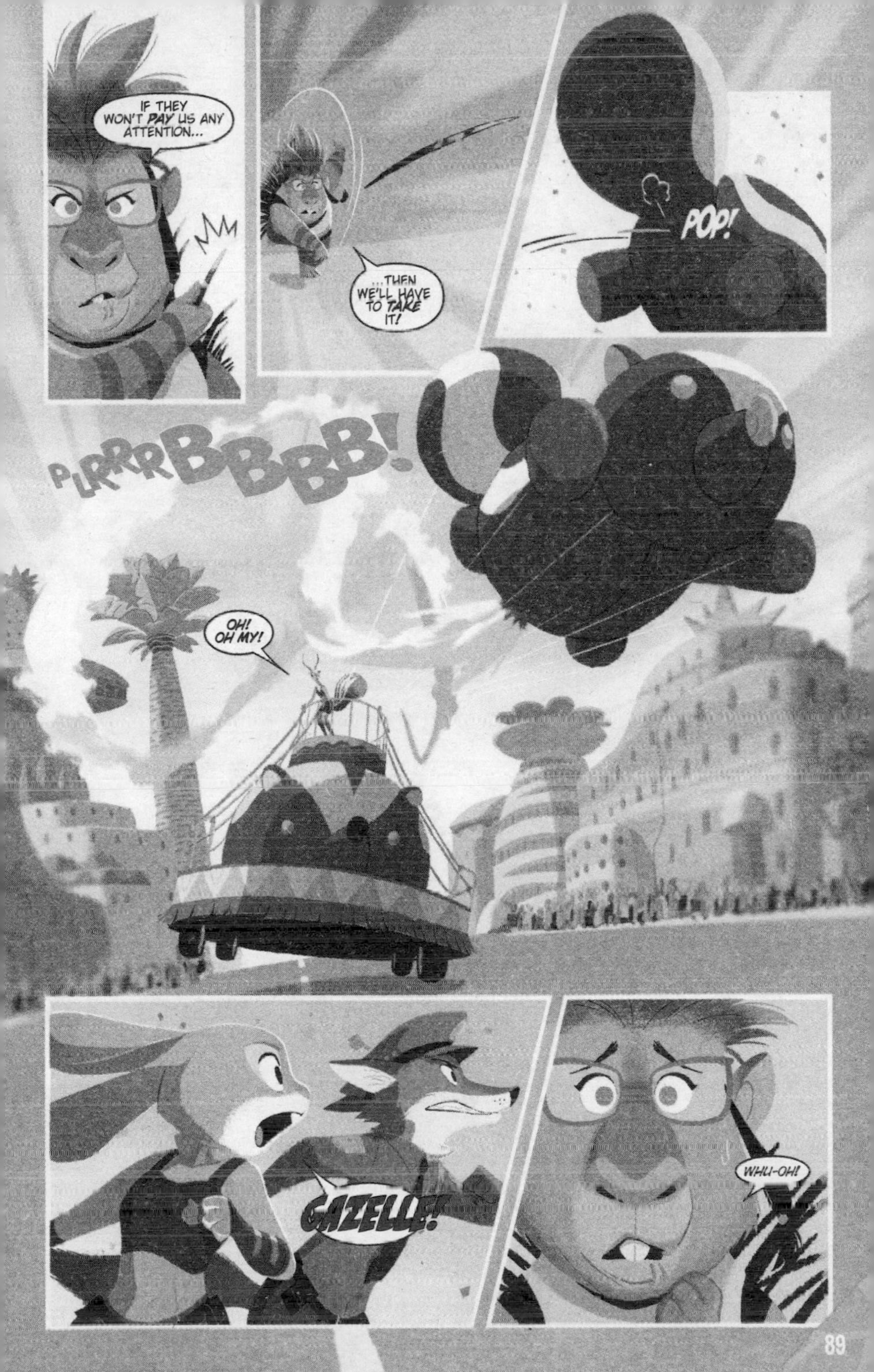
IF THEY WON'T PAY US ANY ATTENTION...
...THEN WE'LL HAVE TO TAKE IT!
POP!
PLRRRRBBBBB!
OH! OH MY!
GAZELLE!
WHU-OH!

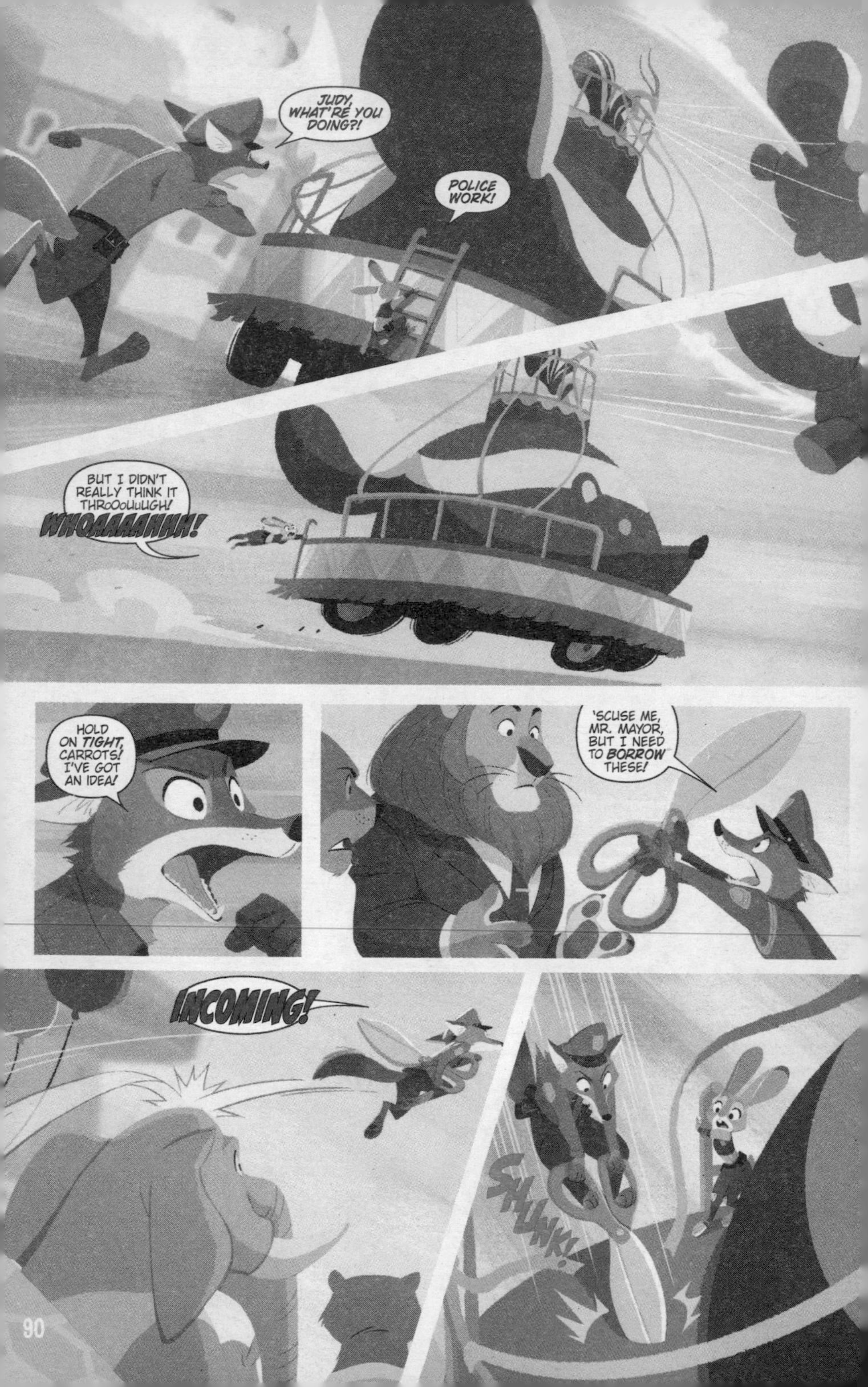
JUDY, WHAT'RE YOU DOING?!
POLICE WORK!
BUT I DIDN'T REALLY THINK IT THROOOUUUGH!
WHOAAAAAHHH!
HOLD ON TIGHT, CARROTS! I'VE GOT AN IDEA!
'SCUSE ME, MR. MAYOR, BUT I NEED TO BORROW THESE!
INCOMING!
SHUNK!

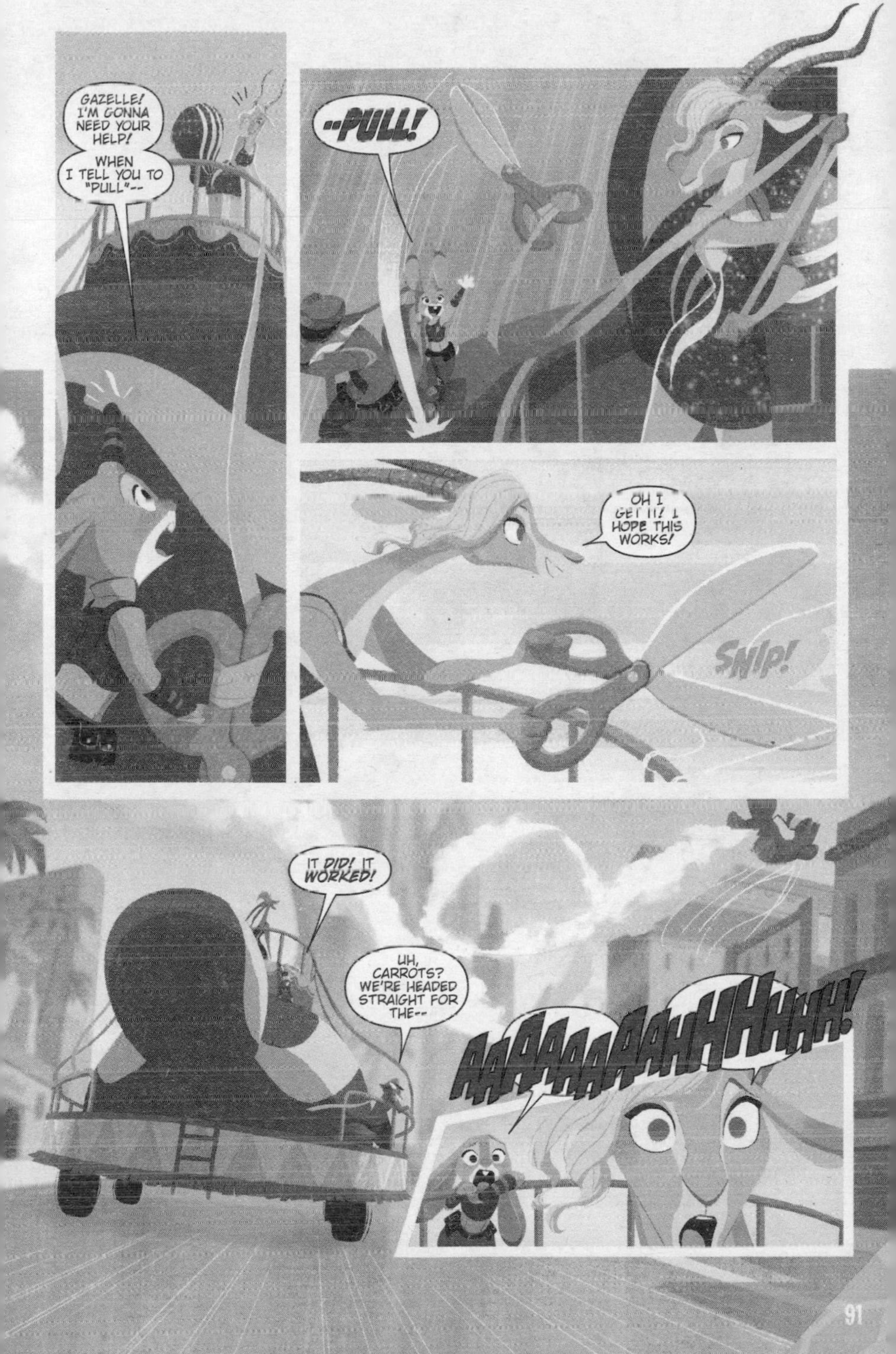
GAZELLE! I'M GONNA NEED YOUR HELP!
WHEN I TELL YOU TO "PULL"--
--PULL!
OH I GET IT! I HOPE THIS WORKS!
SNIP!
IT DID! IT WORKED!
UH, CARROTS? WE'RE HEADED STRAIGHT FOR THE--
AAAAAAAAHHHHHH!

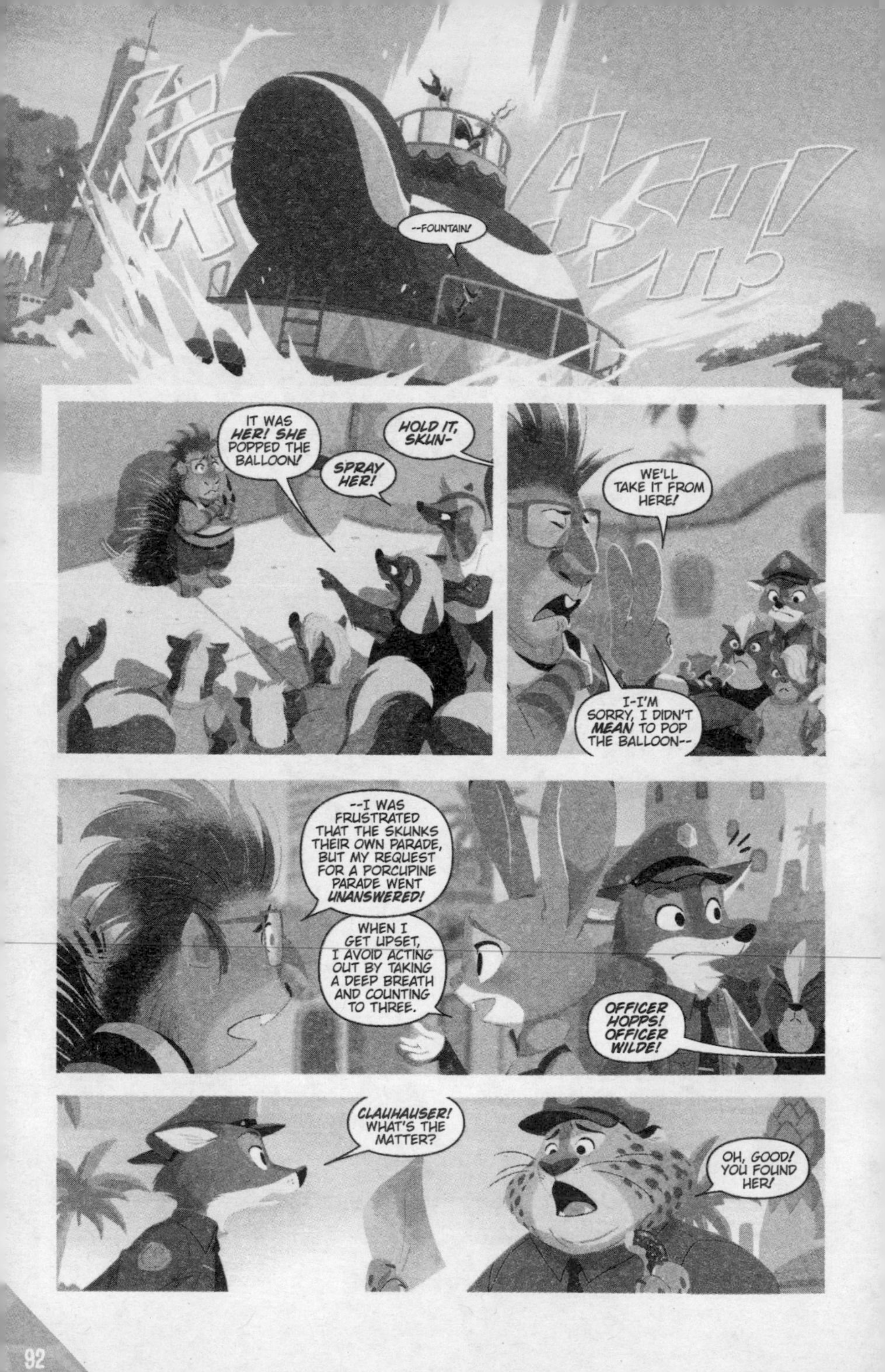
--FOUNTAIN!
IT WAS HER! SHE POPPED THE BALLOON!
SPRAY HER!
HOLD IT, SKUN-
WE'LL TAKE IT FROM HERE!
I-I'M SORRY, I DIDN'T MEAN TO POP THE BALLOON--
--I WAS FRUSTRATED THAT THE SKUNKS THEIR OWN PARADE, BUT MY REQUEST FOR A PORCUPINE PARADE WENT UNANSWERED!
WHEN I GET UPSET, I AVOID ACTING OUT BY TAKING A DEEP BREATH AND COUNTING TO THREE.
OFFICER HOPPS! OFFICER WILDE!
CLAUHAUSER! WHAT'S THE MATTER?
OH, GOOD! YOU FOUND HER!

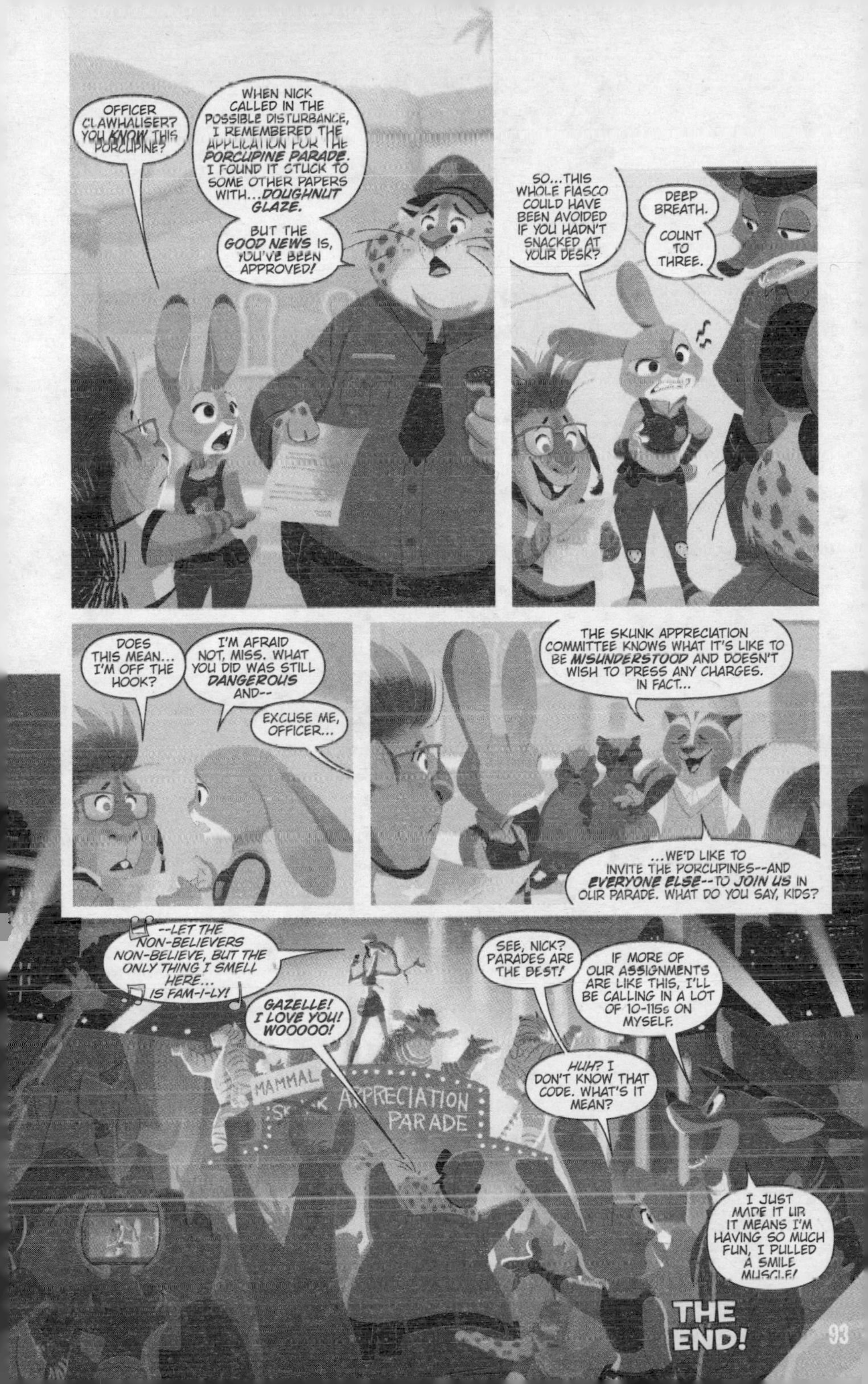
OFFICER CLAWHAUSER? YOU KNOW THIS PORCUPINE?
WHEN NICK CALLED IN THE POSSIBLE DISTURBANCE, I REMEMBERED THE APPLICATION FOR THE PORCUPINE PARADE. I FOUND IT STUCK TO SOME OTHER PAPERS WITH...DOUGHNUT GLAZE.
BUT THE GOOD NEWS IS, YOU'VE BEEN APPROVED!
SO...THIS WHOLE FIASCO COULD HAVE BEEN AVOIDED IF YOU HADN'T SNACKED AT YOUR DESK?
DEEP BREATH.
COUNT TO THREE.
DOES THIS MEAN... I'M OFF THE HOOK?
I'M AFRAID NOT, MISS. WHAT YOU DID WAS STILL DANGEROUS AND--
EXCUSE ME, OFFICER...
THE SKUNK APPRECIATION COMMITTEE KNOWS WHAT IT'S LIKE TO BE MISUNDERSTOOD AND DOESN'T WISH TO PRESS ANY CHARGES. IN FACT...
...WE'D LIKE TO INVITE THE PORCUPINES--AND EVERYONE ELSE--TO JOIN US IN OUR PARADE. WHAT DO YOU SAY, KIDS?
--LET THE NON-BELIEVERS NON-BELIEVE, BUT THE ONLY THING I SMELL HERE... IS FAM-I-LY!
GAZELLE! I LOVE YOU! WOOOOO!
MAMMAL
APPRECIATION PARADE
SEE, NICK? PARADES ARE THE BEST!
IF MORE OF OUR ASSIGNMENTS ARE LIKE THIS, I'LL BE CALLING IN A LOT OF 10-115s ON MYSELF.
HUH? I DON'T KNOW THAT CODE. WHAT'S IT MEAN?
I JUST MADE IT UP. IT MEANS I'M HAVING SO MUCH FUN, I PULLED A SMILE MUSCLE!
THE END!

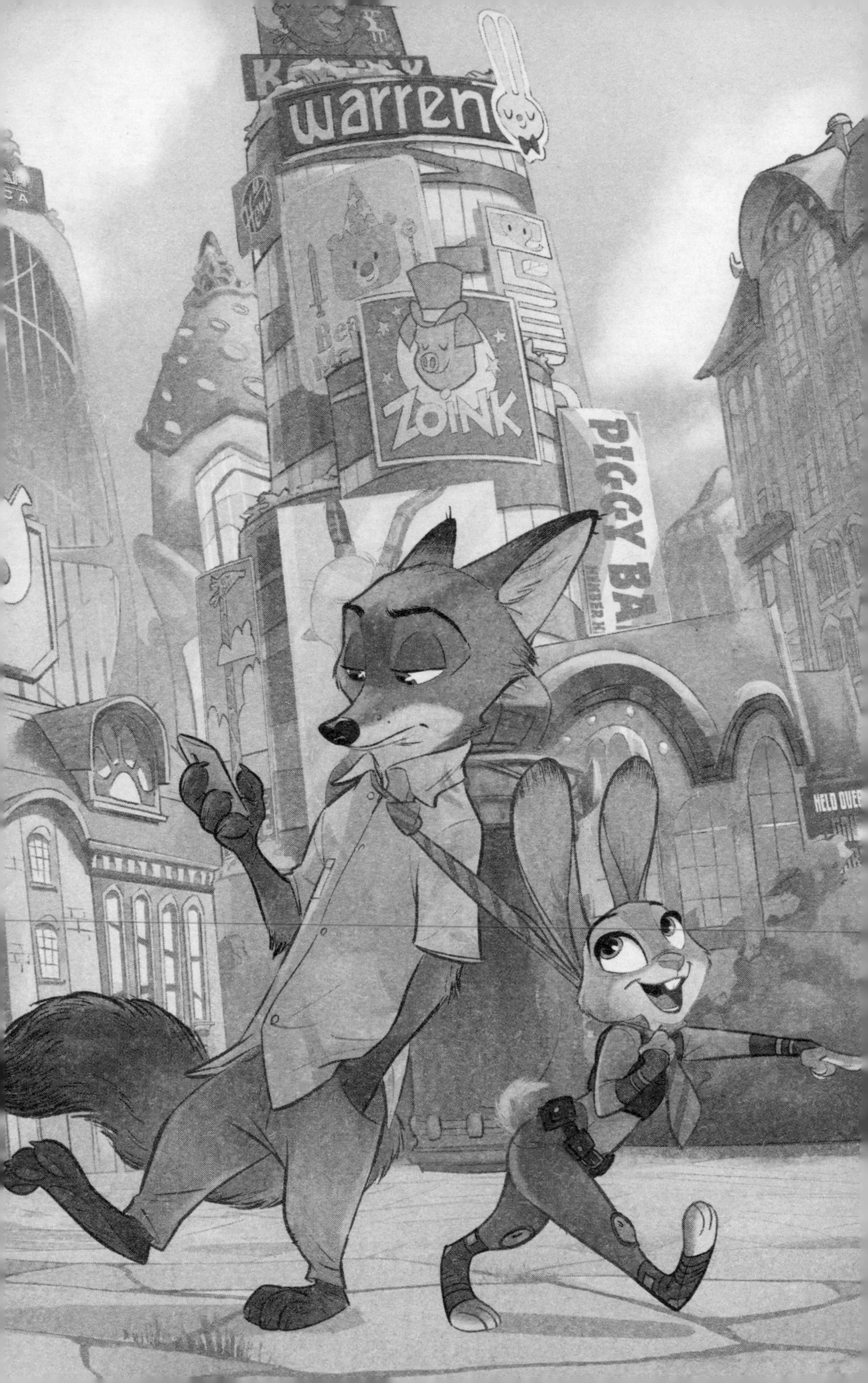
warren
ZOINK
PIGGY BA

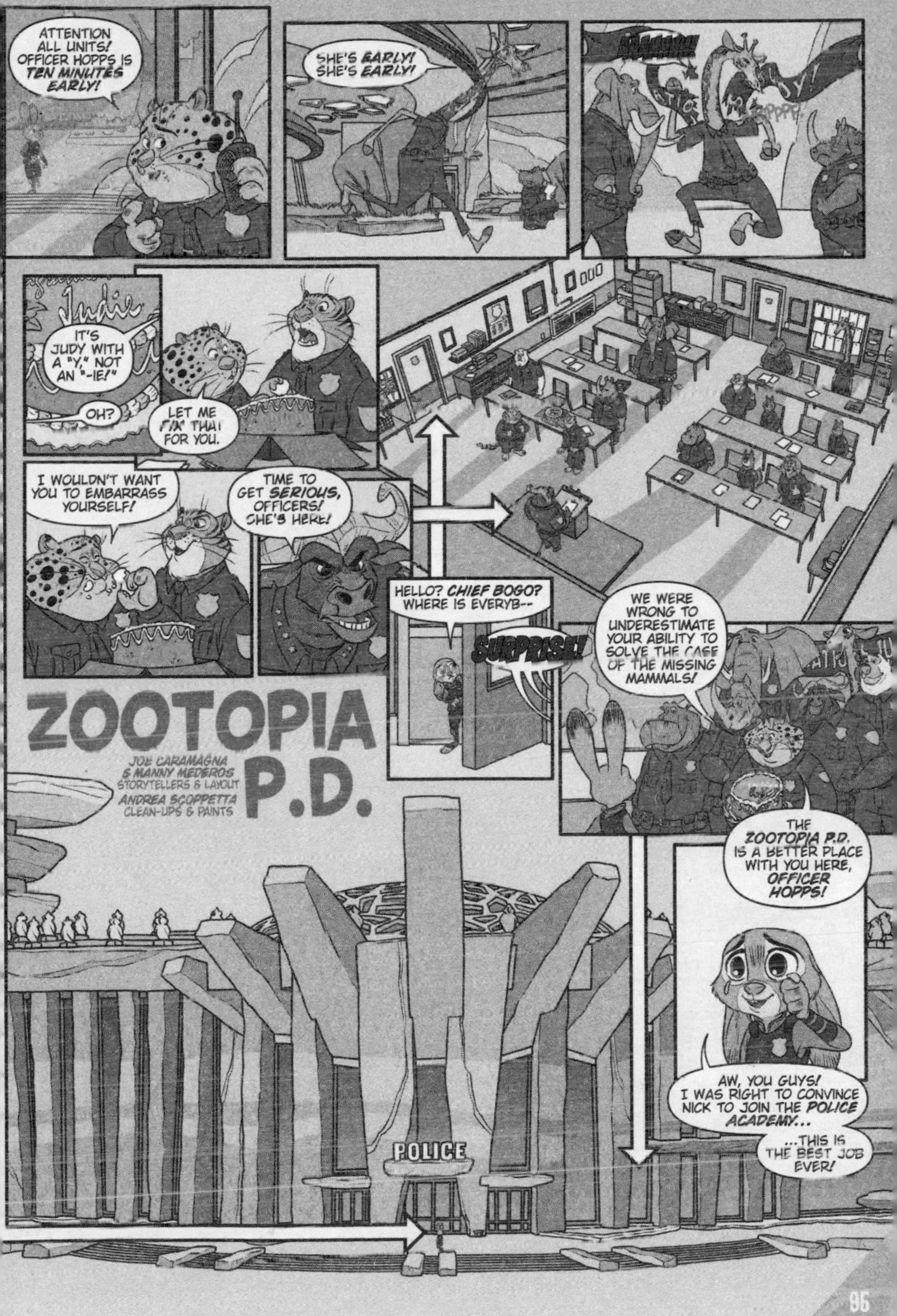
ATTENTION ALL UNITS! OFFICER HOPPS IS TEN MINUTES EARLY!
SHE'S EARLY! SHE'S EARLY!
IT'S JUDY WITH A "Y," NOT AN "-IE!"
OH?
LET ME FIX THAT FOR YOU.
I WOULDN'T WANT YOU TO EMBARRASS YOURSELF!
TIME TO GET SERIOUS, OFFICERS! SHE'S HERE!
HELLO? CHIEF BOGO? WHERE IS EVERYB--
SURPRISE!
WE WERE WRONG TO UNDERESTIMATE YOUR ABILITY TO SOLVE THE CASE OF THE MISSING MAMMALS!
THE ZOOTOPIA P.D. IS A BETTER PLACE WITH YOU HERE, OFFICER HOPPS!
AW, YOU GUYS! I WAS RIGHT TO CONVINCE NICK TO JOIN THE POLICE ACADEMY...
...THIS IS THE BEST JOB EVER!
ZOOTOPIA P.D.
JOE CARAMAGNA & MANNY MEDEROS STORYTELLERS & LAYOUT
ANDREA SCOPPETTA CLEAN-UPS & PAINTS
POLICE

THOUSANDS OF YEARS AGO, THE WORLD WAS DIVIDED IN TWO--VICIOUS PREDATORS AND MEEK PREY. BUT SOME SOUGHT PEACE.

THANKS TO THEM, MAMMALS NO LONGER HAVE TO COWER IN HERDS AND NOW HAVE A MULTITUDE OF OPPORTUNITIES. TO LEARN MORE ABOUT LIFE IN THOSE EARLY DAYS OF CIVILIZATION, THE PEOPLE OF ZOOTOPIA COME HERE: **THE MUSEUM OF NATURAL HISTORY.**

A DAY AT THE MUSEUM

JOE CARAMAGNA & MANNY MEDEROS
STORYTELLERS & LAYOUT

ANDREA SCOPPETTA
CLEAN-UPS & PAINTS

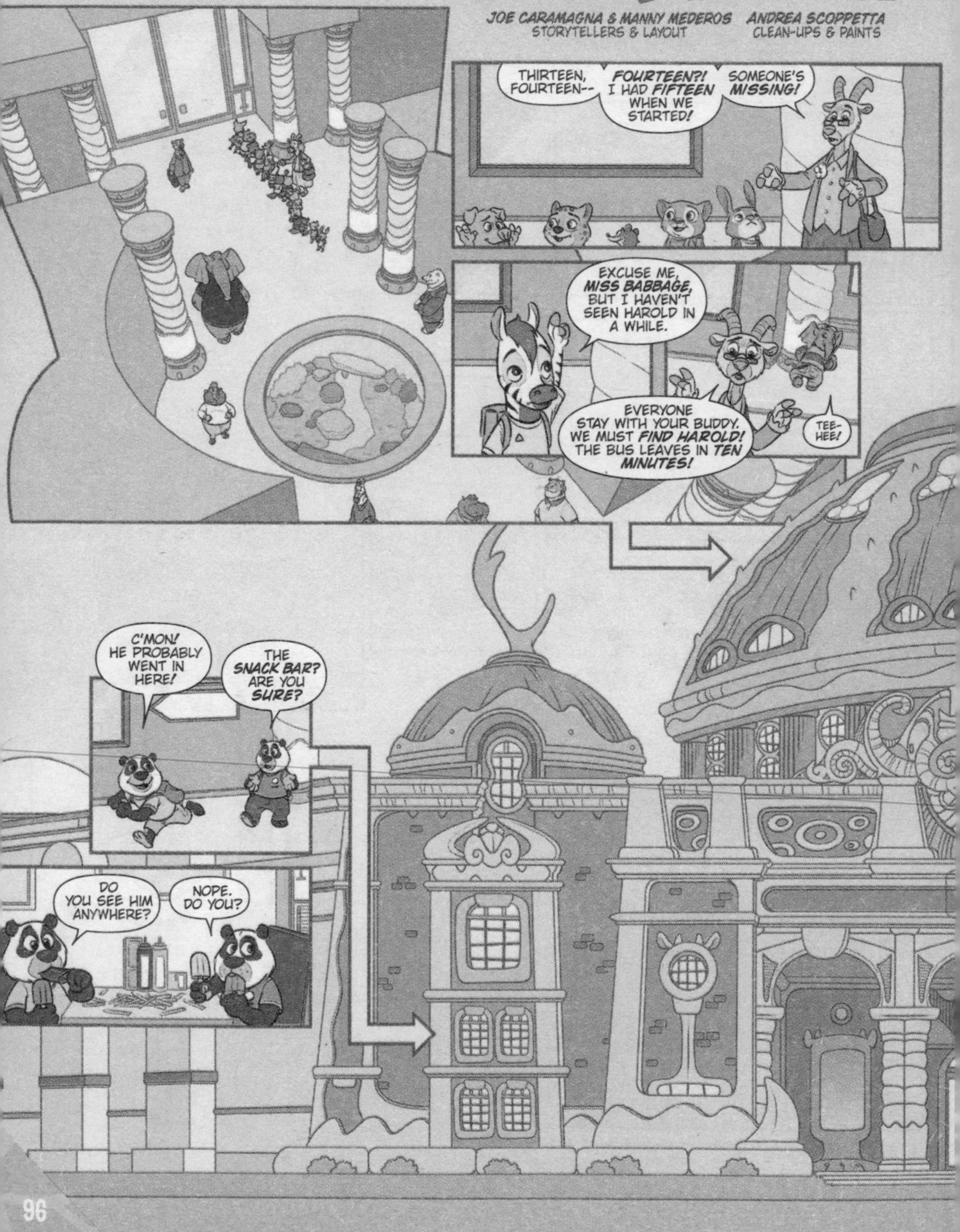
THIRTEEN, FOURTEEN--
FOURTEEN?! I HAD FIFTEEN WHEN WE STARTED!
SOMEONE'S MISSING!
EXCUSE ME, MISS BABBAGE, BUT I HAVEN'T SEEN HAROLD IN A WHILE.
EVERYONE STAY WITH YOUR BUDDY. WE MUST FIND HAROLD! THE BUS LEAVES IN TEN MINUTES!
TEE-HEE!
C'MON! HE PROBABLY WENT IN HERE!
THE SNACK BAR? ARE YOU SURE?
DO YOU SEE HIM ANYWHERE?
NOPE. DO YOU?

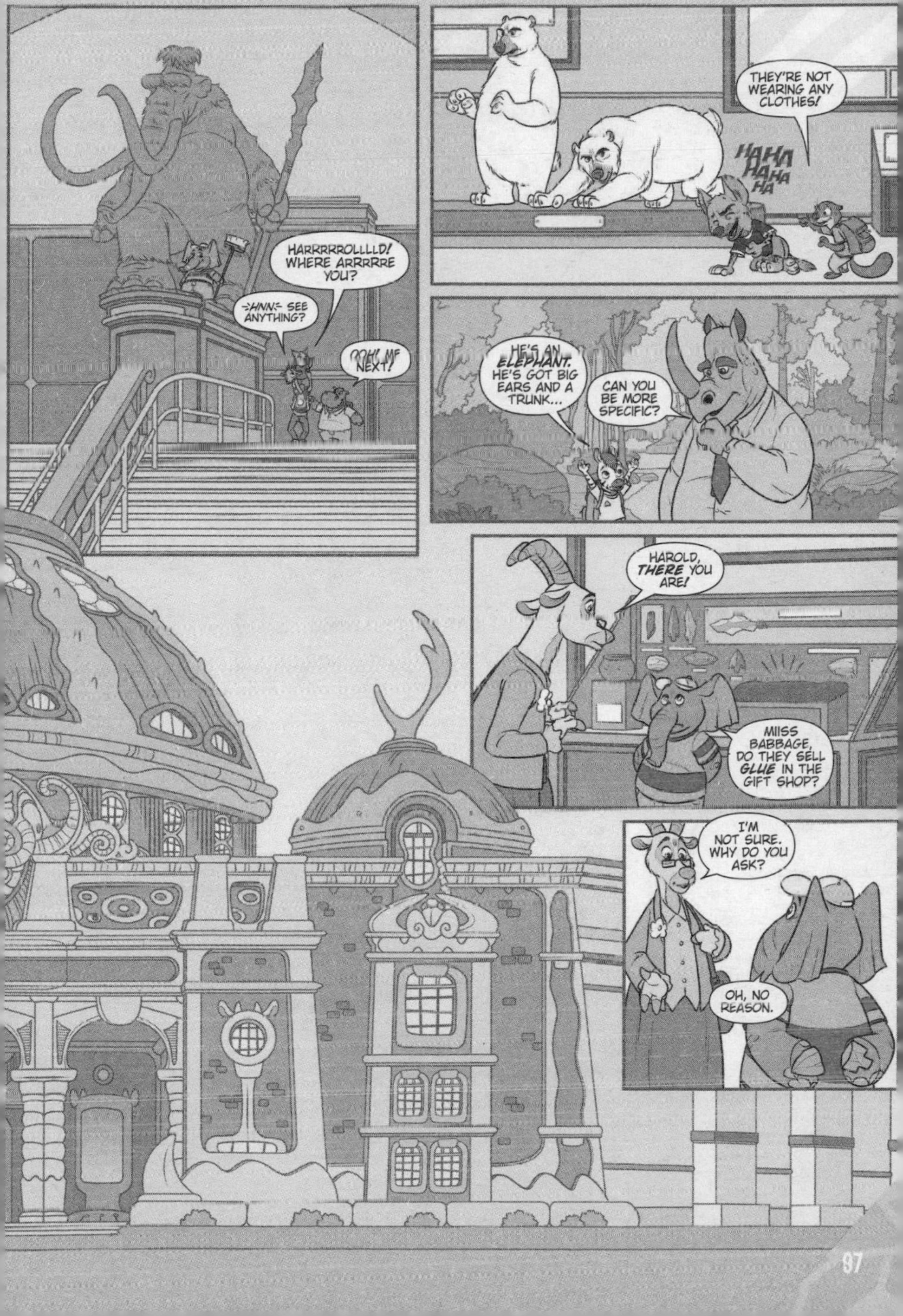
HARRRRROLLLLD! WHERE ARRRRRE YOU?
HNN SEE ANYTHING?
OOH! ME NEXT!
THEY'RE NOT WEARING ANY CLOTHES!
HA HA HA HA HA HA
HE'S AN ELEPHANT. HE'S GOT BIG EARS AND A TRUNK...
CAN YOU BE MORE SPECIFIC?
HAROLD, THERE YOU ARE!
MIISS BABBAGE, DO THEY SELL GLUE IN THE GIFT SHOP?
I'M NOT SURE. WHY DO YOU ASK?
OH, NO REASON.

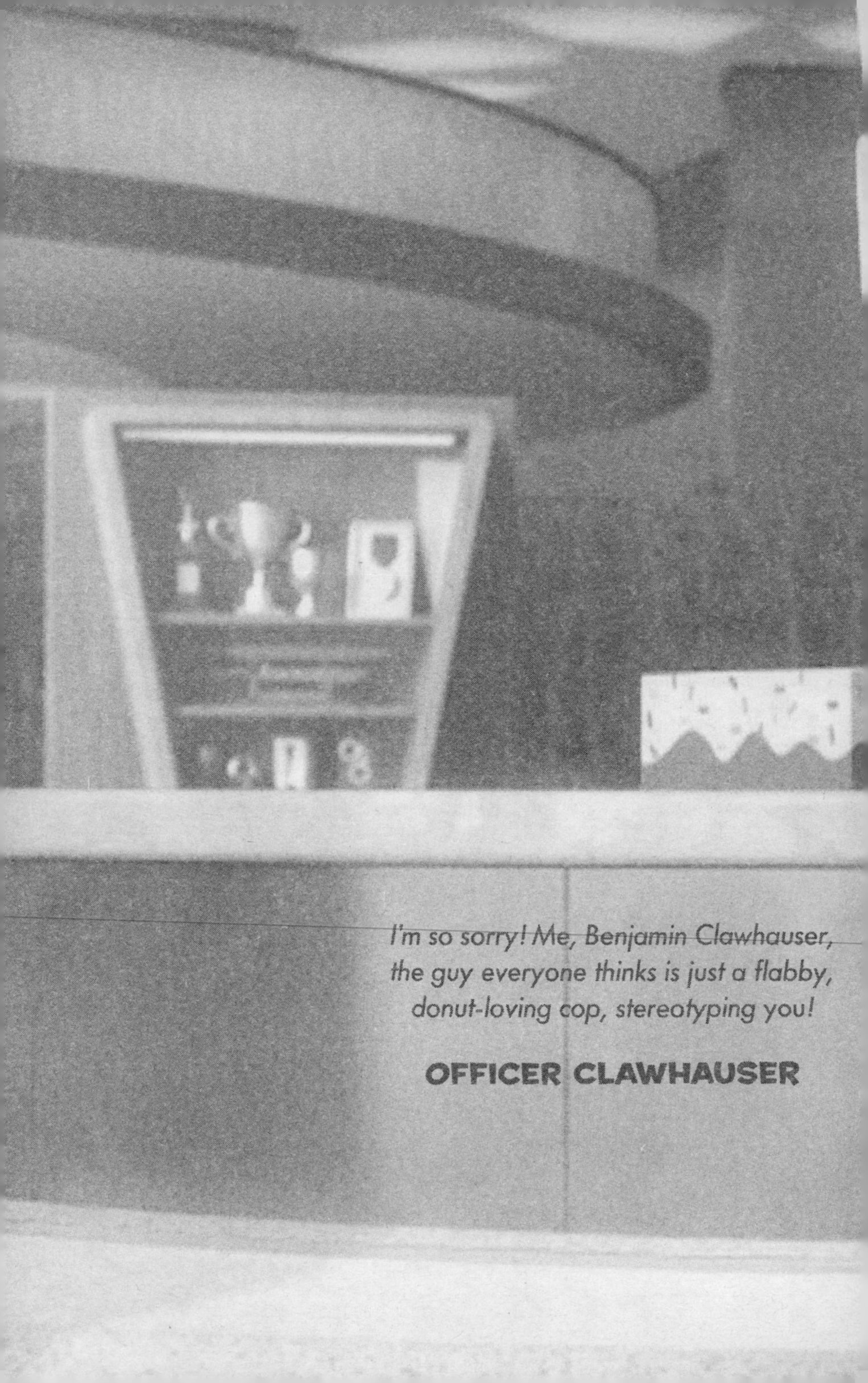

I'm so sorry! Me, Benjamin Clawhauser, the guy everyone thinks is just a flabby, donut-loving cop, stereotyping you!

OFFICER CLAWHAUSER

LIFE IN ZOOTOPIA

A CHANCE MEETING

Judy and Nick's relationship started off in an unusual way. Read on to find out each one's story of how they met.

NICK: Finnick and I were in Jumbeaux's when this cute little bunny meter maid walked in. She was concerned and generous! She fell right into our plan. I realize it wasn't honest, but it all worked out and look at us now!

JUDY: I was busy writing tickets when I noticed a suspicious-looking fox walk into Jumbeaux's Café. When I went inside, I found Nick and his so-called "son" trying to buy an elephant-sized Jumbo-pop. Turned out that he didn't have his wallet, so I helped him out. I couldn't resist! Little did I know that this Jumbo-pop purchase was the beginning of an elaborate scam Nick was running.

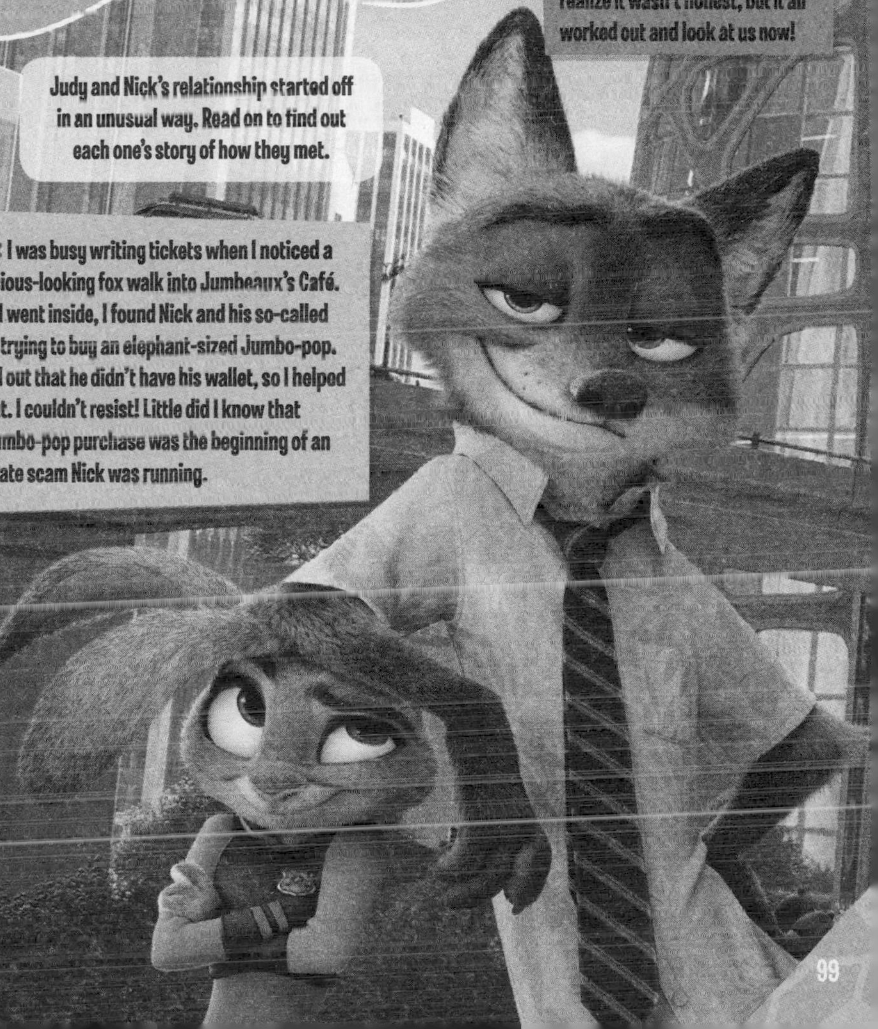

NICK & JUDY'S ZOOTOPIA

In Zootopia, anyone can be anything—but that doesn't mean it's easy. Here are some tips Nick and Judy learned along the way....

RAINFOREST DISTRICT

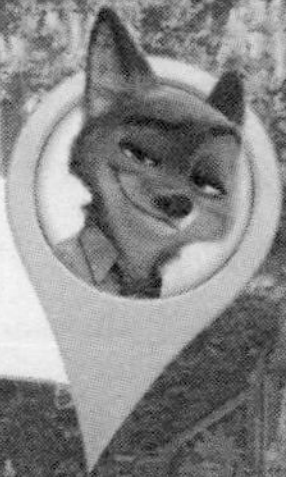

DON'T PRONOUNCE THE "J" IN TUJUNGA. IT'S TU-HUN-GA!

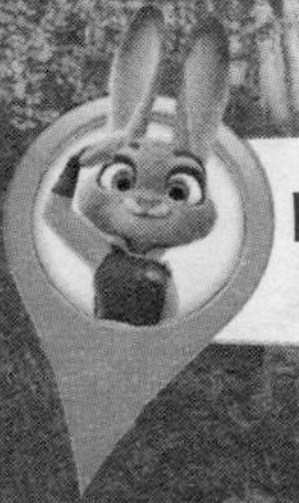

IF YOU'RE GOING TO RAINFOREST DISTRICT... MAKE SURE TO TAKE YOUR RAIN GEAR!

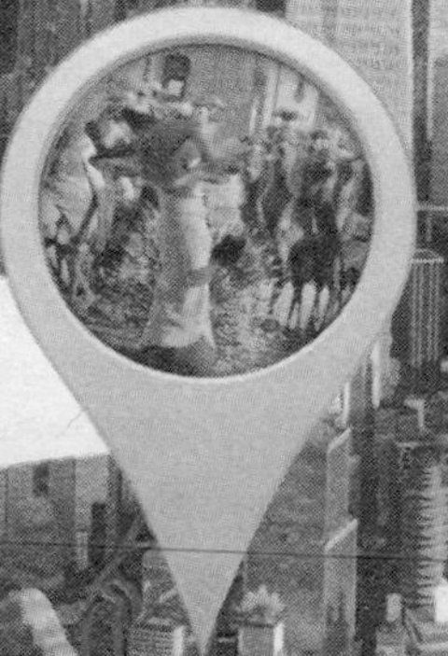

NEED TO CROSS THE STREET DURING RUSH HOUR? JUST FOLLOW THE PORCUPINE!

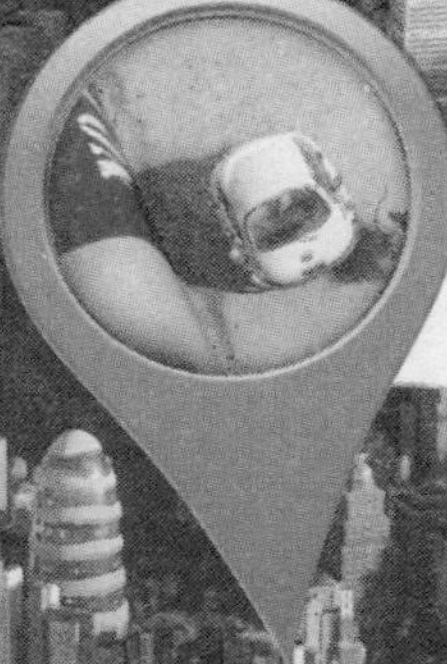

DON'T PARK IN THE RED ZONE. EVEN IF YOUR CAR IS TINY.

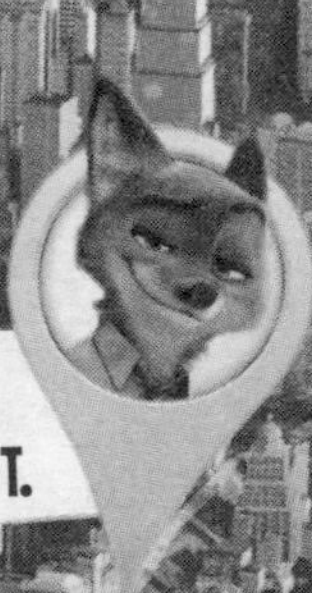

BE VERY CAREFUL WHEN YOU BUY A RUG. IT COULD BE MADE FROM THE FUR OF A SKUNK'S BUTT.

SURVIVAL GUIDE

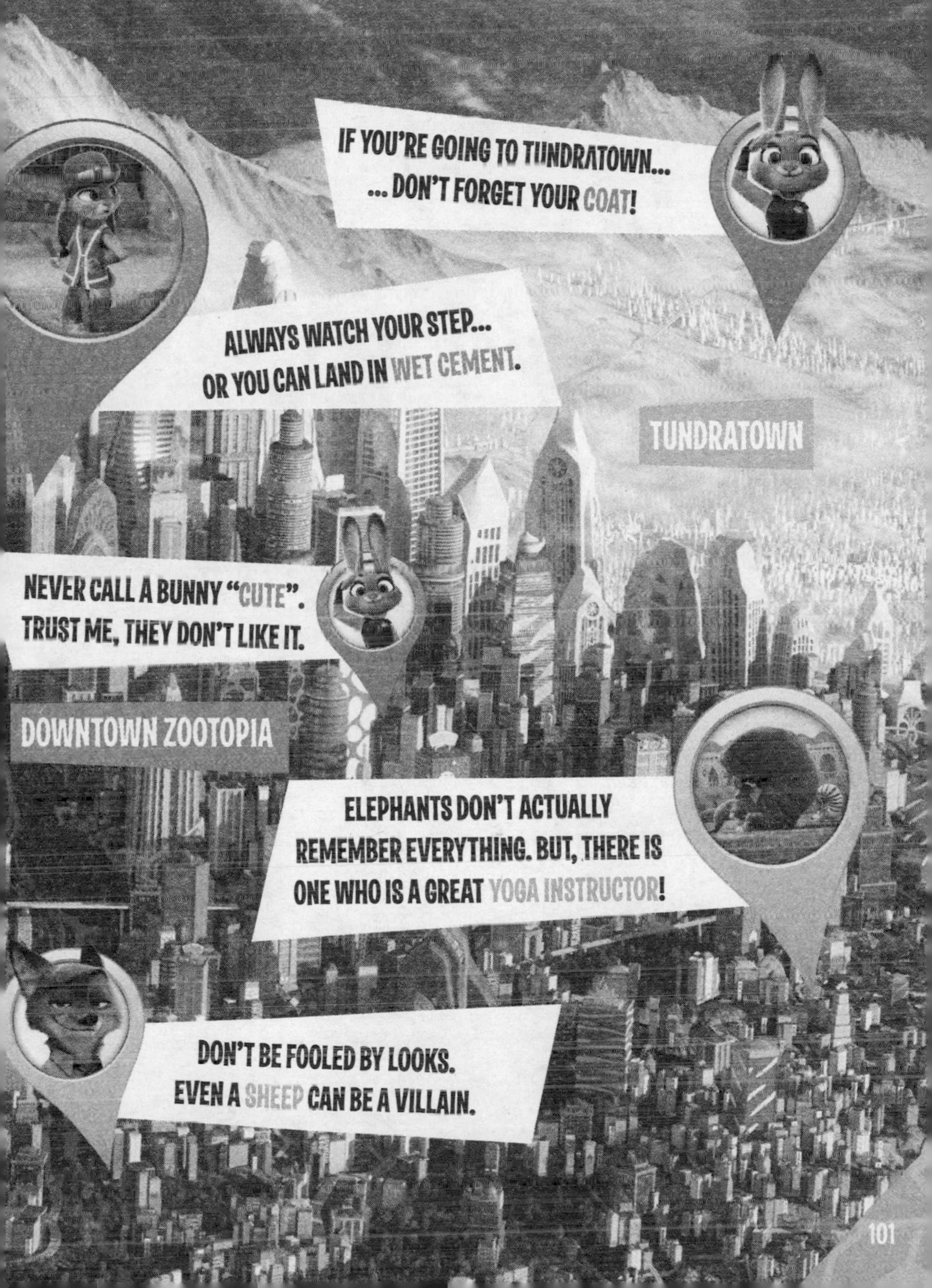
IF YOU'RE GOING TO TUNDRATOWN...
... DON'T FORGET YOUR COAT!
ALWAYS WATCH YOUR STEP...
OR YOU CAN LAND IN WET CEMENT.
TUNDRATOWN
NEVER CALL A BUNNY "CUTE".
TRUST ME, THEY DON'T LIKE IT.
DOWNTOWN ZOOTOPIA
ELEPHANTS DON'T ACTUALLY
REMEMBER EVERYTHING. BUT, THERE IS
ONE WHO IS A GREAT YOGA INSTRUCTOR!
DON'T BE FOOLED BY LOOKS.
EVEN A SHEEP CAN BE A VILLAIN.

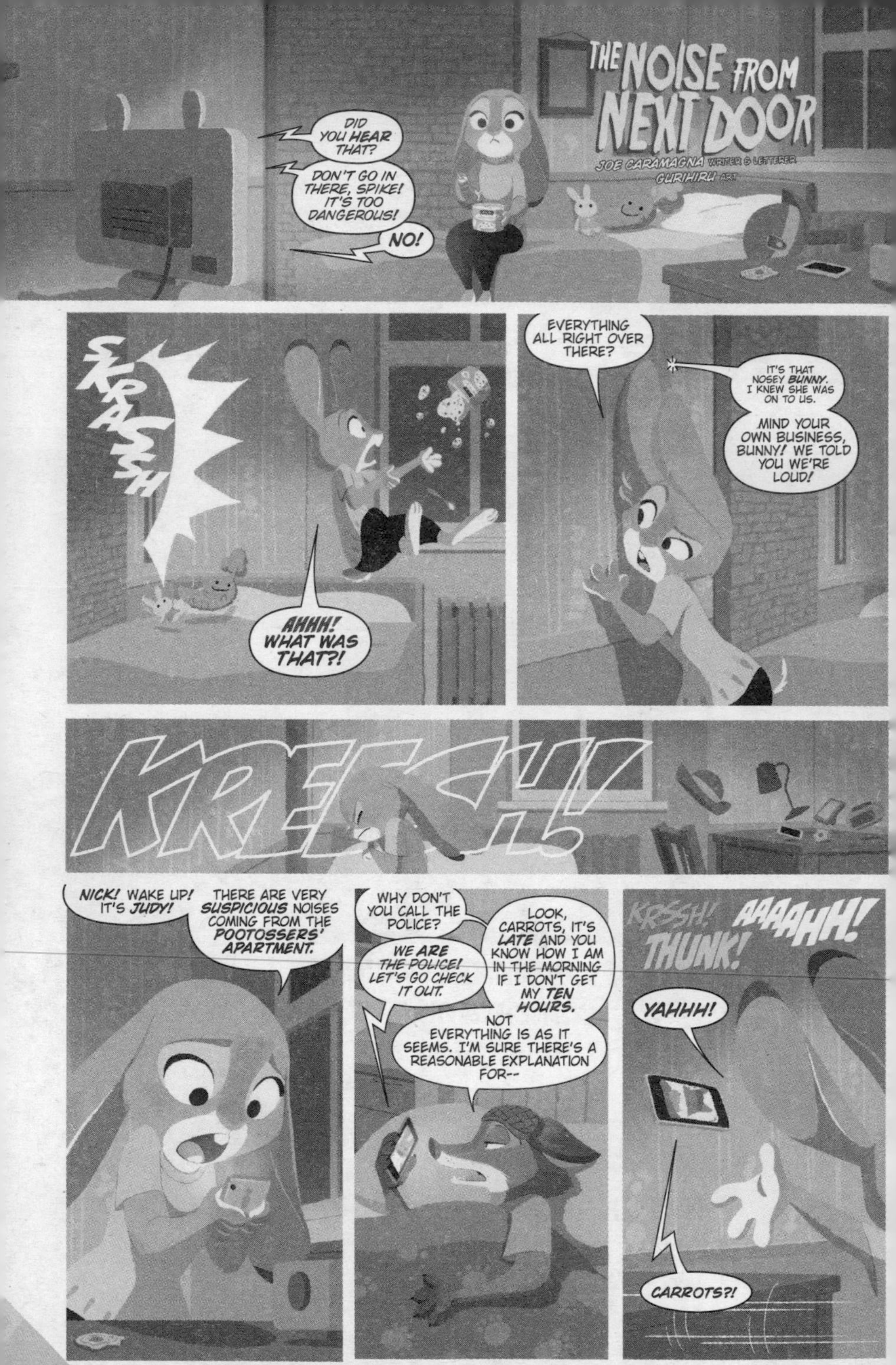
THE NOISE FROM NEXT DOOR
JOE CARAMAGNA WRITER & LETTERER
GURIHIRU ART
DID YOU HEAR THAT?
DON'T GO IN THERE, SPIKE! IT'S TOO DANGEROUS!
NO!
SKRASSH
AHHH! WHAT WAS THAT?!
EVERYTHING ALL RIGHT OVER THERE?
IT'S THAT NOSEY BUNNY. I KNEW SHE WAS ON TO US.
MIND YOUR OWN BUSINESS, BUNNY! WE TOLD YOU WE'RE LOUD!
KRESSH!
NICK! WAKE UP! IT'S JUDY!
THERE ARE VERY SUSPICIOUS NOISES COMING FROM THE POOTOSSERS' APARTMENT.
WHY DON'T YOU CALL THE POLICE?
WE ARE THE POLICE! LET'S GO CHECK IT OUT.
LOOK, CARROTS, IT'S LATE AND YOU KNOW HOW I AM IN THE MORNING IF I DON'T GET MY TEN HOURS.
NOT EVERYTHING IS AS IT SEEMS. I'M SURE THERE'S A REASONABLE EXPLANATION FOR--
KRSSH!
AAAAHH!
THUNK!
YAHHH!
CARROTS?!

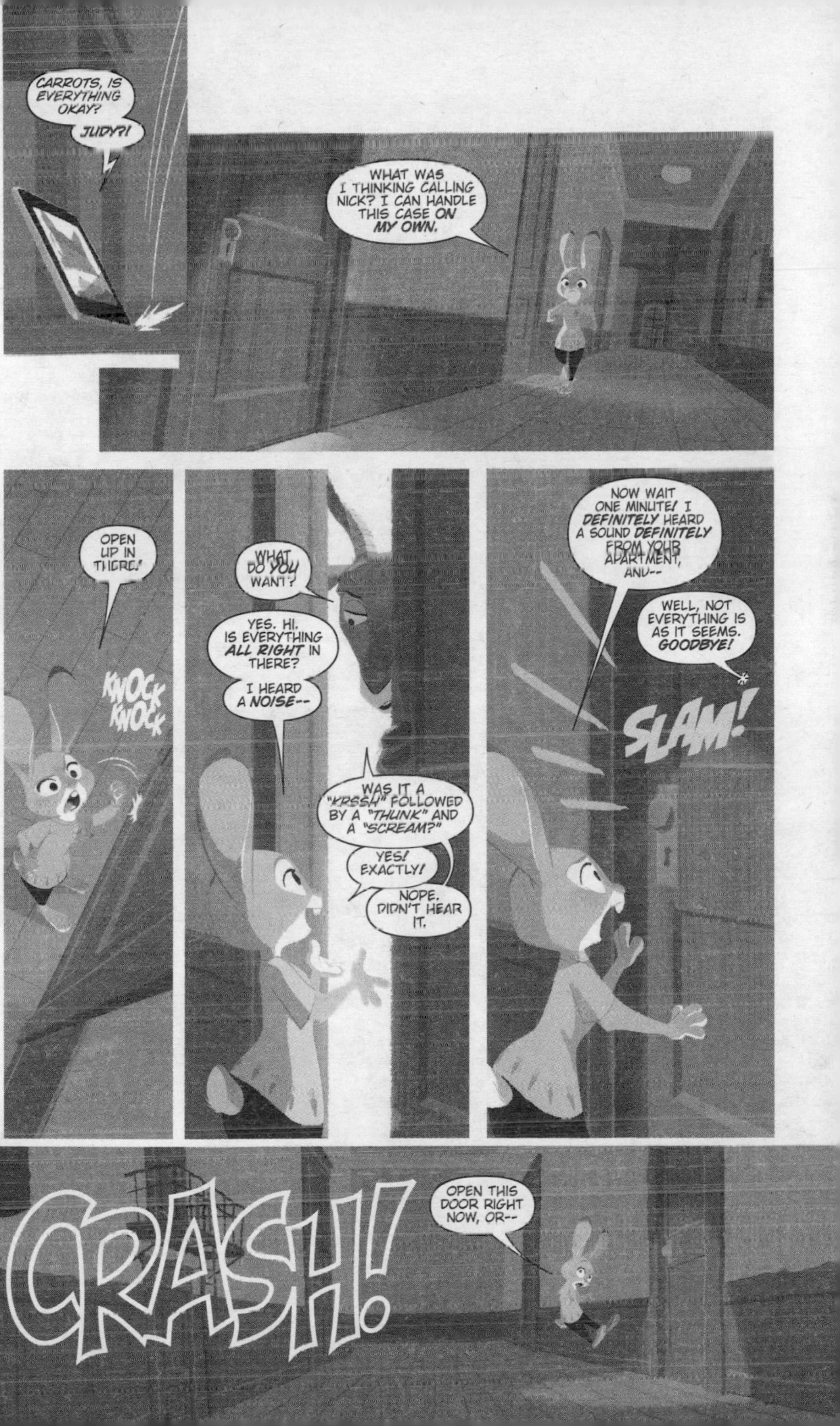

CARROTS, IS EVERYTHING OKAY?
JUDY?!
WHAT WAS I THINKING CALLING NICK? I CAN HANDLE THIS CASE ON MY OWN.
OPEN UP IN THERE!
KNOCK KNOCK
WHAT DO YOU WANT?
YES. HI. IS EVERYTHING ALL RIGHT IN THERE?
I HEARD A NOISE--
WAS IT A "KRSSH" FOLLOWED BY A "THUNK" AND A "SCREAM?"
YES! EXACTLY!
NOPE. DIDN'T HEAR IT.
NOW WAIT ONE MINUTE! I DEFINITELY HEARD A SOUND DEFINITELY FROM YOUR APARTMENT, AND--
WELL, NOT EVERYTHING IS AS IT SEEMS. GOODBYE!
SLAM!
CRASH!
OPEN THIS DOOR RIGHT NOW, OR--

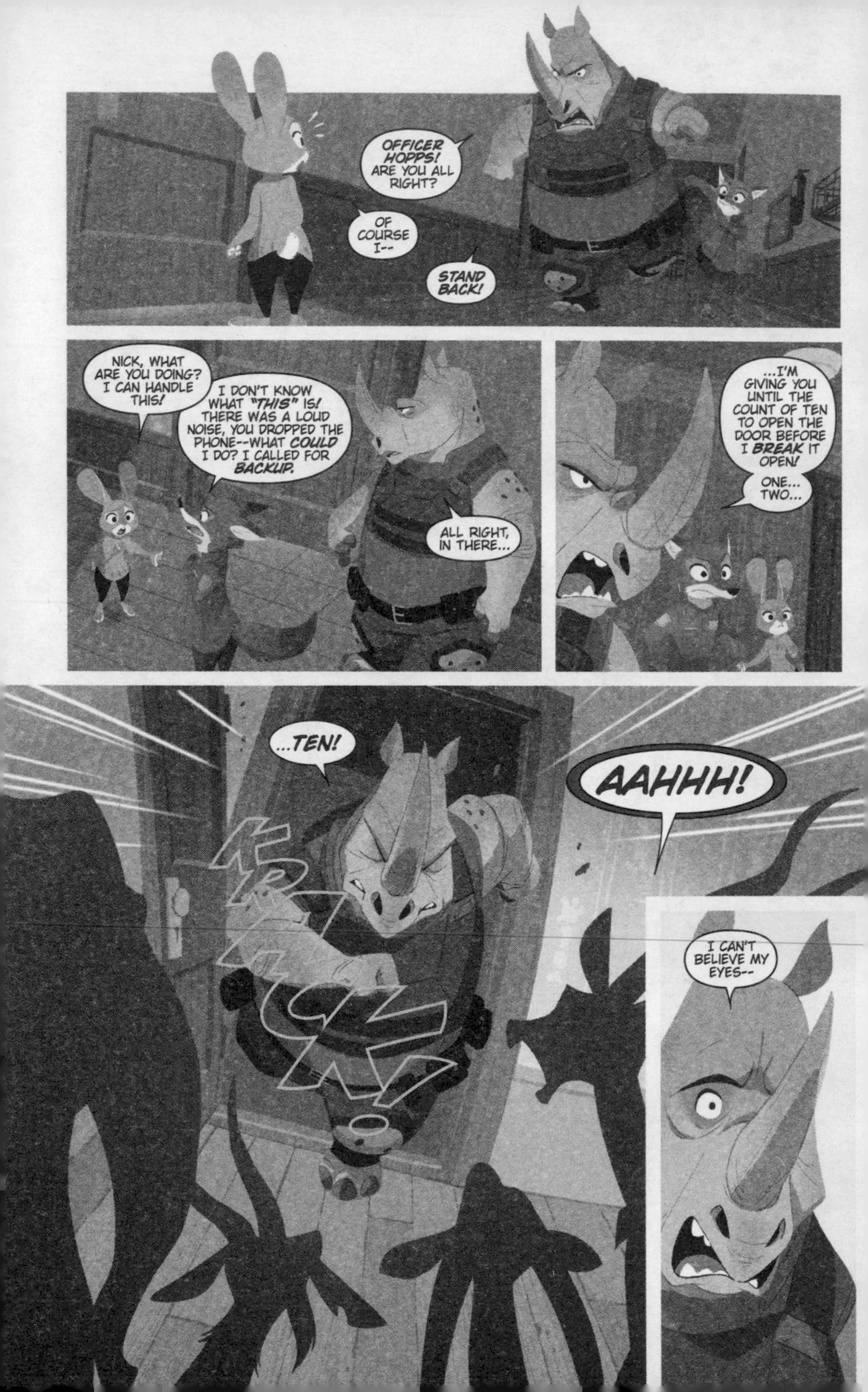
OFFICER HOPPS! ARE YOU ALL RIGHT?
OF COURSE I--
STAND BACK!
NICK, WHAT ARE YOU DOING? I CAN HANDLE THIS!
I DON'T KNOW WHAT "THIS" IS! THERE WAS A LOUD NOISE, YOU DROPPED THE PHONE--WHAT COULD I DO? I CALLED FOR BACKUP.
ALL RIGHT, IN THERE...
...I'M GIVING YOU UNTIL THE COUNT OF TEN TO OPEN THE DOOR BEFORE I BREAK IT OPEN!
ONE... TWO...
...TEN!
KRUNCH!
AAHHH!
I CAN'T BELIEVE MY EYES--

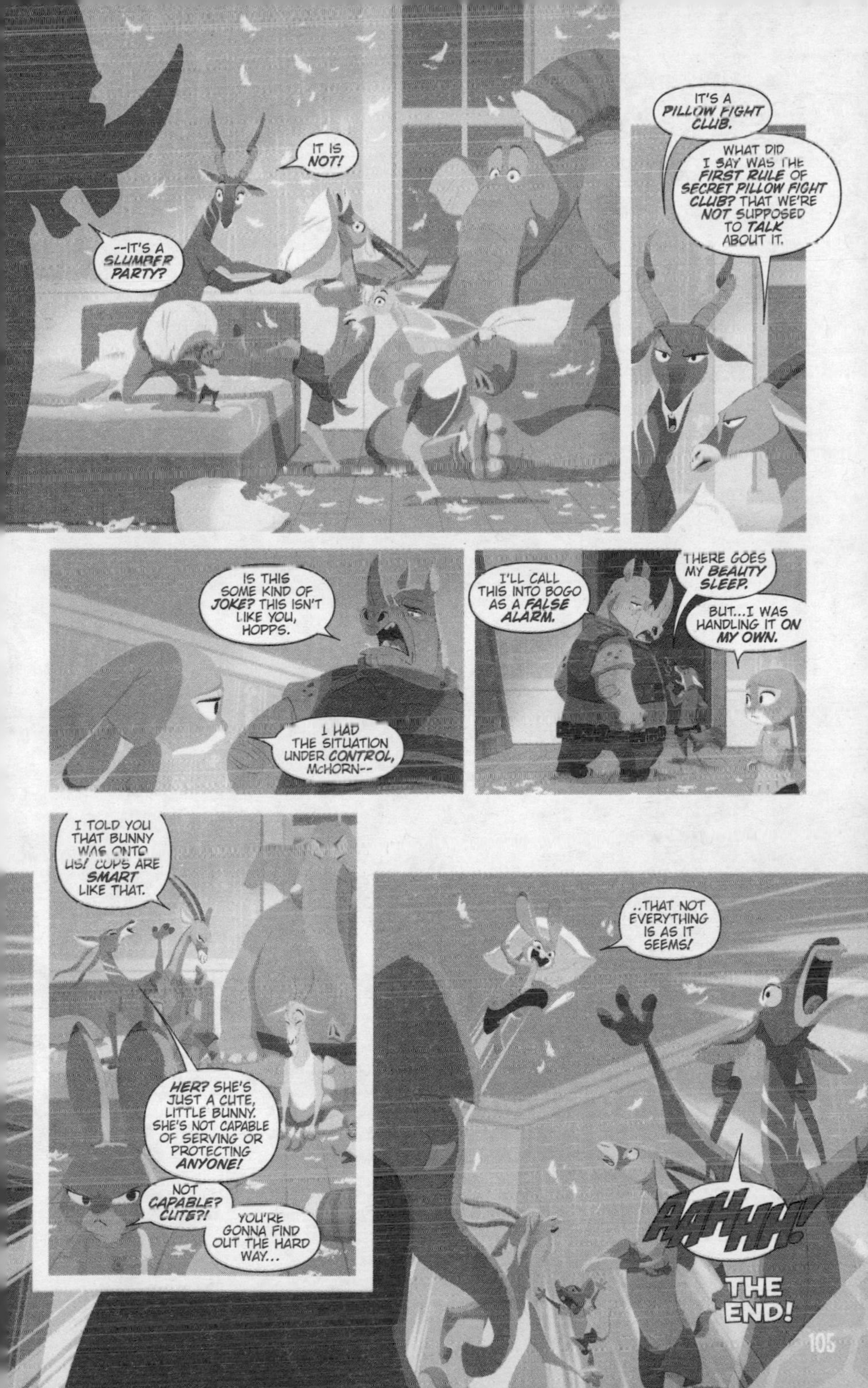

--IT'S A SLUMBER PARTY?
IT IS NOT!
IT'S A PILLOW FIGHT CLUB.
WHAT DID I SAY WAS THE FIRST RULE OF SECRET PILLOW FIGHT CLUB? THAT WE'RE NOT SUPPOSED TO TALK ABOUT IT.
IS THIS SOME KIND OF JOKE? THIS ISN'T LIKE YOU, HOPPS.
I HAD THE SITUATION UNDER CONTROL, McHORN--
I'LL CALL THIS INTO BOGO AS A FALSE ALARM.
THERE GOES MY BEAUTY SLEEP.
BUT...I WAS HANDLING IT ON MY OWN.
I TOLD YOU THAT BUNNY WAS ONTO US! COPS ARE SMART LIKE THAT.
HER? SHE'S JUST A CUTE, LITTLE BUNNY. SHE'S NOT CAPABLE OF SERVING OR PROTECTING ANYONE!
NOT CAPABLE? CUTE?!
YOU'RE GONNA FIND OUT THE HARD WAY...
..THAT NOT EVERYTHING IS AS IT SEEMS!
AAHHH!
THE END!

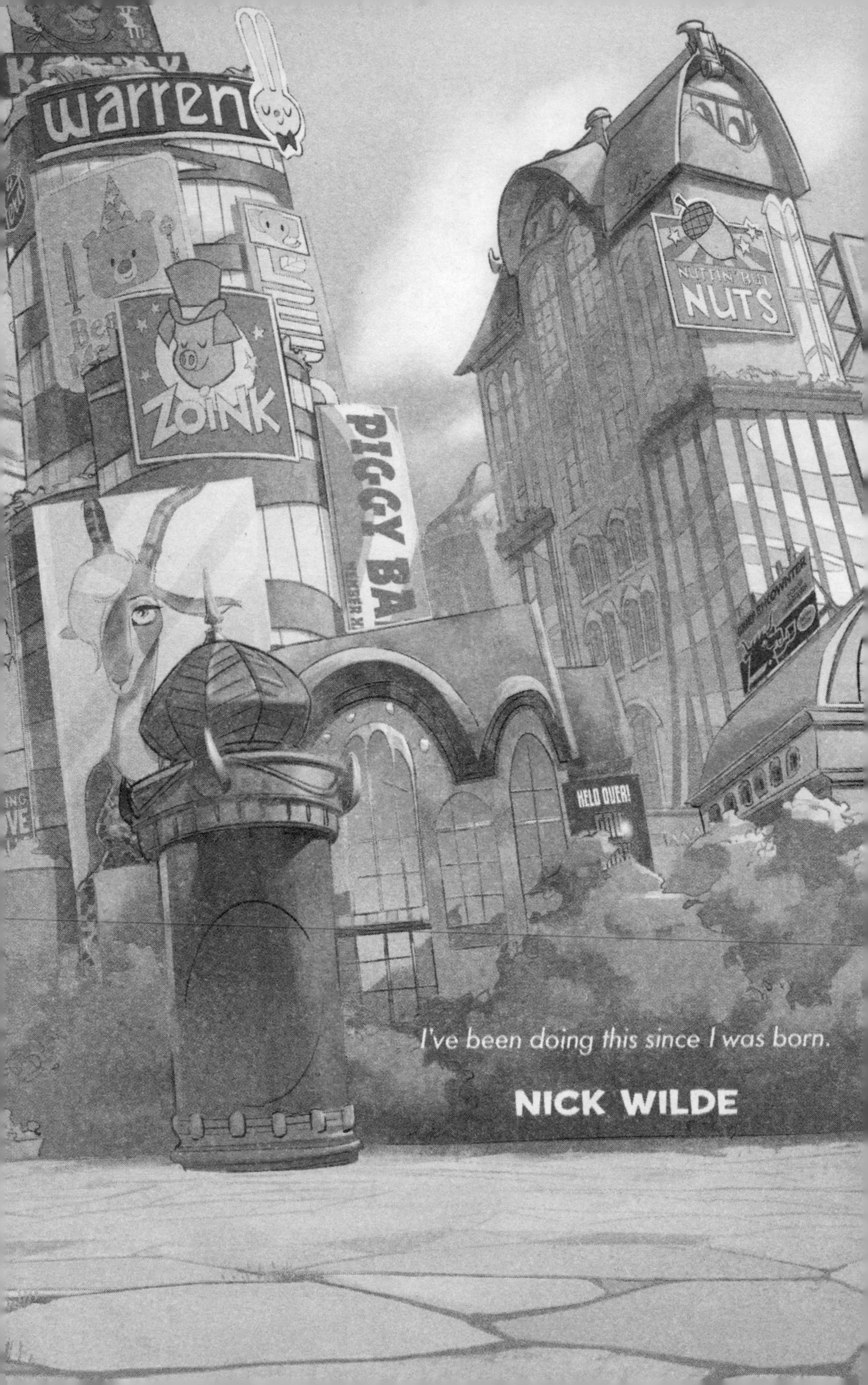
warren
ZOINK
PIGGY BA
NUTTIN' BUT NUTS
HELD OVER!

I've been doing this since I was born.

NICK WILDE

OFFICER IN TRAINING

Quiz yourself and find out which type of police officer you'd most likely be. Answer these questions adding 1 point for each **A**-answer and 2 points for each **B**-answer you give. Then, sum up your points and read the corresponding profile at the bottom of this page.

1 YOUR FIRST ASSIGNMENT IS... WRITING TICKETS FOR ILLEGALLY PARKED CARS.

A. Yes sir! In order to rise to the top of the ranks, you have to start at the bottom.

B. Parking duty - What?! You'll do it, and you'll go above and beyond the call of duty!

2 BY CHANCE, YOU WITNESS AN INJUSTICE. IT'S NOT SOMETHING ILLEGAL, BUT WHAT DO YOU DO?

A. There are clear laws, and if it's not illegal, it isn't up to you to do anything about it. Your job is to uphold the law!

B. No ifs or buts, you can't stand any form of injustice. It's time for action!

3 YOU'VE BEEN ASSIGNED A DIFFFICULT CASE AND YOU NEED A PARTNER...

A. You must only collaborate with a police officer, period!

B. Well, the end justifies the means. You'll do whatever it takes to solve the case, even working with an unconventional partner.

4 YOU CONSIDER TRUSTING SOMEONE YOU DIDN'T TRUST BEFORE...

A. If you've seen them be distrustful before, don't trust them.

B. Everyone deserves a second chance, and you should follow your gut.

5 WHAT WOULD BE YOUR GOAL AS A POLICE OFFICER:

A. To one day be the most firm, honest and loyal police chief the city has ever seen.

B. To make the world a better place.

PROFILES

READY FOR ACTION

8 - 10 POINTS

YOU'RE OPEN-MINDED AND AMBITIOUS. YOU WOULD WORK CLOSELY WITH YOUR PARTNERS WITHOUT ANY BIAS AND ALWAYS BE READY TO REACT TO ANY INJUSTICE.

EXPERIENCED AND FIRM

5 - 7 POINTS

YOU COULD BE A PERFECT LEADER OF A POLICE SQUAD. YOUR LAW-ABIDING SPIRIT AND YOUR SENSE FOR ORDER AND DISCIPLINE WOULD GAIN YOU TRUST AND RESPECT.

MEET THE CHARACTERS

WHO'S WHO IN THE MISSING MAMMAL CASE

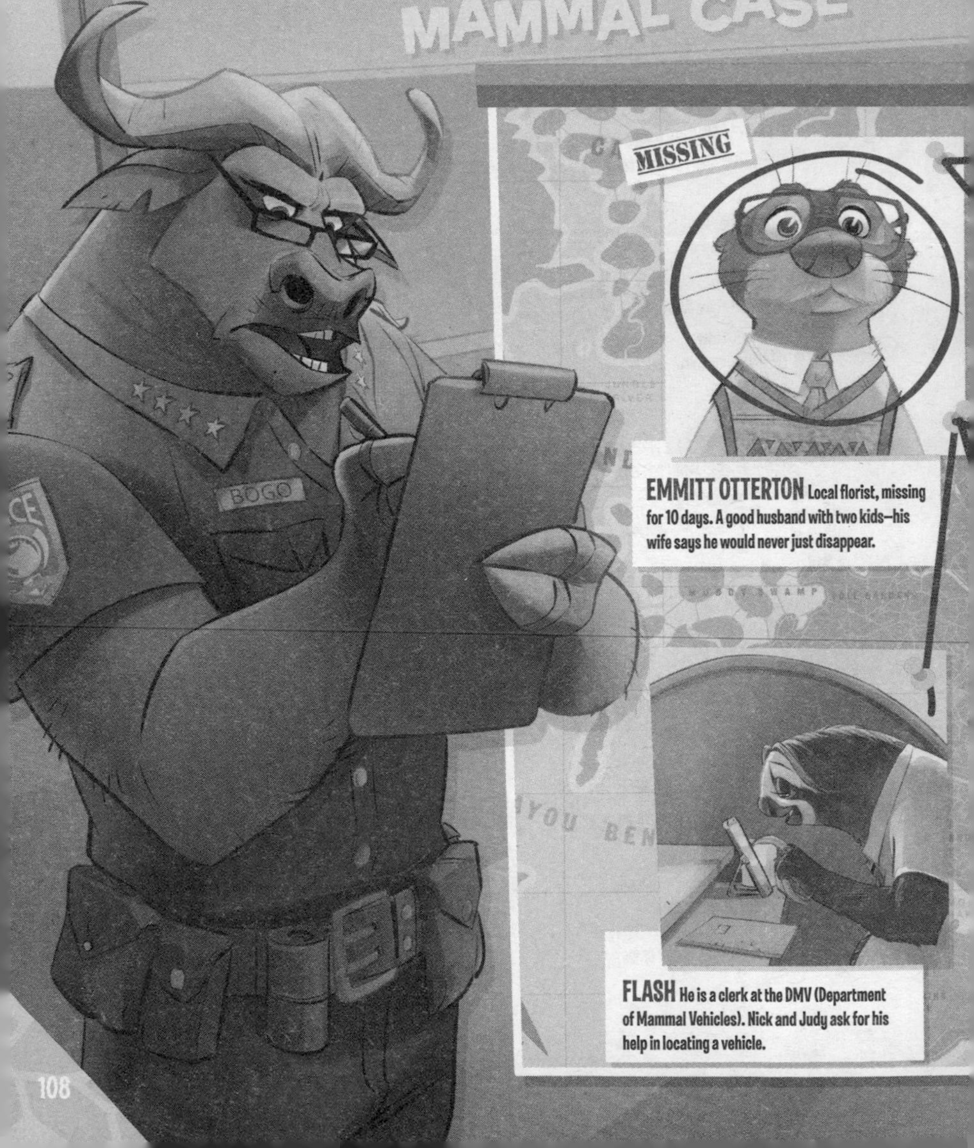
MISSING
BOGO

EMMITT OTTERTON Local florist, missing for 10 days. A good husband with two kids—his wife says he would never just disappear.

FLASH He is a clerk at the DMV (Department of Mammal Vehicles). Nick and Judy ask for his help in locating a vehicle.

What do all of these mammals below have in common? They were all part of Zootopia's missing mammal case! Each one gave Judy important clues that helped her solve the case. Read on to find Who's Who in in this big mystery.

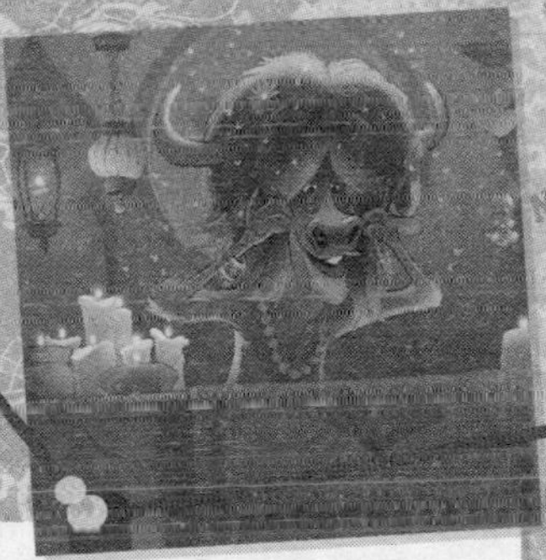

YAX This hippie Yak works the front desk at the Mystic Spring Oasis naturalist club. Mr. Otterton used to frequent the establishment.

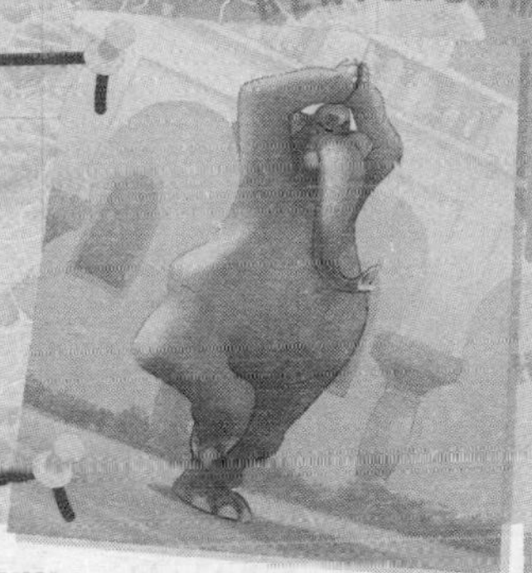

NANGI Yoga instructor at the Mystic Spring Oasis. Contrary to the stereotype, elephants can be forgetful like any other mammal.

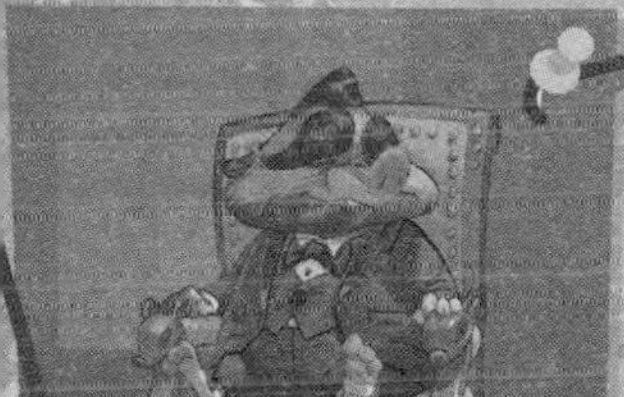

MR. BIG A dangerous crime boss in Tundratown! He runs a limo service, and Emmitt Otterton was his florist.

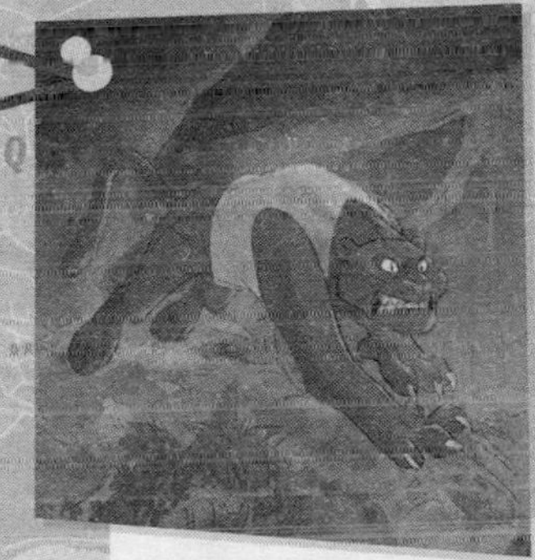

MANCHAS A jaguar living in the Rainforest District. He's a driver who works for Mr. Big. He drove Otterton, but then what happened?

ZOOTOPIA

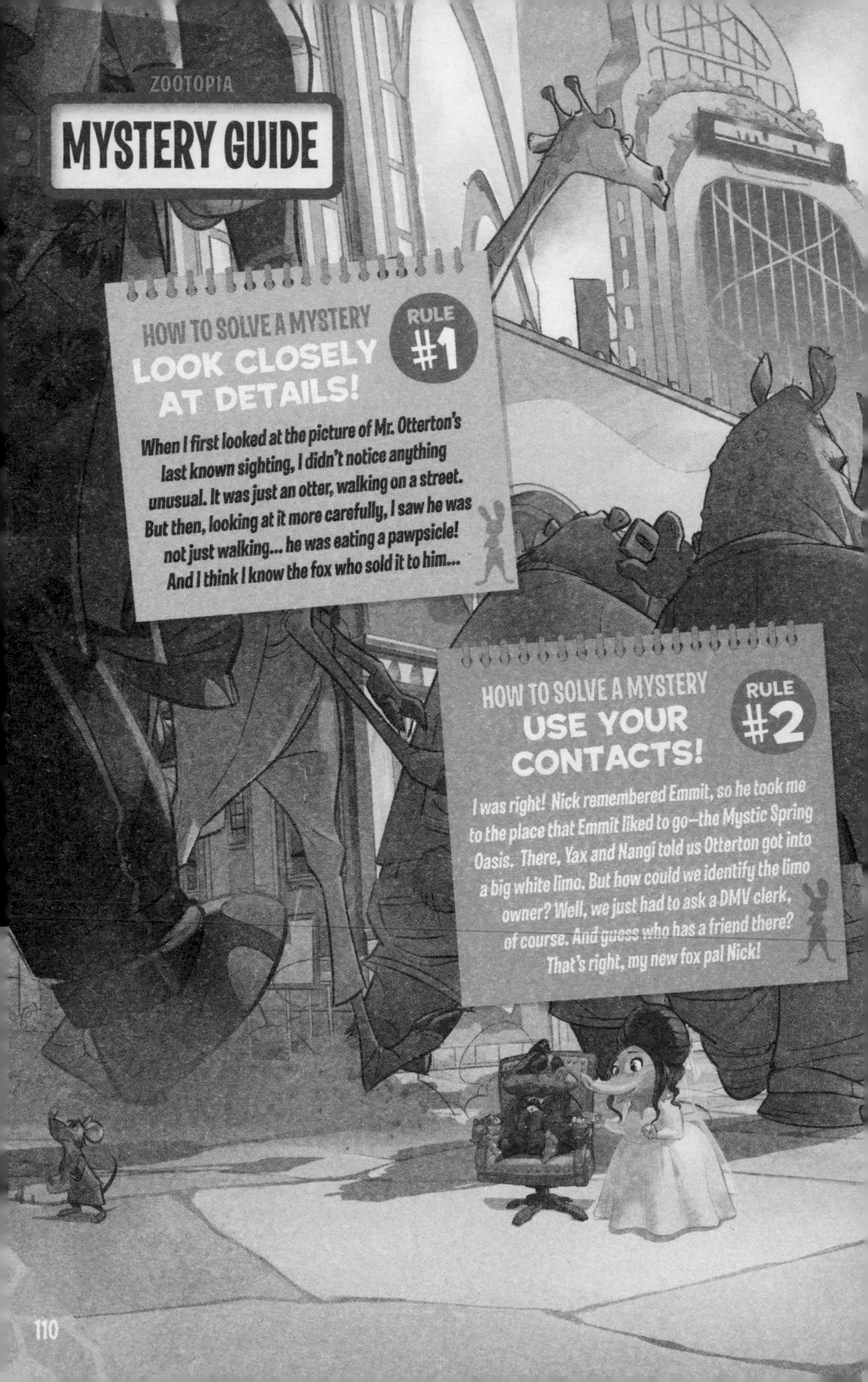

ZOOTOPIA

MYSTERY GUIDE

HOW TO SOLVE A MYSTERY

RULE #1

LOOK CLOSELY AT DETAILS!

When I first looked at the picture of Mr. Otterton's last known sighting, I didn't notice anything unusual. It was just an otter, walking on a street. But then, looking at it more carefully, I saw he was not just walking... he was eating a pawpsicle! And I think I know the fox who sold it to him...

HOW TO SOLVE A MYSTERY

RULE #2

USE YOUR CONTACTS!

I was right! Nick remembered Emmit, so he took me to the place that Emmit liked to go—the Mystic Spring Oasis. There, Yax and Nangi told us Otterton got into a big white limo. But how could we identify the limo owner? Well, we just had to ask a DMV clerk, of course. And guess who has a friend there? That's right, my new fox pal Nick!

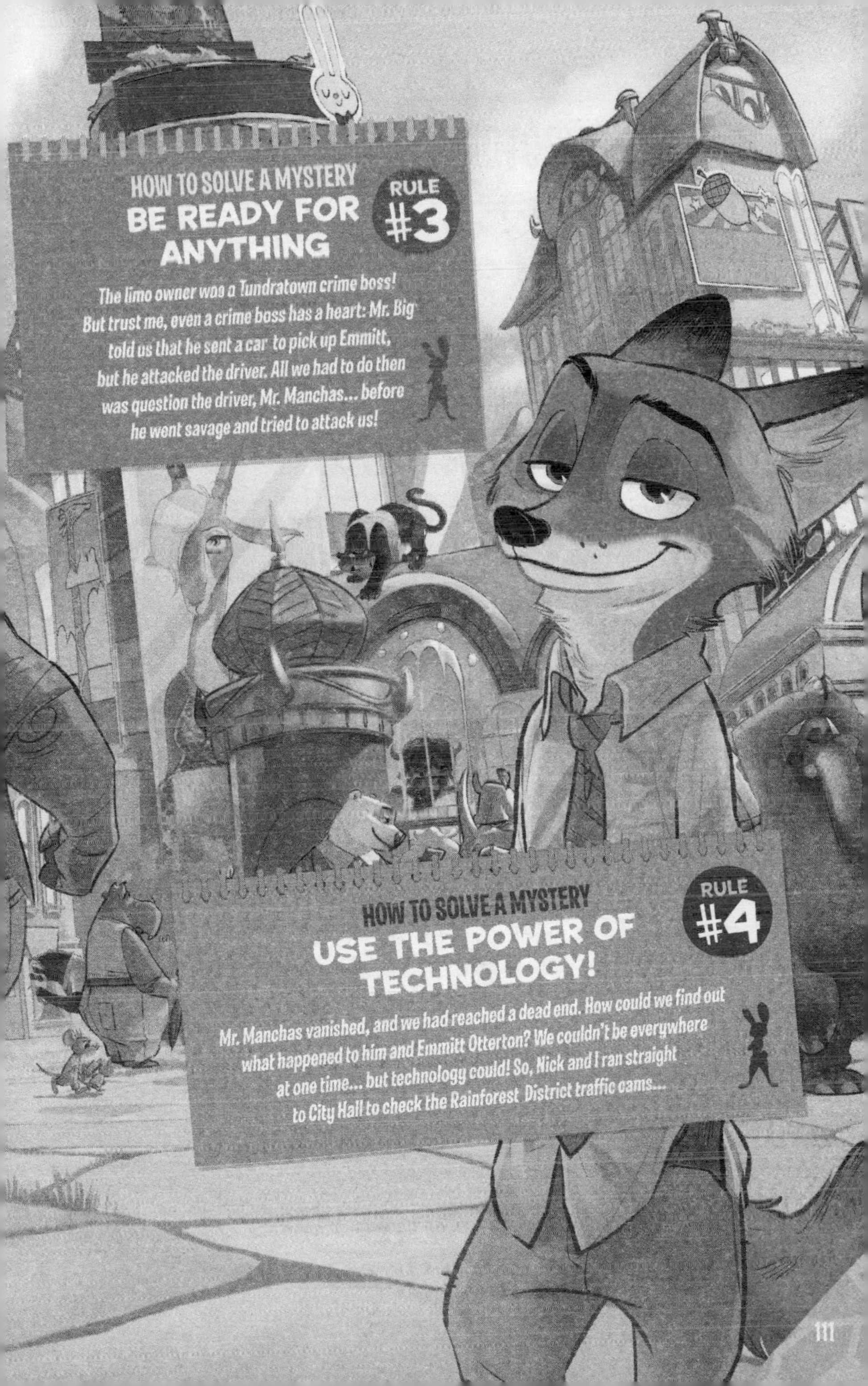

HOW TO SOLVE A MYSTERY

BE READY FOR ANYTHING

RULE #3

The limo owner was a Tundratown crime boss! But trust me, even a crime boss has a heart: Mr. Big told us that he sent a car to pick up Emmitt, but he attacked the driver. All we had to do then was question the driver, Mr. Manchas... before he went savage and tried to attack us!

HOW TO SOLVE A MYSTERY

USE THE POWER OF TECHNOLOGY!

RULE #4

Mr. Manchas vanished, and we had reached a dead end. How could we find out what happened to him and Emmitt Otterton? We couldn't be everywhere at one time... but technology could! So, Nick and I ran straight to City Hall to check the Rainforest District traffic cams...

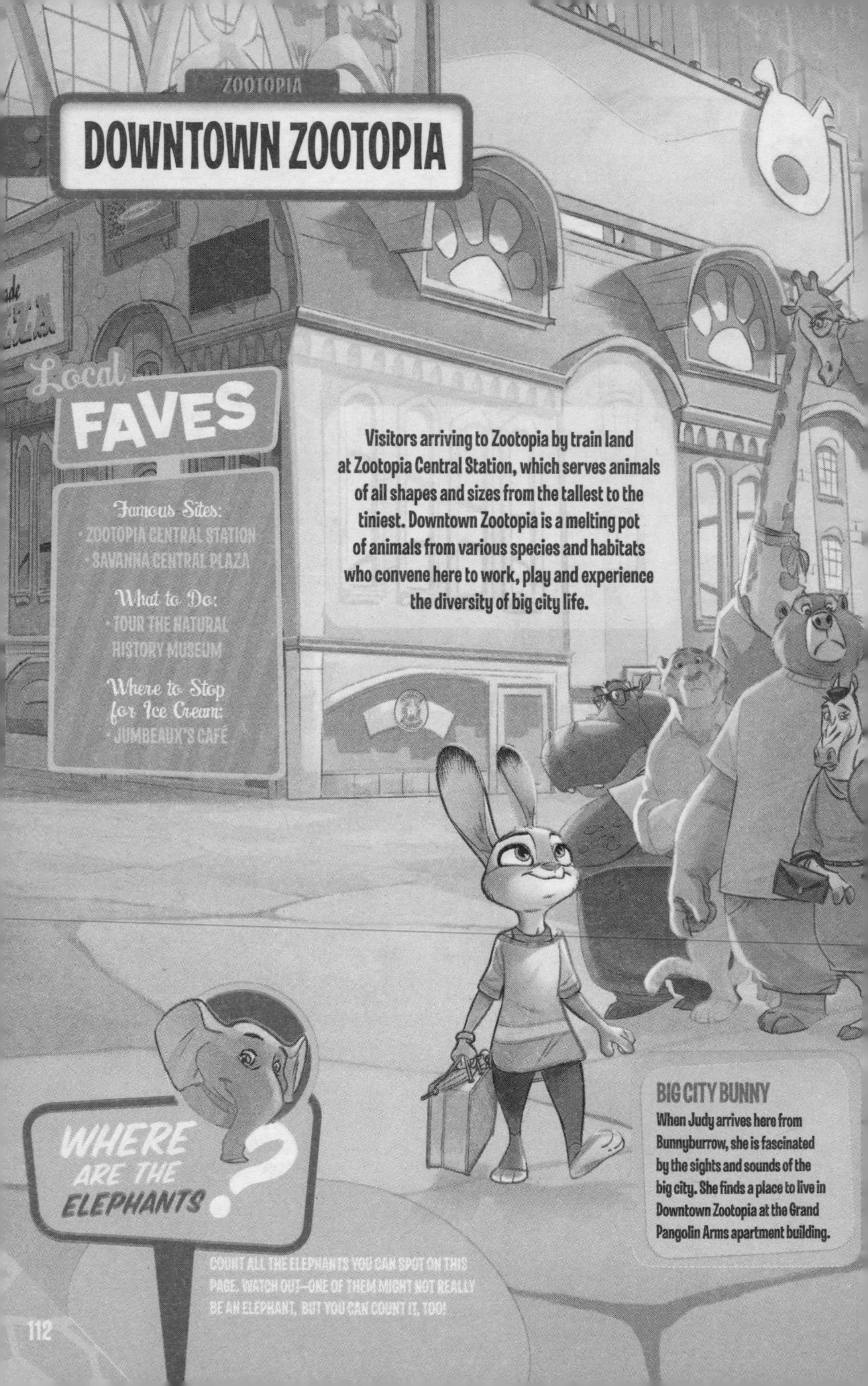

ZOOTOPIA

DOWNTOWN ZOOTOPIA

Local FAVES

Famous Sites:
- ZOOTOPIA CENTRAL STATION
- SAVANNA CENTRAL PLAZA

What to Do:
- TOUR THE NATURAL HISTORY MUSEUM

Where to Stop for Ice Cream:
- JUMBEAUX'S CAFÉ

Visitors arriving to Zootopia by train land at Zootopia Central Station, which serves animals of all shapes and sizes from the tallest to the tiniest. Downtown Zootopia is a melting pot of animals from various species and habitats who convene here to work, play and experience the diversity of big city life.

BIG CITY BUNNY

When Judy arrives here from Bunnyburrow, she is fascinated by the sights and sounds of the big city. She finds a place to live in Downtown Zootopia at the Grand Pangolin Arms apartment building.

WHERE ARE THE ELEPHANTS?

COUNT ALL THE ELEPHANTS YOU CAN SPOT ON THIS PAGE. WATCH OUT—ONE OF THEM MIGHT NOT REALLY BE AN ELEPHANT, BUT YOU CAN COUNT IT, TOO!

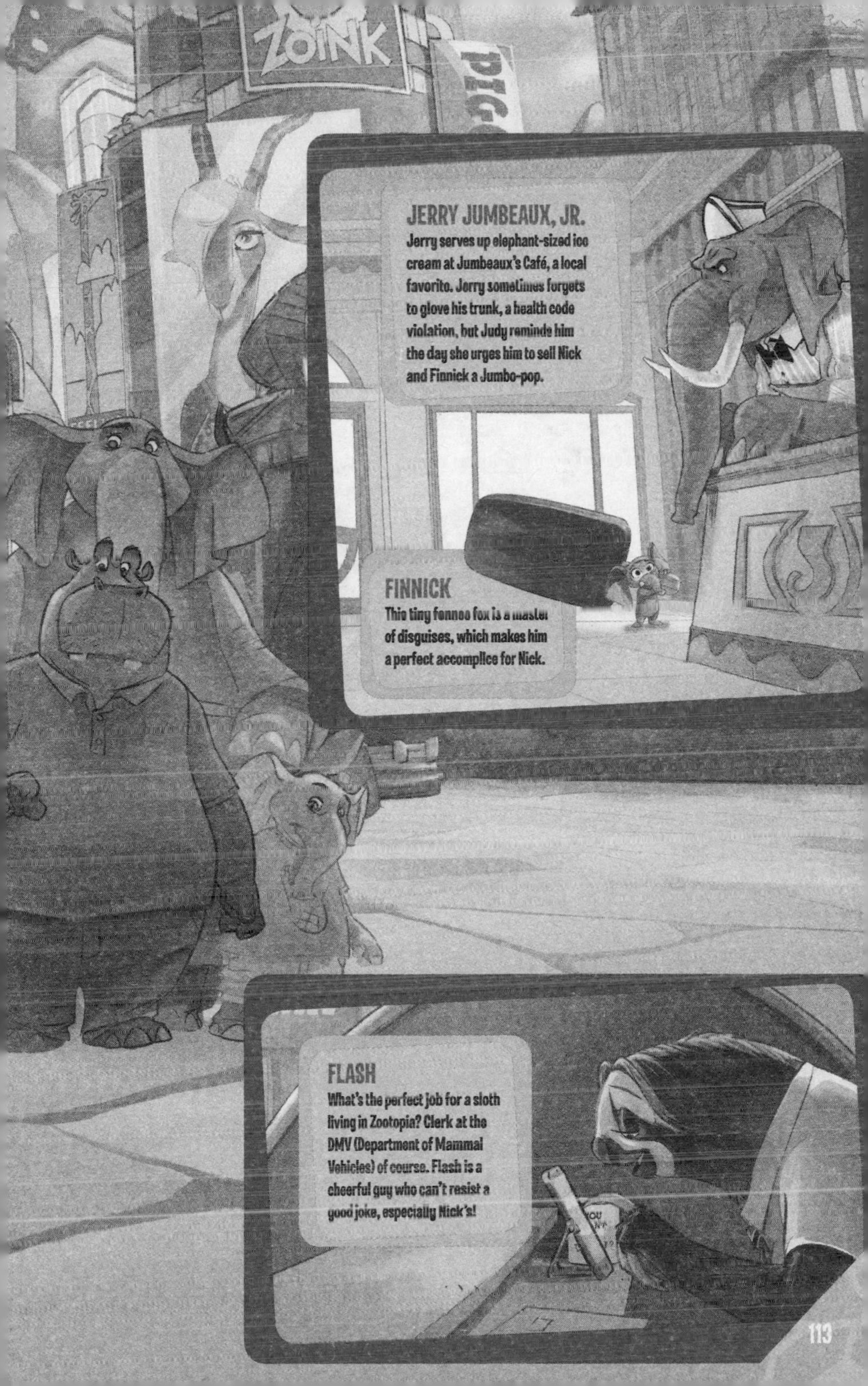
ZOINK

JERRY JUMBEAUX, JR.

Jerry serves up elephant-sized ice cream at Jumbeaux's Café, a local favorite. Jerry sometimes forgets to glove his trunk, a health code violation, but Judy reminds him the day she urges him to sell Nick and Finnick a Jumbo-pop.

FINNICK

This tiny fennec fox is a master of disguises, which makes him a perfect accomplice for Nick.

FLASH

What's the perfect job for a sloth living in Zootopia? Clerk at the DMV (Department of Mammal Vehicles) of course. Flash is a cheerful guy who can't resist a good joke, especially Nick's!

ZOOTOPIA

MEET THE CHARACTERS

ZOOTOPIANS AT WORK

Sloths make up the entire work force at the Zootopia Department of Mammal Vehicles. Surprisingly, a lot gets done in this very busy place!

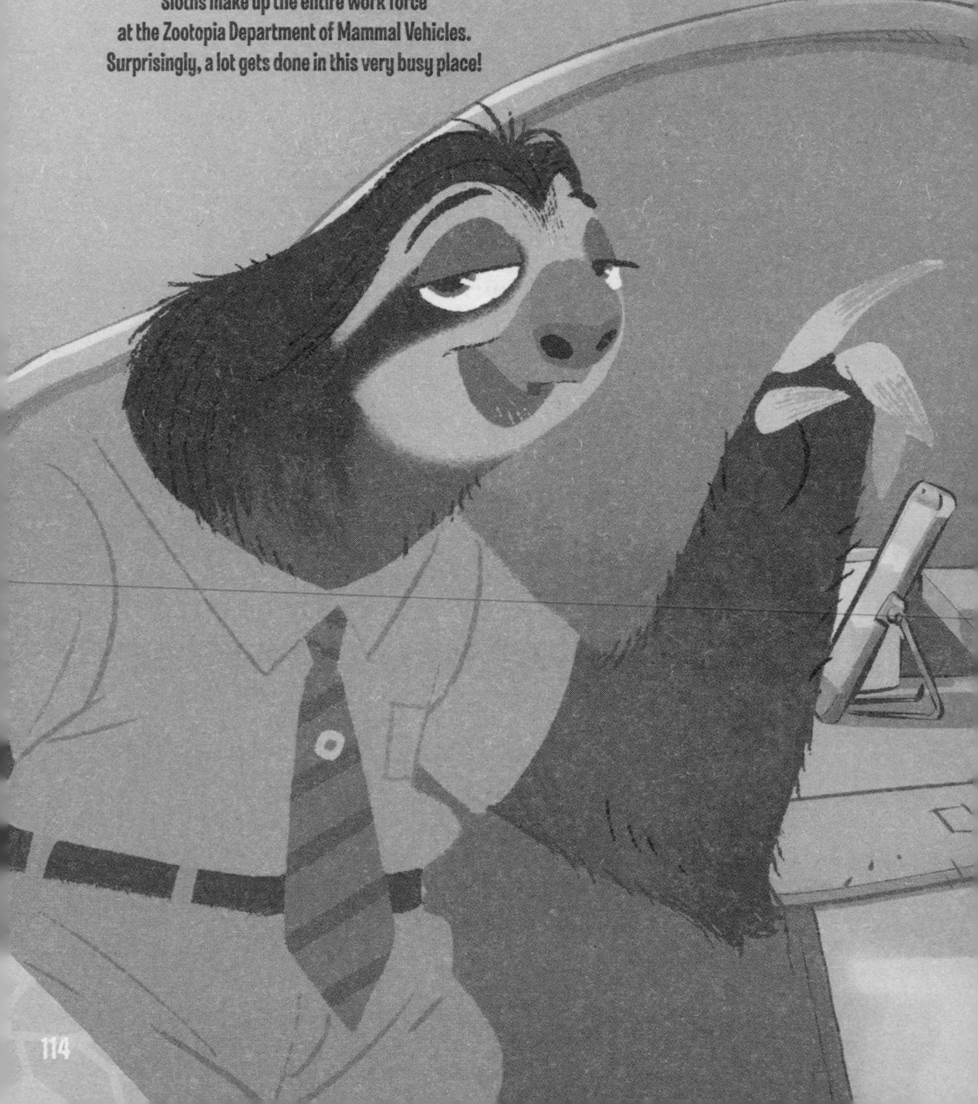

FLASH

As his friend Nick always says, Flash is the one you call when you need something done. Well, if you don't need it fast. Like all his colleagues at the Zootopia Department of Mammal Vehicles (DMV), Flash is a sloth: he works, laughs, moves and talks at his own pace. He is friendly and helpful, and he can... not... resist... a... joke!

PRISCILLA

Priscilla is Flash's colleague at the Zootopia DMV and sits next to him. Like all employees at the DMV, she's a sloth, too.

ZOOTOPIA DMV

Mammals in Zootopia may drive a wide variety of vehicles, but all drivers get their driver's licenses and license plates in the same place: the Zootopia DMV. It's easy, but not quick (they are all sloths, after all!).

A LONG WAIT

When Judy was trying to solve the missing mammal case, she needed to run a plate and Nick took her to Flash. When Judy got out it was night already.... but thanks to Flash she found the car she was looking for!

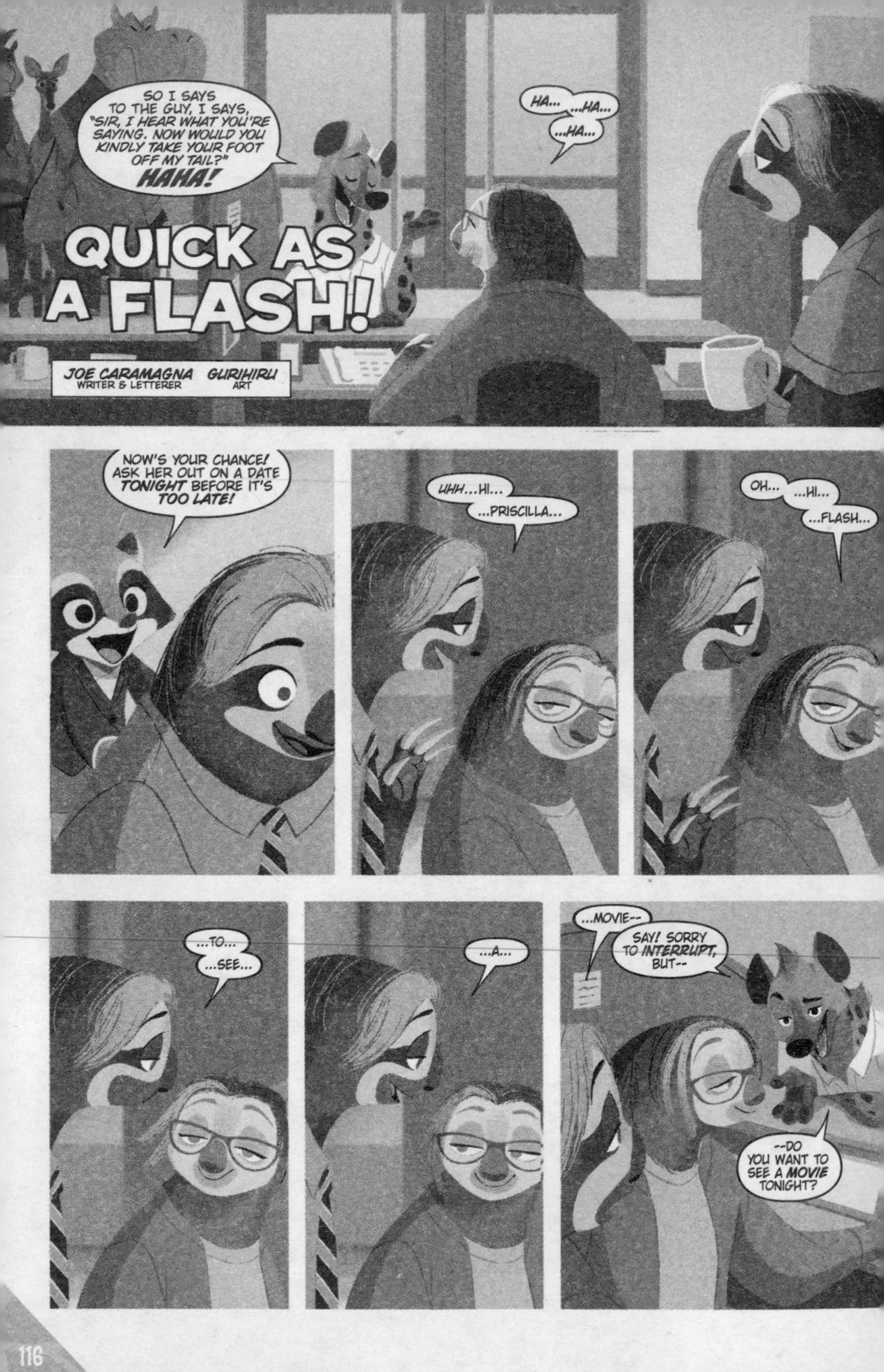
SO I SAYS TO THE GUY, I SAYS, "SIR, I HEAR WHAT YOU'RE SAYING. NOW WOULD YOU KINDLY TAKE YOUR FOOT OFF MY TAIL?" HAHA!
HA... ...HA... ...HA...
QUICK AS A FLASH!
JOE CARAMAGNA WRITER & LETTERER
GURIHIRU ART
NOW'S YOUR CHANCE! ASK HER OUT ON A DATE TONIGHT BEFORE IT'S TOO LATE!
UHH...HI...
...PRISCILLA...
OH...
...HI...
...FLASH...
...TO...
...SEE...
...A...
...MOVIE--
SAY! SORRY TO INTERRUPT, BUT--
--DO YOU WANT TO SEE A MOVIE TONIGHT?

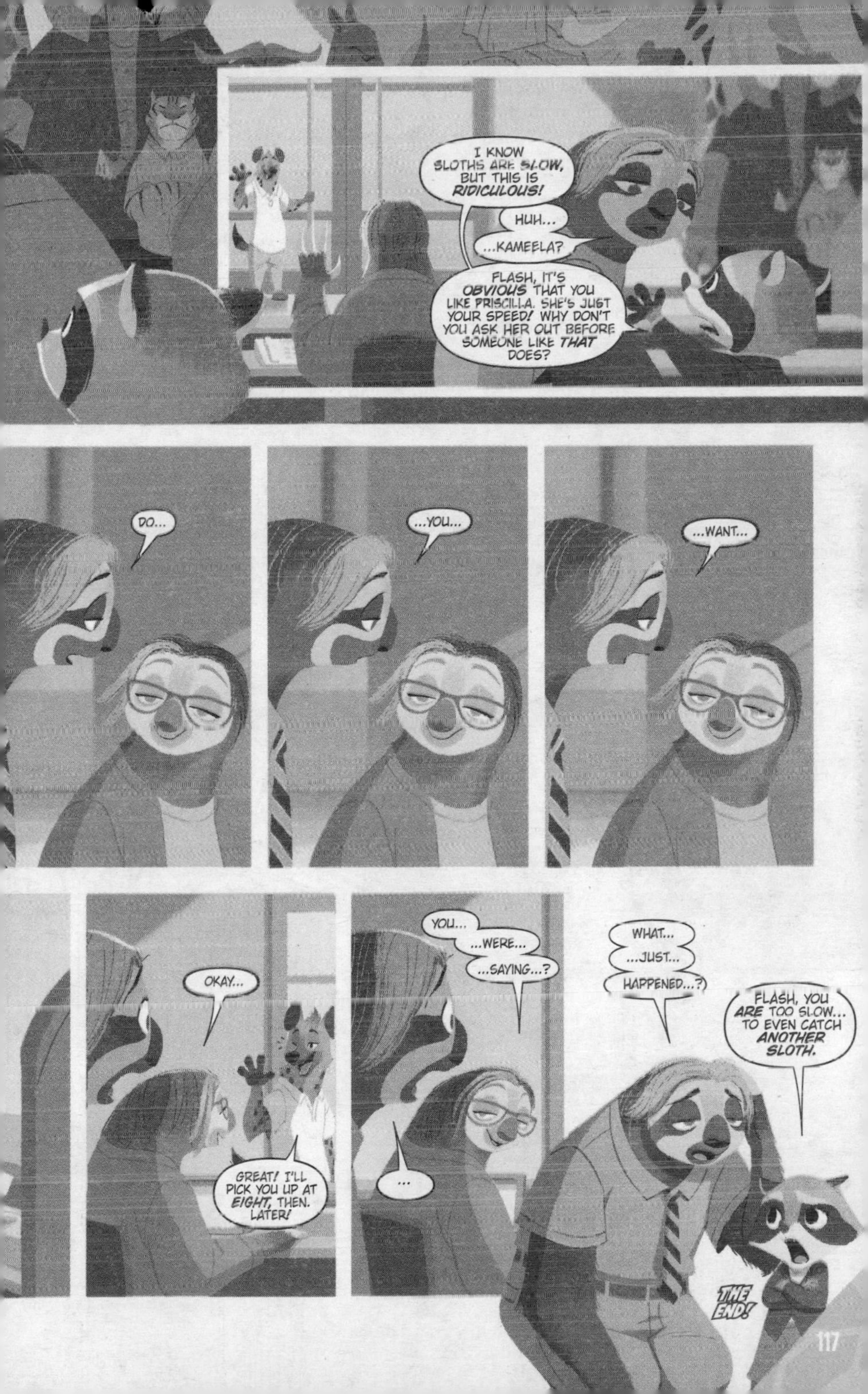
I KNOW SLOTHS ARE SLOW, BUT THIS IS RIDICULOUS!
HUH...
...KAMEELA?
FLASH, IT'S OBVIOUS THAT YOU LIKE PRISCILLA. SHE'S JUST YOUR SPEED! WHY DON'T YOU ASK HER OUT BEFORE SOMEONE LIKE THAT DOES?
DO...
...YOU...
...WANT...
OKAY...
GREAT! I'LL PICK YOU UP AT EIGHT, THEN. LATER!
YOU...
...WERE...
...SAYING...?
...
WHAT...
...JUST...
HAPPENED...?
FLASH, YOU ARE TOO SLOW... TO EVEN CATCH ANOTHER SLOTH.
THE END!

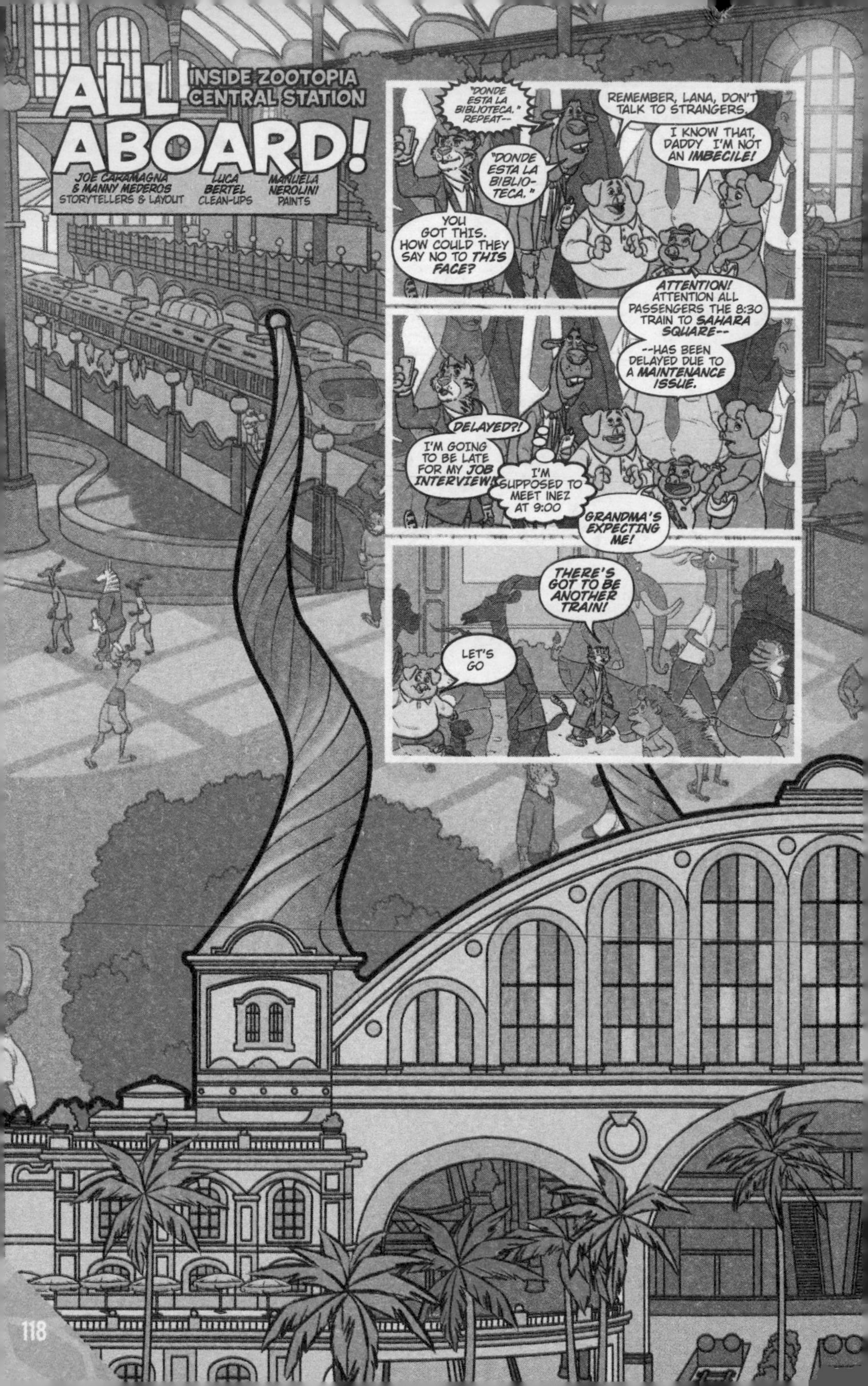
ALL ABOARD!
INSIDE ZOOTOPIA CENTRAL STATION
JOE CARAMAGNA & MANNY MEDEROS STORYTELLERS & LAYOUT
LUCA BERTEL CLEAN-UPS
MANUELA NEROLINI PAINTS
"DONDE ESTA LA BIBLIOTECA." REPEAT--
"DONDE ESTA LA BIBLIO-TECA."
YOU GOT THIS. HOW COULD THEY SAY NO TO THIS FACE?
REMEMBER, LANA, DON'T TALK TO STRANGERS.
I KNOW THAT, DADDY. I'M NOT AN IMBECILE!
ATTENTION! ATTENTION ALL PASSENGERS THE 8:30 TRAIN TO SAHARA SQUARE--
--HAS BEEN DELAYED DUE TO A MAINTENANCE ISSUE.
DELAYED?!
I'M GOING TO BE LATE FOR MY JOB INTERVIEW!
I'M SUPPOSED TO MEET INEZ AT 9:00
GRANDMA'S EXPECTING ME!
THERE'S GOT TO BE ANOTHER TRAIN!
LET'S GO

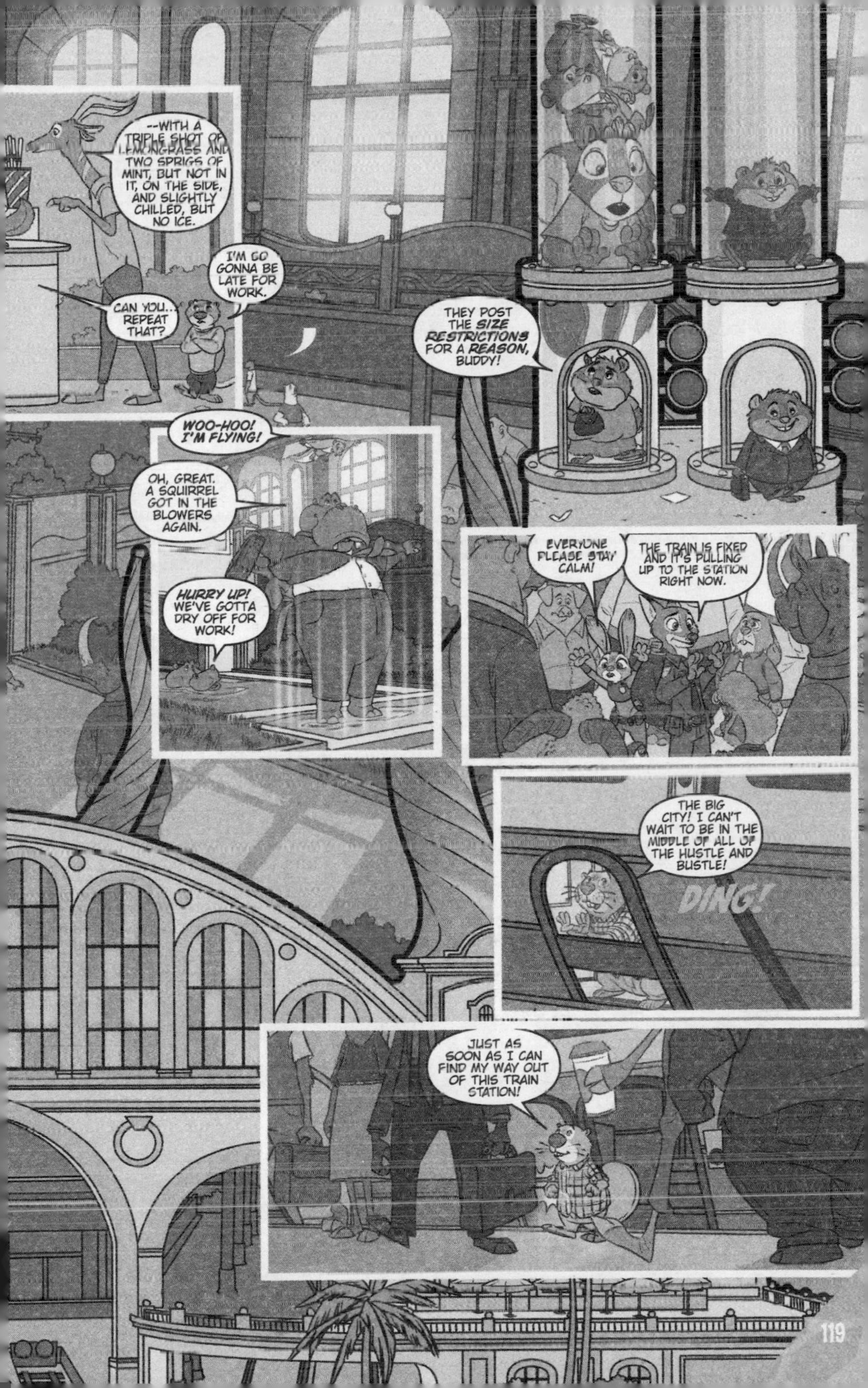
--WITH A TRIPLE SHOT OF LEMONGRASS AND TWO SPRIGS OF MINT, BUT NOT IN IT, ON THE SIDE, AND SLIGHTLY CHILLED, BUT NO ICE.
CAN YOU... REPEAT THAT?
I'M SO GONNA BE LATE FOR WORK.
THEY POST THE SIZE RESTRICTIONS FOR A REASON, BUDDY!
WOO-HOO! I'M FLYING!
OH, GREAT. A SQUIRREL GOT IN THE BLOWERS AGAIN.
HURRY UP! WE'VE GOTTA DRY OFF FOR WORK!
EVERYONE PLEASE STAY CALM!
THE TRAIN IS FIXED AND IT'S PULLING UP TO THE STATION RIGHT NOW.
THE BIG CITY! I CAN'T WAIT TO BE IN THE MIDDLE OF ALL OF THE HUSTLE AND BUSTLE!
DING!
JUST AS SOON AS I CAN FIND MY WAY OUT OF THIS TRAIN STATION!

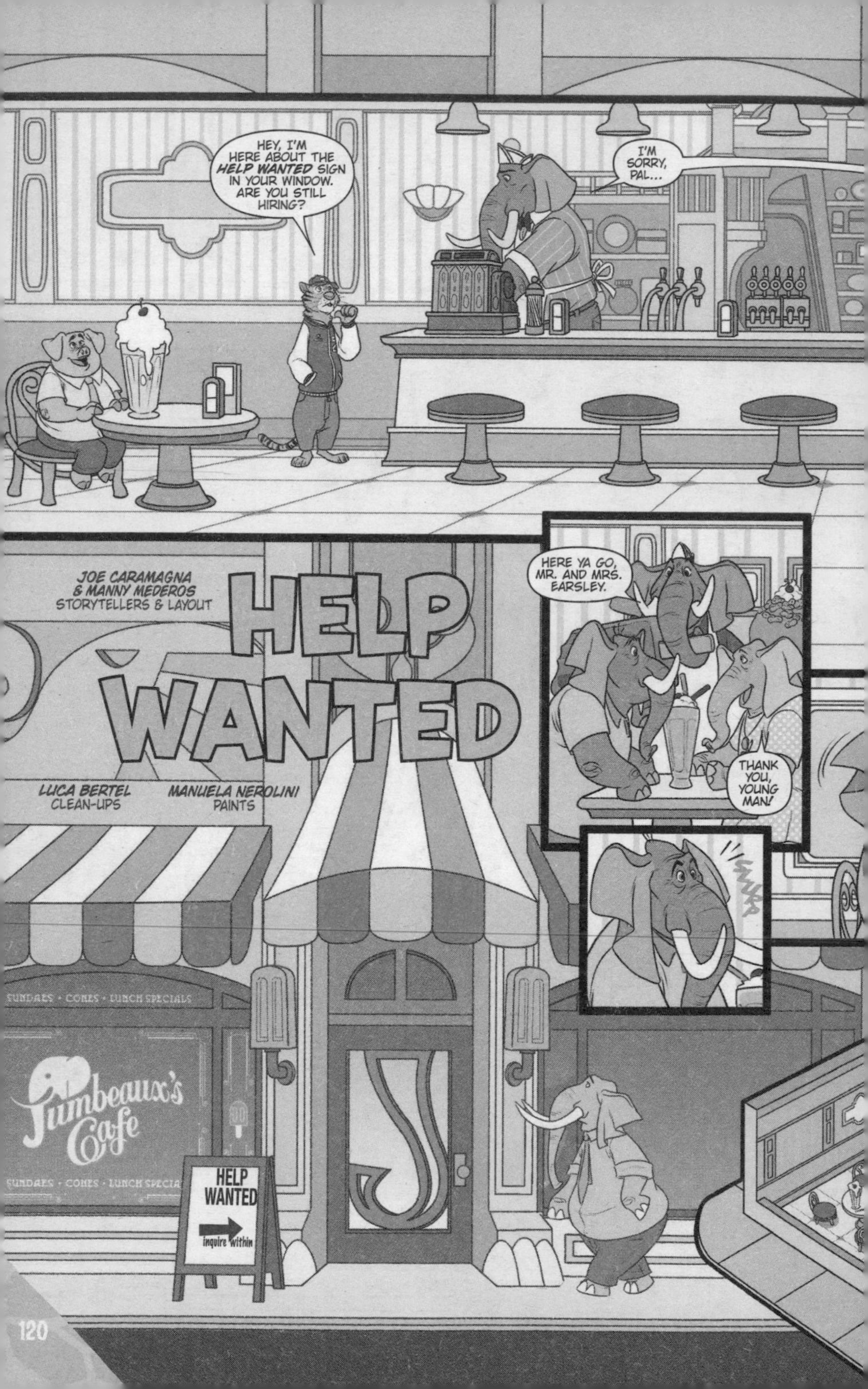
HEY, I'M HERE ABOUT THE *HELP WANTED* SIGN IN YOUR WINDOW. ARE YOU STILL HIRING?
I'M SORRY, PAL...
JOE CARAMAGNA & MANNY MEDEROS
STORYTELLERS & LAYOUT
HELP WANTED
LUCA BERTEL
CLEAN-UPS
MANUELA NEROLINI
PAINTS
HERE YA GO, MR. AND MRS. EARSLEY.
THANK YOU, YOUNG MAN!
SUNDAES · CONES · LUNCH SPECIALS
Jumbeaux's Cafe
HELP WANTED
inquire within

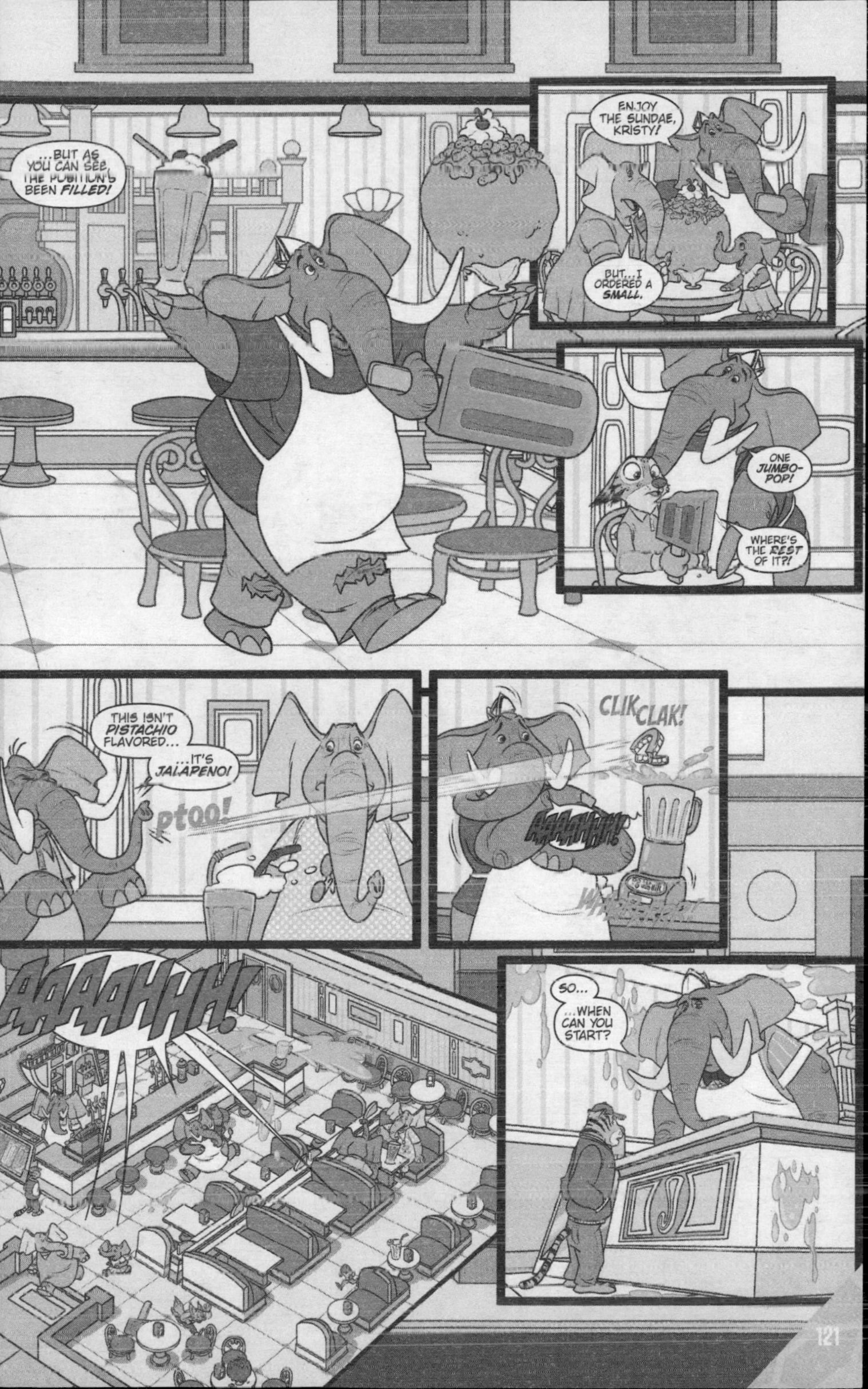
...BUT AS YOU CAN SEE, THE POSITION'S BEEN *FILLED!*
ENJOY THE SUNDAE, KRISTY!
BUT... I ORDERED A *SMALL.*
ONE *JUMBO-POP!*
WHERE'S THE *REST* OF IT?!
THIS ISN'T *PISTACHIO* FLAVORED...
...IT'S *JALAPENO!*
ptoo!
CLIK CLAK!
AAAAHHH!
SO...
...WHEN CAN YOU START?

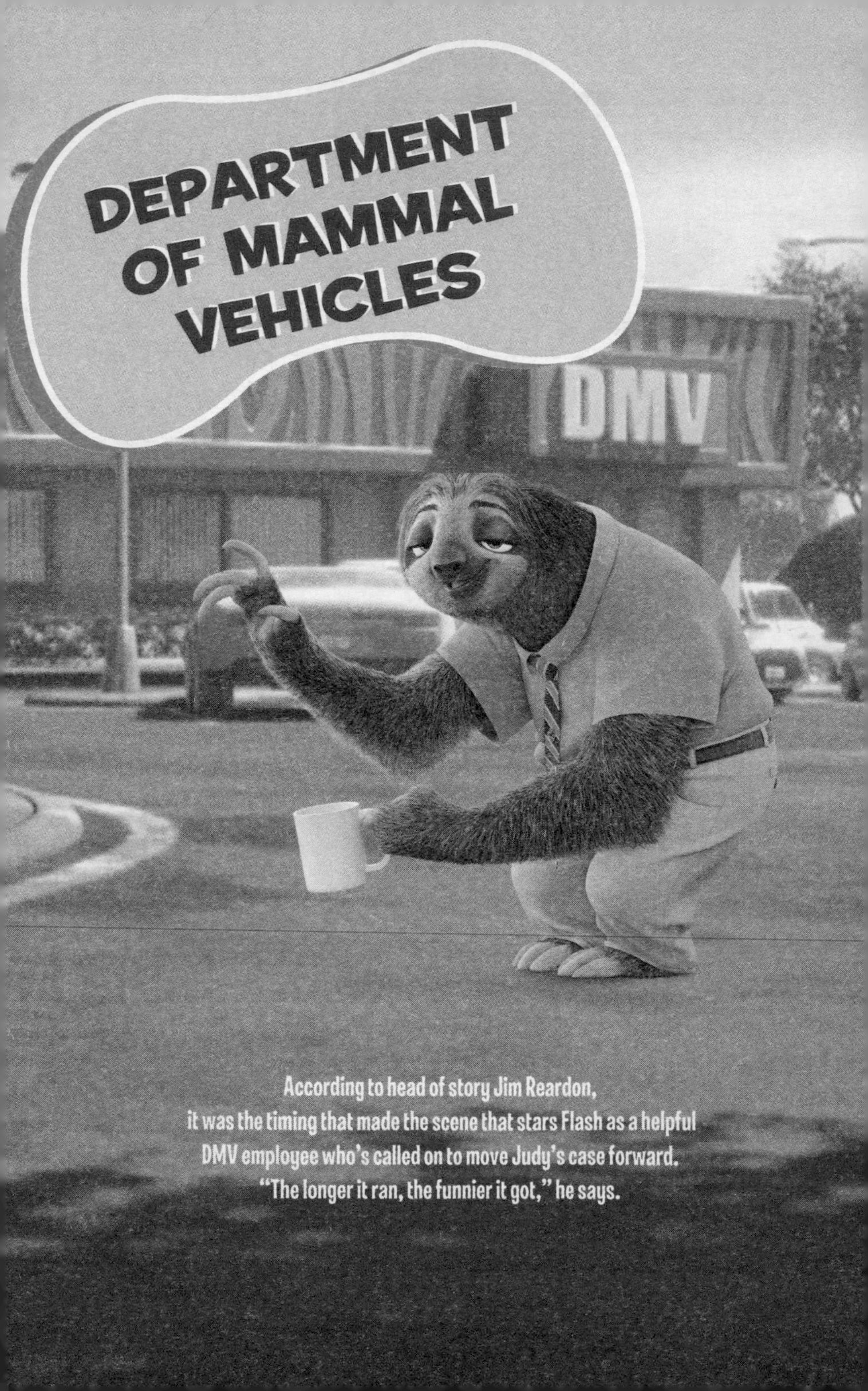
DEPARTMENT OF MAMMAL VEHICLES
DMV

According to head of story Jim Reardon, it was the timing that made the scene that stars Flash as a helpful DMV employee who's called on to move Judy's case forward. "The longer it ran, the funnier it got," he says.

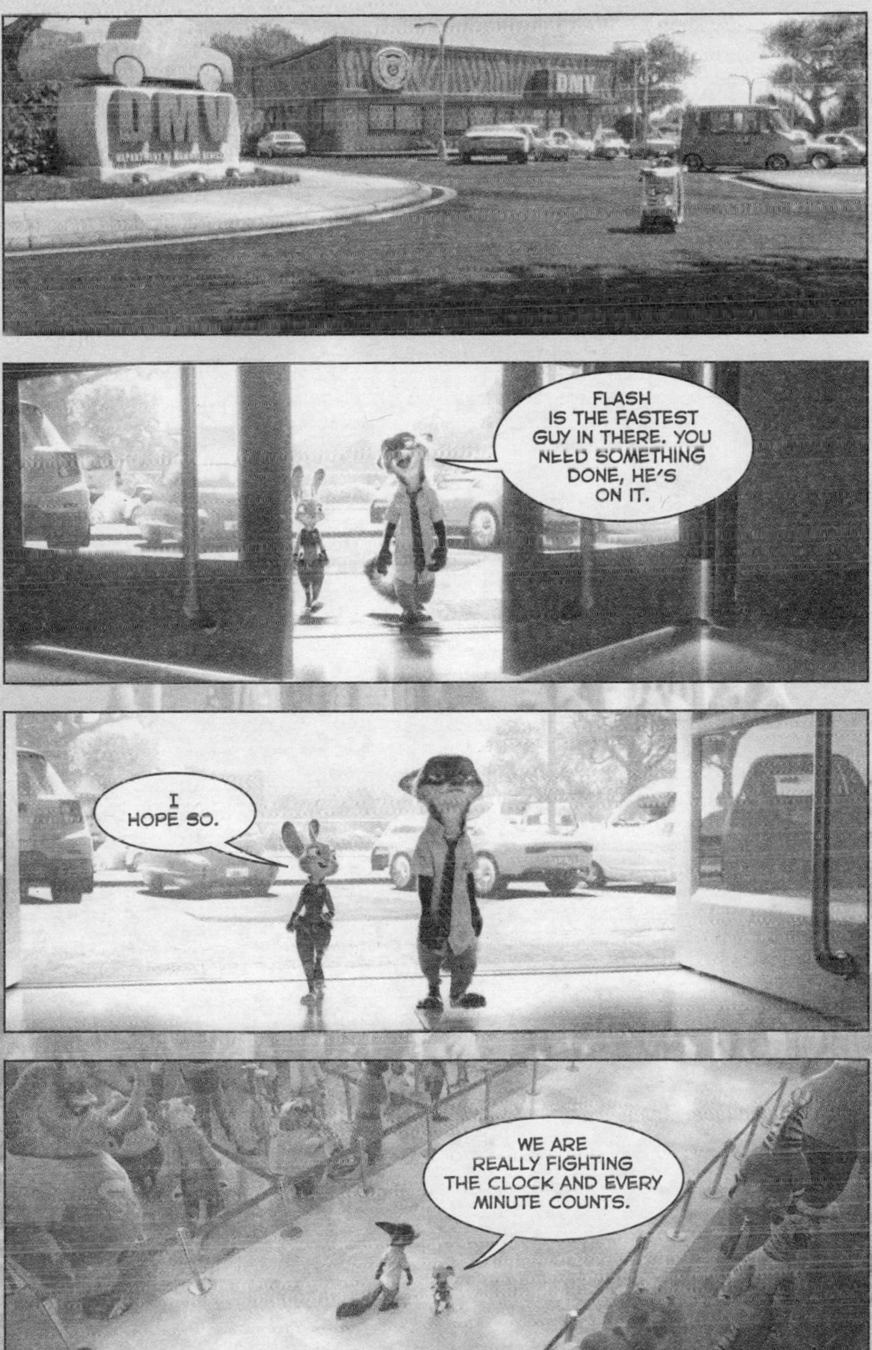
DMV
DMV
FLASH IS THE FASTEST GUY IN THERE. YOU NEED SOMETHING DONE, HE'S ON IT.
I HOPE SO.
WE ARE REALLY FIGHTING THE CLOCK AND EVERY MINUTE COUNTS.

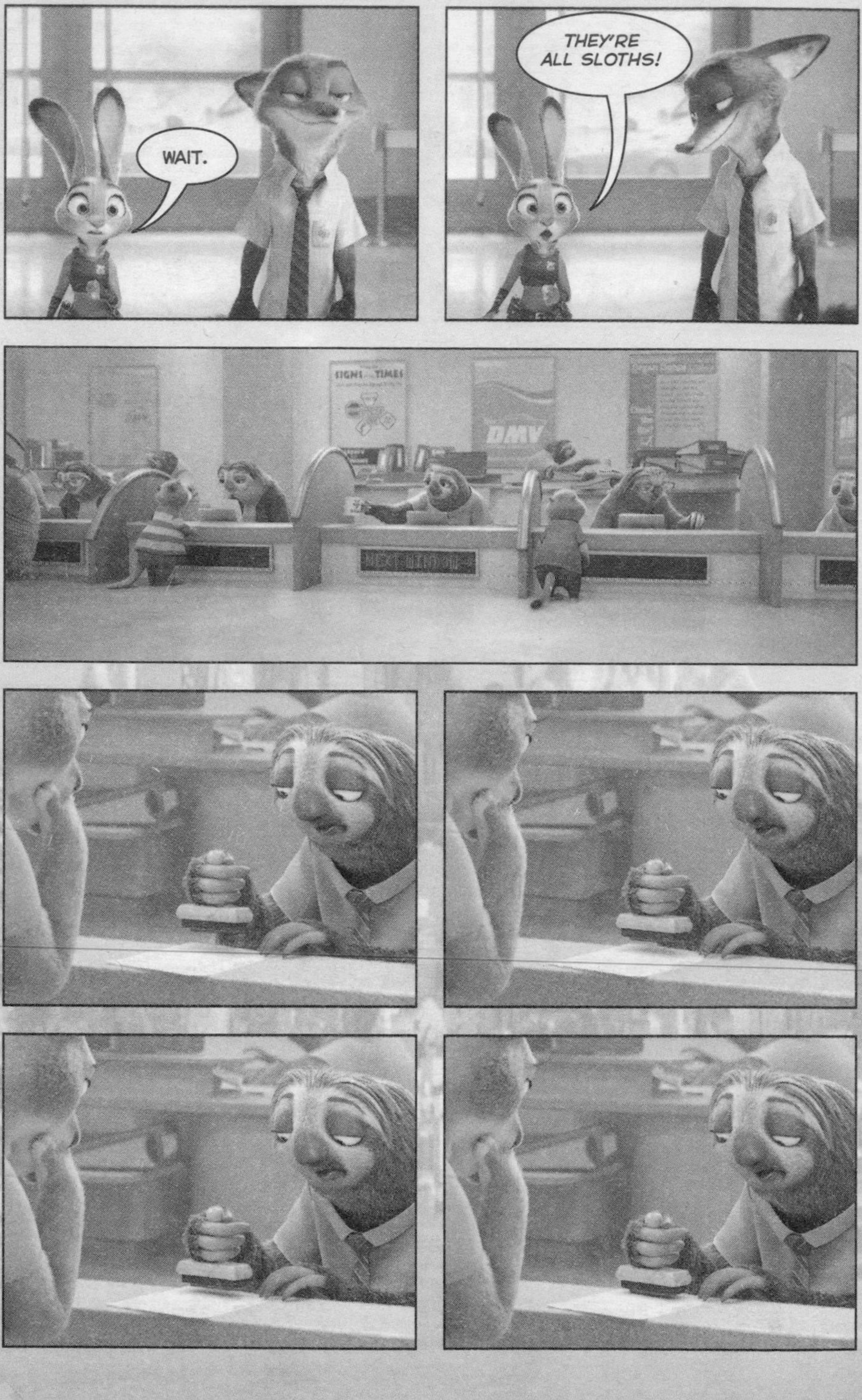
WAIT.
THEY'RE ALL SLOTHS!

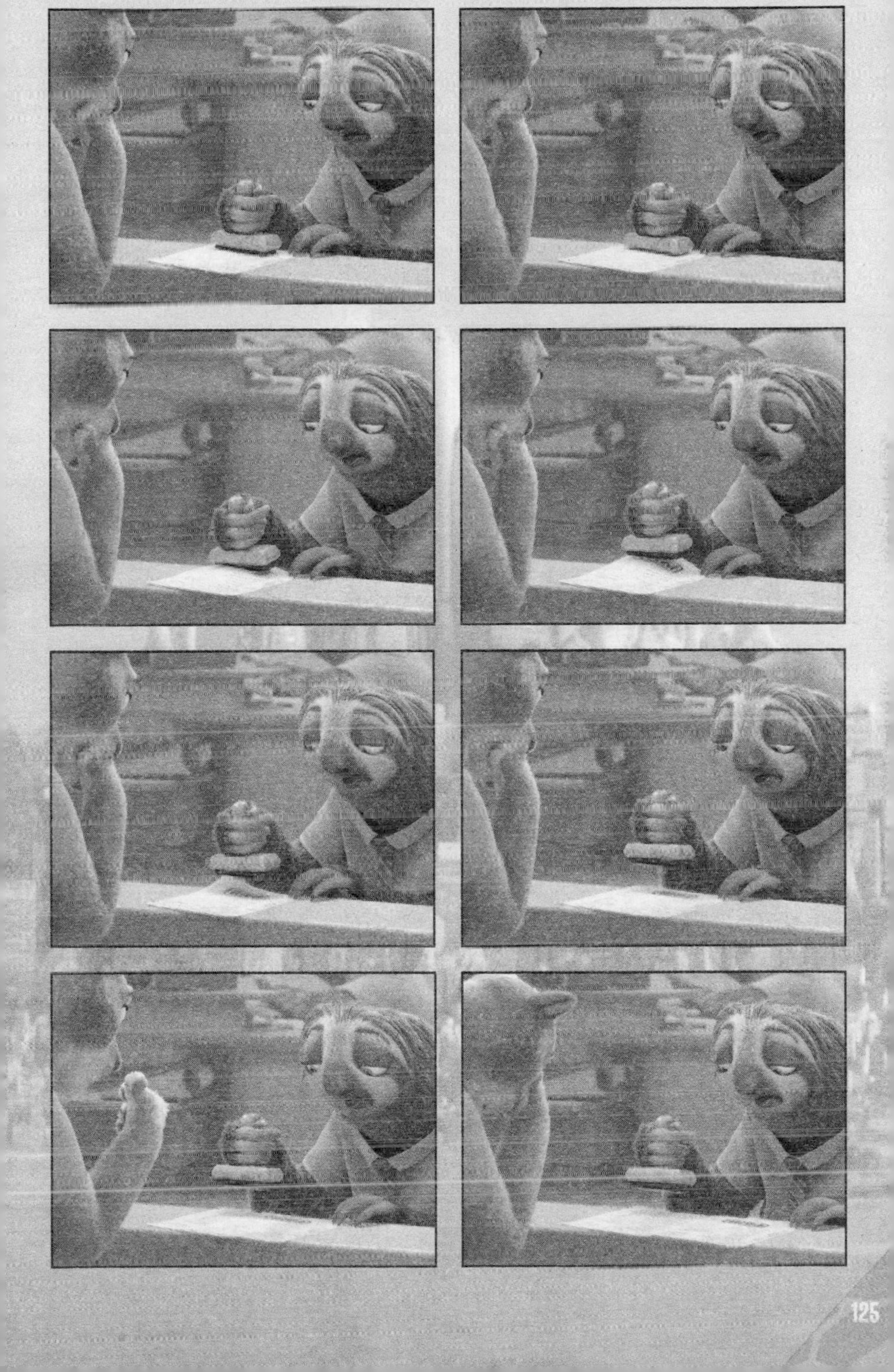

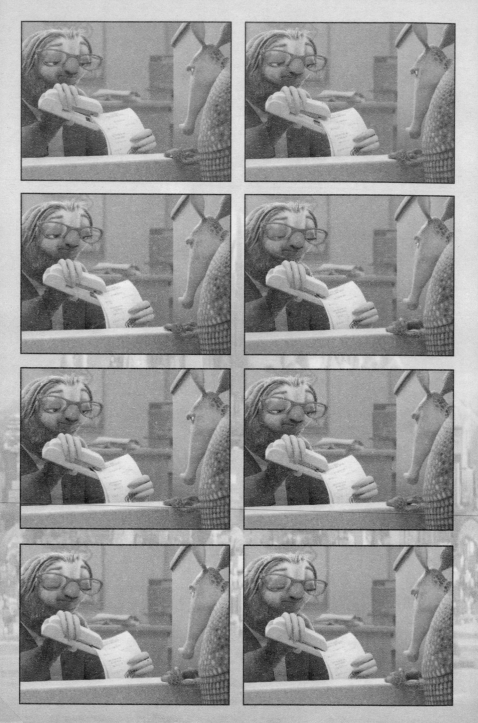

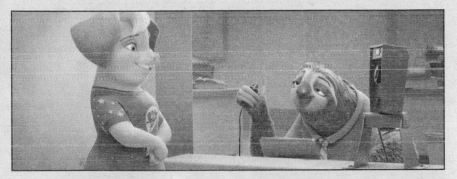

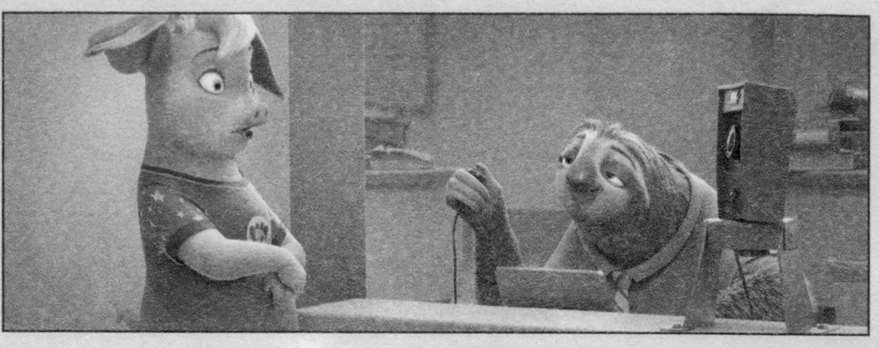

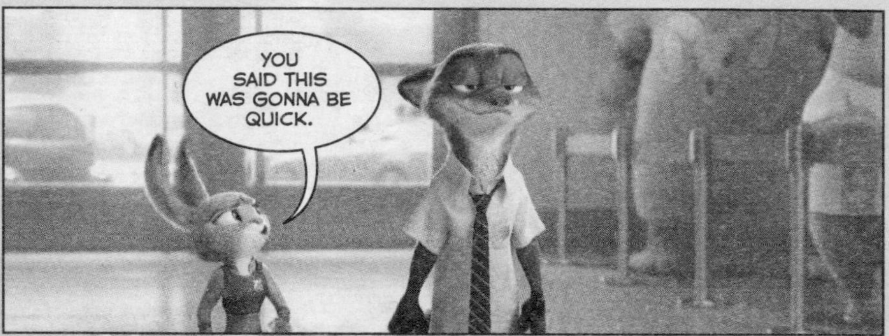
YOU SAID THIS WAS GONNA BE QUICK.

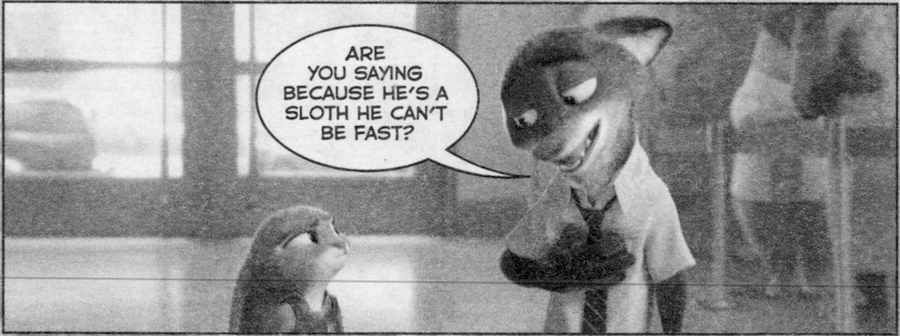
ARE YOU SAYING BECAUSE HE'S A SLOTH HE CAN'T BE FAST?

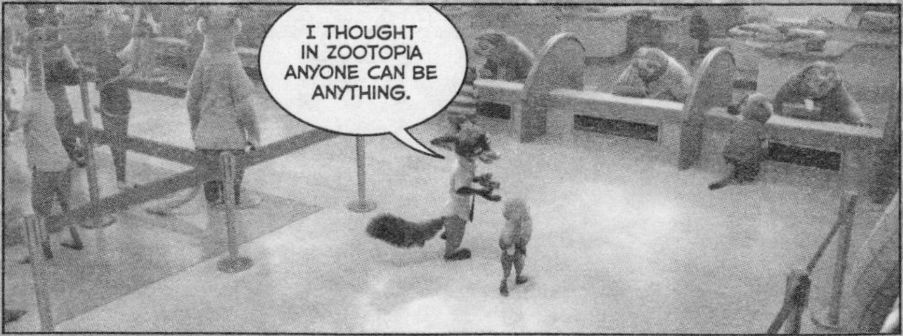
I THOUGHT IN ZOOTOPIA ANYONE CAN BE ANYTHING.

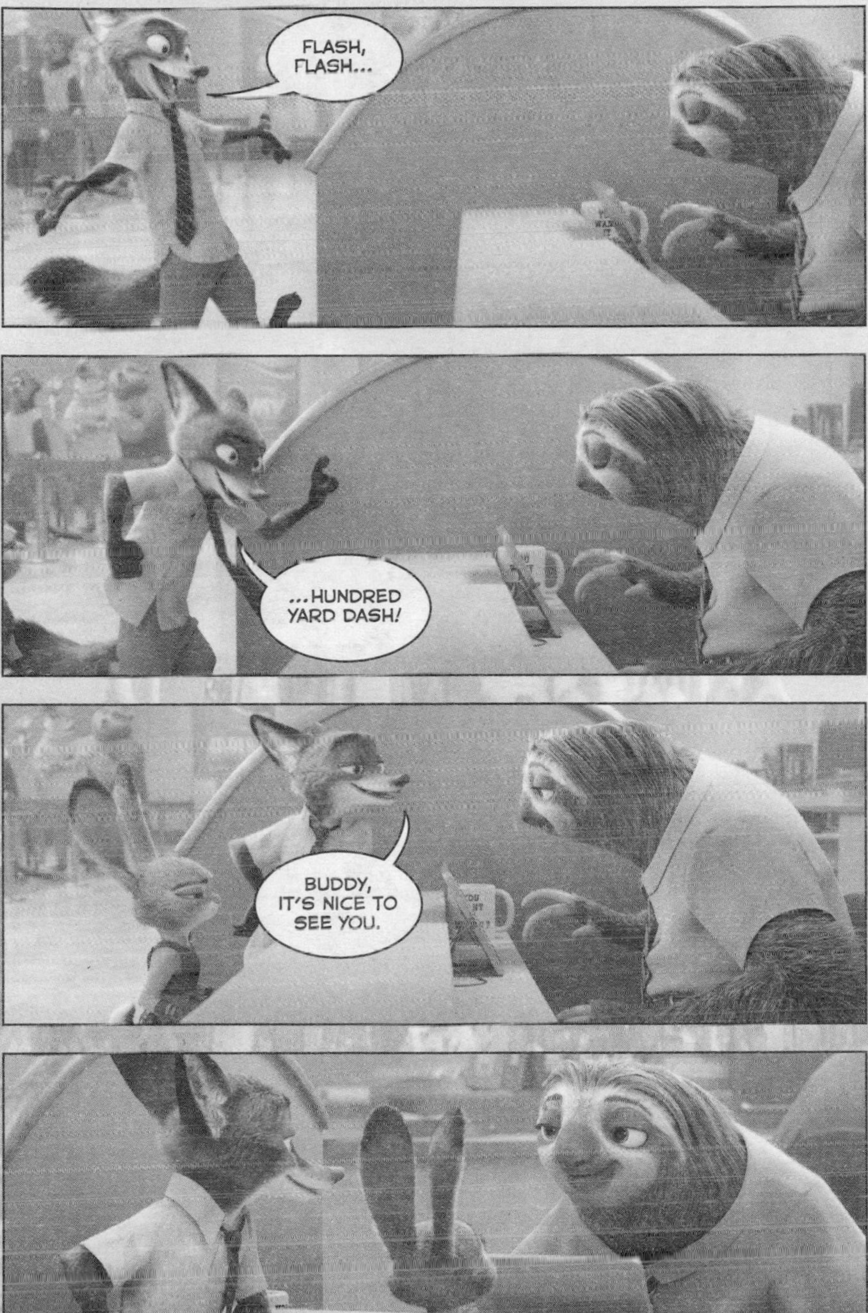
FLASH, FLASH...
...HUNDRED YARD DASH!
BUDDY, IT'S NICE TO SEE YOU.

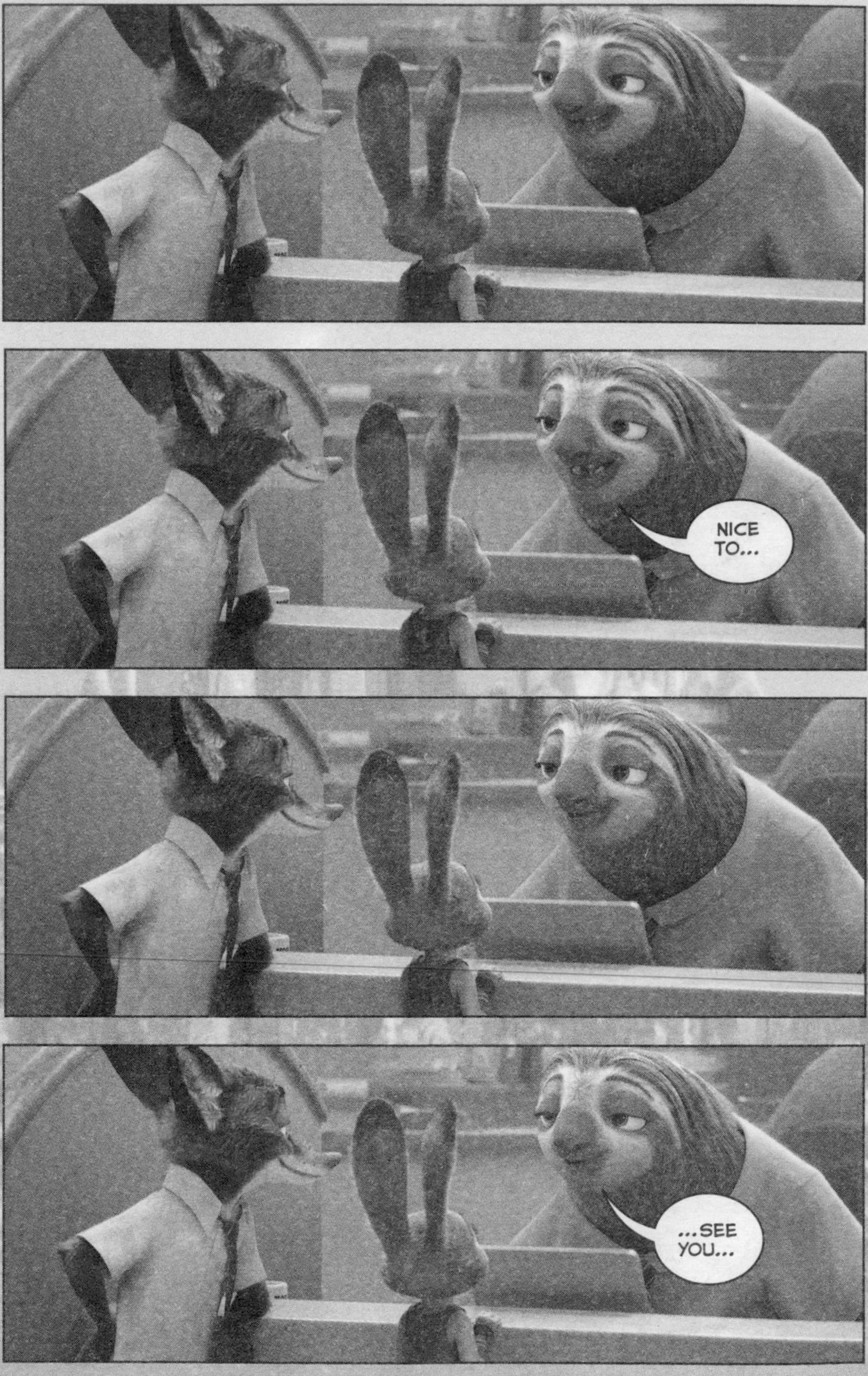
NICE TO...
...SEE YOU...

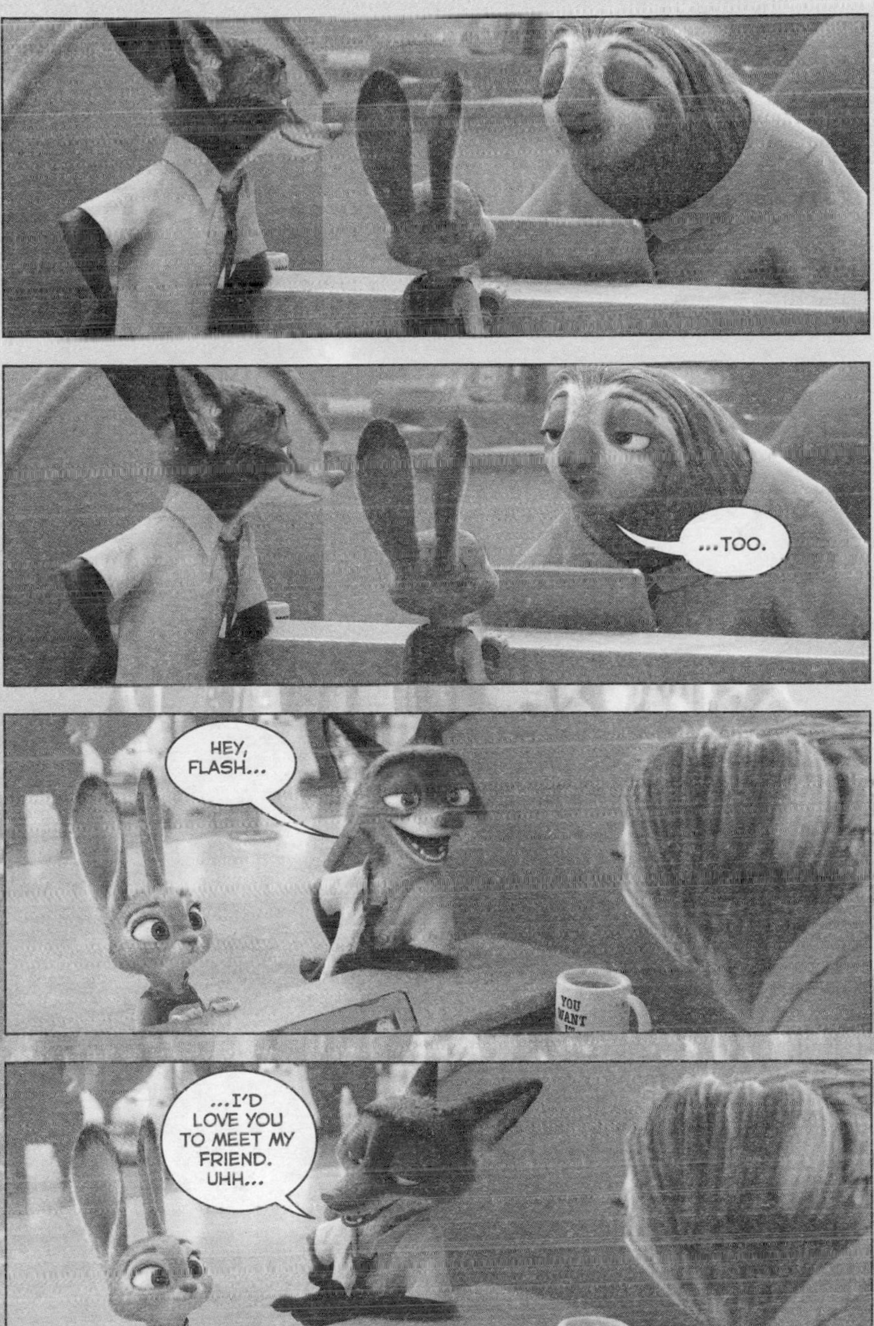
...TOO.
HEY, FLASH...
YOU WANT
...I'D LOVE YOU TO MEET MY FRIEND. UHH...
YOU WANT

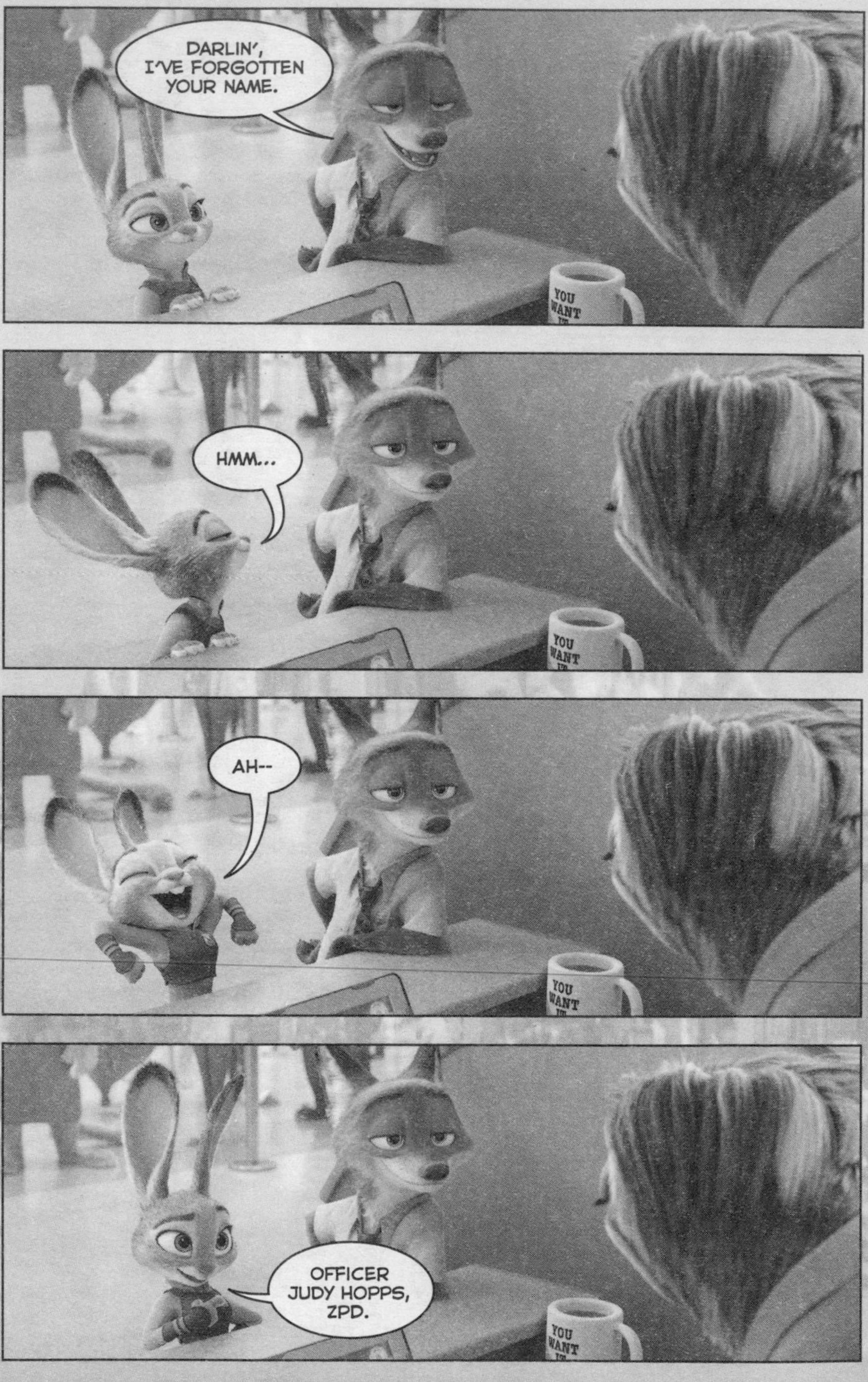
DARLIN', I'VE FORGOTTEN YOUR NAME.
YOU WANT
HMM...
YOU WANT
AH--
YOU WANT
OFFICER JUDY HOPPS, ZPD.
YOU WANT

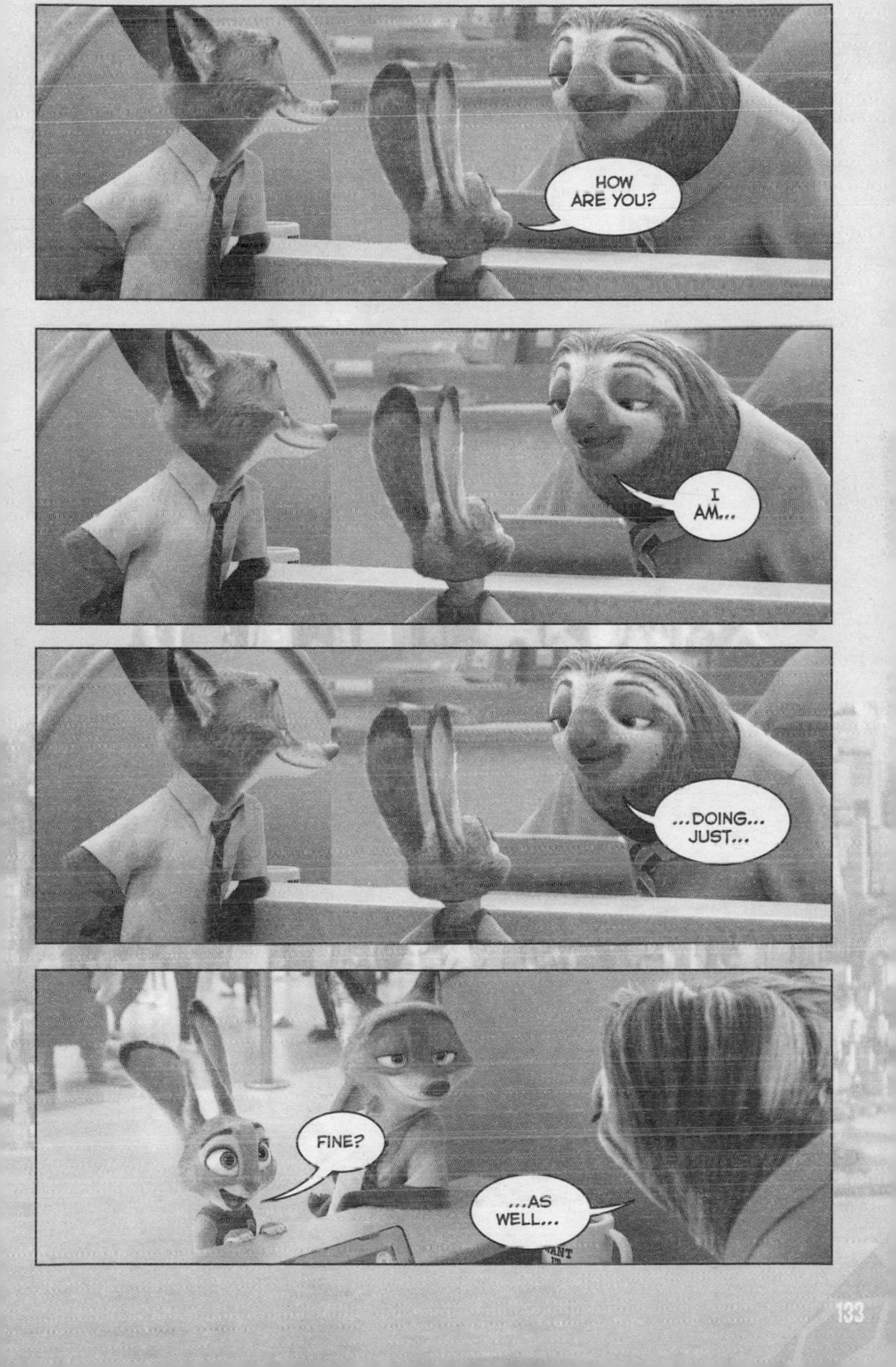
HOW ARE YOU?
I AM...
...DOING... JUST...
FINE?
...AS WELL...

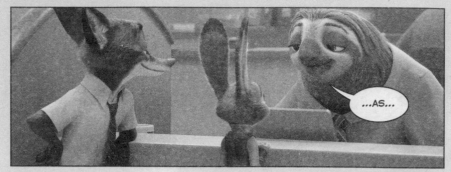

...AS...

...I CAN...

HMM?

...BE.

HANG IN THERE.

WHAT...

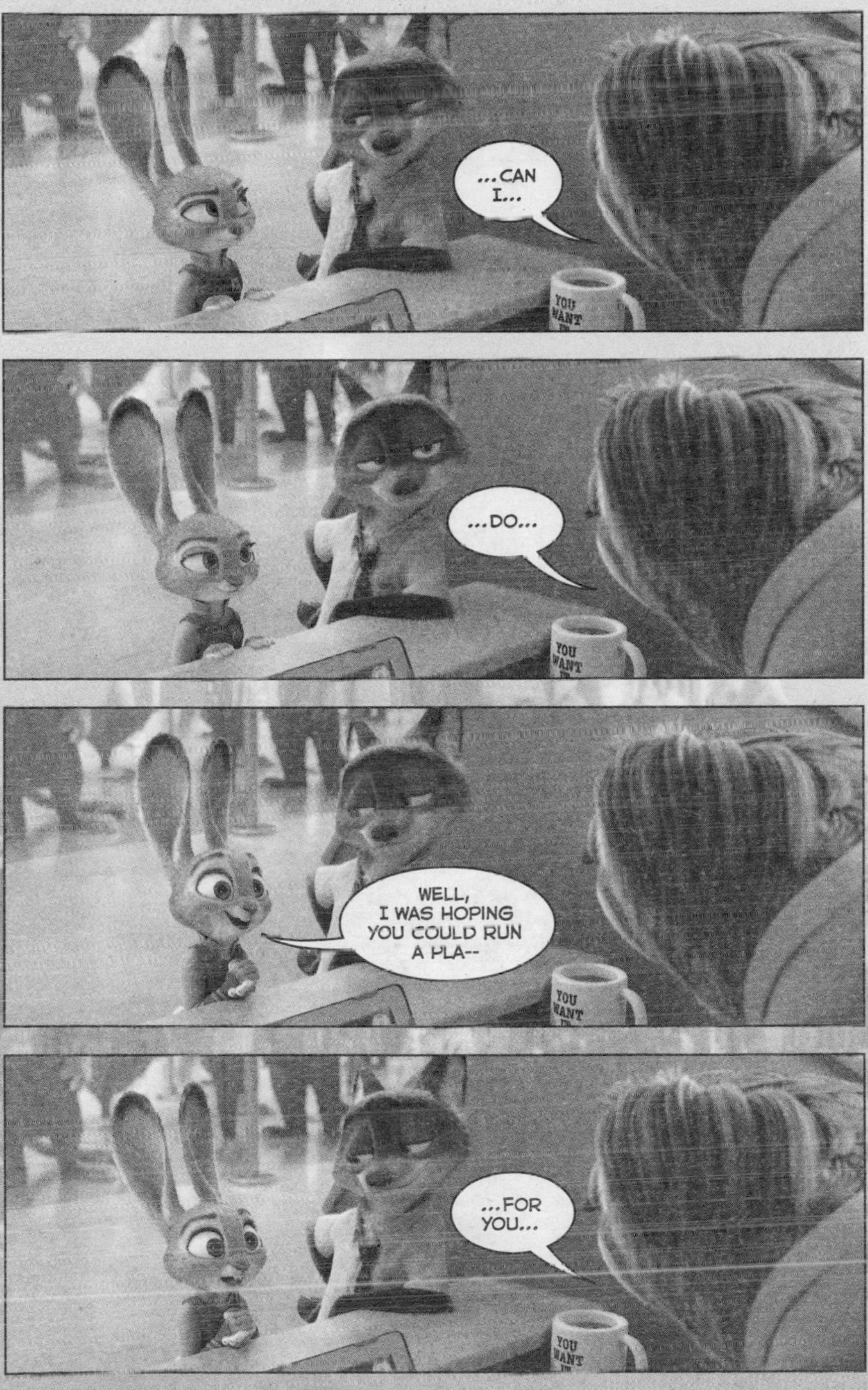
...CAN I...
...DO...
WELL, I WAS HOPING YOU COULD RUN A PLA--
...FOR YOU...

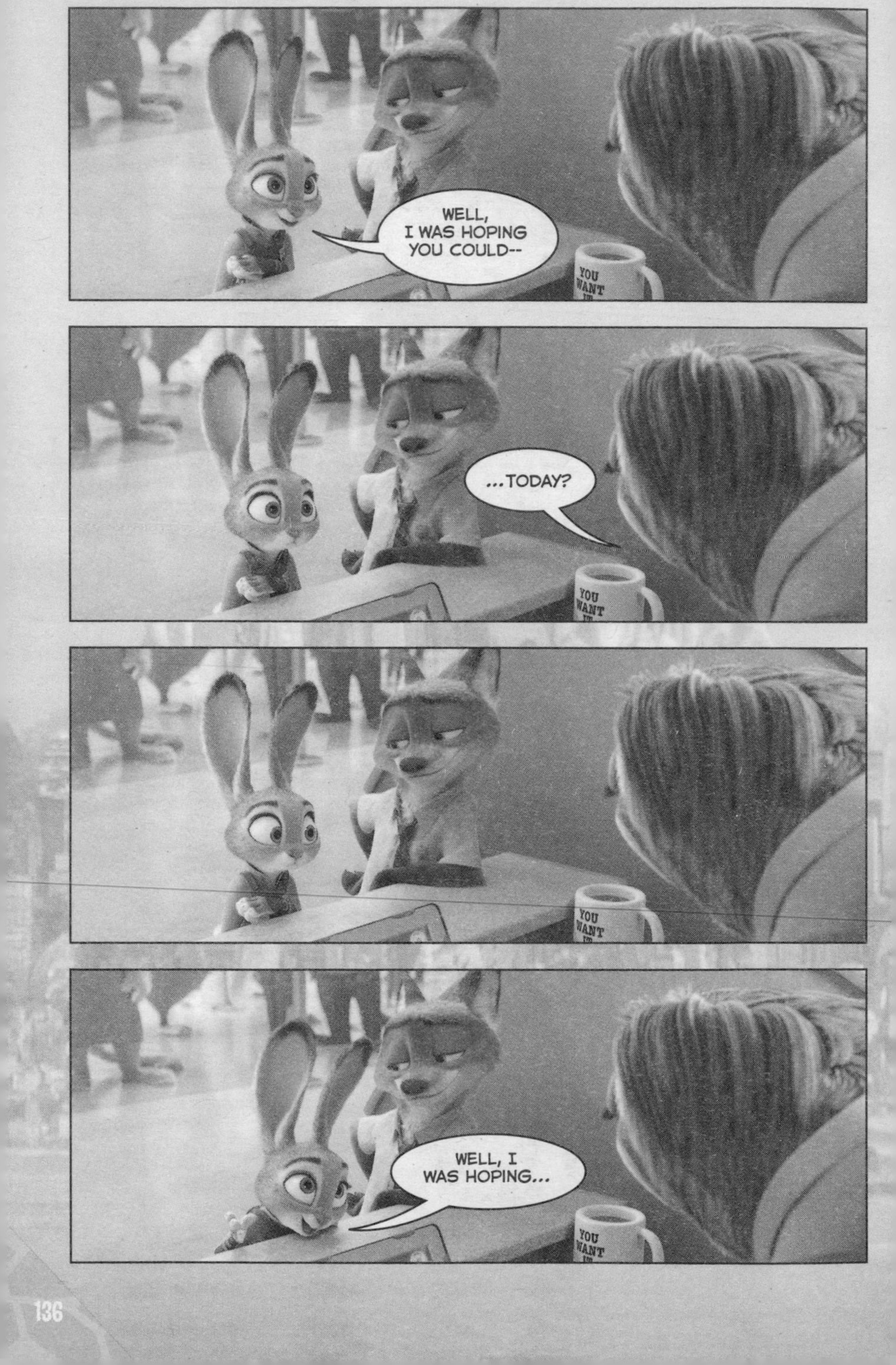
WELL, I WAS HOPING YOU COULD--
YOU WANT
...TODAY?
WELL, I WAS HOPING...

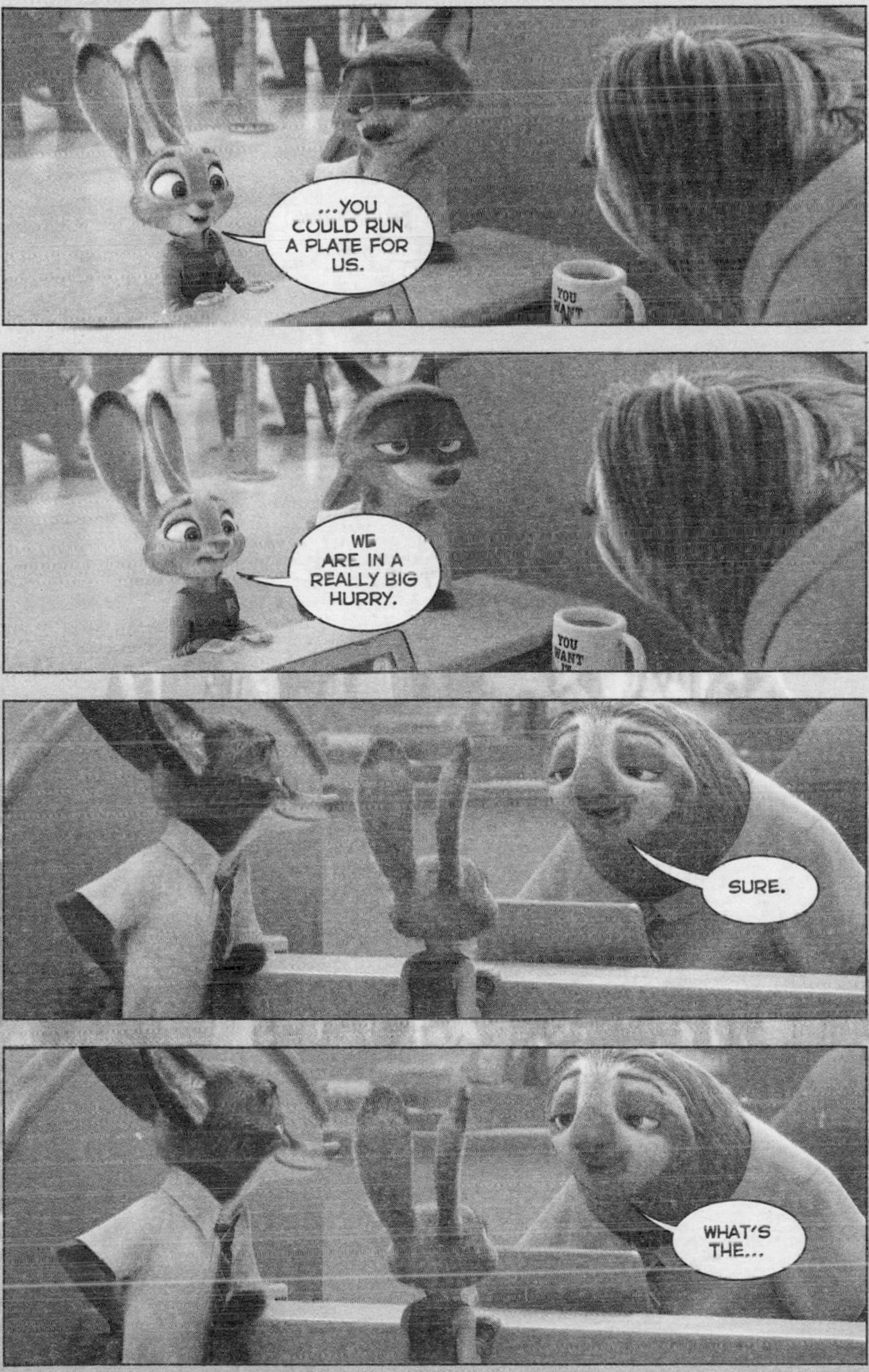
...YOU COULD RUN A PLATE FOR US.
WE ARE IN A REALLY BIG HURRY.
SURE.
WHAT'S THE...

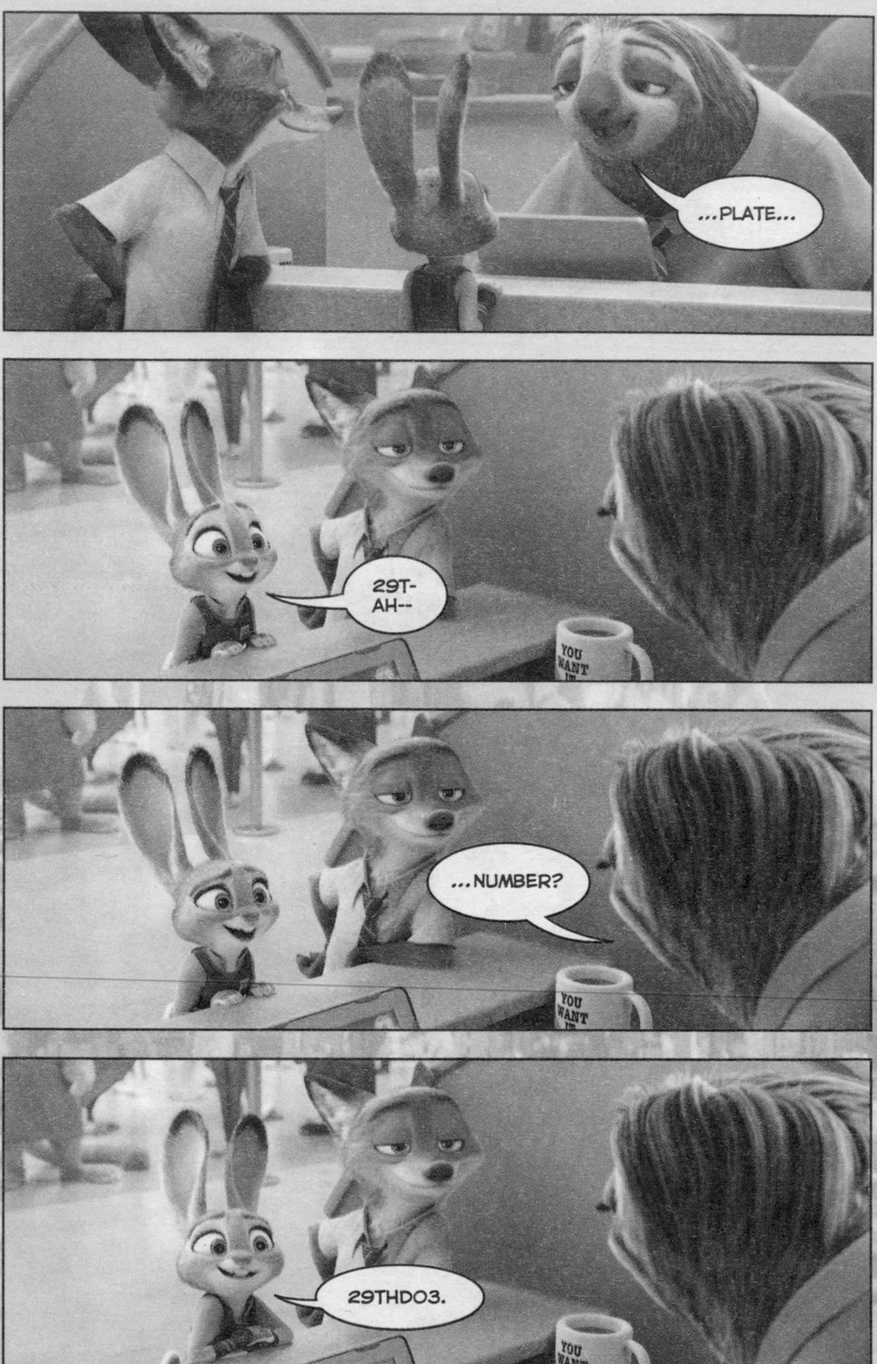
...PLATE...
29T-
AH--
...NUMBER?
29THD03.

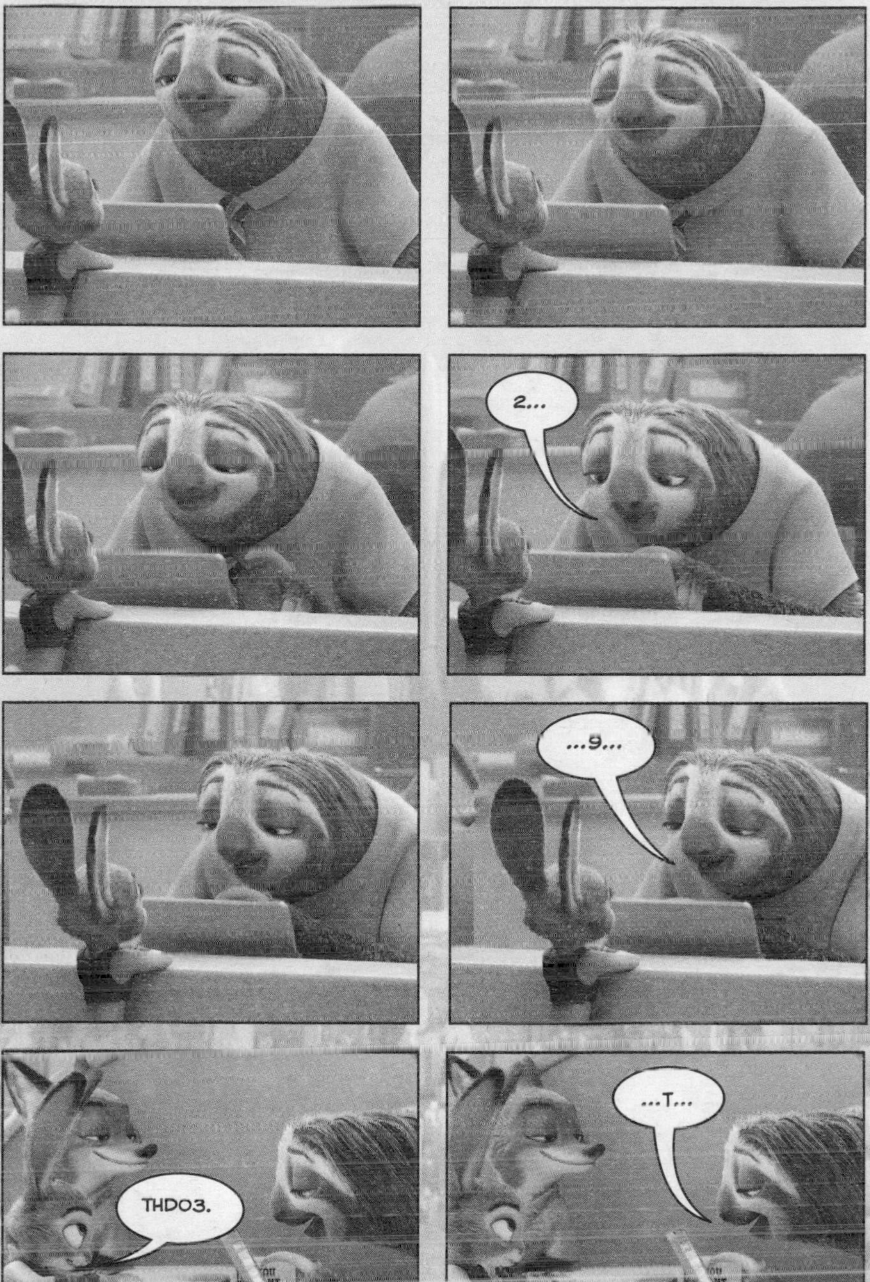
2...
...9...
THDO3.
...T...

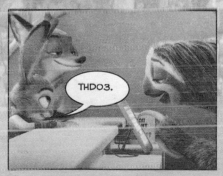

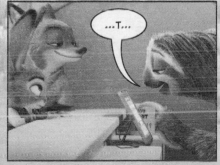

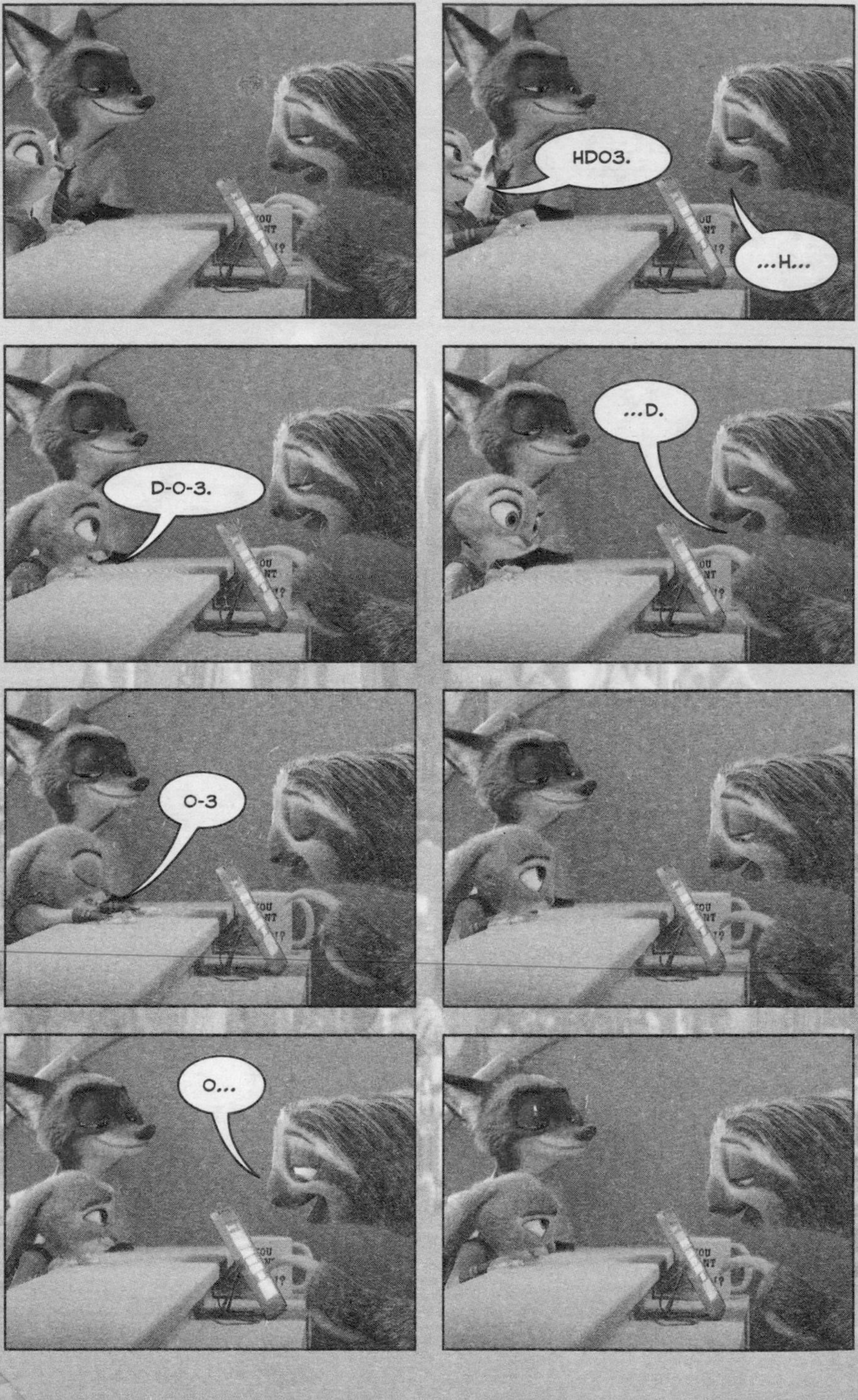
HDO3.
...H...
D-O-3.
...D.
O-3
O...

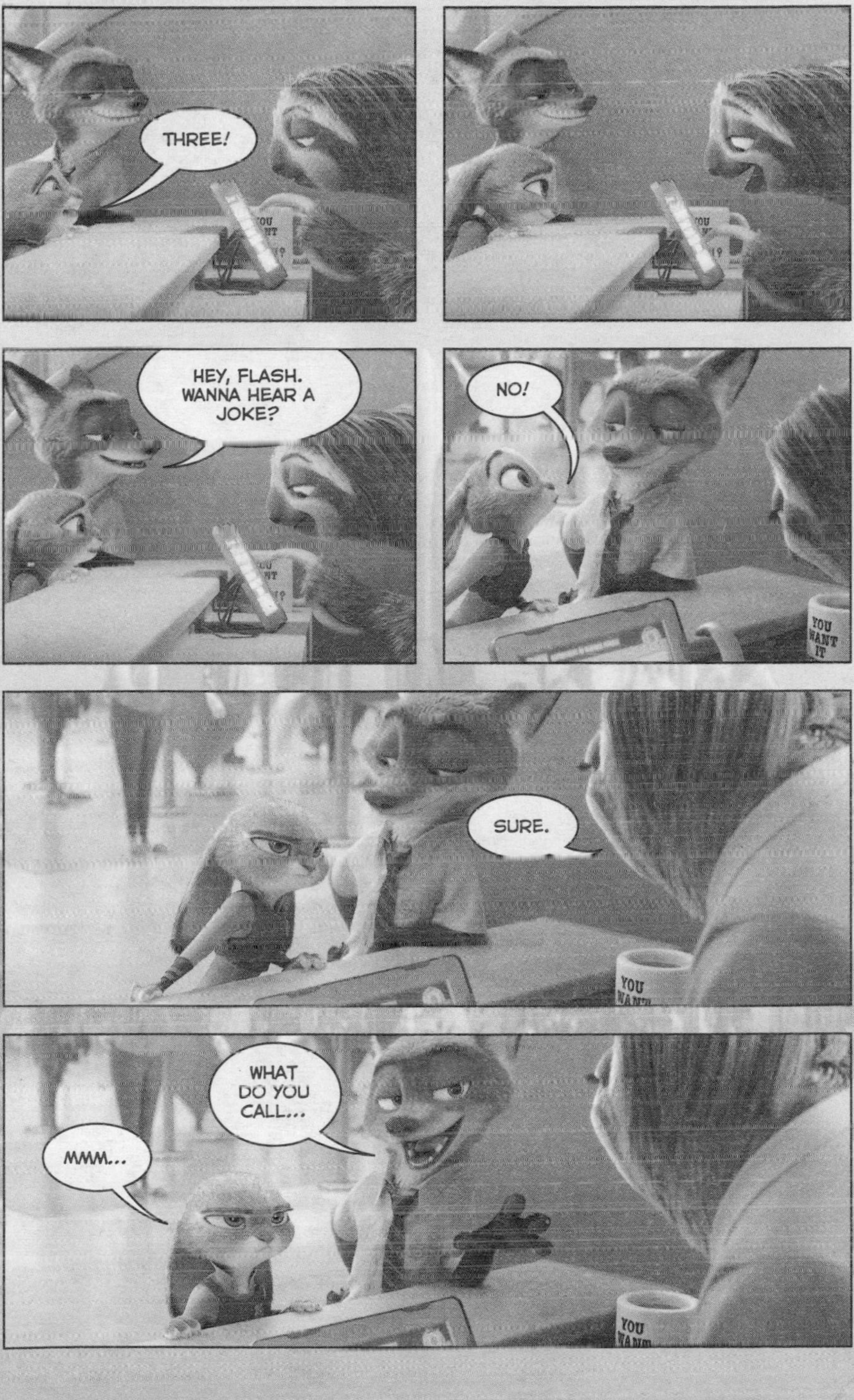
THREE!
HEY, FLASH. WANNA HEAR A JOKE?
NO!
YOU WANT IT
SURE.
WHAT DO YOU CALL...
MMM...

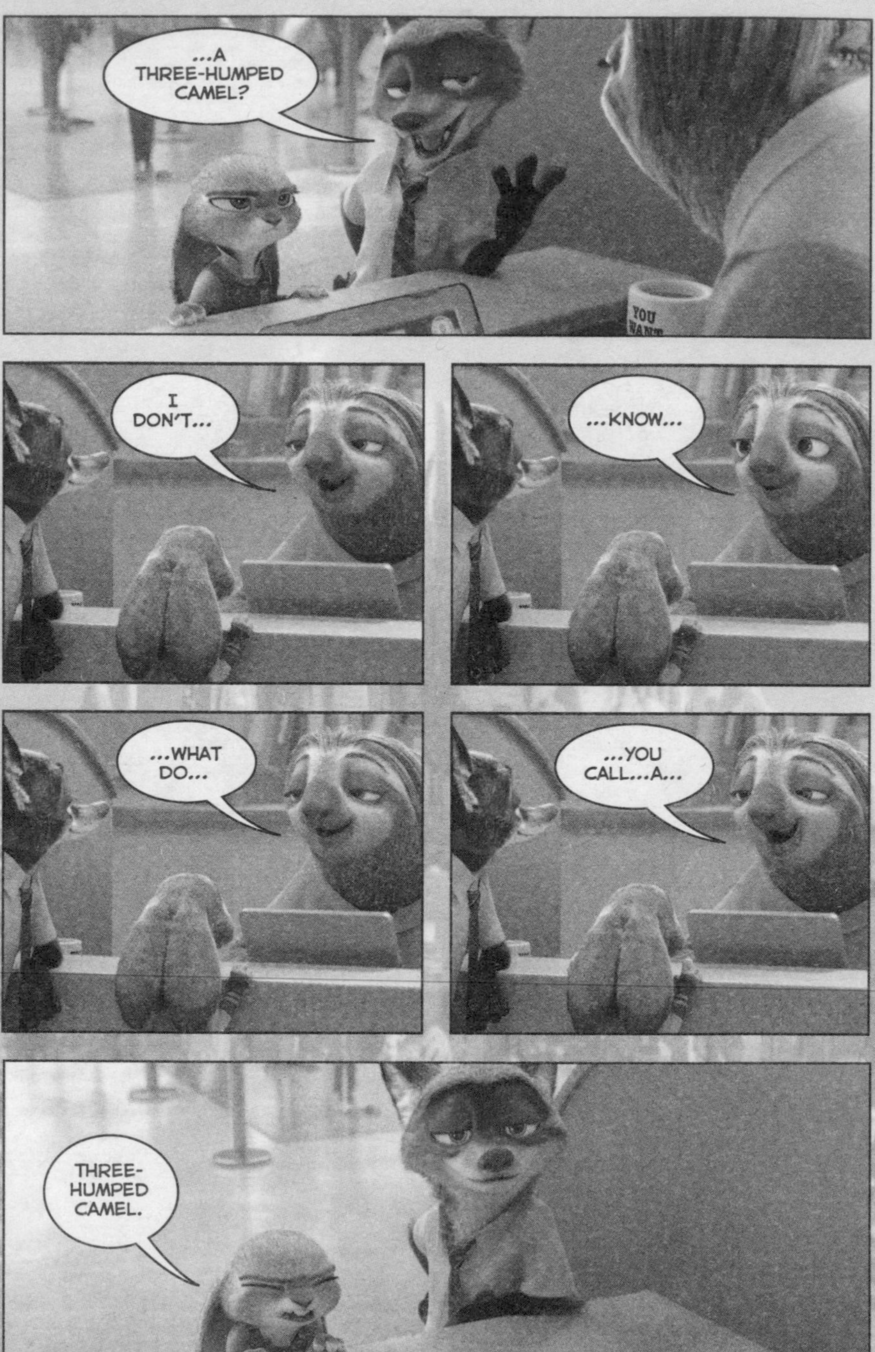
...A THREE-HUMPED CAMEL?
I DON'T...
...KNOW...
...WHAT DO...
...YOU CALL...A...
THREE-HUMPED CAMEL.
YOU WANT

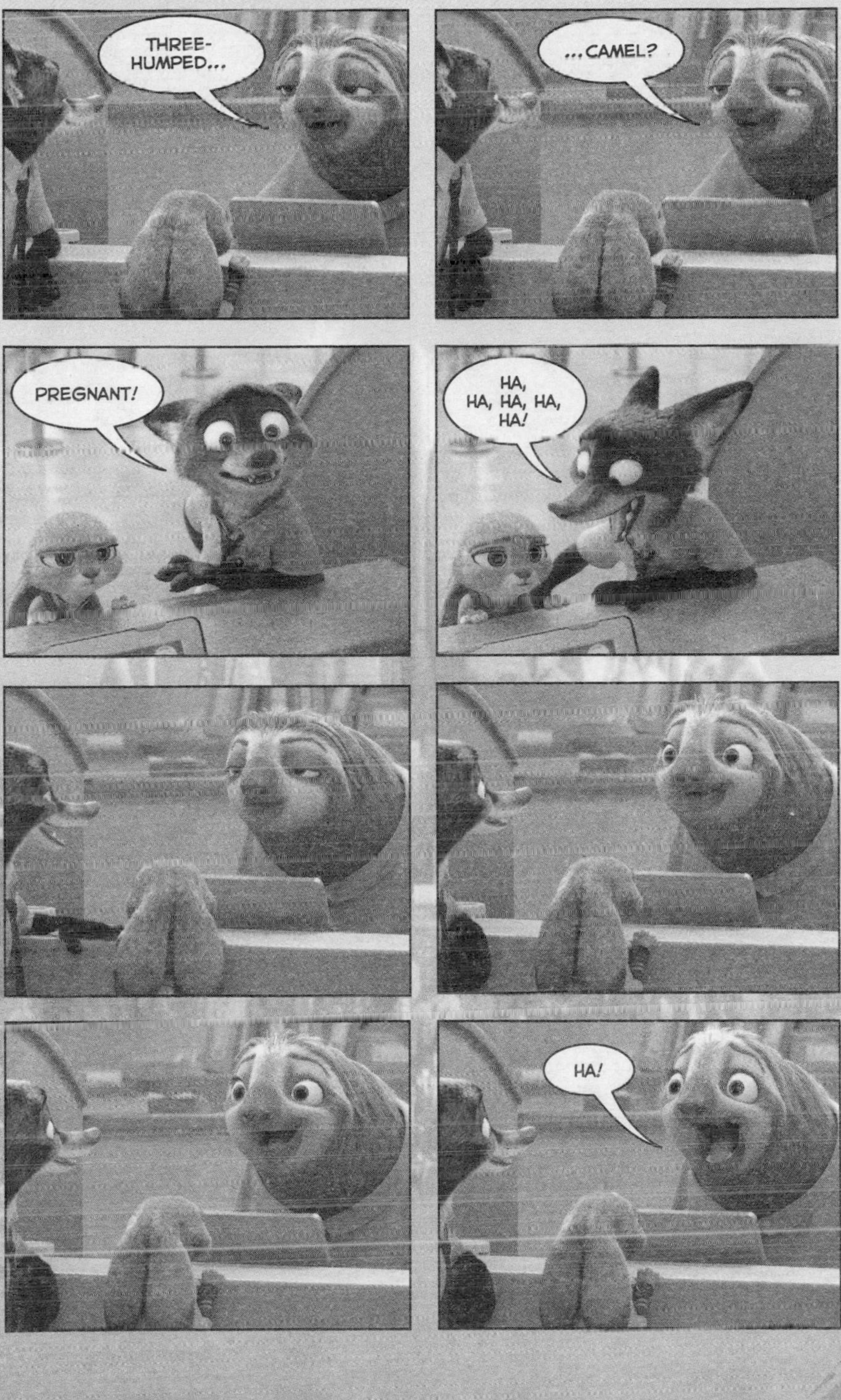
THREE-HUMPED...
...CAMEL?
PREGNANT!
HA, HA, HA, HA, HA!
HA!

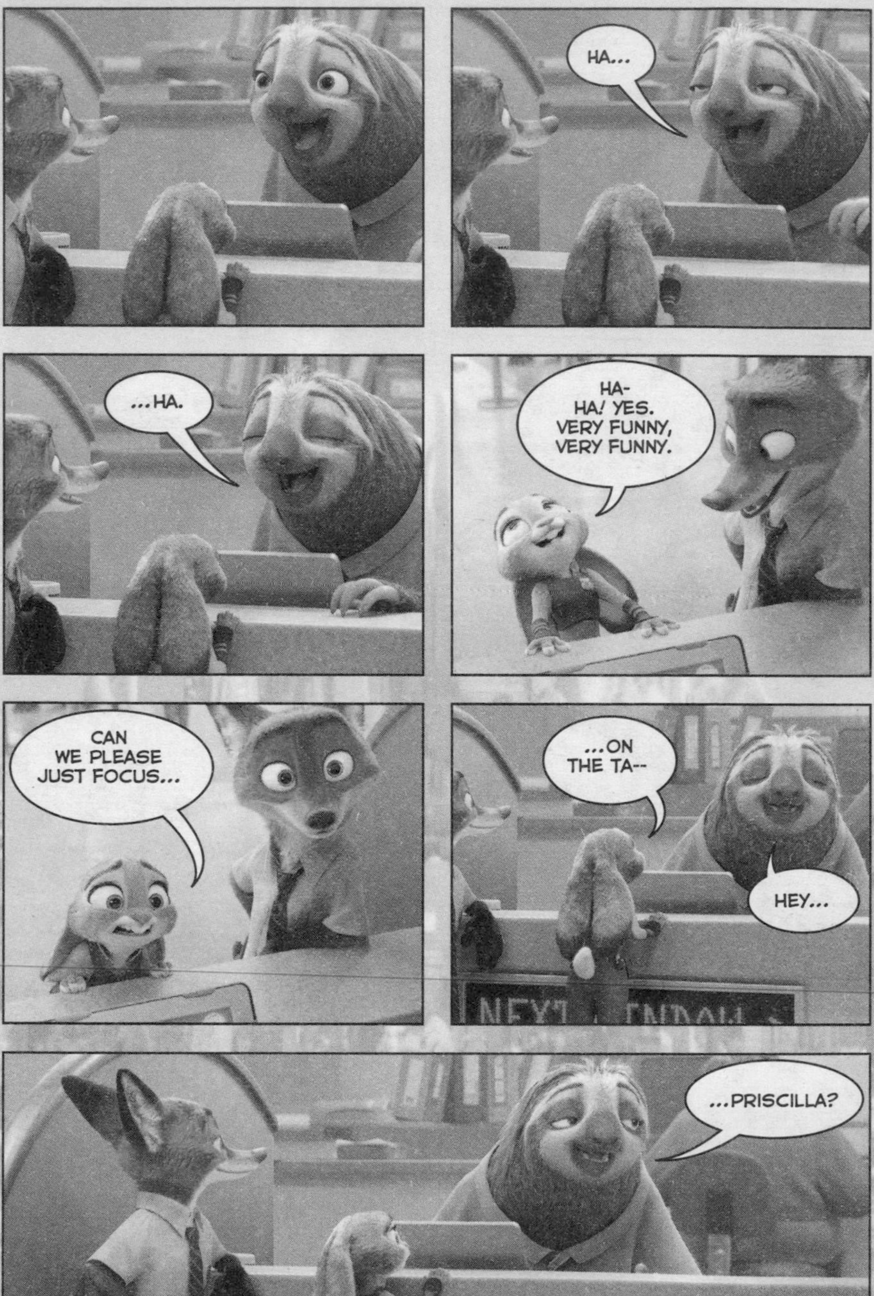
HA...
...HA.
HA- HA! YES. VERY FUNNY, VERY FUNNY.
CAN WE PLEASE JUST FOCUS...
...ON THE TA--
HEY...
...PRISCILLA?

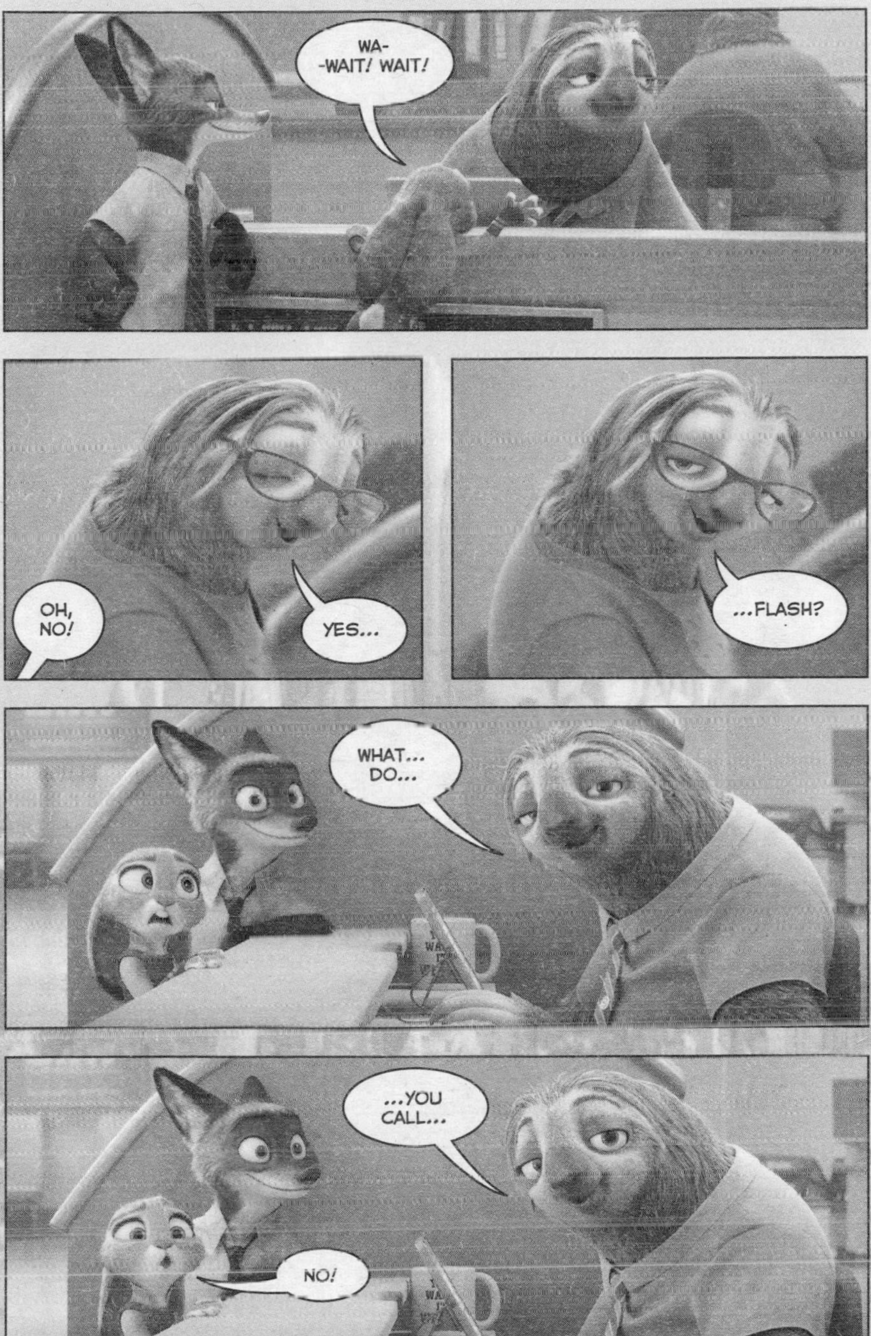
WA-
-WAIT! WAIT!
OH, NO!
YES...
...FLASH?
WHAT... DO...
...YOU CALL...
NO!

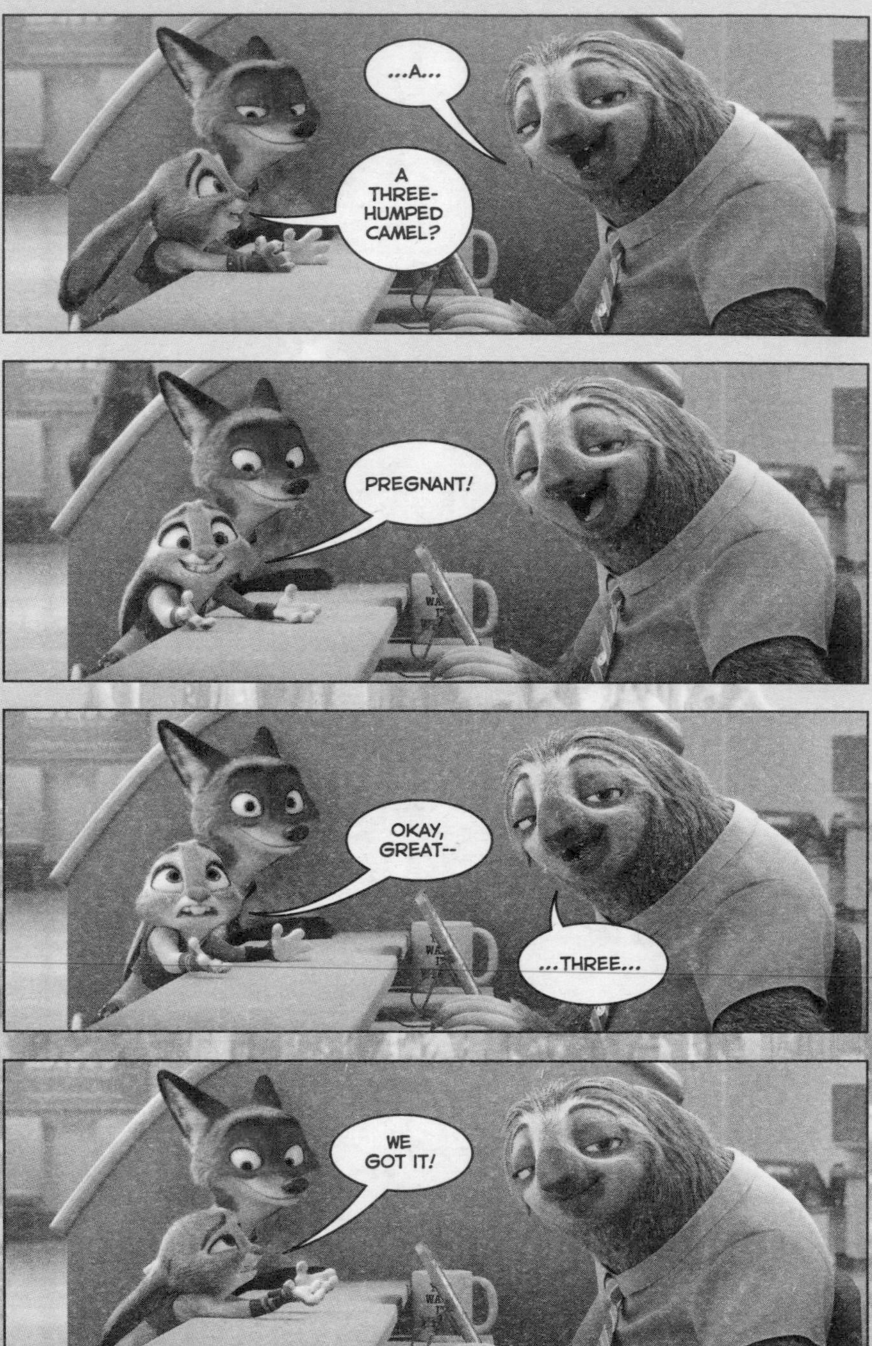
...A...
A THREE-HUMPED CAMEL?
PREGNANT!
OKAY, GREAT--
...THREE...
WE GOT IT!

...HUMPED...
PLEASE, JUST--
UGHH!
CITY OF ZOOTOPIA
DEPARTMENT OF MAMMAL VEHICLES
OWNER: TUNDRATOWN LIMO SERVICE
TUNDRATOWN, ZOOTOPIA

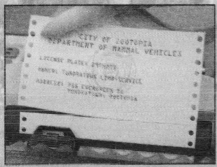

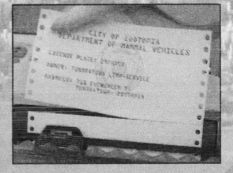

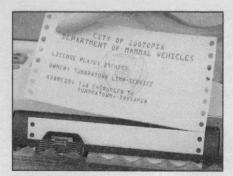
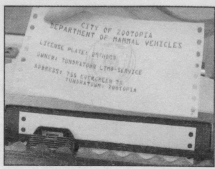

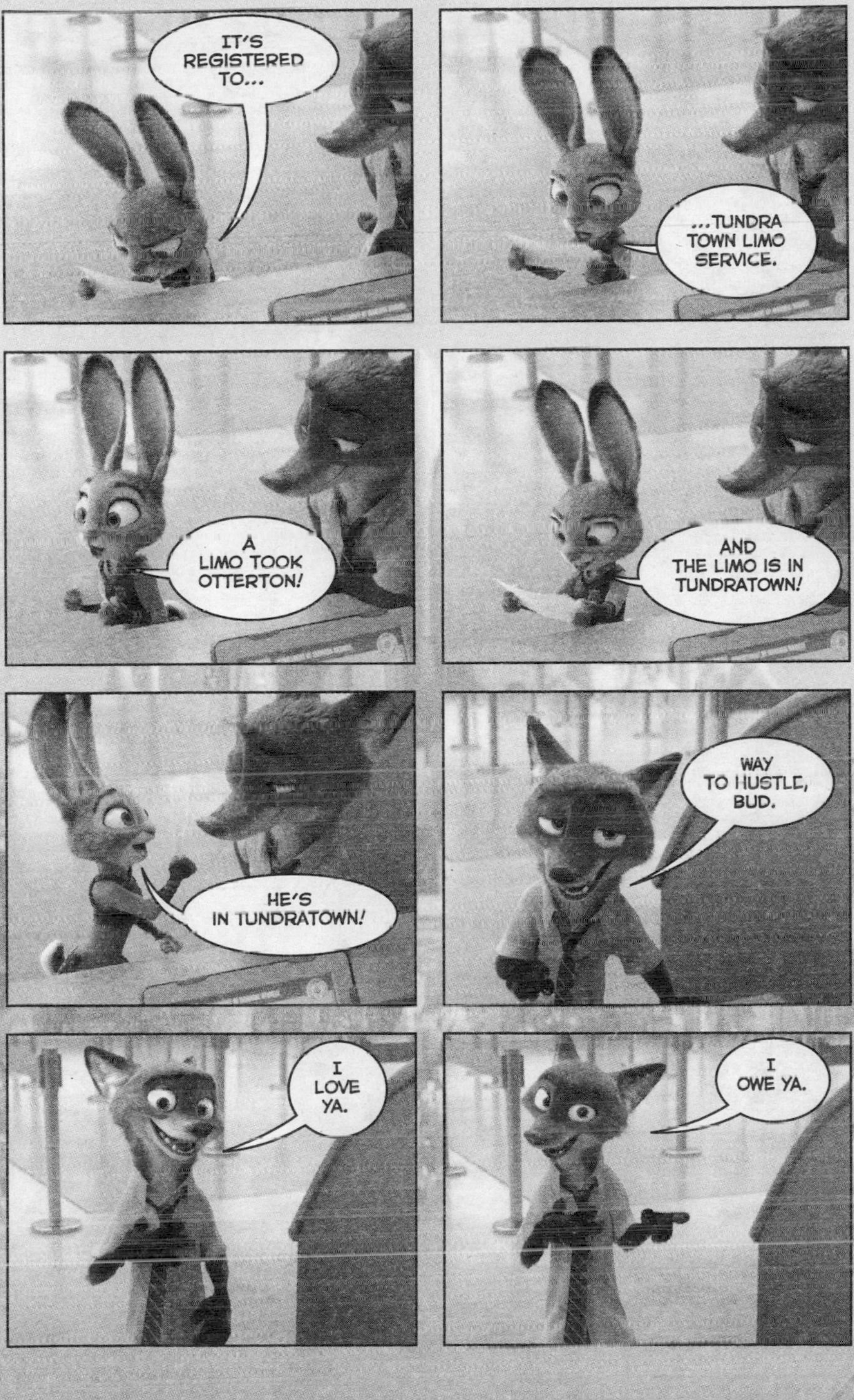
IT'S REGISTERED TO...
...TUNDRA TOWN LIMO SERVICE.
A LIMO TOOK OTTERTON!
AND THE LIMO IS IN TUNDRATOWN!
HE'S IN TUNDRATOWN!
WAY TO HUSTLE, BUD.
I LOVE YA.
I OWE YA.

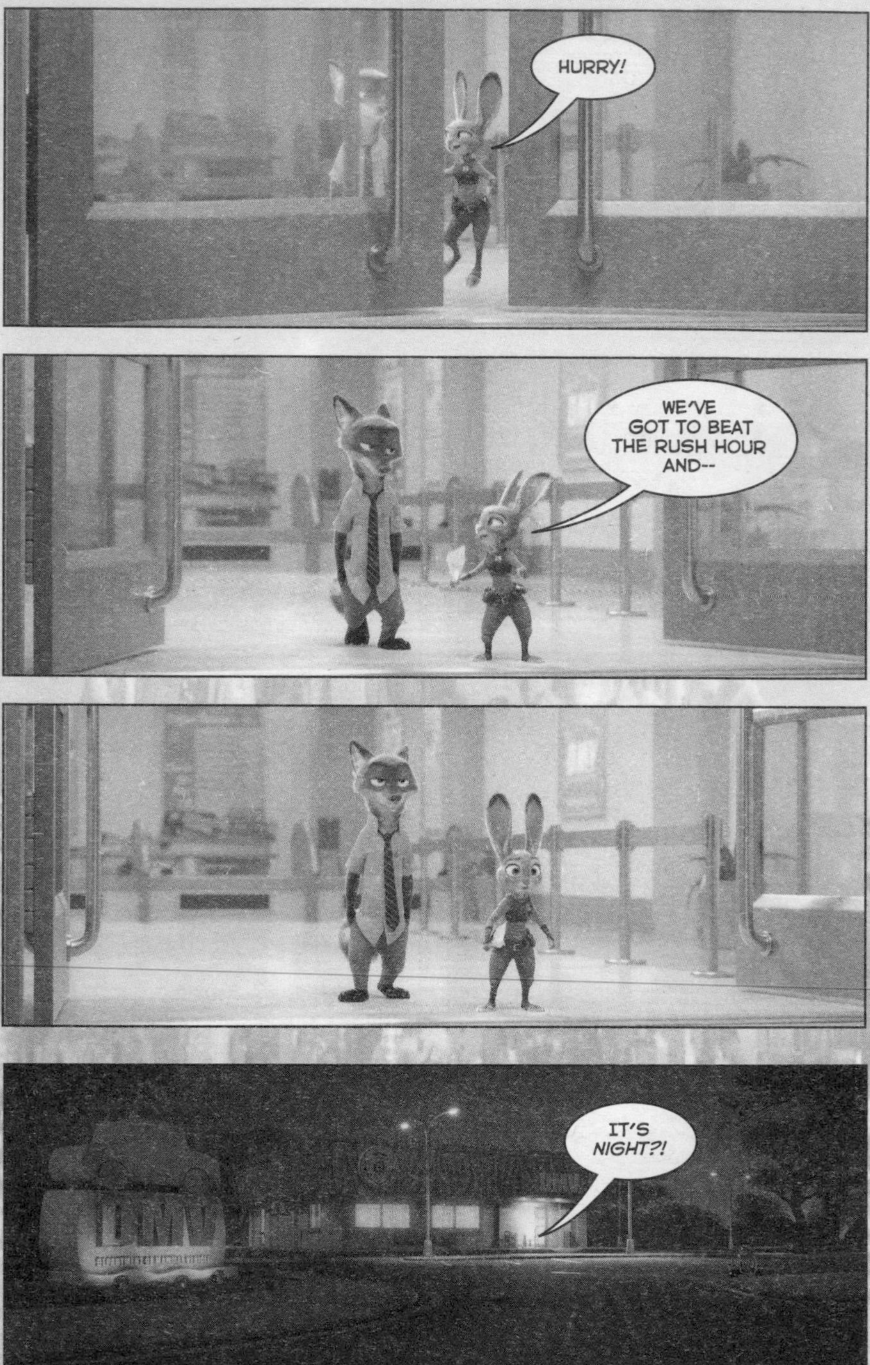
HURRY!
WE'VE GOT TO BEAT THE RUSH HOUR AND--
IT'S NIGHT?!

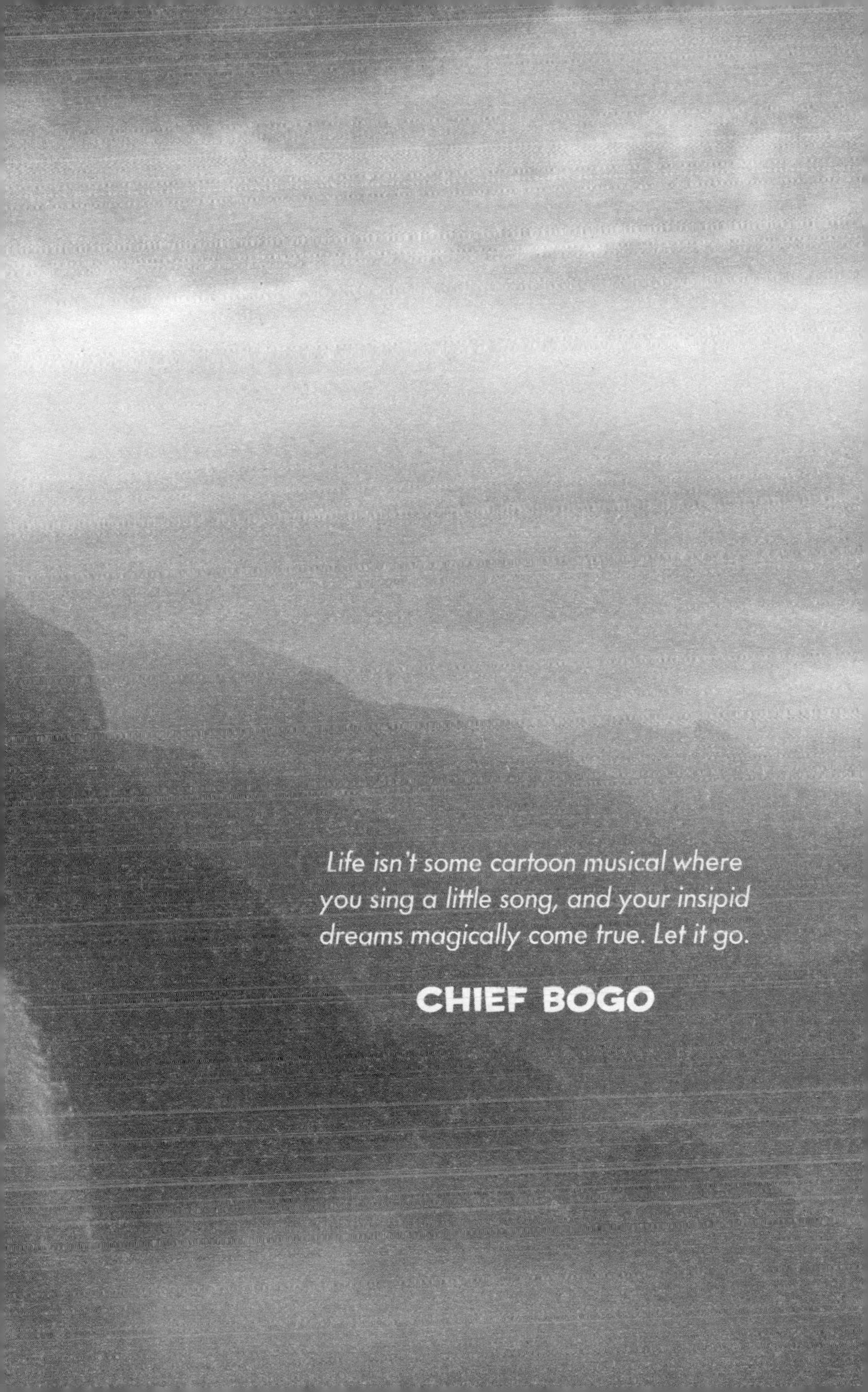

Life isn't some cartoon musical where you sing a little song, and your insipid dreams magically come true. Let it go.

CHIEF BOGO

ZOOTOPIA

BUNNYBURROW

Bunnyburrow is a suburb about 200 miles outside of the city of Zootopia. This quaint, small-town getaway is a refuge from the hustle and bustle of big city life. It's home to a large population of bunnies, most of whom are carrot farmers, just like Judy's family.

Judy loves her home and family, but she doesn't want to live the life of a carrot farmer. When things get tough in Zootopia, Judy returns home, and her family welcomes her with open paws! She doesn't stay long, though, because she discovers an important clue!

Local FAVES

Where to Go:

- VISIT BUNNYBURROW DURING THE CARROT DAYS FESTIVAL AND GET A FULL DOSE OF LOCAL FLAVOR

What to Eat:

- TRY SOME DELICIOUS CARROTS FROM THE HOPPS FAMILY FARM VEGETABLE STAND

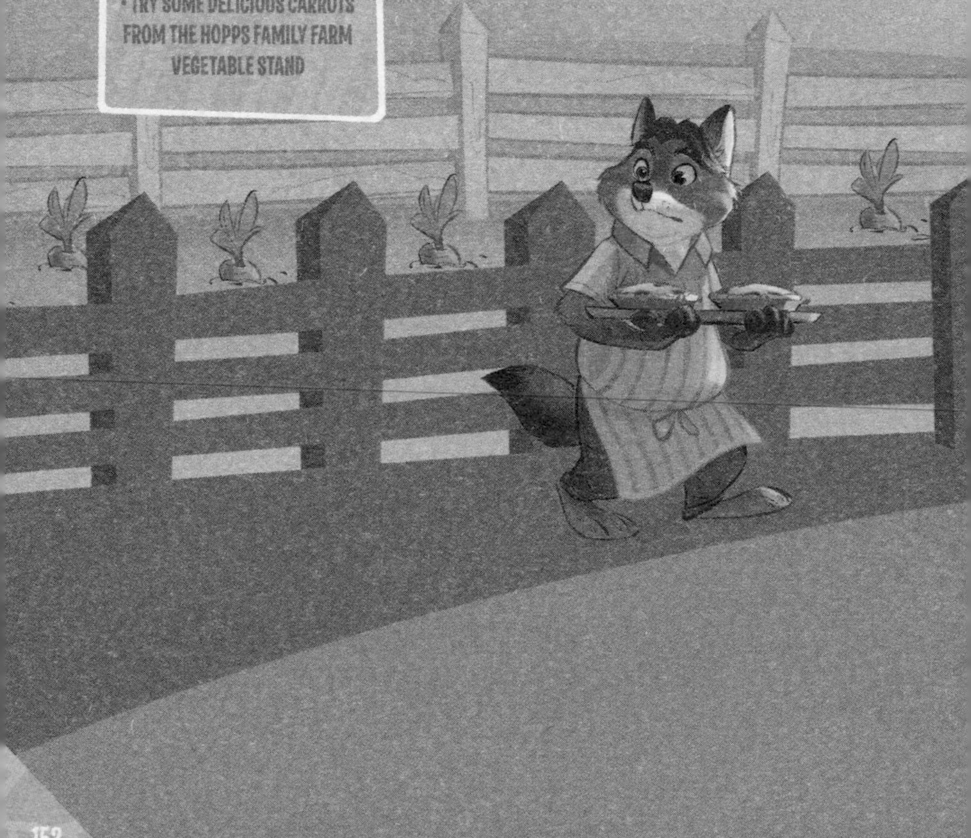

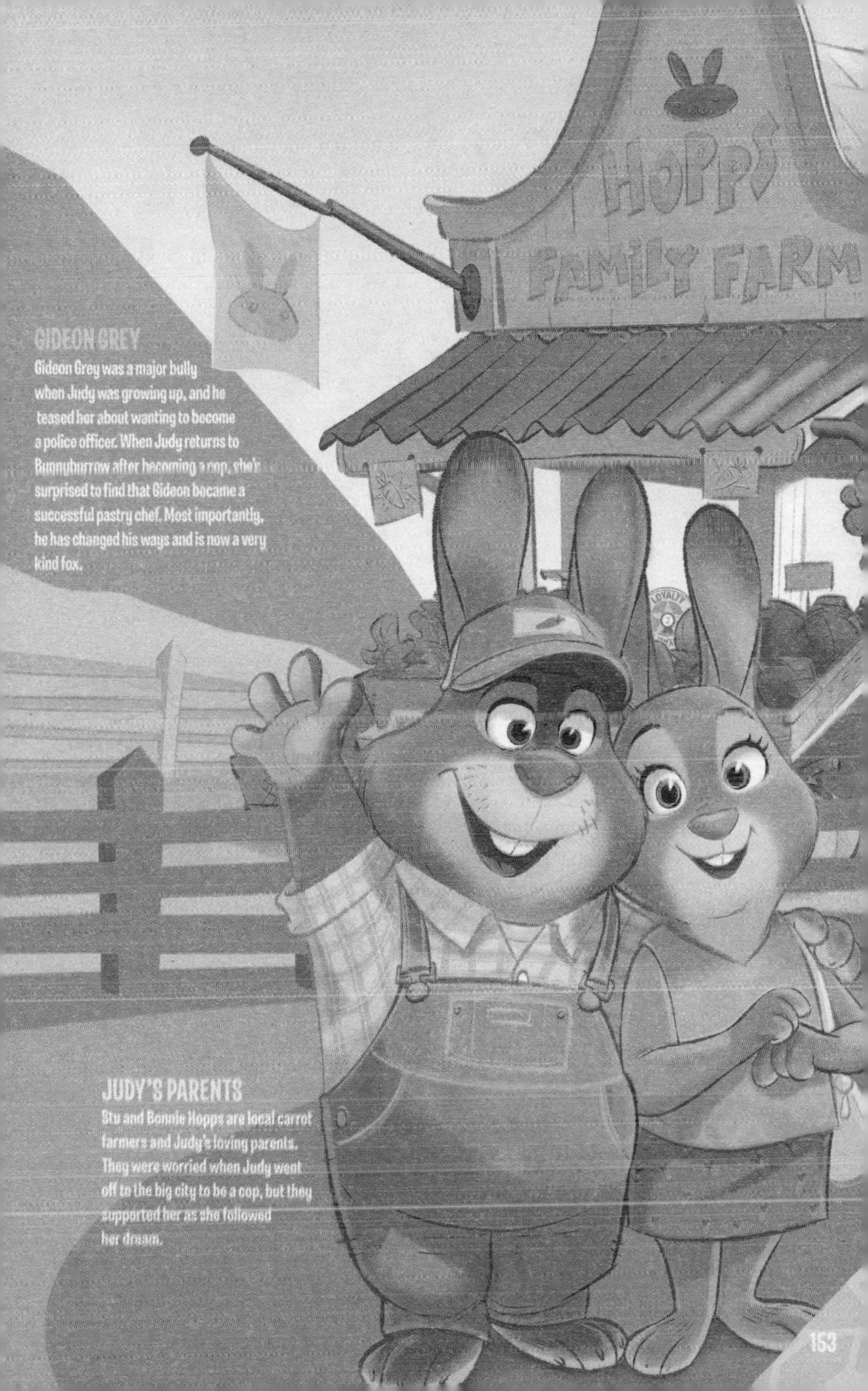
HOPPS'
FAMILY FARM
LOYALTY

GIDEON GREY

Gideon Grey was a major bully when Judy was growing up, and he teased her about wanting to become a police officer. When Judy returns to Bunnyburrow after becoming a cop, she's surprised to find that Gideon became a successful pastry chef. Most importantly, he has changed his ways and is now a very kind fox.

JUDY'S PARENTS

Stu and Bonnie Hopps are local carrot farmers and Judy's loving parents. They were worried when Judy went off to the big city to be a cop, but they supported her as she followed her dream.

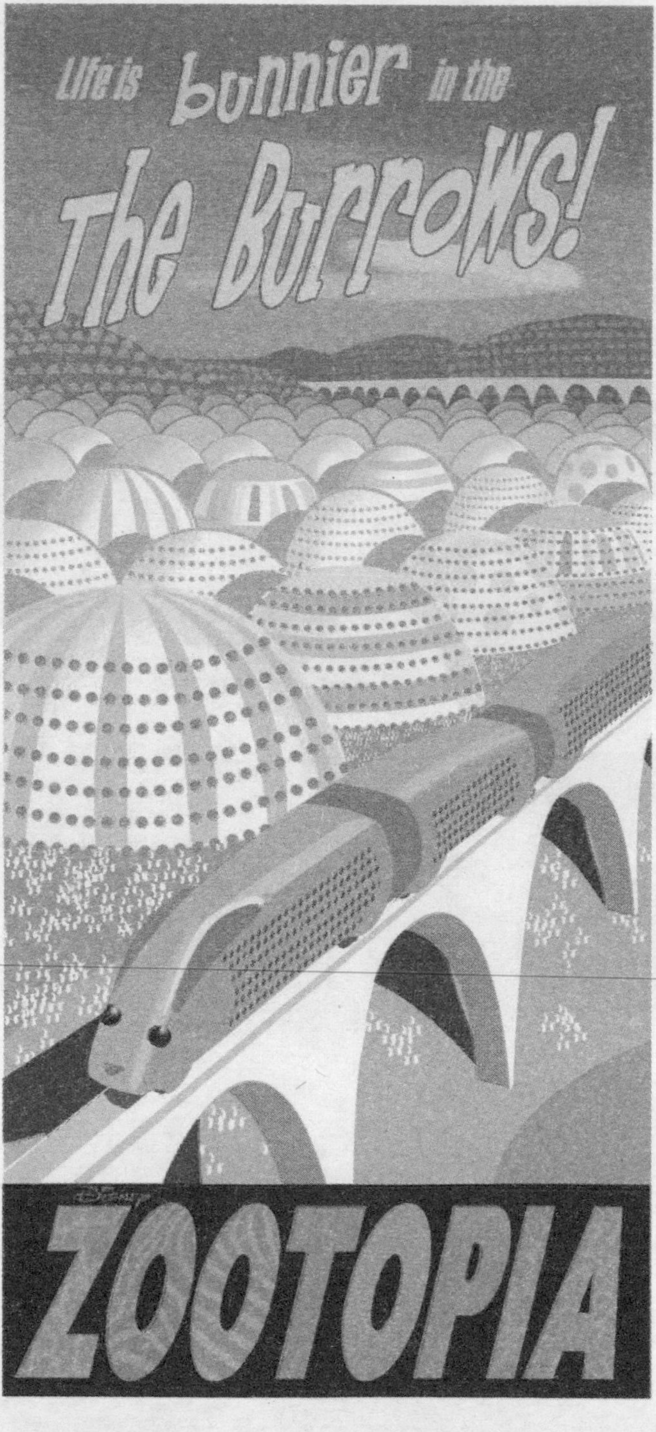
Life is bunnier in the
The Burrows!
Disney
ZOOTOPIA

LIFE IS SWEETER IN
BUNNYBURROW!

October

SUN	MON	TUES	WED	THURS	FRI	SAT
			1	2	3	4
1	2	3	4	5	6	7
8	9	10	11	12	13	14
15	16	17	18	19	20	21
22 Carrot Days Festival	23	24	25	26	27	28
29	30	31				

DID YOU KNOW?

- Bunnyburrow, Judy Hopps' hometown, is a suburb 200 miles from the city. Vast, sprawling open space contrasts with the busy city streets of Zootopia.
- Bunnies are born there and live out their lives there. Nobody quite understands why in the world Judy would want to leave— and move to the big city of all places.

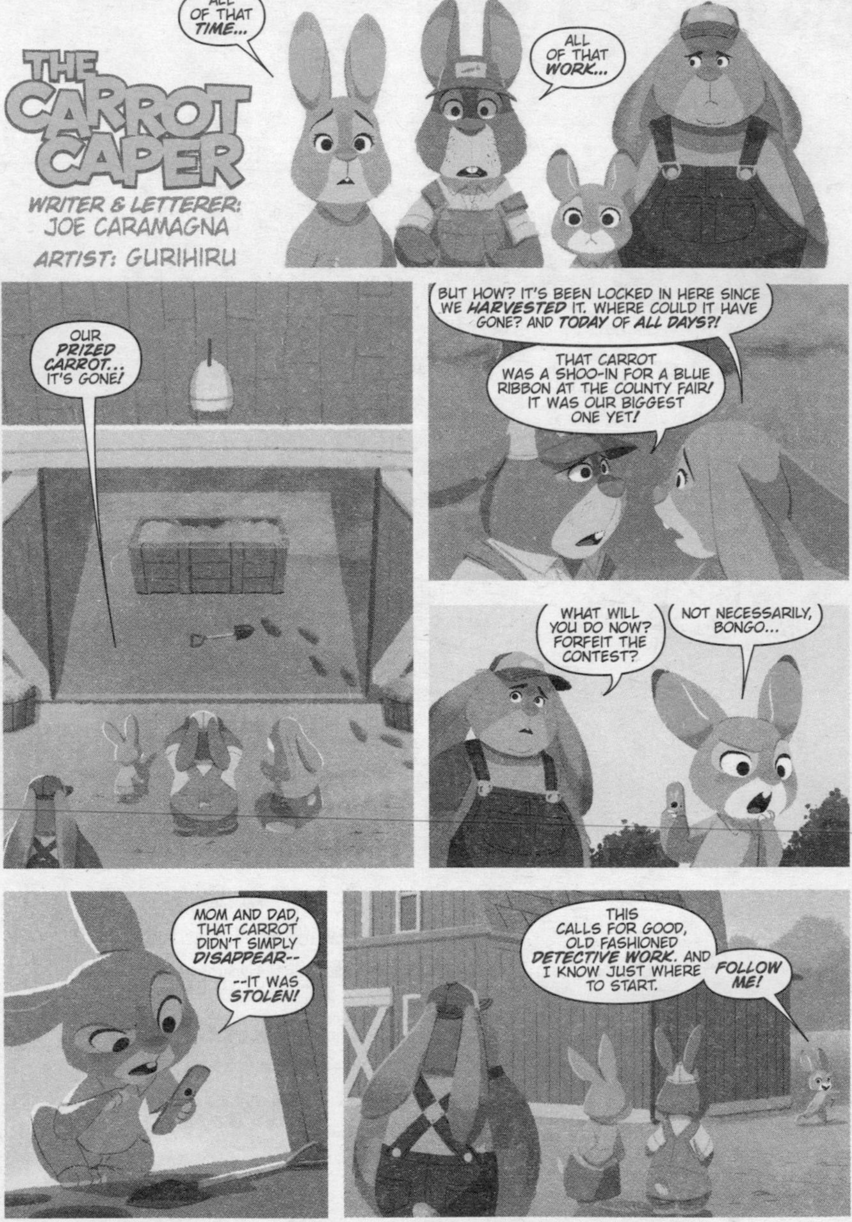
THE CARROT CAPER
WRITER & LETTERER: JOE CARAMAGNA
ARTIST: GURIHIRU
ALL OF THAT TIME...
ALL OF THAT WORK...
OUR PRIZED CARROT... IT'S GONE!
BUT HOW? IT'S BEEN LOCKED IN HERE SINCE WE HARVESTED IT. WHERE COULD IT HAVE GONE? AND TODAY OF ALL DAYS?!
THAT CARROT WAS A SHOO-IN FOR A BLUE RIBBON AT THE COUNTY FAIR! IT WAS OUR BIGGEST ONE YET!
WHAT WILL YOU DO NOW? FORFEIT THE CONTEST?
NOT NECESSARILY, BONGO...
MOM AND DAD, THAT CARROT DIDN'T SIMPLY DISAPPEAR--
--IT WAS STOLEN!
THIS CALLS FOR GOOD, OLD FASHIONED DETECTIVE WORK. AND I KNOW JUST WHERE TO START.
FOLLOW ME!

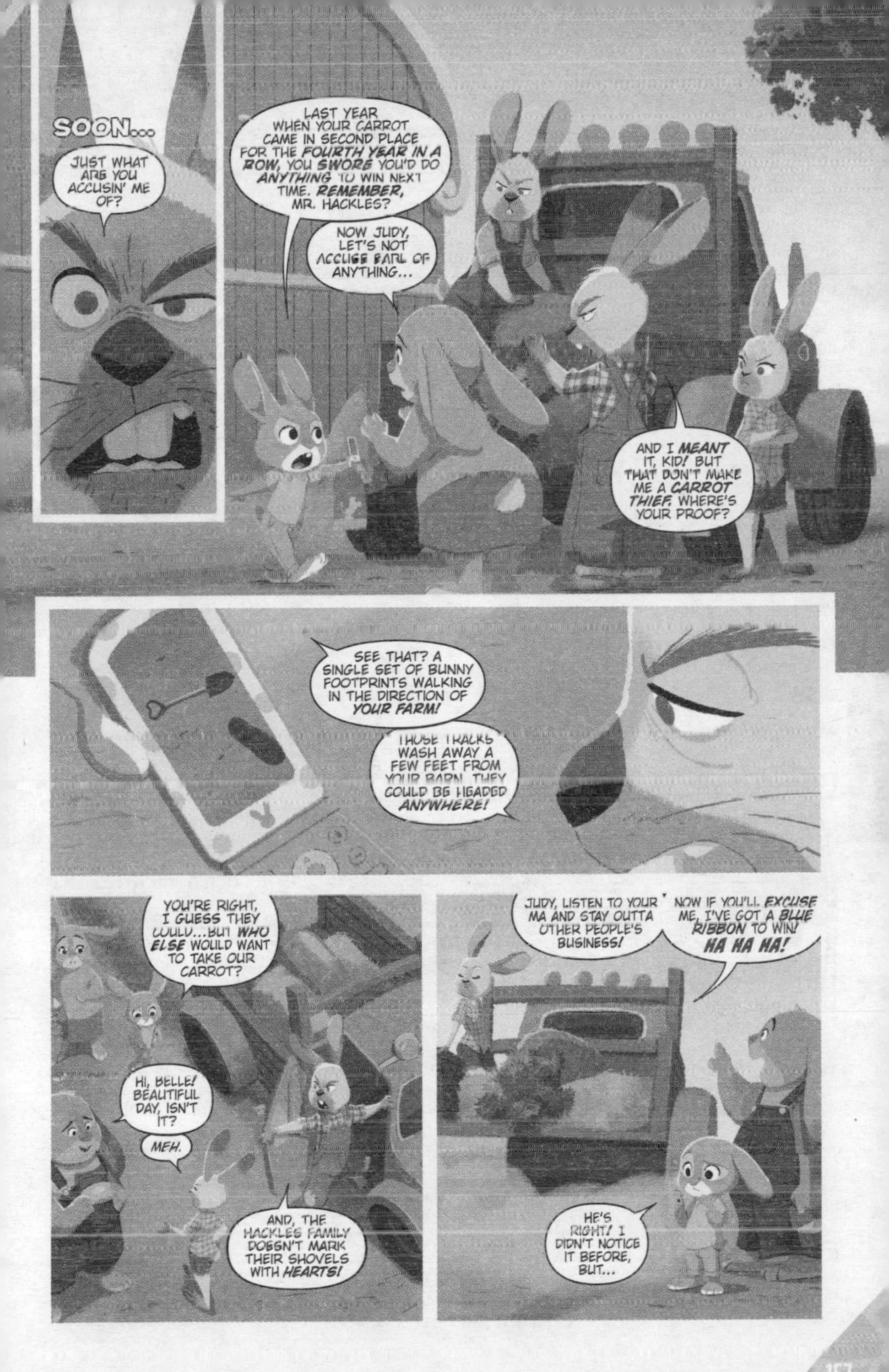
SOON...
JUST WHAT ARE YOU ACCUSIN' ME OF?
LAST YEAR WHEN YOUR CARROT CAME IN SECOND PLACE FOR THE FOURTH YEAR IN A ROW, YOU SWORE YOU'D DO ANYTHING TO WIN NEXT TIME. REMEMBER, MR. HACKLES?
NOW JUDY, LET'S NOT ACCUSE EARL OF ANYTHING...
AND I MEANT IT, KID! BUT THAT DON'T MAKE ME A CARROT THIEF. WHERE'S YOUR PROOF?
SEE THAT? A SINGLE SET OF BUNNY FOOTPRINTS WALKING IN THE DIRECTION OF YOUR FARM!
THOSE TRACKS WASH AWAY A FEW FEET FROM YOUR BARN. THEY COULD BE HEADED ANYWHERE!
YOU'RE RIGHT, I GUESS THEY COULD...BUT WHO ELSE WOULD WANT TO TAKE OUR CARROT?
HI, BELLE! BEAUTIFUL DAY, ISN'T IT?
MEH.
AND, THE HACKLES FAMILY DOESN'T MARK THEIR SHOVELS WITH HEARTS!
JUDY, LISTEN TO YOUR MA AND STAY OUTTA OTHER PEOPLE'S BUSINESS!
NOW IF YOU'LL EXCUSE ME, I'VE GOT A BLUE RIBBON TO WIN! HA HA HA!
HE'S RIGHT! I DIDN'T NOTICE IT BEFORE, BUT...

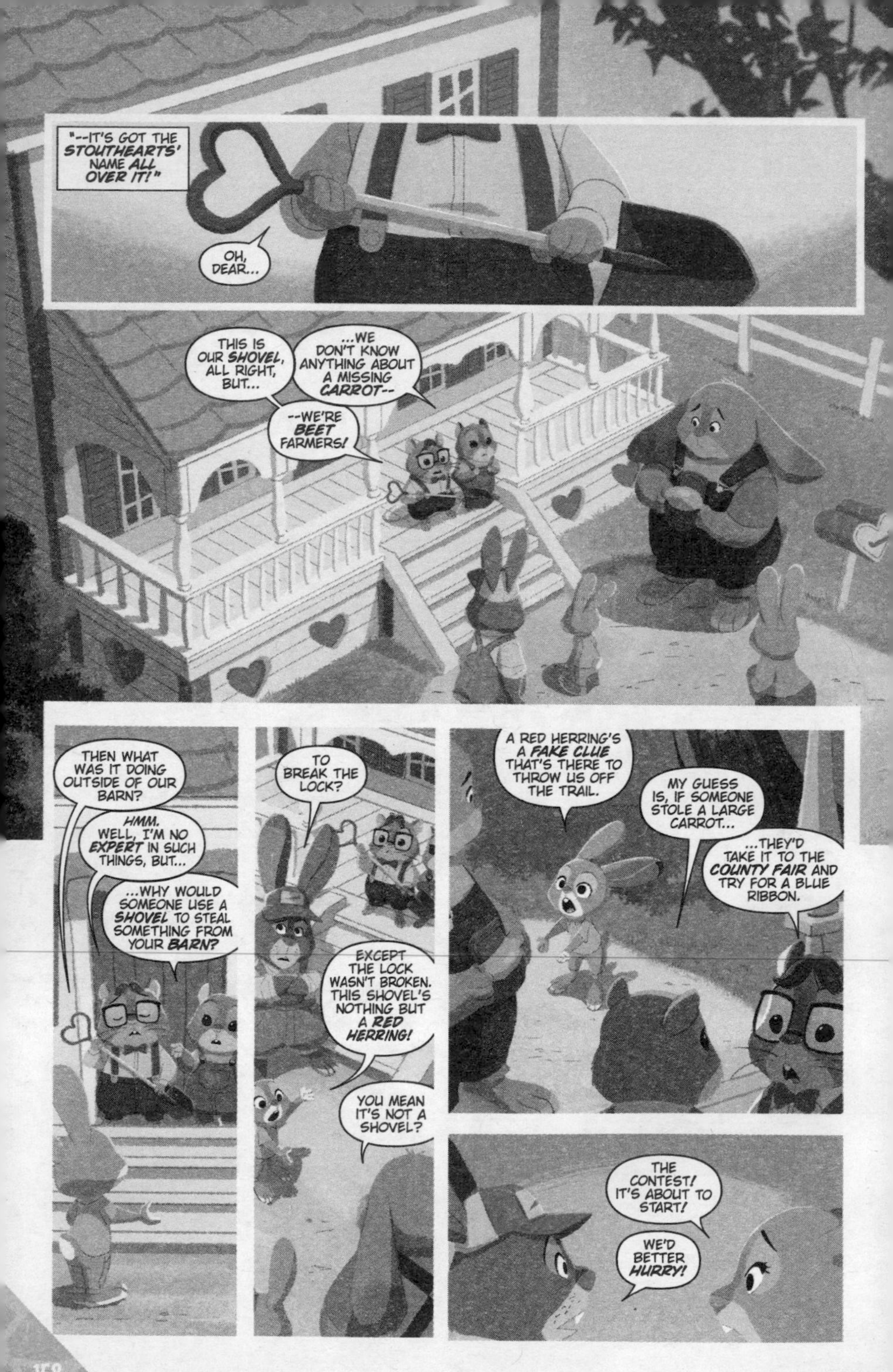
"--IT'S GOT THE STOUTHEARTS' NAME ALL OVER IT!"
OH, DEAR...
THIS IS OUR SHOVEL, ALL RIGHT, BUT...
...WE DON'T KNOW ANYTHING ABOUT A MISSING CARROT--
--WE'RE BEET FARMERS!
THEN WHAT WAS IT DOING OUTSIDE OF OUR BARN?
HMM. WELL, I'M NO EXPERT IN SUCH THINGS, BUT...
...WHY WOULD SOMEONE USE A SHOVEL TO STEAL SOMETHING FROM YOUR BARN?
TO BREAK THE LOCK?
EXCEPT THE LOCK WASN'T BROKEN. THIS SHOVEL'S NOTHING BUT A RED HERRING!
YOU MEAN IT'S NOT A SHOVEL?
A RED HERRING'S A FAKE CLUE THAT'S THERE TO THROW US OFF THE TRAIL.
MY GUESS IS, IF SOMEONE STOLE A LARGE CARROT...
...THEY'D TAKE IT TO THE COUNTY FAIR AND TRY FOR A BLUE RIBBON.
THE CONTEST! IT'S ABOUT TO START!
WE'D BETTER HURRY!

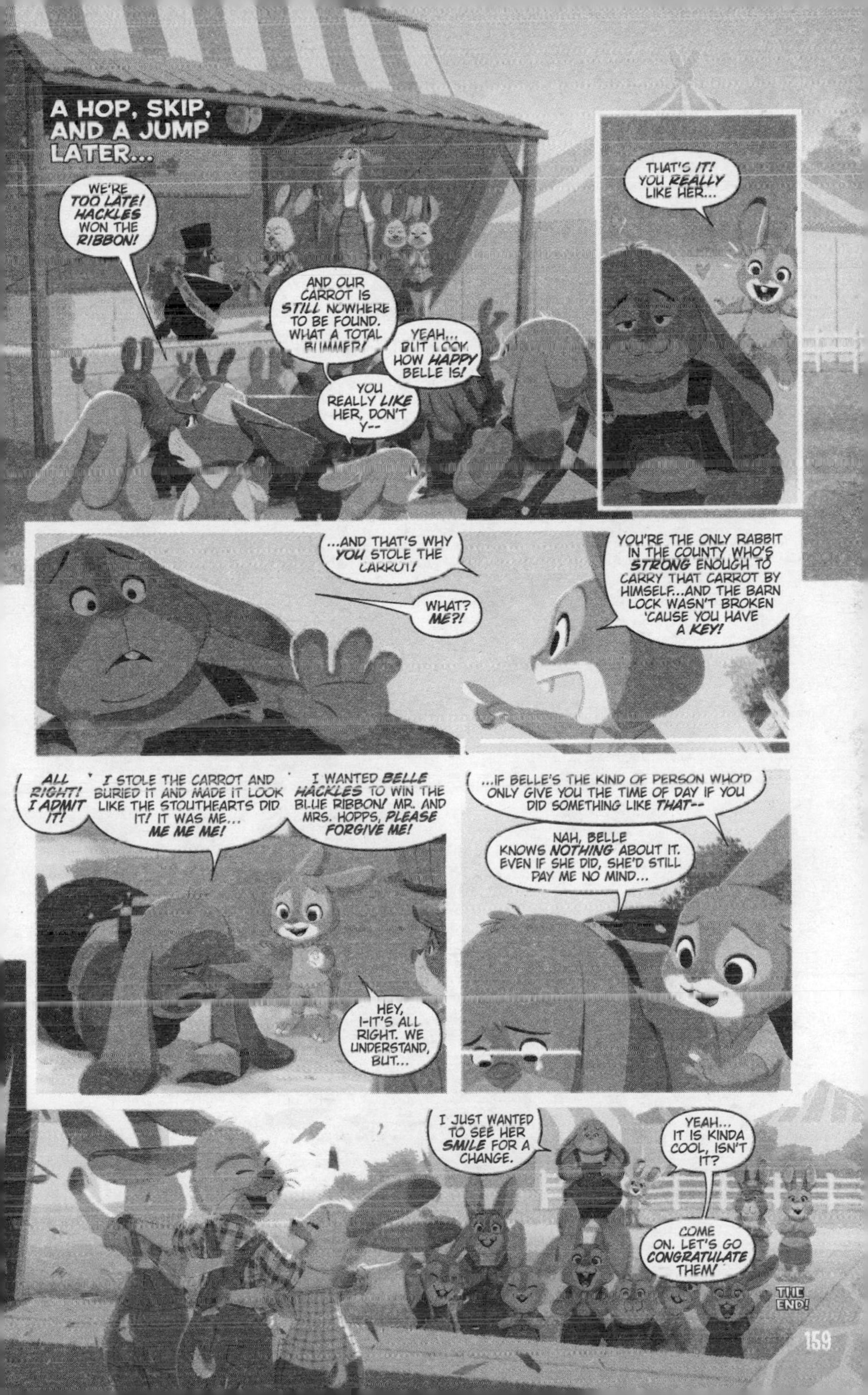
A HOP, SKIP, AND A JUMP LATER...
WE'RE TOO LATE! HACKLES WON THE RIBBON!
AND OUR CARROT IS STILL NOWHERE TO BE FOUND. WHAT A TOTAL BUMMER!
YEAH... BUT LOOK HOW HAPPY BELLE IS!
YOU REALLY LIKE HER, DON'T Y--
THAT'S IT! YOU REALLY LIKE HER...
...AND THAT'S WHY YOU STOLE THE CARROT!
WHAT? ME?!
YOU'RE THE ONLY RABBIT IN THE COUNTY WHO'S STRONG ENOUGH TO CARRY THAT CARROT BY HIMSELF...AND THE BARN LOCK WASN'T BROKEN 'CAUSE YOU HAVE A KEY!
ALL RIGHT! I ADMIT IT!
I STOLE THE CARROT AND BURIED IT AND MADE IT LOOK LIKE THE STOUTHEARTS DID IT! IT WAS ME... ME ME ME!
I WANTED BELLE HACKLES TO WIN THE BLUE RIBBON! MR. AND MRS. HOPPS, PLEASE FORGIVE ME!
HEY, I-IT'S ALL RIGHT. WE UNDERSTAND, BUT...
...IF BELLE'S THE KIND OF PERSON WHO'D ONLY GIVE YOU THE TIME OF DAY IF YOU DID SOMETHING LIKE THAT--
NAH, BELLE KNOWS NOTHING ABOUT IT. EVEN IF SHE DID, SHE'D STILL PAY ME NO MIND...
I JUST WANTED TO SEE HER SMILE FOR A CHANGE.
YEAH... IT IS KINDA COOL, ISN'T IT?
COME ON. LET'S GO CONGRATULATE THEM!
THE END!

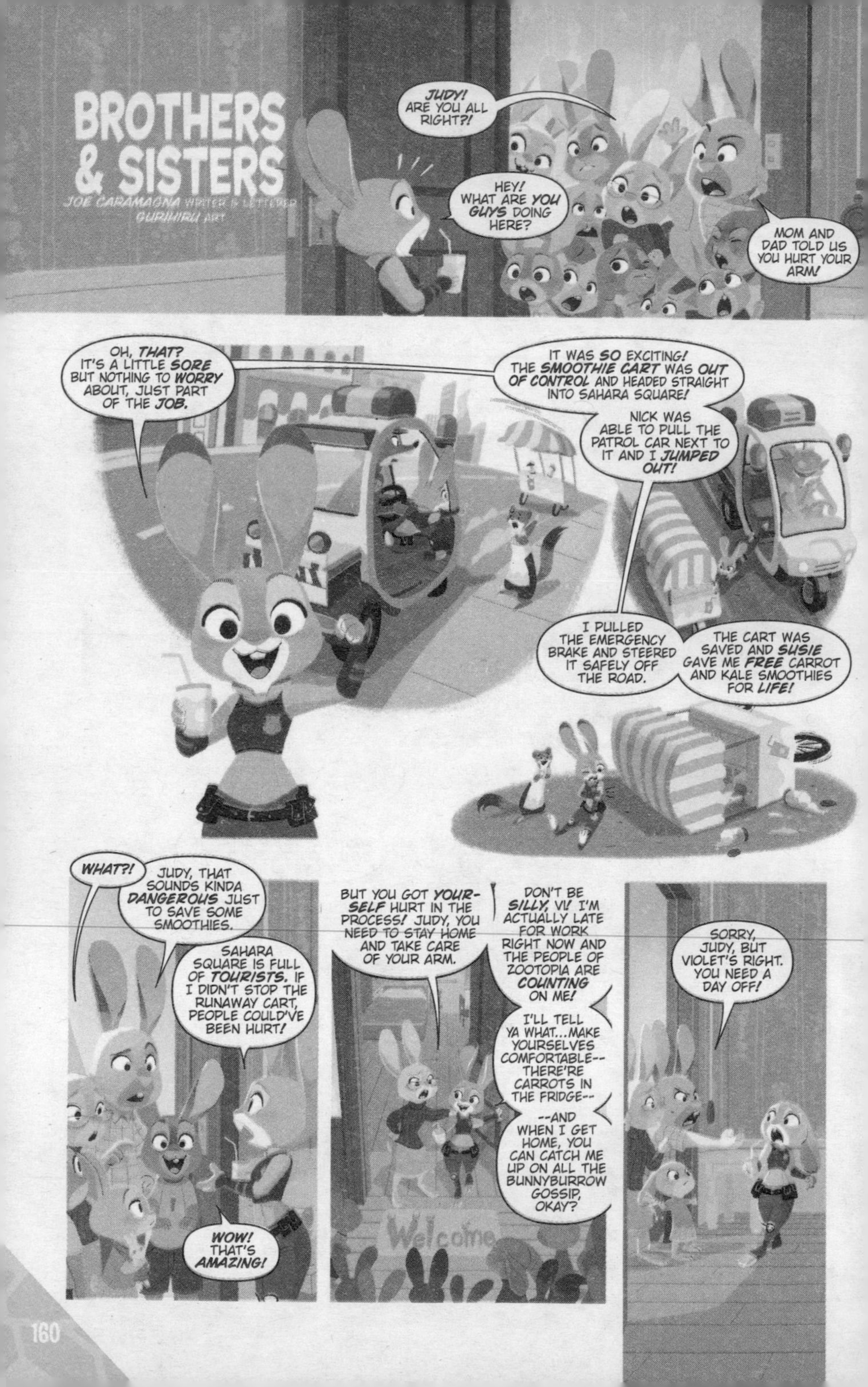
BROTHERS & SISTERS
JOE CARAMAGNA WRITER & LETTERER
GURIHIRU ART
JUDY! ARE YOU ALL RIGHT?!
HEY! WHAT ARE YOU GUYS DOING HERE?
MOM AND DAD TOLD US YOU HURT YOUR ARM!
OH, THAT? IT'S A LITTLE SORE BUT NOTHING TO WORRY ABOUT, JUST PART OF THE JOB.
IT WAS SO EXCITING! THE SMOOTHIE CART WAS OUT OF CONTROL AND HEADED STRAIGHT INTO SAHARA SQUARE!
NICK WAS ABLE TO PULL THE PATROL CAR NEXT TO IT AND I JUMPED OUT!
I PULLED THE EMERGENCY BRAKE AND STEERED IT SAFELY OFF THE ROAD.
THE CART WAS SAVED AND SUSIE GAVE ME FREE CARROT AND KALE SMOOTHIES FOR LIFE!
WHAT?!
JUDY, THAT SOUNDS KINDA DANGEROUS JUST TO SAVE SOME SMOOTHIES.
SAHARA SQUARE IS FULL OF TOURISTS. IF I DIDN'T STOP THE RUNAWAY CART, PEOPLE COULD'VE BEEN HURT!
WOW! THAT'S AMAZING!
BUT YOU GOT YOURSELF HURT IN THE PROCESS! JUDY, YOU NEED TO STAY HOME AND TAKE CARE OF YOUR ARM.
DON'T BE SILLY, VI! I'M ACTUALLY LATE FOR WORK RIGHT NOW AND THE PEOPLE OF ZOOTOPIA ARE COUNTING ON ME!
I'LL TELL YA WHAT...MAKE YOURSELVES COMFORTABLE-- THERE'RE CARROTS IN THE FRIDGE--
--AND WHEN I GET HOME, YOU CAN CATCH ME UP ON ALL THE BUNNYBURROW GOSSIP, OKAY?
Welcome
SORRY, JUDY, BUT VIOLET'S RIGHT. YOU NEED A DAY OFF!

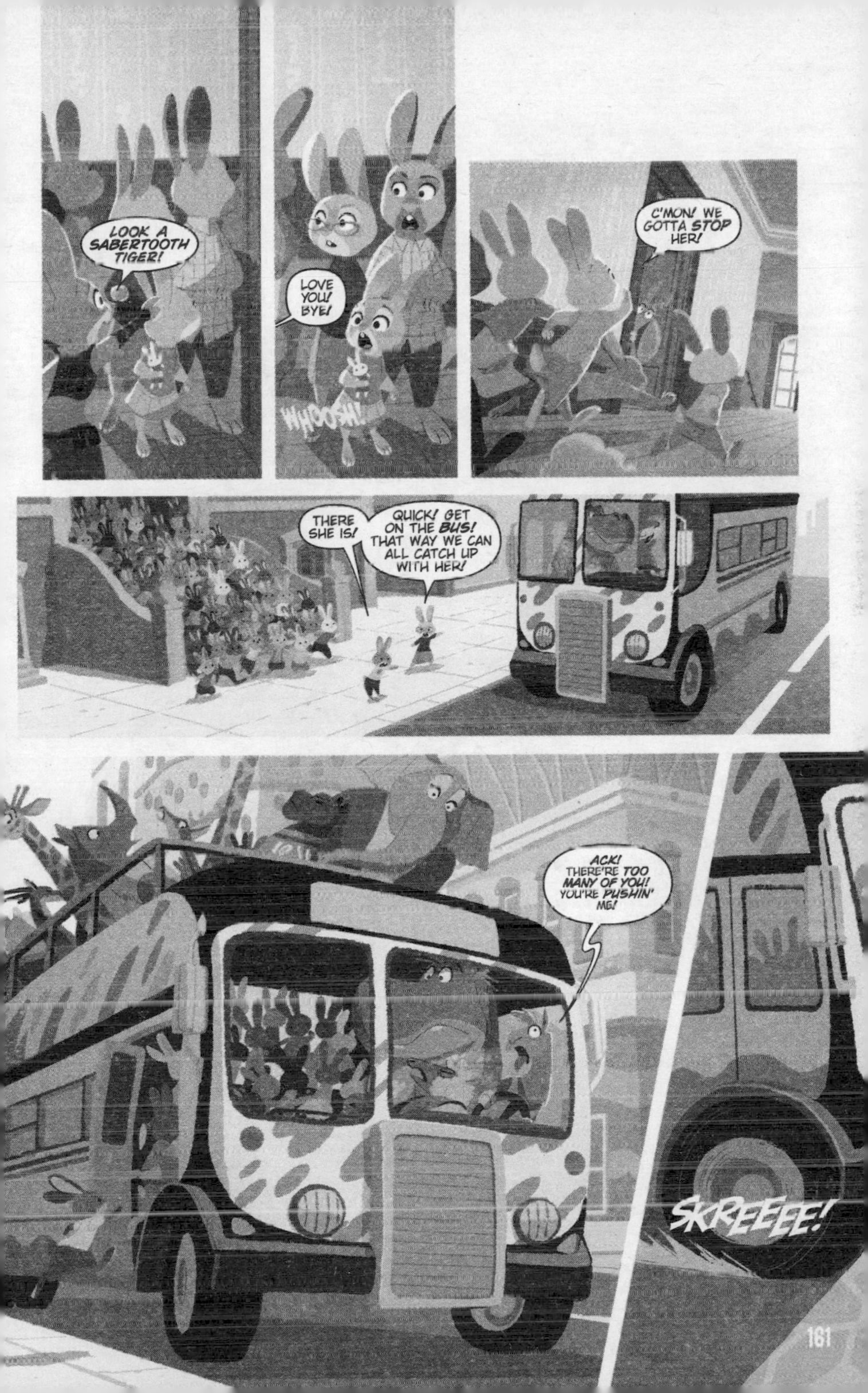
LOOK A SABERTOOTH TIGER!
LOVE YOU! BYE!
WHOOSH!
C'MON! WE GOTTA STOP HER!
THERE SHE IS!
QUICK! GET ON THE BUS! THAT WAY WE CAN ALL CATCH UP WITH HER!
ACK! THERE'RE TOO MANY OF YOU! YOU'RE PUSHIN' ME!
SKREEEEE!

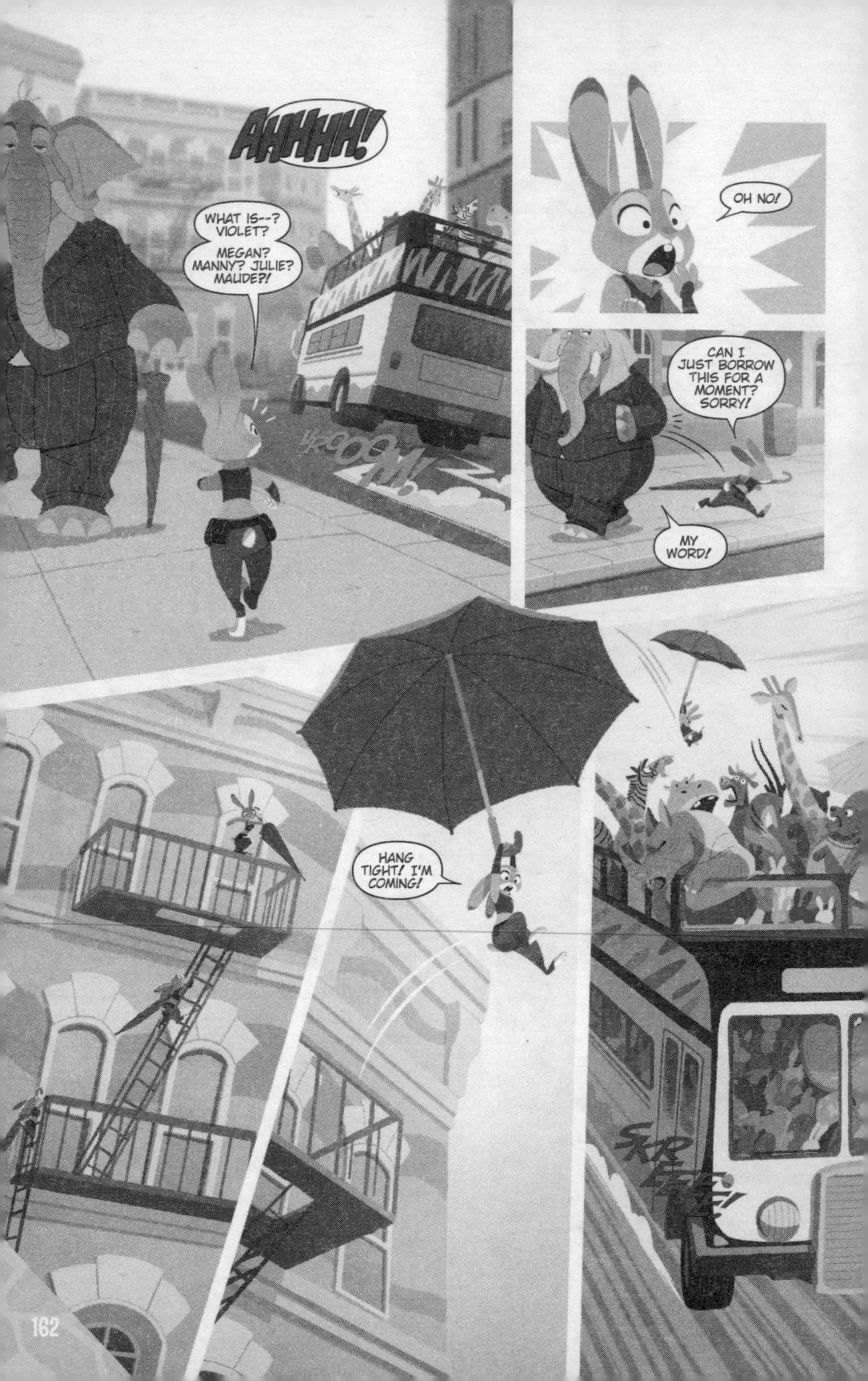
AHHHH!
WHAT IS--? VIOLET? MEGAN? MANNY? JULIE? MAUDE?!
VROOOOM!
OH NO!
CAN I JUST BORROW THIS FOR A MOMENT? SORRY!
MY WORD!
HANG TIGHT! I'M COMING!
SKREEEE!

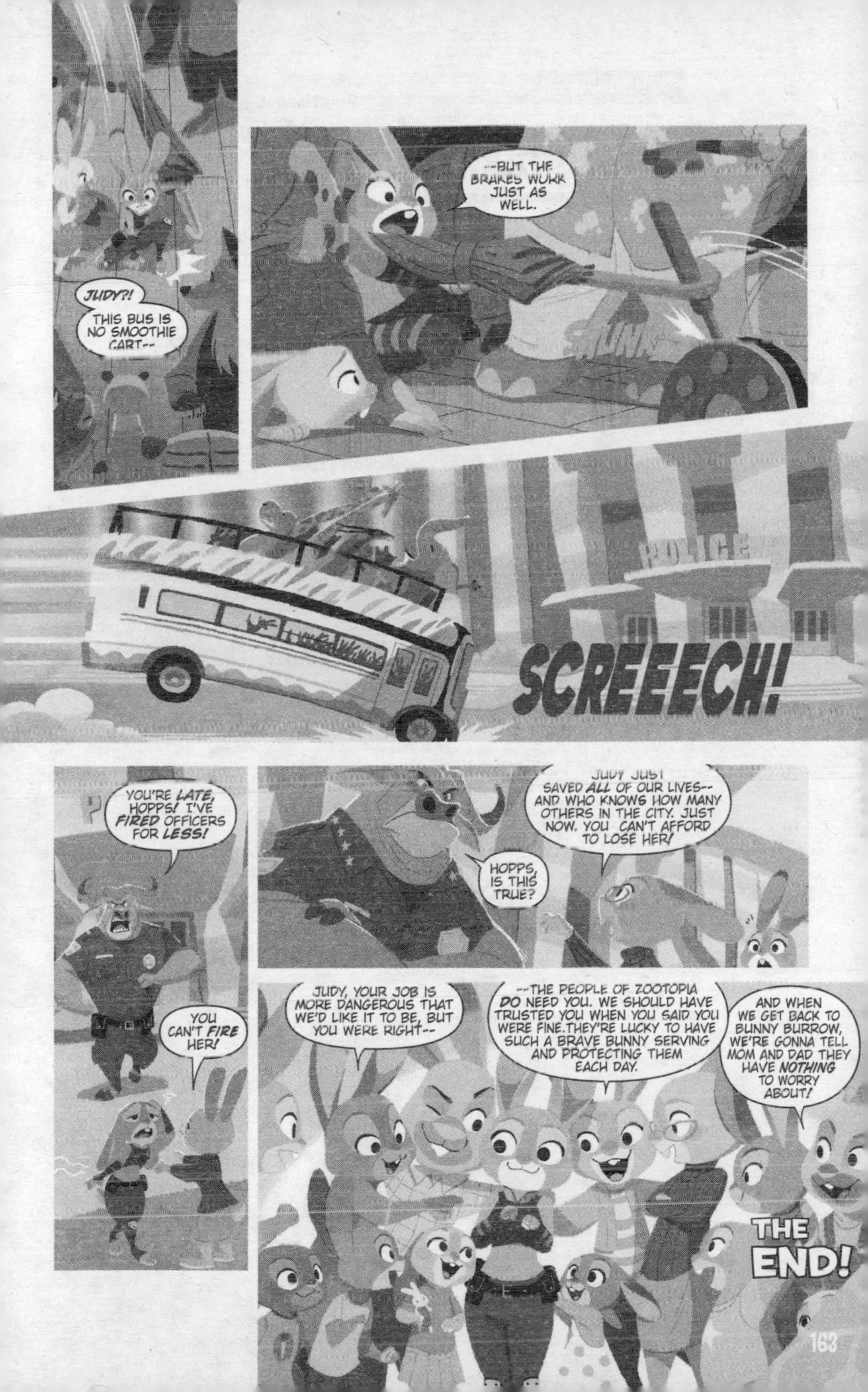
JUDY?!
THIS BUS IS NO SMOOTHIE CART--
--BUT THE BRAKES WORK JUST AS WELL.
SCREEECH!
POLICE
YOU'RE LATE, HOPPS! I'VE FIRED OFFICERS FOR LESS!
YOU CAN'T FIRE HER!
HOPPS, IS THIS TRUE?
JUDY JUST SAVED ALL OF OUR LIVES--AND WHO KNOWS HOW MANY OTHERS IN THE CITY. JUST NOW. YOU CAN'T AFFORD TO LOSE HER!
JUDY, YOUR JOB IS MORE DANGEROUS THAT WE'D LIKE IT TO BE, BUT YOU WERE RIGHT--
--THE PEOPLE OF ZOOTOPIA DO NEED YOU. WE SHOULD HAVE TRUSTED YOU WHEN YOU SAID YOU WERE FINE. THEY'RE LUCKY TO HAVE SUCH A BRAVE BUNNY SERVING AND PROTECTING THEM EACH DAY.
AND WHEN WE GET BACK TO BUNNY BURROW, WE'RE GONNA TELL MOM AND DAD THEY HAVE NOTHING TO WORRY ABOUT!
THE END!

ZOOTOPIA

SAHARA SQUARE

Separated from Tundratown by a climate wall, Sahara Square is a desert oasis and popular resort destination. It's a vacation spot for both Zootopians and tourists. Two of the area's hottest spots are the Palm Hotel and the Mystic Spring Oasis.

Local FAVES

What to Do:
- VISIT THE SUNDAY MEERKAT MARKET FOR LIVE MUSIC AND TASTY TREATS

Where to Relax:
- MYSTIC SPRING OASIS

Where to Stay:
- THE PALM HOTEL

The possibilities for fun and entertainment are limitless in Sahara Square. But Nick and Judy don't come here for play—they get an important lead in their case that brings them here.

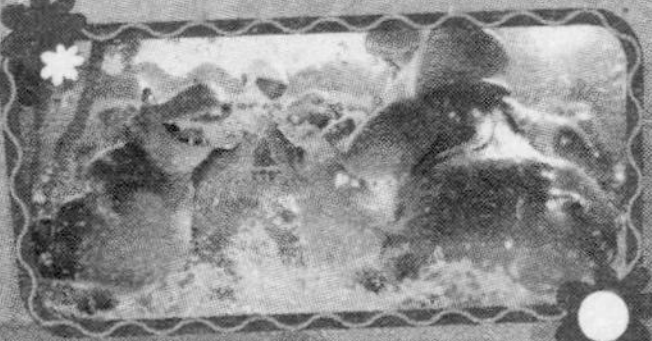

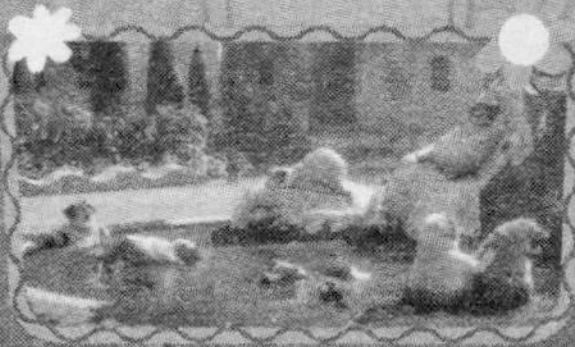

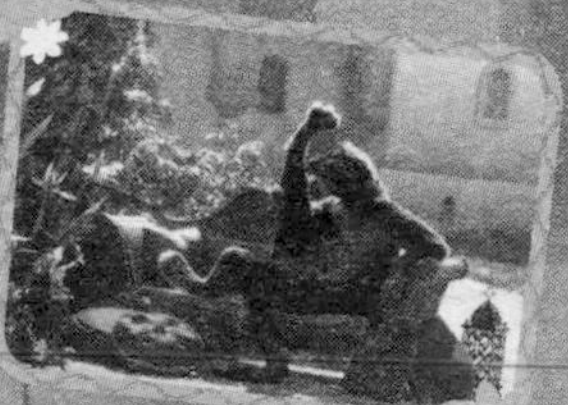

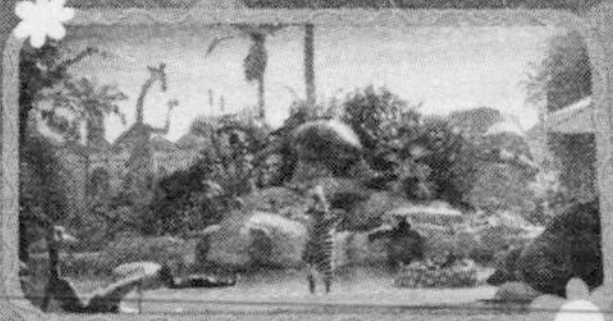

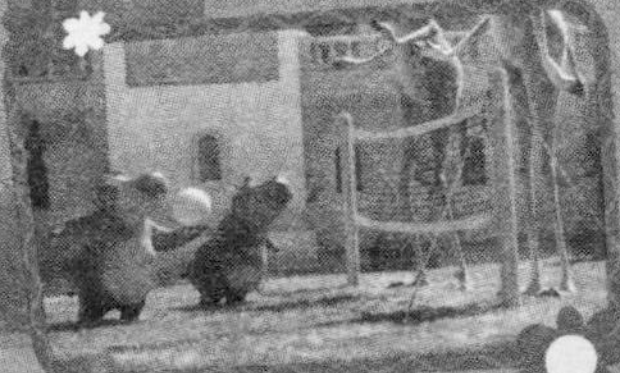

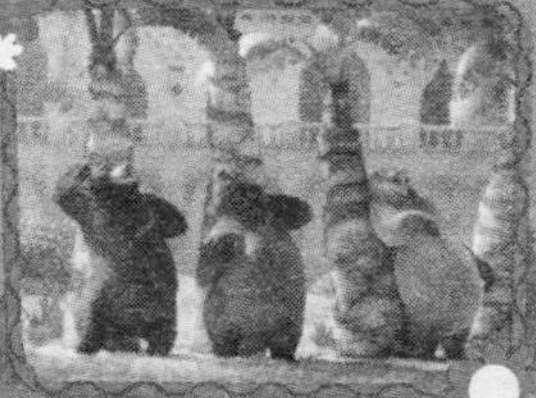

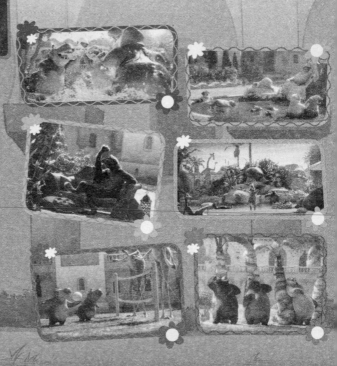

Zootopians sometimes need to escape the stress of big-city life. One place to find peace in Zootopia is at Mystic Spring Oasis, the naturalist club. Here, animals can take a yoga class, relax in the pool and are free to be themselves! Guests at Mystic Spring don't even need to wear clothes! Judy and Nick pay a visit to Mystic Spring Oasis, where missing Emmitt Otterton liked to go to relax. There they meet Yax and Nangi, who turn out to be very helpful!

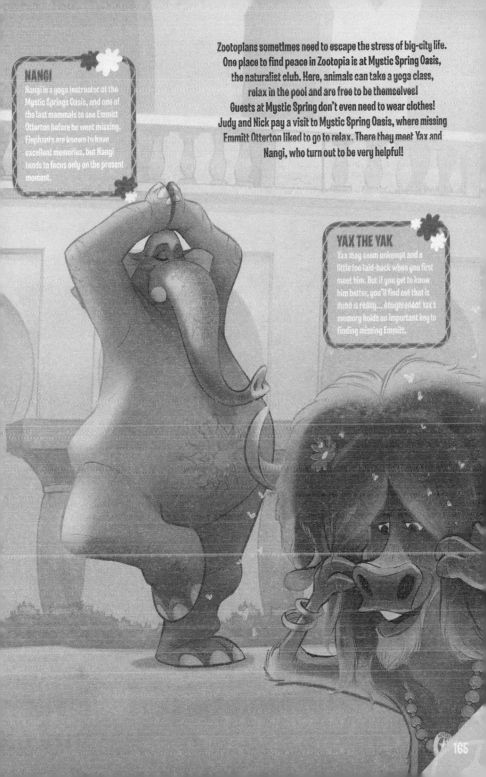

NANGI

Nangi is a yoga instructor at the Mystic Springs Oasis, and one of the last mammals to see Emmitt Otterton before he went missing. Elephants are known to have excellent memories, but Nangi tends to focus only on the present moment.

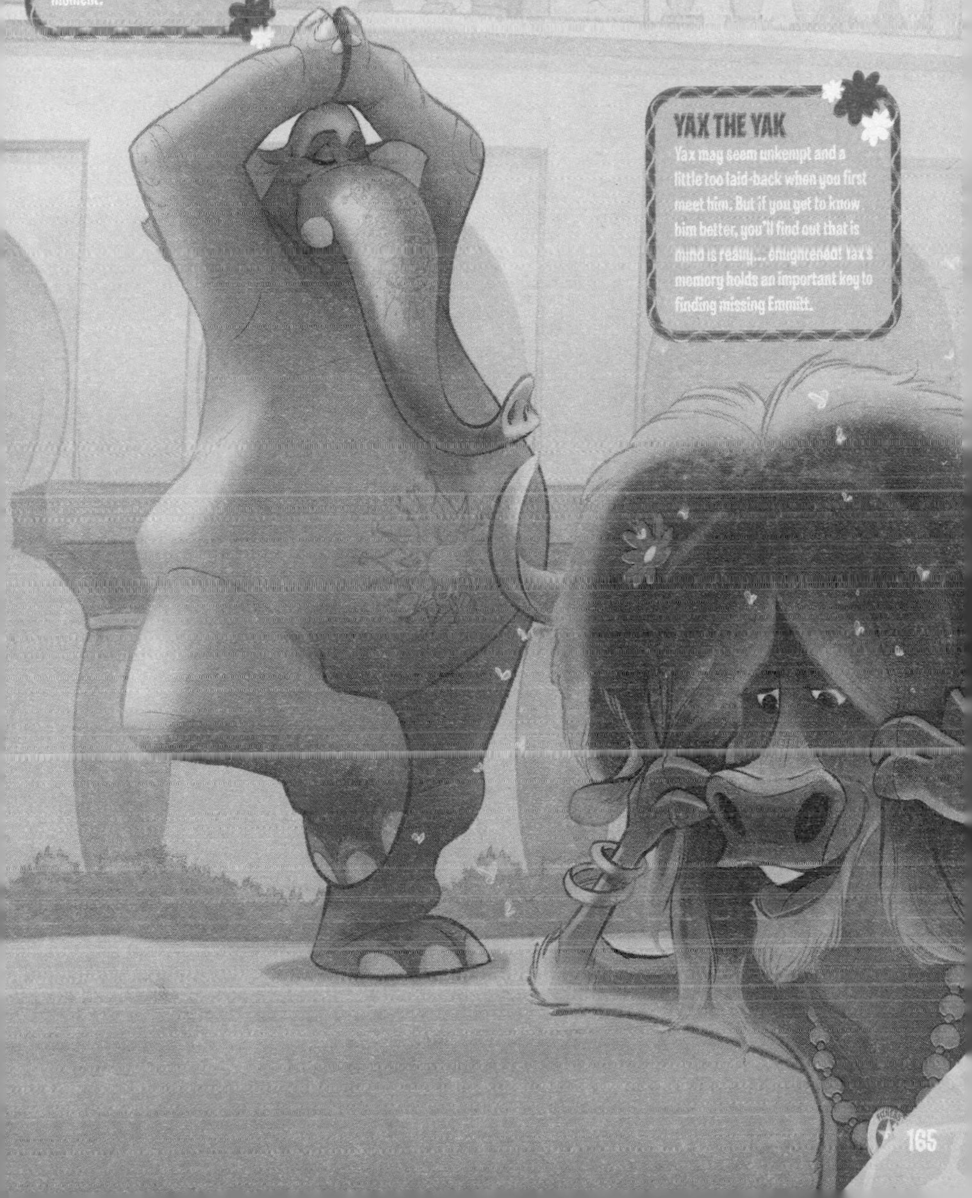

YAX THE YAK

Yax may seem unkempt and a little too laid-back when you first meet him. But if you get to know him better, you'll find out that is mind is really... enlightened! Yax's memory holds an important key to finding missing Emmitt.

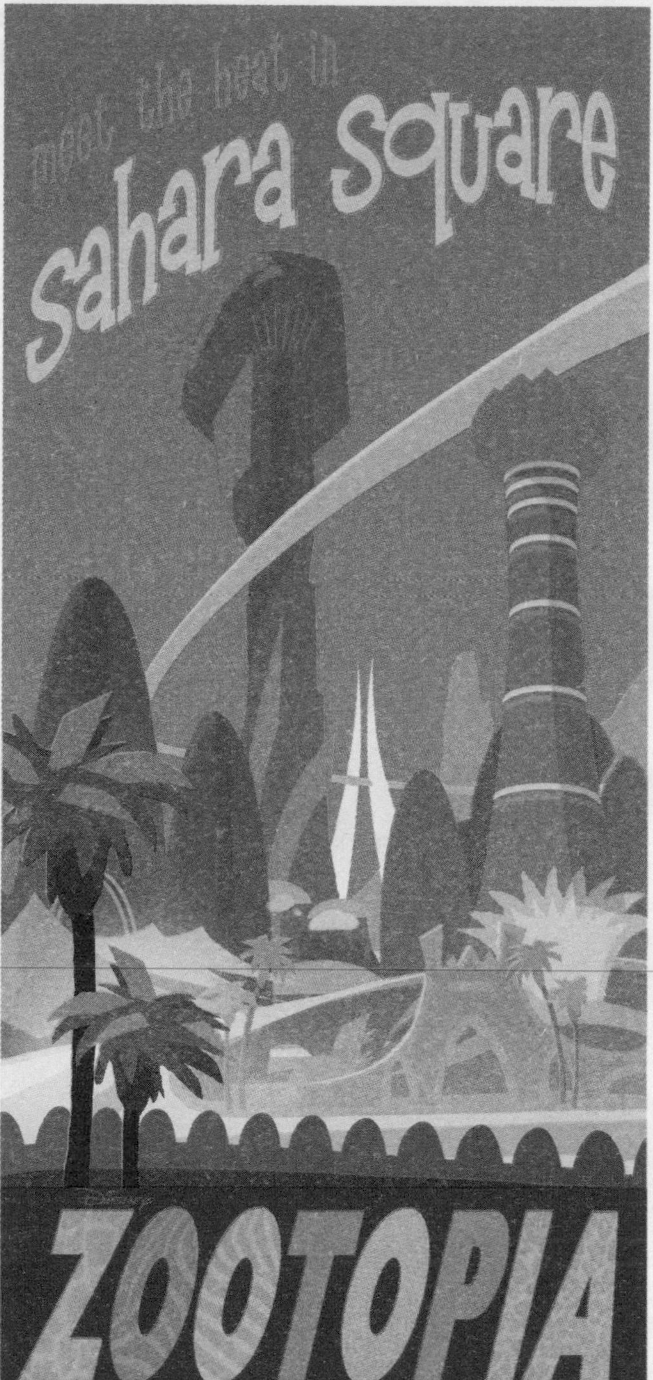
meet the heat in
sahara square
ZOOTOPIA

The Heat Is On In SAHARA SQUARE!

WEATHER REPORT!

Today's weather in SAHARA SQUARE is 95% chance of HOT! HOT! HOT! sun and clear skies! Actually, it's 99%! Okay, it's 100%.

Here in Sahara Square, the days are so hot, most of the residents prefer the exciting nightlife instead! Stay at the world-famous PALM HOTEL! Enjoy the casinos, the Meerkat Market and much, much more!

If you need to chill out in the hot daylight, come to the Mystic Springs Oasis and reclaim your natural self! *Dude!*

DID YOU KNOW?

- Sahara Square is made up of sand dunes and buildings that are shaped like sand dunes.
- Sahara Square features a warm palette of reds, oranges and yellows.

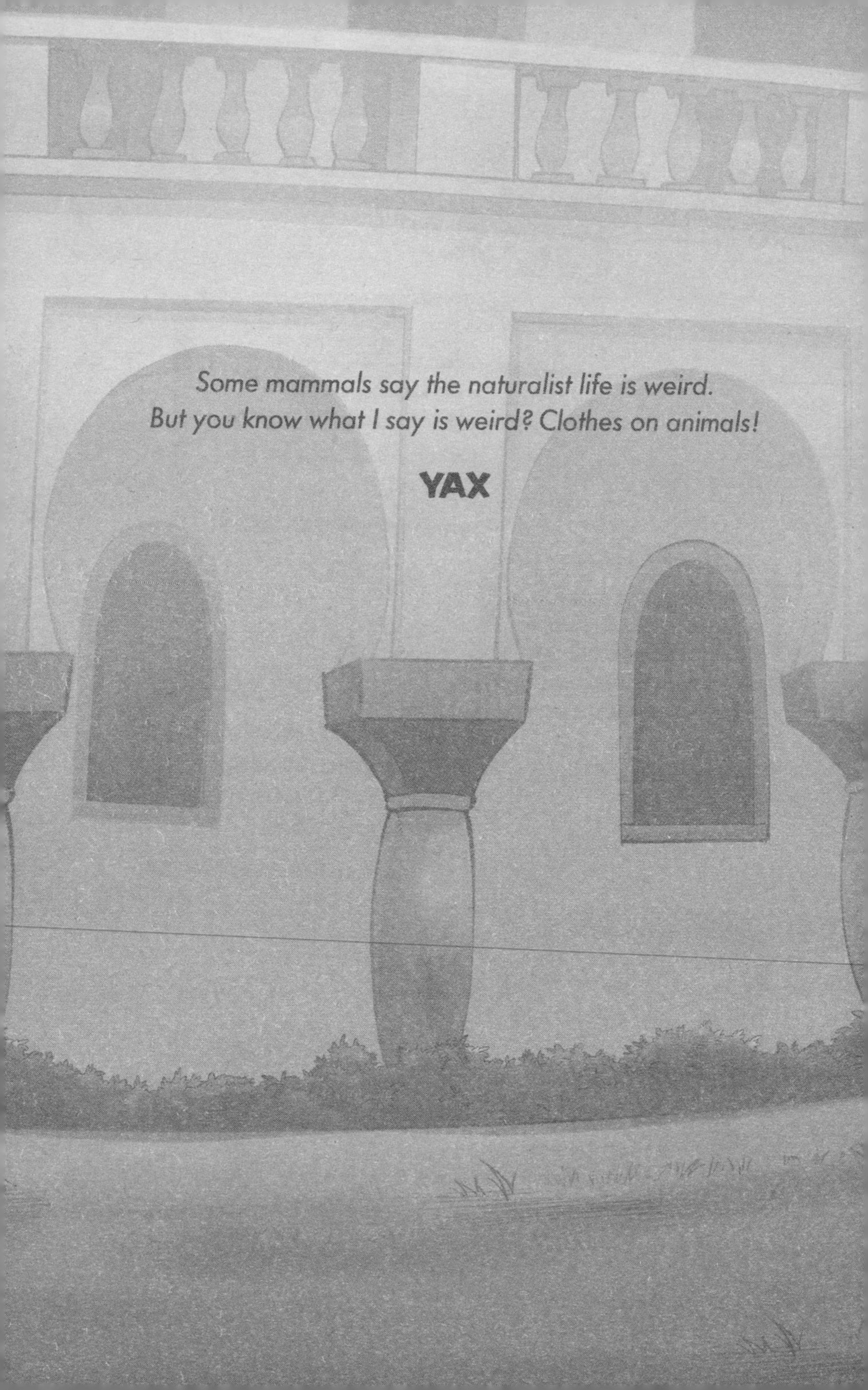

*Some mammals say the naturalist life is weird.
But you know what I say is weird? Clothes on animals!*

YAX

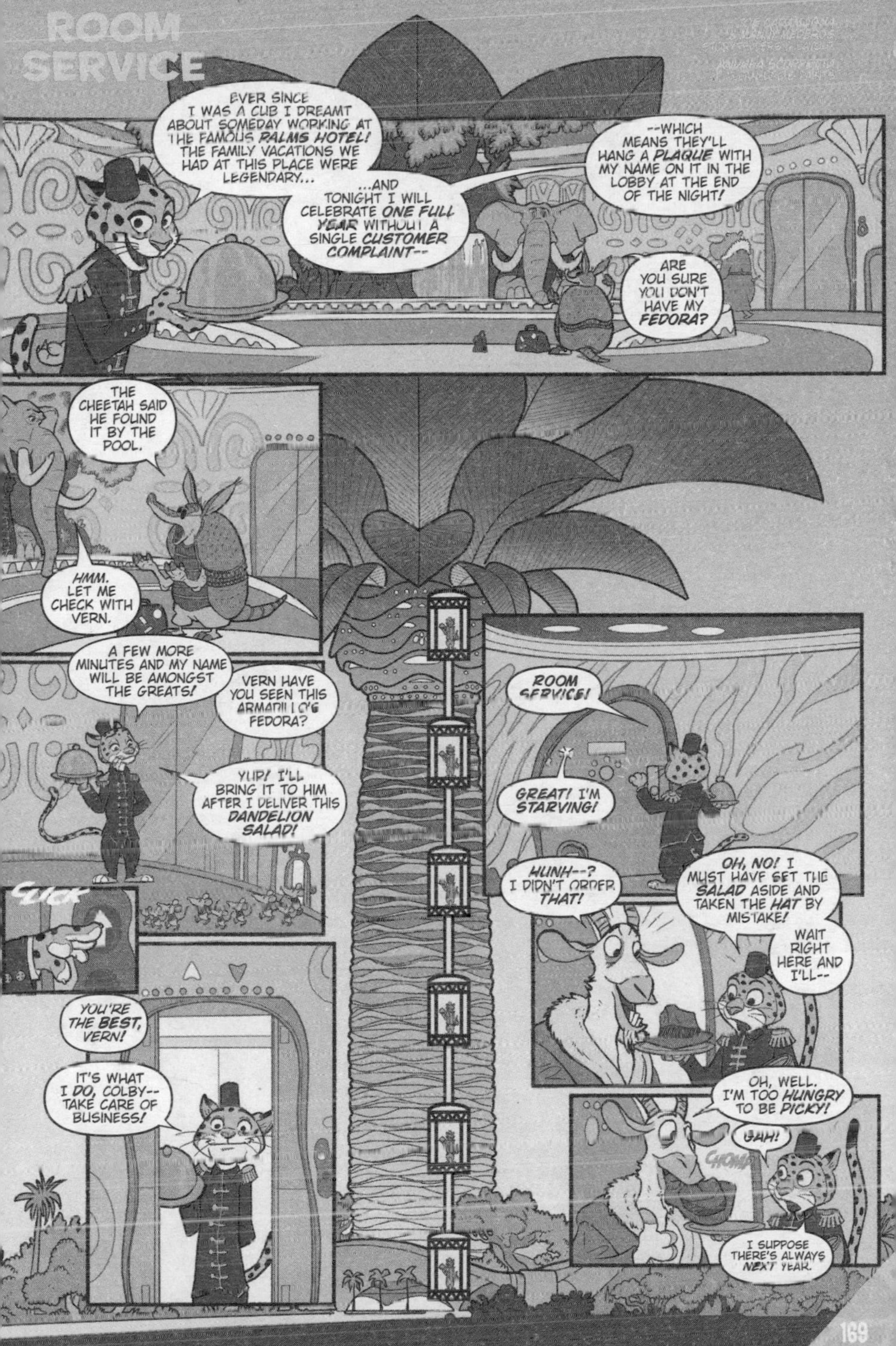
ROOM SERVICE
EVER SINCE I WAS A CUB I DREAMT ABOUT SOMEDAY WORKING AT THE FAMOUS PALMS HOTEL! THE FAMILY VACATIONS WE HAD AT THIS PLACE WERE LEGENDARY...
...AND TONIGHT I WILL CELEBRATE ONE FULL YEAR WITHOUT A SINGLE CUSTOMER COMPLAINT--
--WHICH MEANS THEY'LL HANG A PLAQUE WITH MY NAME ON IT IN THE LOBBY AT THE END OF THE NIGHT!
ARE YOU SURE YOU DON'T HAVE MY FEDORA?
THE CHEETAH SAID HE FOUND IT BY THE POOL.
HMM. LET ME CHECK WITH VERN.
A FEW MORE MINUTES AND MY NAME WILL BE AMONGST THE GREATS!
VERN HAVE YOU SEEN THIS ARMADILLO'S FEDORA?
YUP! I'LL BRING IT TO HIM AFTER I DELIVER THIS DANDELION SALAD!
CLICK
YOU'RE THE BEST, VERN!
IT'S WHAT I DO, COLBY-- TAKE CARE OF BUSINESS!
ROOM SERVICE!
GREAT! I'M STARVING!
HUNH--? I DIDN'T ORDER THAT!
OH, NO! I MUST HAVE SET THE SALAD ASIDE AND TAKEN THE HAT BY MISTAKE!
WAIT RIGHT HERE AND I'LL--
OH, WELL. I'M TOO HUNGRY TO BE PICKY!
GAH!
CHOMP
I SUPPOSE THERE'S ALWAYS NEXT YEAR.

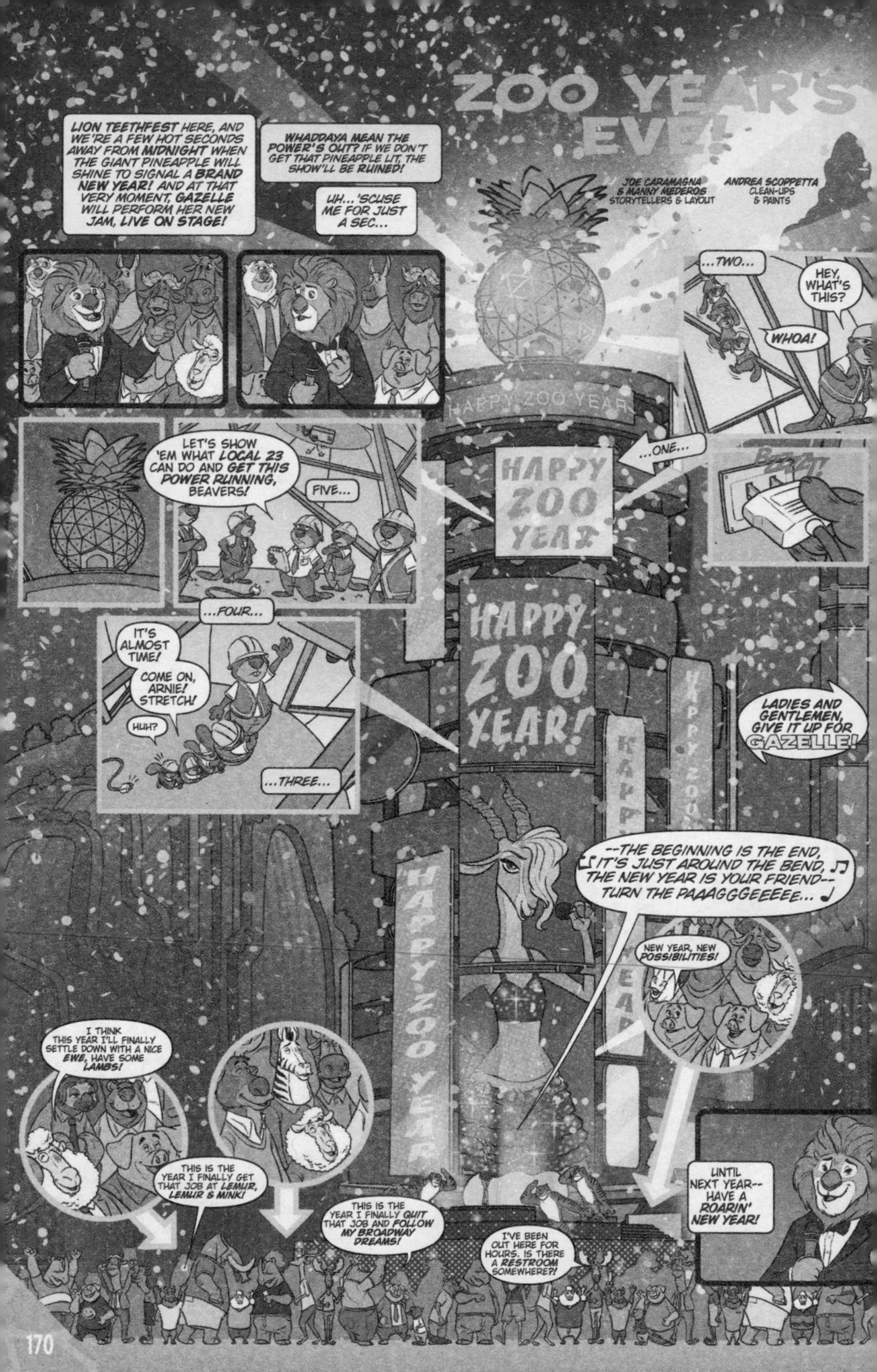
ZOO YEAR'S EVE!
JOE CARAMAGNA & MANNY MEDEROS STORYTELLERS & LAYOUT
ANDREA SCOPPETTA CLEAN-UPS & PAINTS
LION TEETHFEST HERE, AND WE'RE A FEW HOT SECONDS AWAY FROM MIDNIGHT WHEN THE GIANT PINEAPPLE WILL SHINE TO SIGNAL A BRAND NEW YEAR! AND AT THAT VERY MOMENT, GAZELLE WILL PERFORM HER NEW JAM, LIVE ON STAGE!
WHADDAYA MEAN THE POWER'S OUT? IF WE DON'T GET THAT PINEAPPLE LIT, THE SHOW'LL BE RUINED!
UH... 'SCUSE ME FOR JUST A SEC...
HAPPY ZOO YEAR
LET'S SHOW 'EM WHAT LOCAL 23 CAN DO AND GET THIS POWER RUNNING, BEAVERS!
FIVE...
...FOUR...
IT'S ALMOST TIME!
COME ON, ARNIE! STRETCH!
HUH?
...THREE...
...TWO...
HEY, WHAT'S THIS?
WHOA!
...ONE...
HAPPY ZOO YEAR
HAPPY ZOO YEAR!
LADIES AND GENTLEMEN, GIVE IT UP FOR GAZELLE!
--THE BEGINNING IS THE END, IT'S JUST AROUND THE BEND, THE NEW YEAR IS YOUR FRIEND-- TURN THE PAAAGGGEEEEE...
NEW YEAR, NEW POSSIBILITIES!
I THINK THIS YEAR I'LL FINALLY SETTLE DOWN WITH A NICE EWE, HAVE SOME LAMBS!
THIS IS THE YEAR I FINALLY GET THAT JOB AT LEMUR, LEMUR & MINK!
THIS IS THE YEAR I FINALLY QUIT THAT JOB AND FOLLOW MY BROADWAY DREAMS!
I'VE BEEN OUT HERE FOR HOURS. IS THERE A RESTROOM SOMEWHERE?!
UNTIL NEXT YEAR-- HAVE A ROARIN' NEW YEAR!

LITTLE RODENTIA

DON'T TREAD ON US!

It's your big day! As you get ready to make that mouse your spouse, be sure you brush up that fur! Styling services available only at Mousy's. Exclusive appointments requested and preferred.

The tubes are ready for transit! When you need to get to that big interview with Lemming Brothers, take the tubes today! Your career is sure to shoot ahead!

DID YOU KNOW?

- Little Rodentia is where Zootopia's smallest mammals reside.
- It may be small, but Little Rodentia has all of the big-city luxuries, including a chic hair salon that caters to tiny high-end clientele.

ZOOTOPIA

LITTLE RODENTIA

Little Rodentia is a gated area of Downtown reserved for the tiniest of Zootopia's residents. Here you'll find some of the finest shops and restaurants around. Anyone who's small enough to squeeze inside can experience all the area has to offer.

Local FAVES

Famous Sites:

- THE BIG DONUT

What to Do:

- IF YOU'RE SMALL ENOUGH... GO FOR A STROLL DOWN MAIN STREET AND PICK UP SOME FRESH FRUITS AND VEGGIES ALONG THE WAY

Where to Eat:

- CHEZ CHEEZ

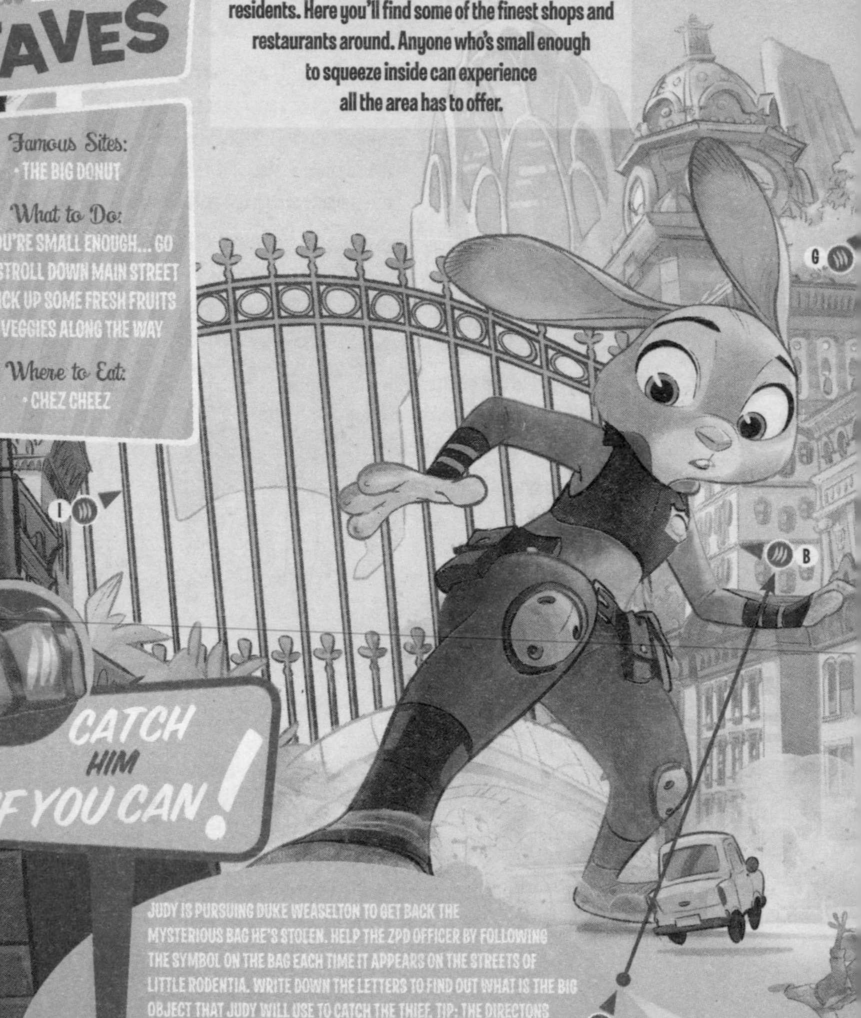
G
I
B
A

CATCH HIM IF YOU CAN!

JUDY IS PURSUING DUKE WEASELTON TO GET BACK THE MYSTERIOUS BAG HE'S STOLEN. HELP THE ZPD OFFICER BY FOLLOWING THE SYMBOL ON THE BAG EACH TIME IT APPEARS ON THE STREETS OF LITTLE RODENTIA. WRITE DOWN THE LETTERS TO FIND OUT WHAT IS THE BIG OBJECT THAT JUDY WILL USE TO CATCH THE THIEF. TIP: THE DIRECTONS OF THE ARROWS WILL LEAD YOU TO THE GOAL. STARTING RIGHT... HERE!

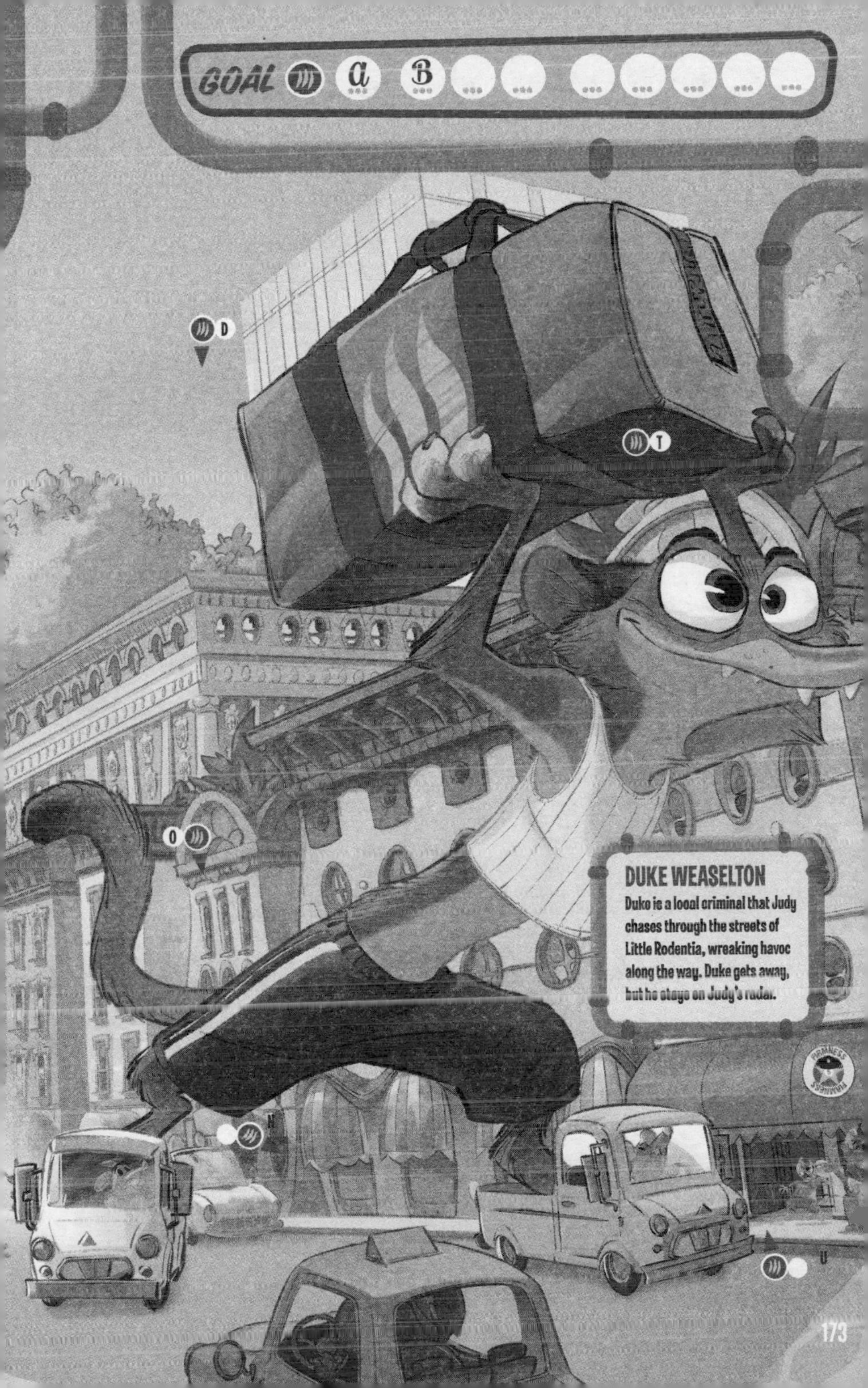
GOAL
a
B
D
T
O
PIRANESS

DUKE WEASELTON

Duke is a local criminal that Judy chases through the streets of Little Rodentia, wreaking havoc along the way. Duke gets away, but he stays on Judy's radar.

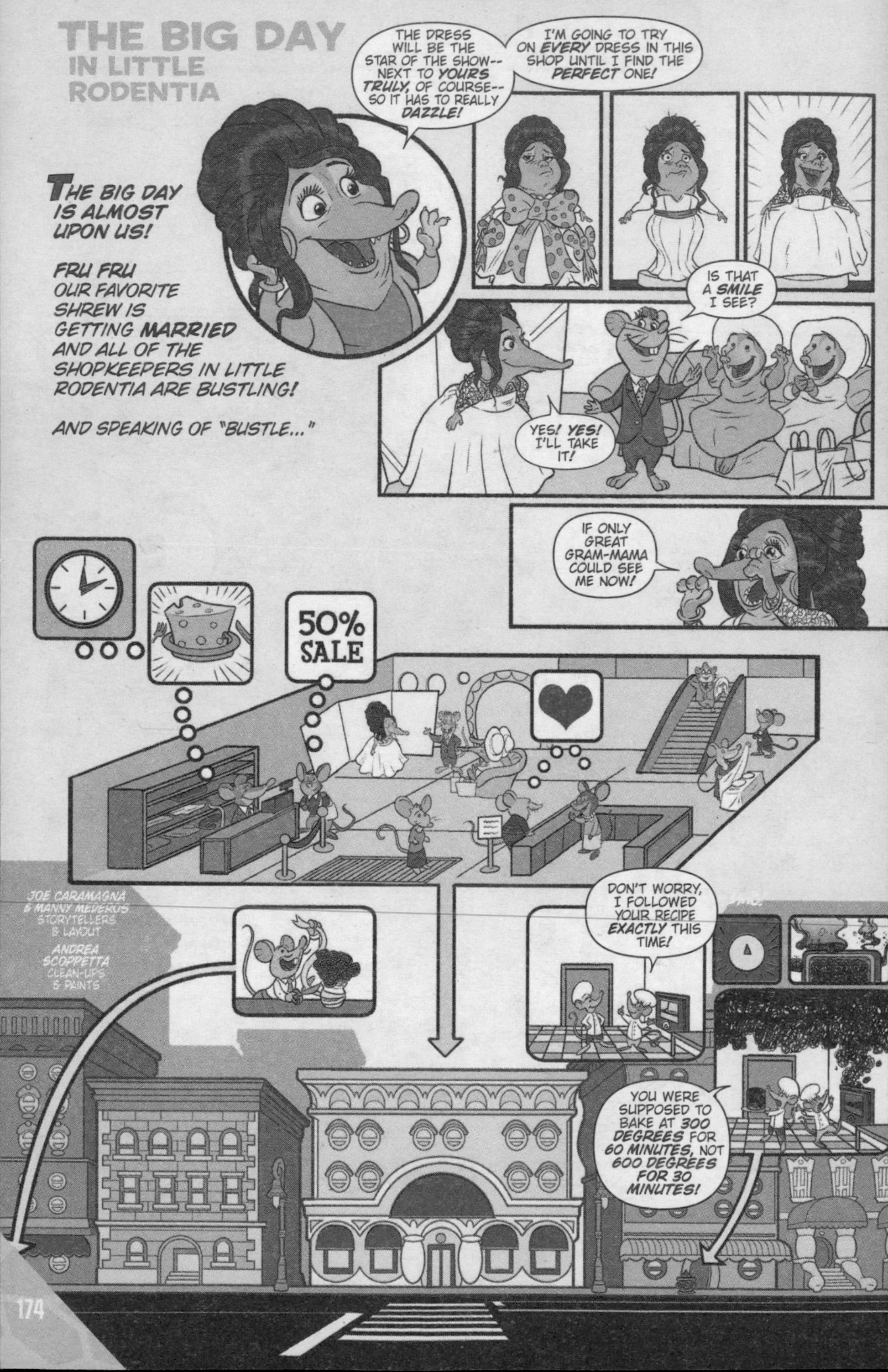
THE BIG DAY IN LITTLE RODENTIA
THE BIG DAY IS ALMOST UPON US!
FRU FRU OUR FAVORITE SHREW IS GETTING MARRIED AND ALL OF THE SHOPKEEPERS IN LITTLE RODENTIA ARE BUSTLING!
AND SPEAKING OF "BUSTLE..."
THE DRESS WILL BE THE STAR OF THE SHOW-- NEXT TO YOURS TRULY, OF COURSE-- SO IT HAS TO REALLY DAZZLE!
I'M GOING TO TRY ON EVERY DRESS IN THIS SHOP UNTIL I FIND THE PERFECT ONE!
IS THAT A SMILE I SEE?
YES! YES! I'LL TAKE IT!
IF ONLY GREAT GRAM-MAMA COULD SEE ME NOW!
50% SALE
DON'T WORRY, I FOLLOWED YOUR RECIPE EXACTLY THIS TIME!
YOU WERE SUPPOSED TO BAKE AT 300 DEGREES FOR 60 MINUTES, NOT 600 DEGREES FOR 30 MINUTES!
JOE CARAMAGNA & MANNY MEDEROS STORYTELLERS & LAYOUT
ANDREA SCOPPETTA CLEAN-UPS & PAINTS

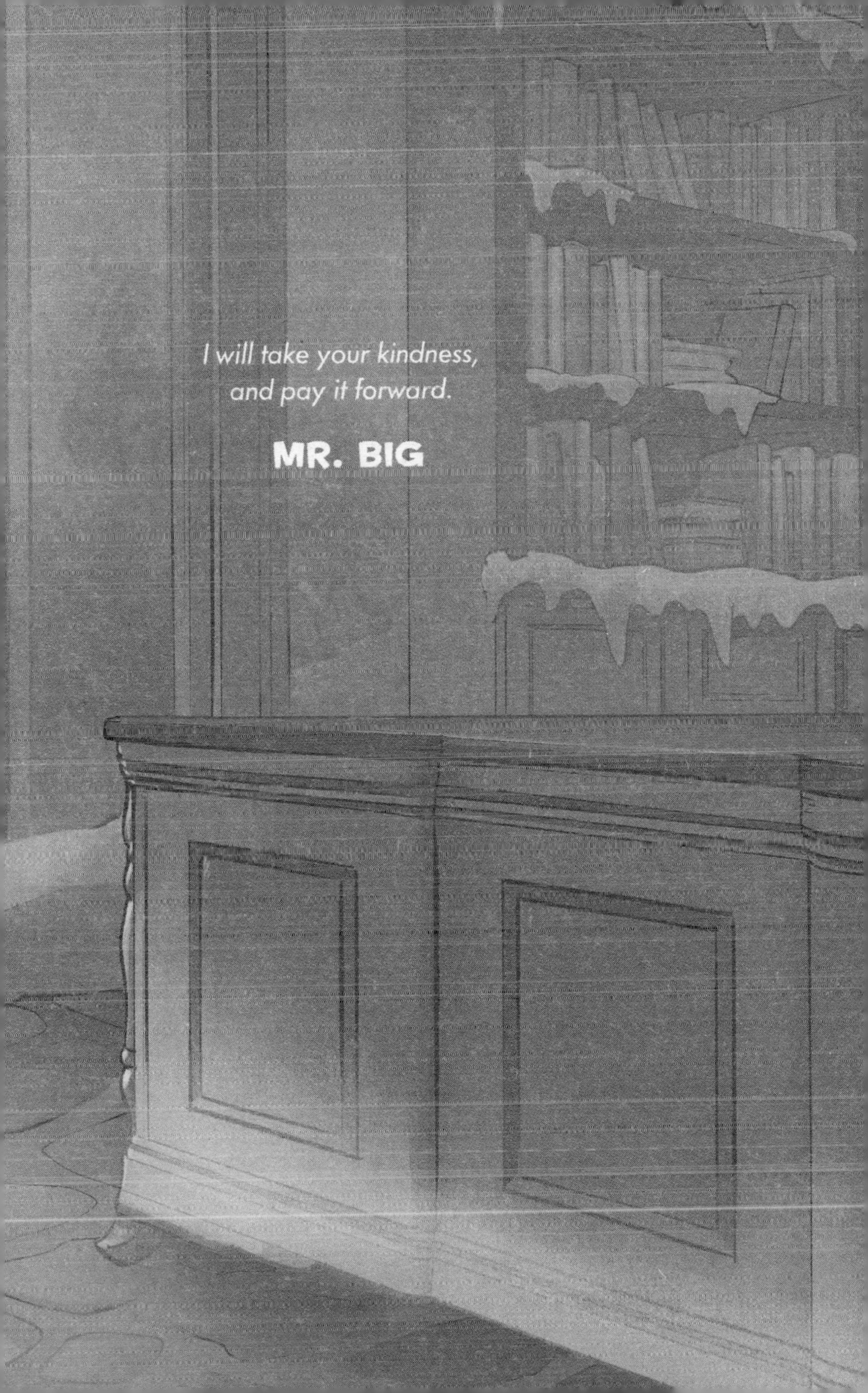

*I will take your kindness,
and pay it forward.*

MR. BIG

RAINFOREST DISTRICT

Local FAVES

What to Do:

- TAKE A RIDE ON THE GONDOLA TO EXPLORE THE DISTRICT'S LUSH CANOPY AND EXTRAORDINARY TREETOP HOMES

Where to Eat:

- MISTY'S ON THE VINE

Don't Forget:

- YOUR UMBRELLA

There's so much to see in the Rainforest District, from the very top of its canopy to the river far below. This area is known for its soaring trees, steamy wet climate and beautiful vegetation. Here you will also find some of Zootopia's most incredible homes perched high in the treetops. Judy and Nick take a trip to the Rainforest District following a big lead in their missing mammal case. But they get all tangled up in the process!

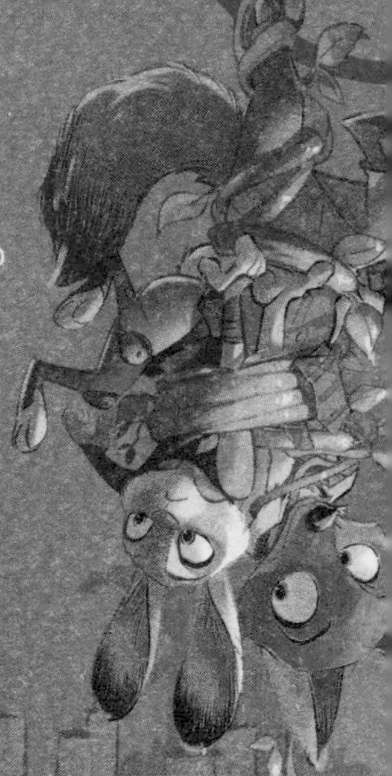

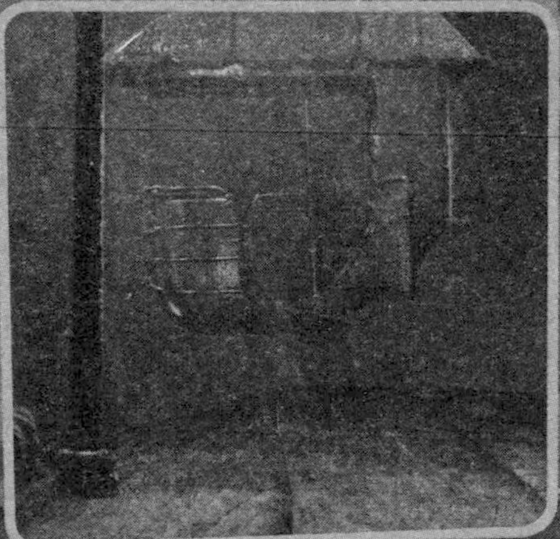

GO GONDOLA!

Escape the traffic by taking the gondola. Whether you're sightseeing or commuting, you won't get a better view.

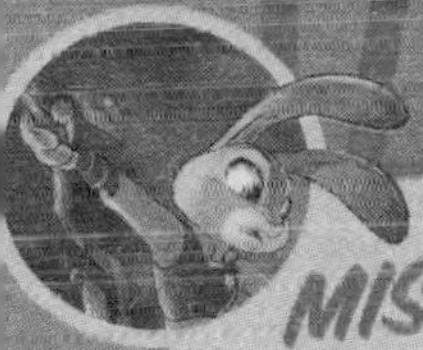

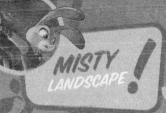

MISTY LANDSCAPE!

IT'S EASY TO GET CONFUSED IN A RAINFOREST ENVIRONMENT FULL OF TANGLED VINES AND THICK MIST. SPOT THE 5 DIFFERENCES BETWEEN THESE TWO PICTURES.

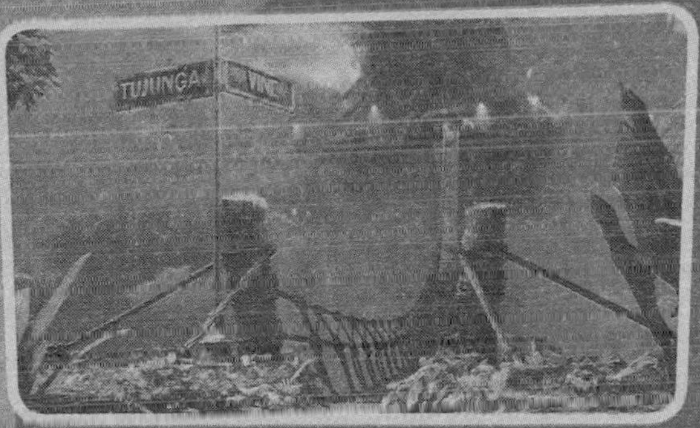
TUJUNGA
VINE

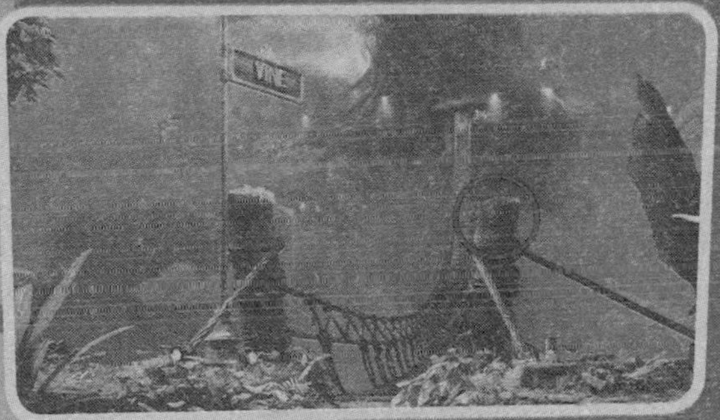
VINE

MANCHAS

Manchas is a Rainforest District resident and Mr. Big's driver. When Nick and Judy pay him a visit, they get a big surprise—he goes savage right before their eyes!

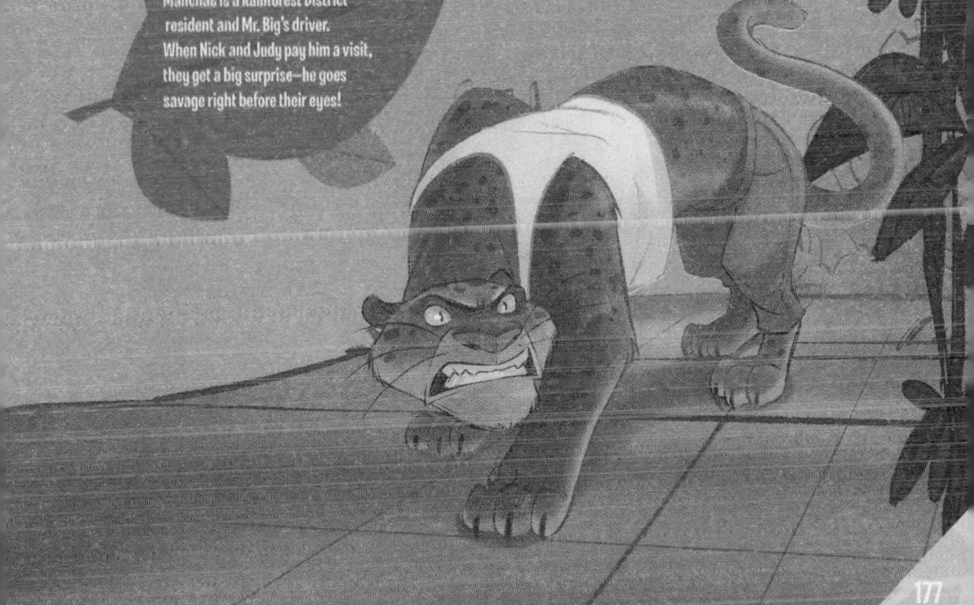

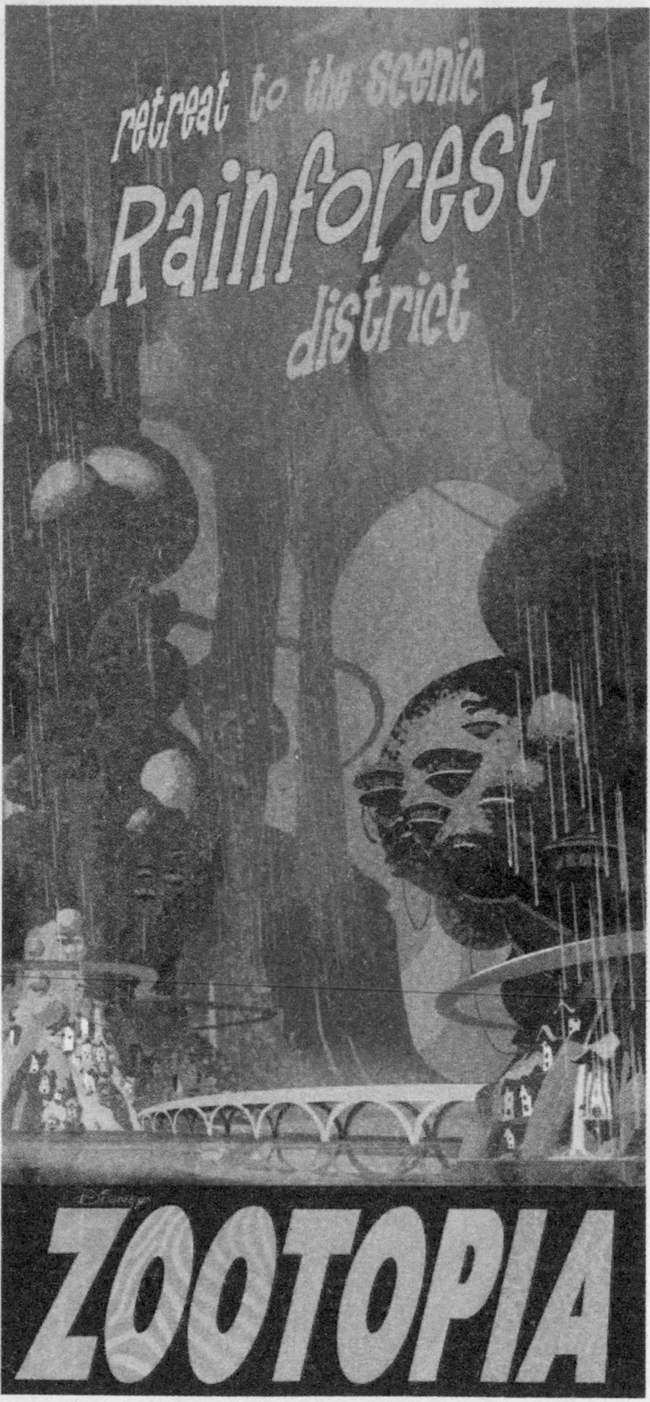
retreat to the scenic
Rainforest
district
ZOOTOPIA

Welcome to the RAINFOREST DISTRICT!

In the Rainforest District, you can glide over the jungle canopy completely at ease in a gondola built for two! It's the best when you have to make a dramatic exit in front of your boss who may or may not have just fired you.

DID YOU KNOW?

- The Rainforest District is home to hundreds of giant, bright, jungle-green steamer trees—artificial trees that mechanically suck up water from a river to create the steamy atmosphere required by the locals.
- The rainforest has cool tones and heavy humidity.

ZOOTOPIA

TUNDRATOWN

Local FAVES

What to Do:
- SHOP TILL YOU DROP IN THE FASHION DISTRICT

Getting Around:
- TUNDRATOWN LIMO-SERVICE
- GONDOLAS

Where to Eat:
- HALIBUTS

Tundratown is cooled to freezing temperatures, so it glistens with snow and ice all year long! This winter wonderland is home to polar bears, wolves, moose, reindeer and other cold-loving animals. Here you can marvel at the stunning architecture made entirely out of ice, explore the mountainous surroundings or take a ride on the gondola.

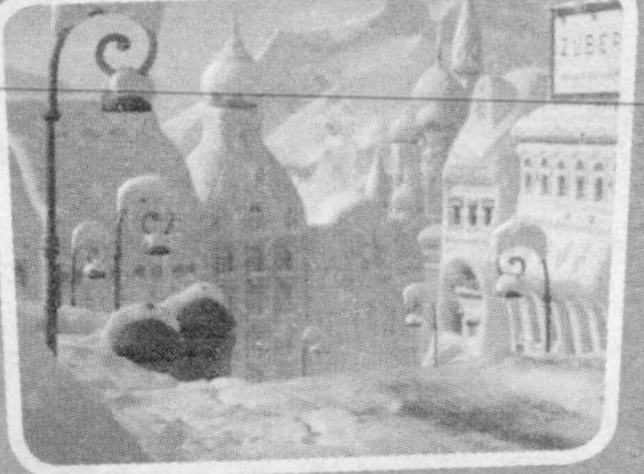

THE CLIMATE WALL

This feat of engineering that separates the boroughs of Tundratown and Sahara Square keeps Tundratown chilled out while blowing hot air on Sahara Square, keeping it dry and toasty warm.

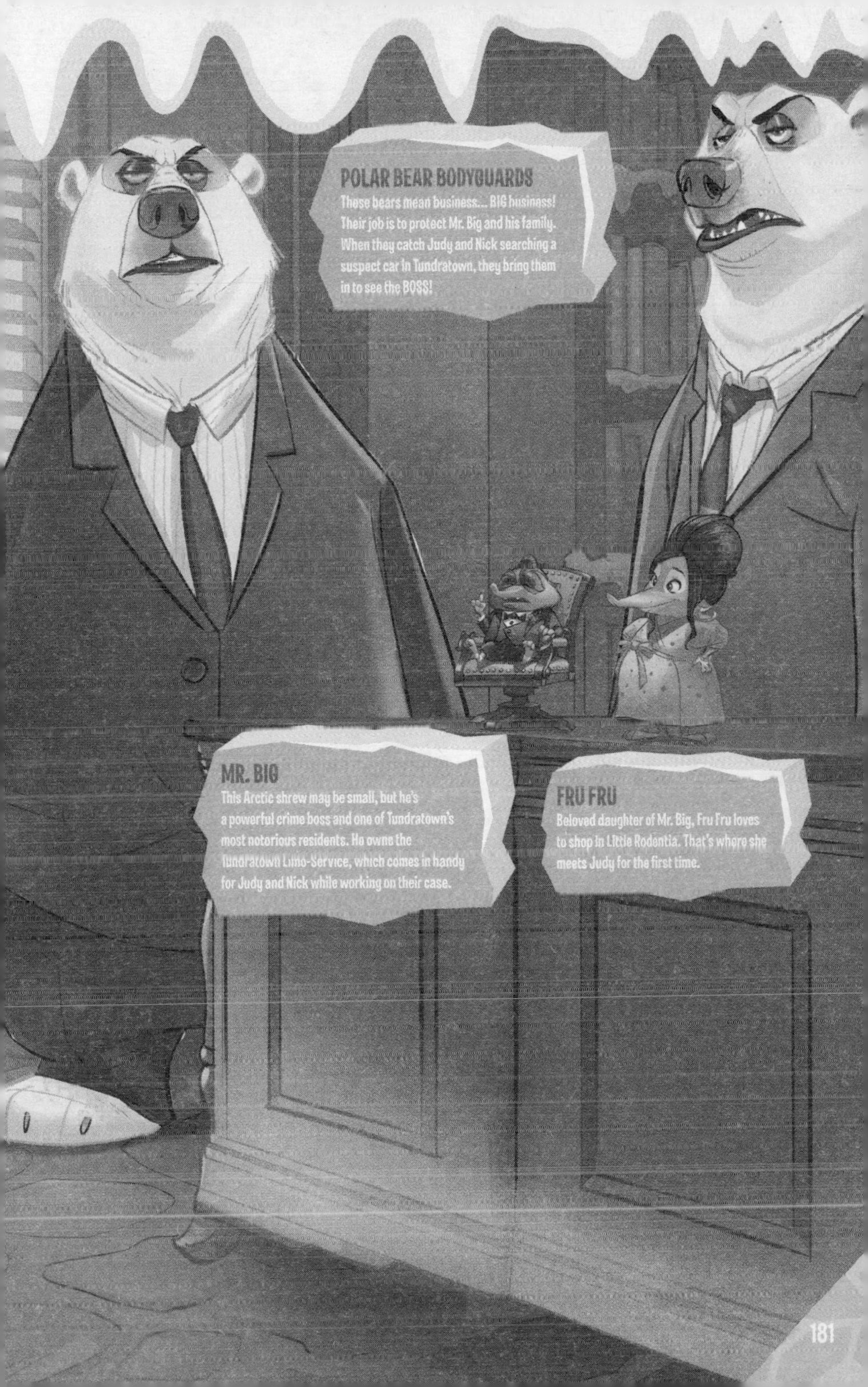

POLAR BEAR BODYGUARDS

These bears mean business... BIG business! Their job is to protect Mr. Big and his family. When they catch Judy and Nick searching a suspect car in Tundratown, they bring them in to see the BOSS!

MR. BIG

This Arctic shrew may be small, but he's a powerful crime boss and one of Tundratown's most notorious residents. He owns the Tundratown Limo-Service, which comes in handy for Judy and Nick while working on their case.

FRU FRU

Beloved daughter of Mr. Big, Fru Fru loves to shop in Little Rodentia. That's where she meets Judy for the first time.

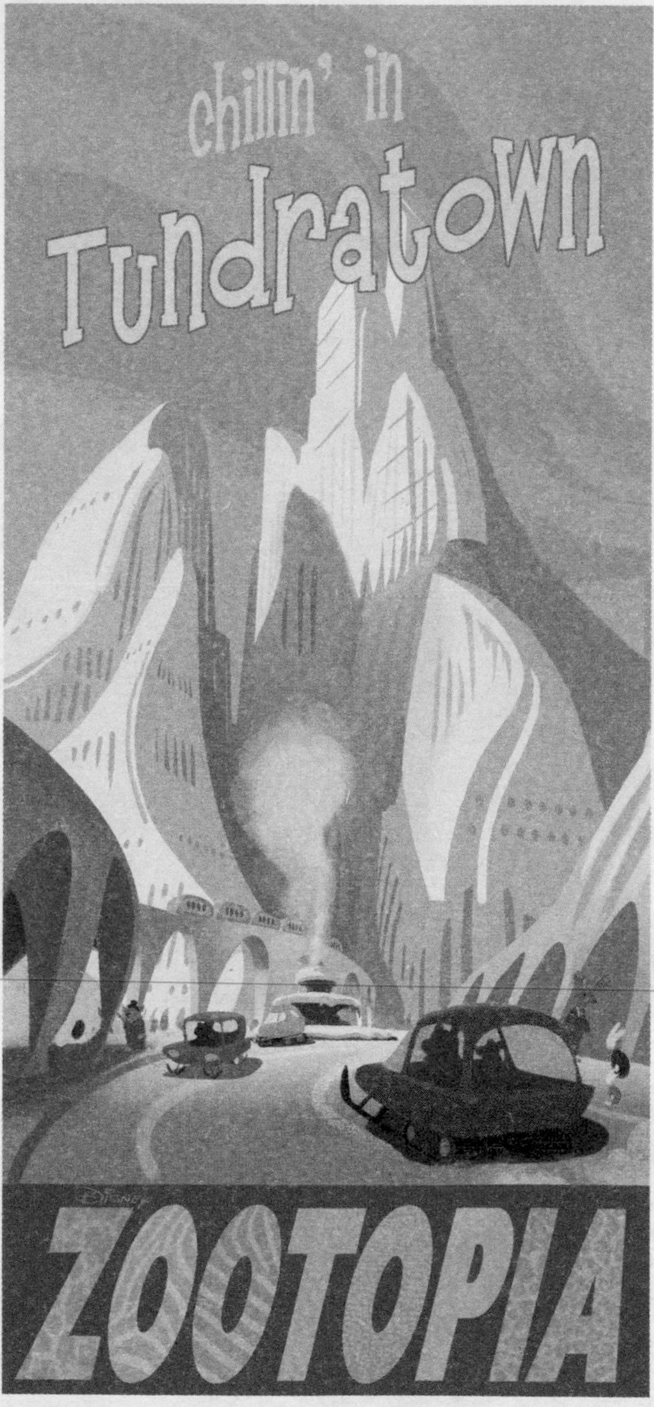
chillin' in
Tundratown
Disney
ZOOTOPIA

Welcome to TUNDRATOWN!

"I'LL MAKE YOU AN OFFER YOU CAN'T REFUSE."

Mr. Big welcomes you to Tundratown—as long you don't cause any trouble, *capiche?* Otherwise, you'll get taken for a ride. Watch out for icy conditions!

TRAFFIC REPORT

The snow blowers are working at full capacity today, so make sure you keep on the sideblocks if you're walking around today. And make sure the skis on your vehicles are freshly waxed!

TUNDRATOWN UPDATE

DID YOU KNOW?

- Tundratown is constructed mainly of snow and ice, and features a cool color palette with blues and teals.
- There are giant snow blowers that go off periodically—they're part of the climate control. Nothing ever thaws. There are floating blocks of ice instead of moving sidewalks and cars are on skis.

TAKE YOUR CUB TO WORK DAY!

JOE CARAMAGNA & MANNY MEDEROS
STORYTELLERS & LAYOUT

ANDREA SCOPPETTA
CLEAN-UPS & PAINTS

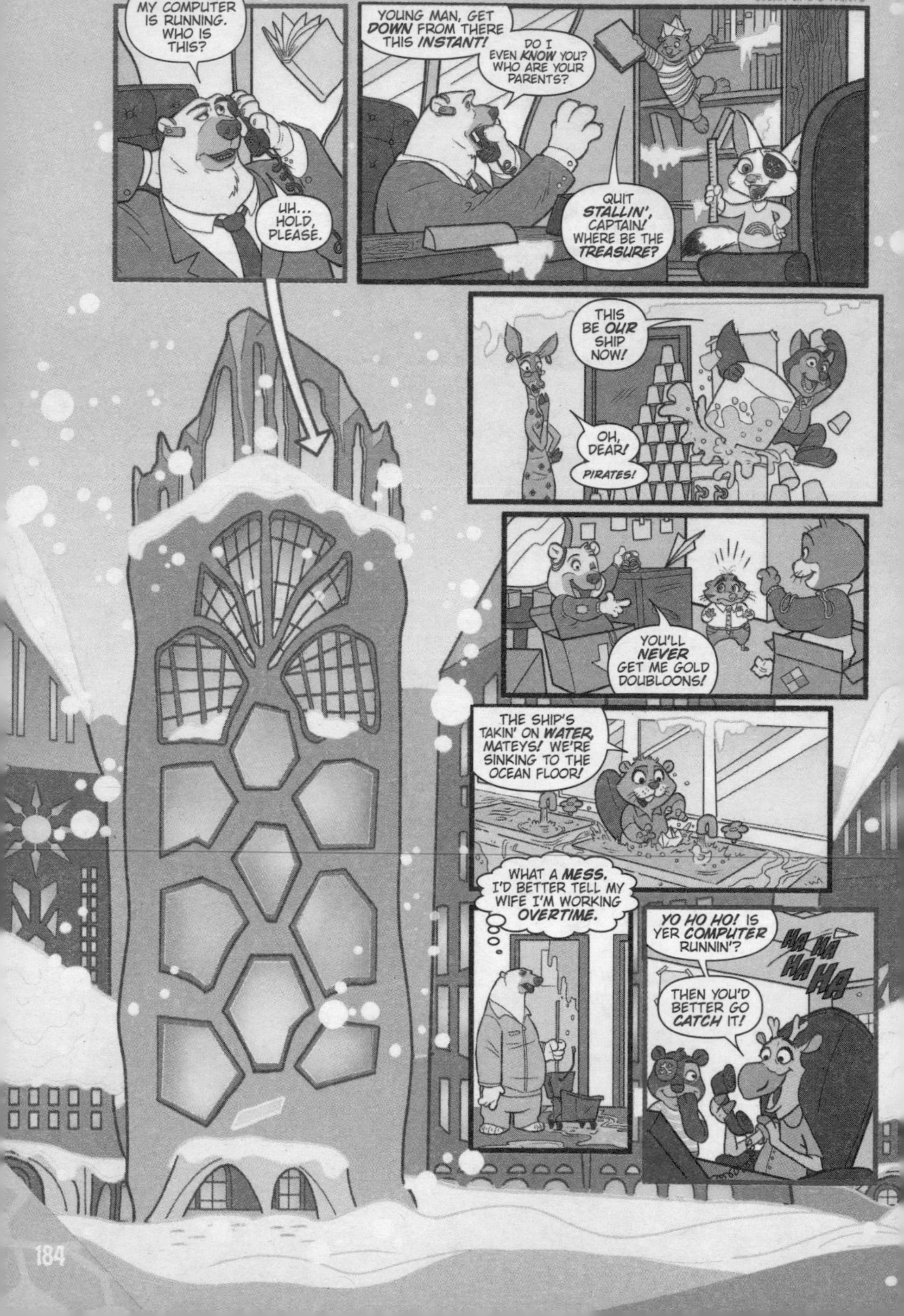
OF COURSE MY COMPUTER IS RUNNING. WHO IS THIS?
UH... HOLD, PLEASE.
YOUNG MAN, GET DOWN FROM THERE THIS INSTANT!
DO I EVEN KNOW YOU? WHO ARE YOUR PARENTS?
QUIT STALLIN', CAPTAIN! WHERE BE THE TREASURE?
THIS BE OUR SHIP NOW!
OH, DEAR!
PIRATES!
YOU'LL NEVER GET ME GOLD DOUBLOONS!
THE SHIP'S TAKIN' ON WATER, MATEYS! WE'RE SINKING TO THE OCEAN FLOOR!
WHAT A MESS. I'D BETTER TELL MY WIFE I'M WORKING OVERTIME.
YO HO HO! IS YER COMPUTER RUNNIN'?
THEN YOU'D BETTER GO CATCH IT!
HA HA HA HA

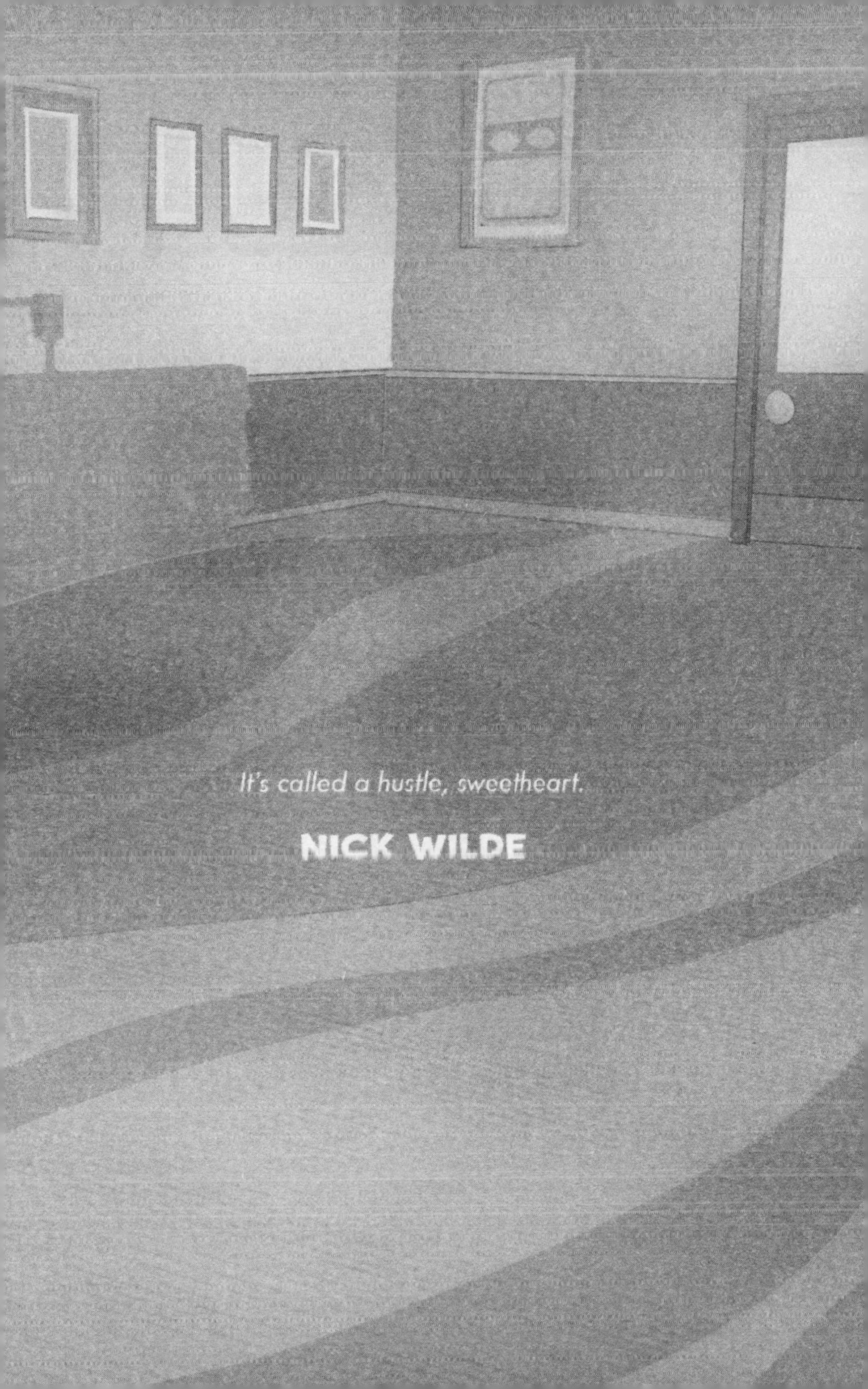

It's called a hustle, sweetheart.

NICK WILDE

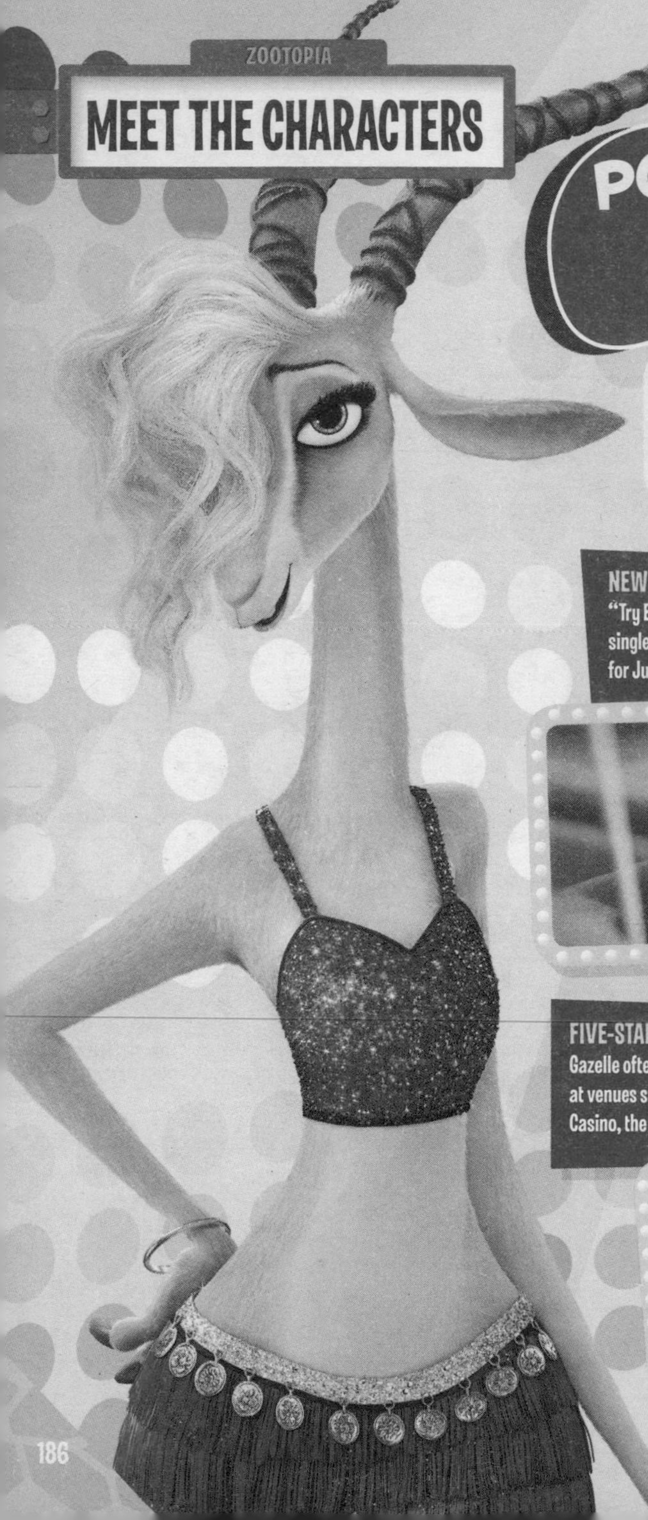

POWERFUL PREY

The one and only Gazelle! This international pop star is an influential singer and performer who has fans from Tundratown to Bunnyburrow.

NEW LIFE, NEW SONG

"Try Everything," Gazelle's hit single, is the perfect soundtrack for Judy's journey into town.

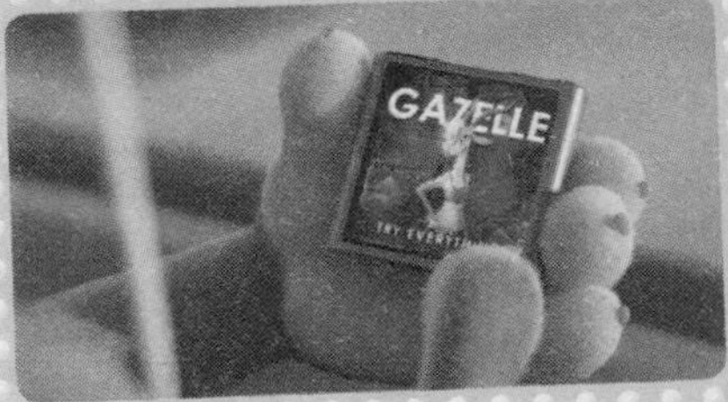
GAZELLE

FIVE-STAR ZOOTOPIAN

Gazelle often performs live in Zootopia at venues such as the Palm Hotel and Casino, the jewel of Sahara Square.

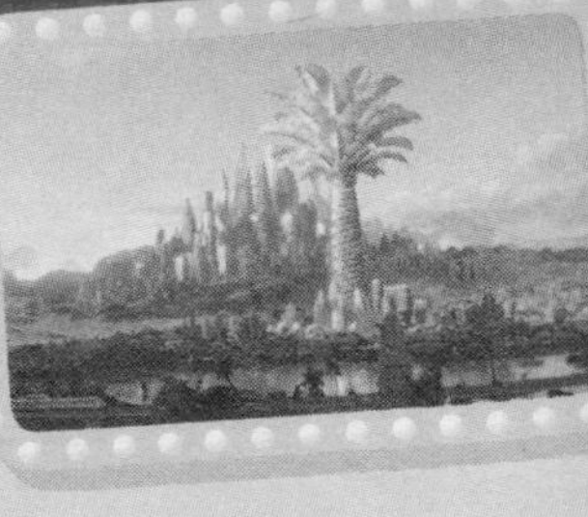

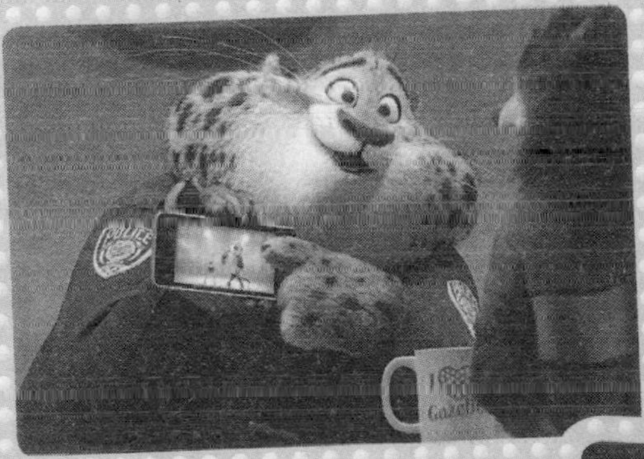

NUMBER ONE FAN

Many ZPD officers love Gazelle's music, Chief Bogo included, but there's only one who believes Gazelle is the greatest singer ever, an angel with horns: Clawhauser!

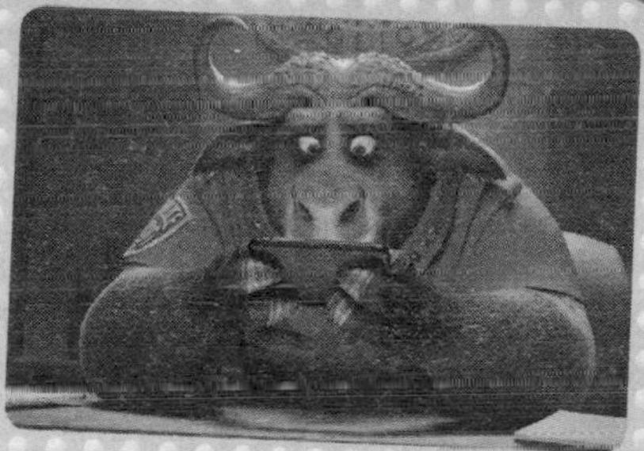

UNITY AND HARMONY

Gazelle really cares about mammal equality. When Mayor Lionheart was arrested and predators were seen as a threat, Gazelle and her Tigers led a rally: they encouraged predators and prey to leave any prejudice behind and live together in peace.

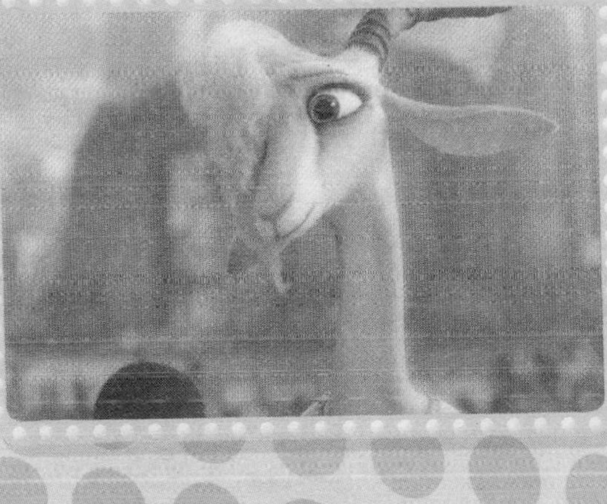

ZOOTOPIA

MEET THE CHARACTERS LOVEABLE

Benjamin Clawhauser works at the front desk of the Zootopia Police Department. His job, Gazelle and donuts are a few of his favorite things!

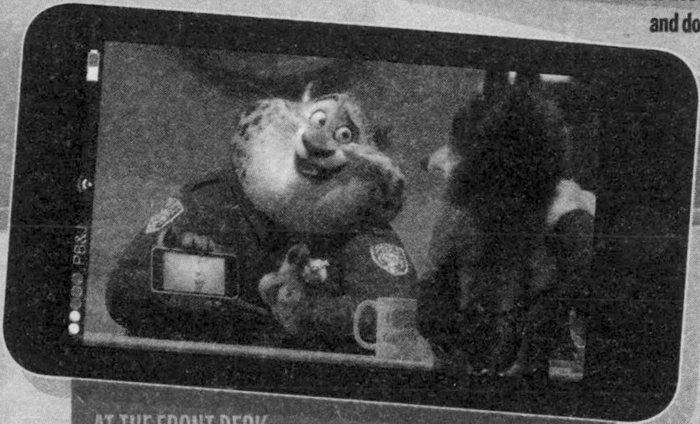
PB&J

AT THE FRONT DESK

Clawhauser is the first officer visitors to the ZPD see when they walk in the door; his kindness and sense of humor can put anyone at ease, criminals included. More than just a donut-loving cop, Clawhauser helps Judy and Nick when they run into trouble.

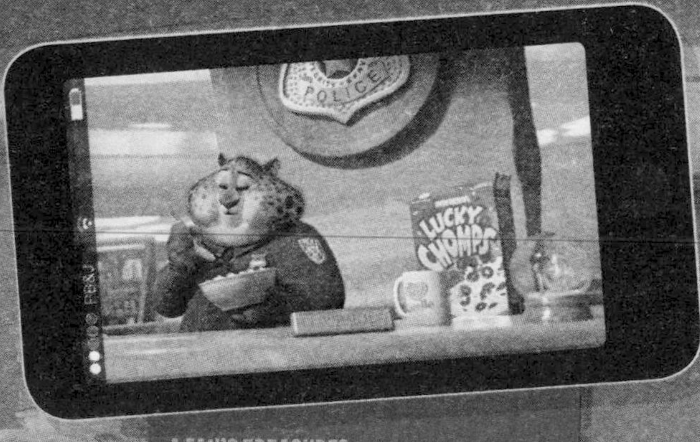
POLICE
LUCKY CHOMPS
PB&J

A FAN'S TREASURES

Along with candy, cereal and donuts, Clawhauser keeps a few souvenirs on his desk to show that he's a big fan of Gazelle.

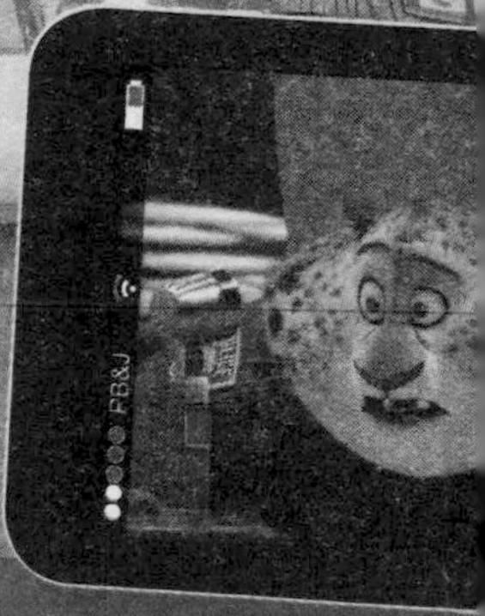
PB&J

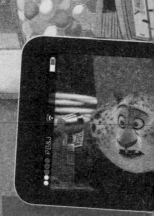

CALL THE COPS!

Clawhauser takes emergency calls when the other cops need help. When Officer Judy Hopps and Nick Wilde discover a jaguar gone savage, he sends help!

PREDATOR

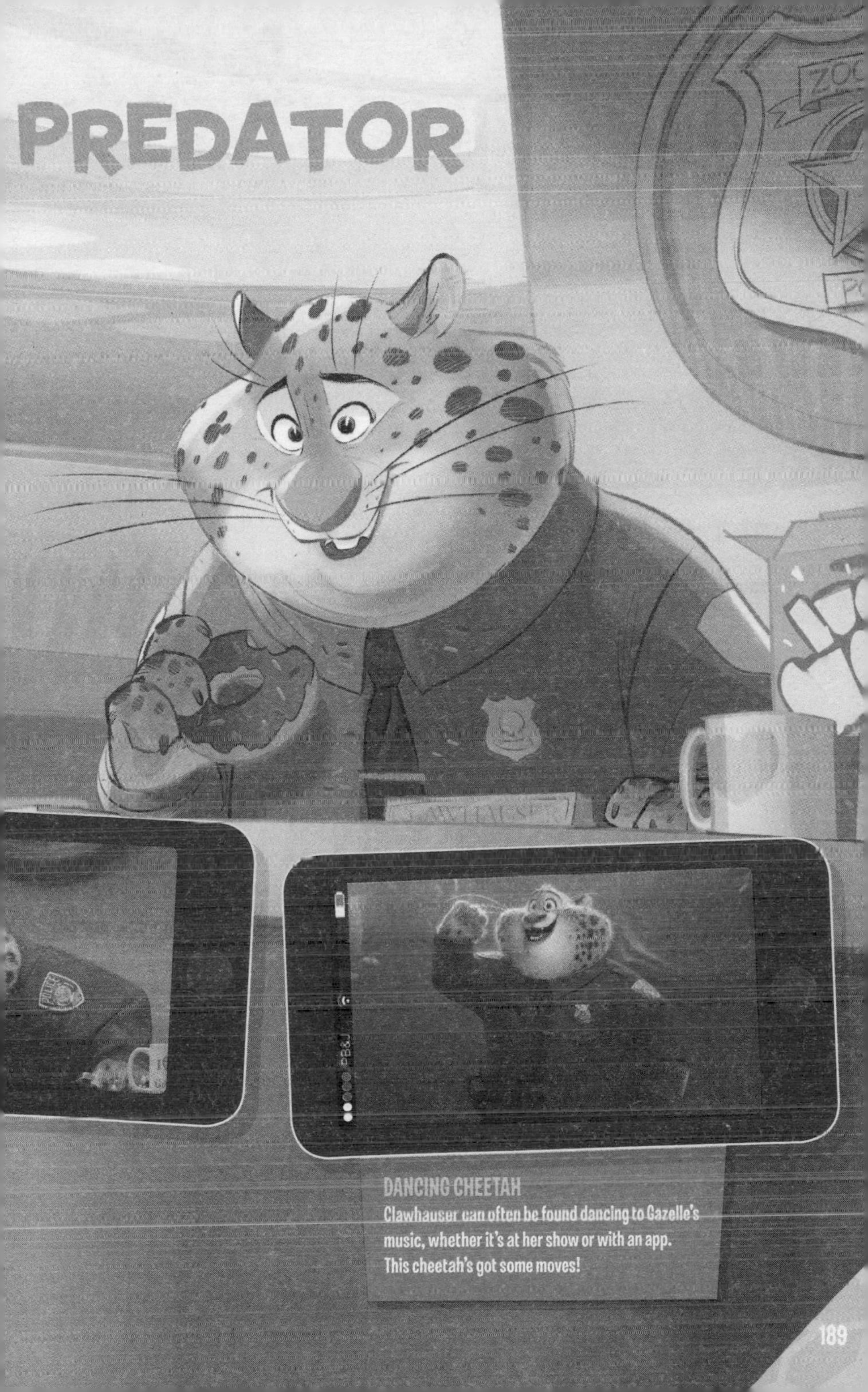

DANCING CHEETAH
Clawhauser can often be found dancing to Gazelle's music, whether it's at her show or with an app. This cheetah's got some moves!

LIVING IN HARMONY

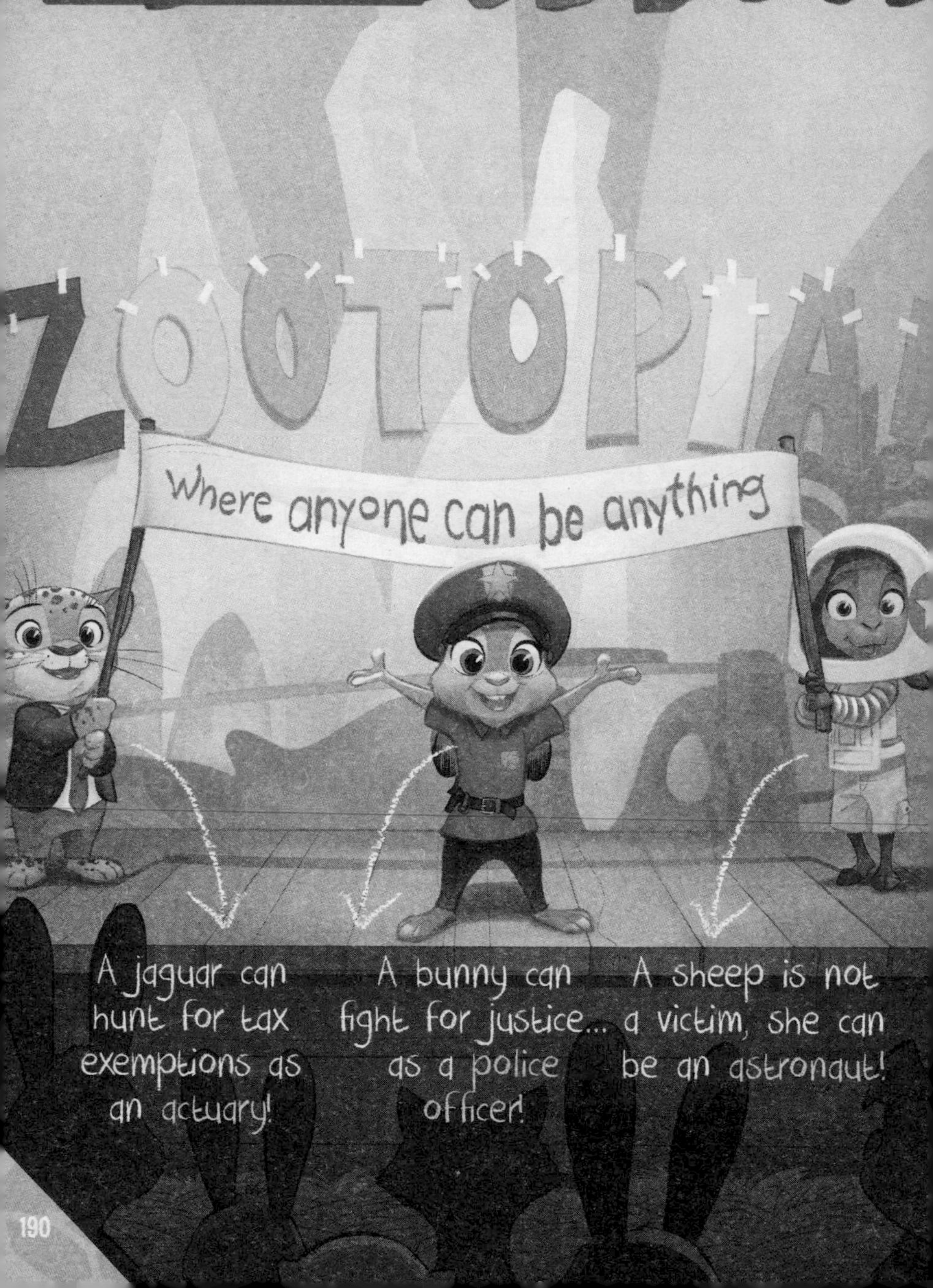
ZOOTOPIA
Where anyone can be anything

A jaguar can hunt for tax exemptions as an actuary!

A bunny can fight for justice... as a police officer!

A sheep is not a victim, she can be an astronaut!

A DREAM COME TRUE

Long before Zootopia even existed, prey were living in fear and predators ruled the world. But then some sought peace and things changed forever. Now, young mammals like Judy Hopps and her friends from school learn at an early age that predators and prey live in harmony... and that anyone can be anything they want!

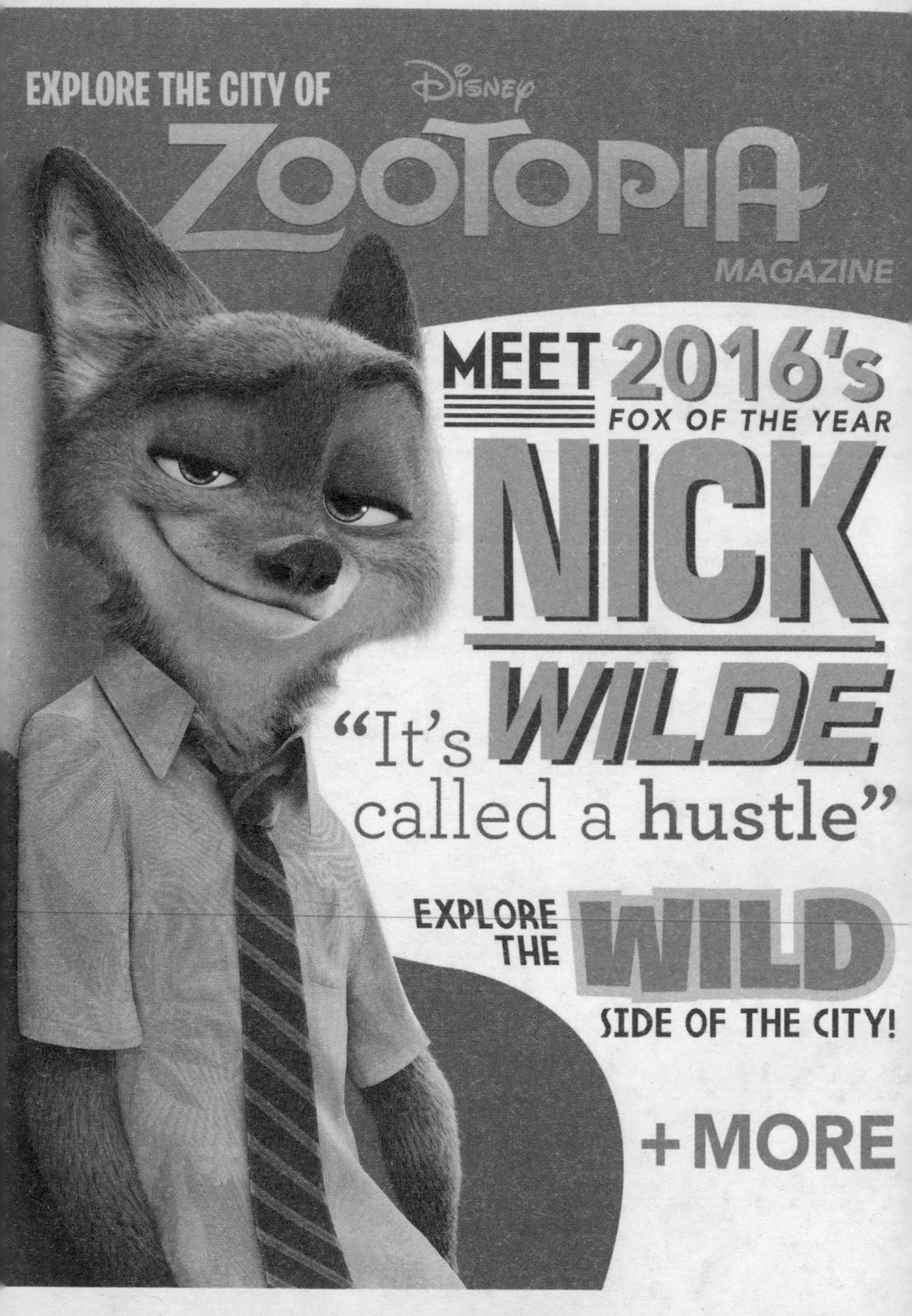
EXPLORE THE CITY OF
DISNEY
ZOOTOPIA
MAGAZINE
MEET 2016's
FOX OF THE YEAR
NICK WILDE
"It's called a hustle"
EXPLORE THE WILD SIDE OF THE CITY!
+MORE

IT'S CALLED A HUSTLE

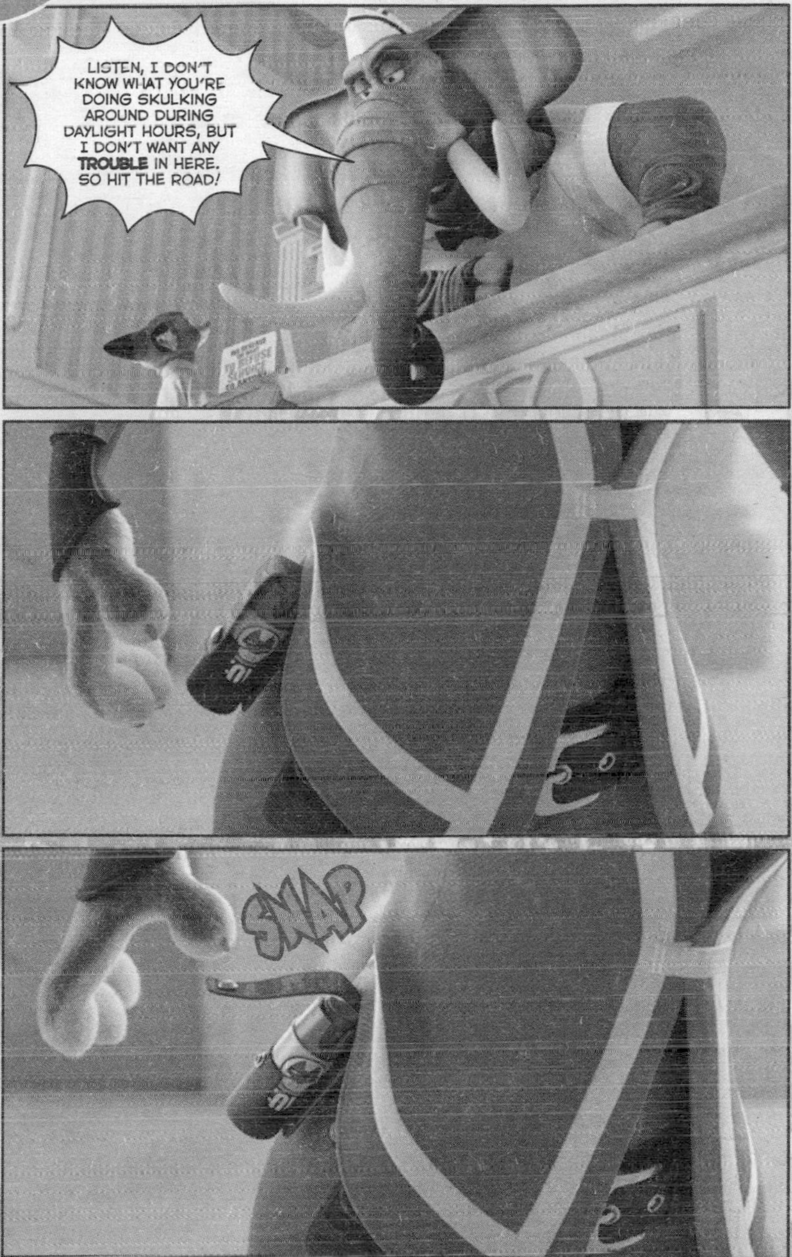
LISTEN, I DON'T KNOW WHAT YOU'RE DOING SKULKING AROUND DURING DAYLIGHT HOURS, BUT I DON'T WANT ANY **TROUBLE** IN HERE. SO HIT THE ROAD!
SNAP

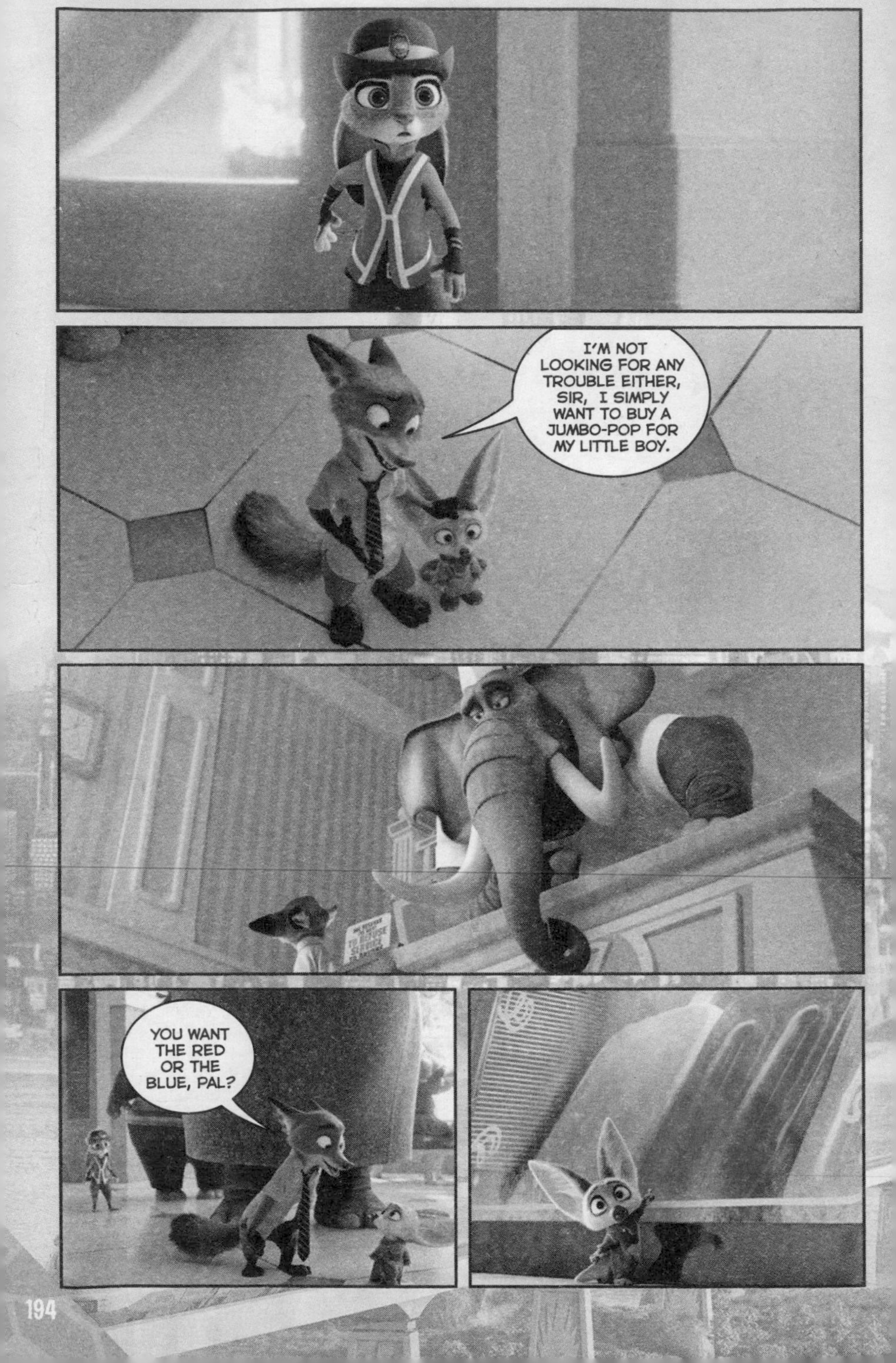
I'M NOT LOOKING FOR ANY TROUBLE EITHER, SIR, I SIMPLY WANT TO BUY A JUMBO-POP FOR MY LITTLE BOY.
YOU WANT THE RED OR THE BLUE, PAL?

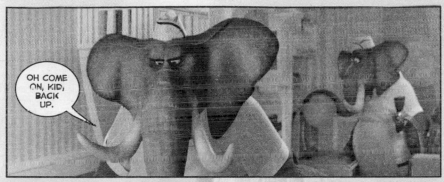

OH COME ON, KID, BACK UP.

I'M **SUCH** A --

LISTEN, BUDDY, WHAT? THERE AREN'T ANY **FOX** ICE CREAM JOINTS IN YOUR PART OF TOWN?

UH, NO, NO, THERE ARE. IT'S JUST, MY BOY -- THIS GOOFY LITTLE STINKER -- HE **LOVES** ALL THINGS ELEPHANT. WANTS TO BE ONE WHEN HE GROWS UP. ISN'T THAT ADORABLE?

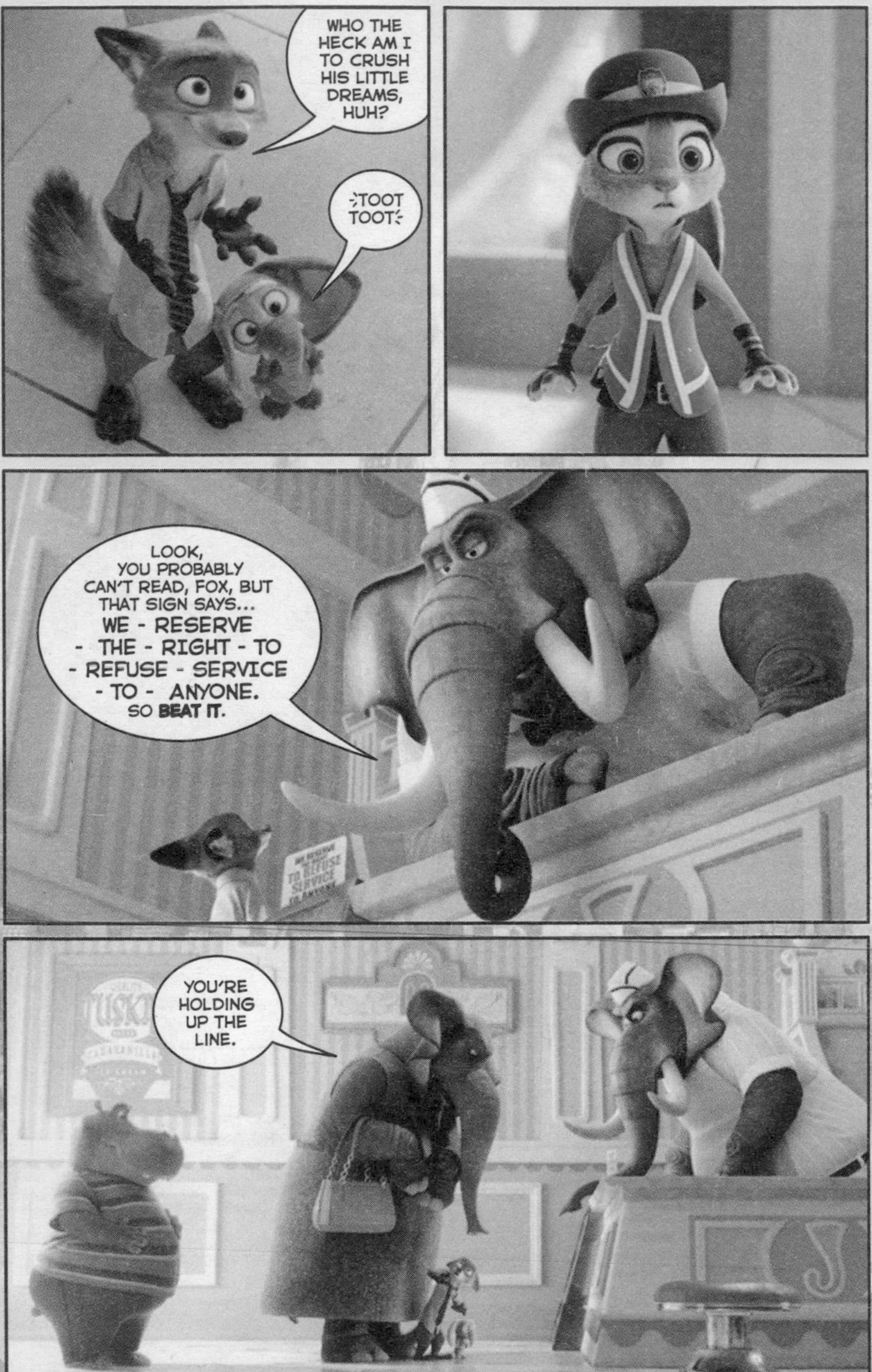
WHO THE HECK AM I TO CRUSH HIS LITTLE DREAMS, HUH?
TOOT TOOT
LOOK, YOU PROBABLY CAN'T READ, FOX, BUT THAT SIGN SAYS... WE - RESERVE - THE - RIGHT - TO - REFUSE - SERVICE - TO - ANYONE. SO BEAT IT.
YOU'RE HOLDING UP THE LINE.

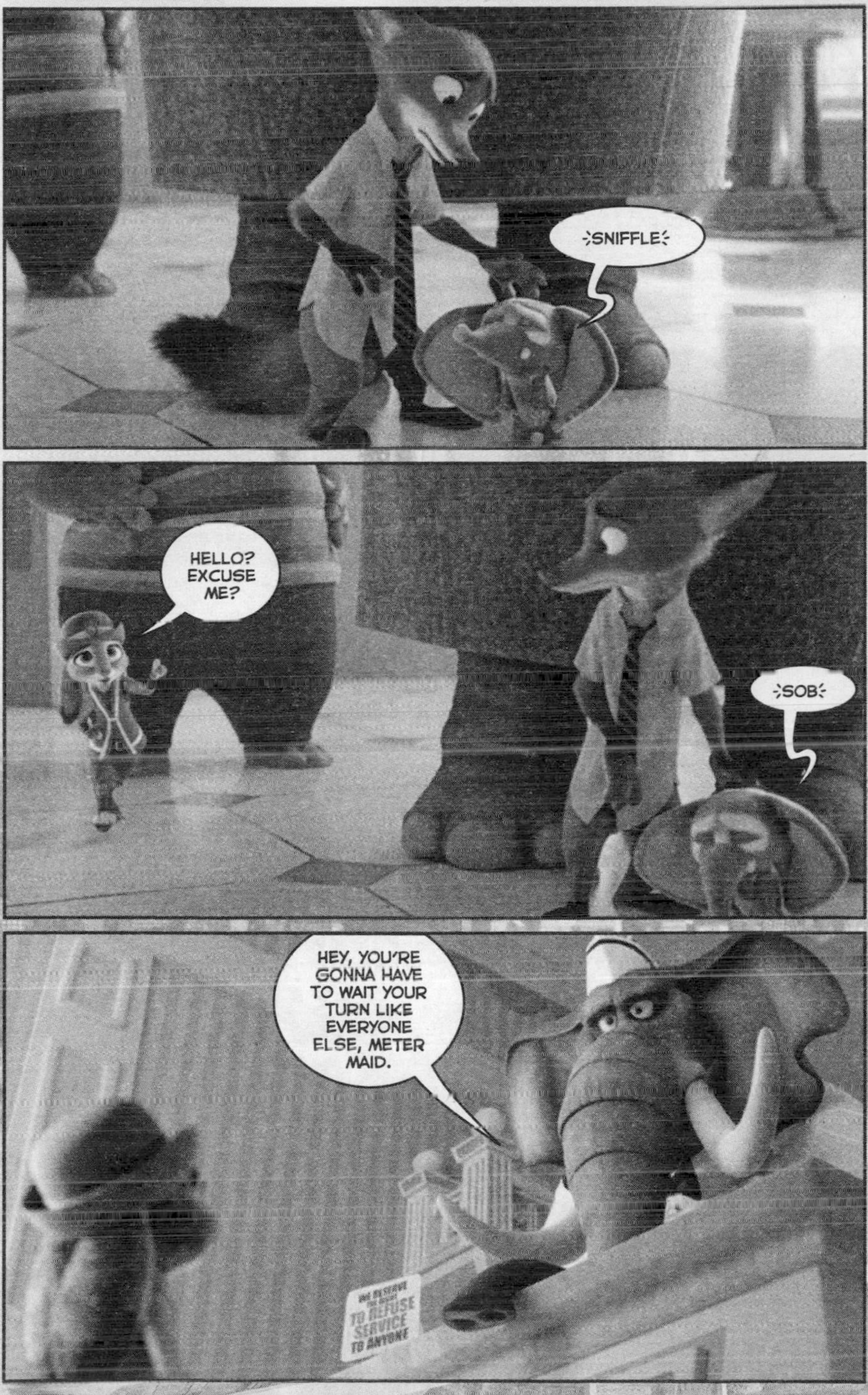

SNIFFLE
HELLO? EXCUSE ME?
SOB
HEY, YOU'RE GONNA HAVE TO WAIT YOUR TURN LIKE EVERYONE ELSE, METER MAID.
WE RESERVE THE RIGHT TO REFUSE SERVICE TO ANYONE

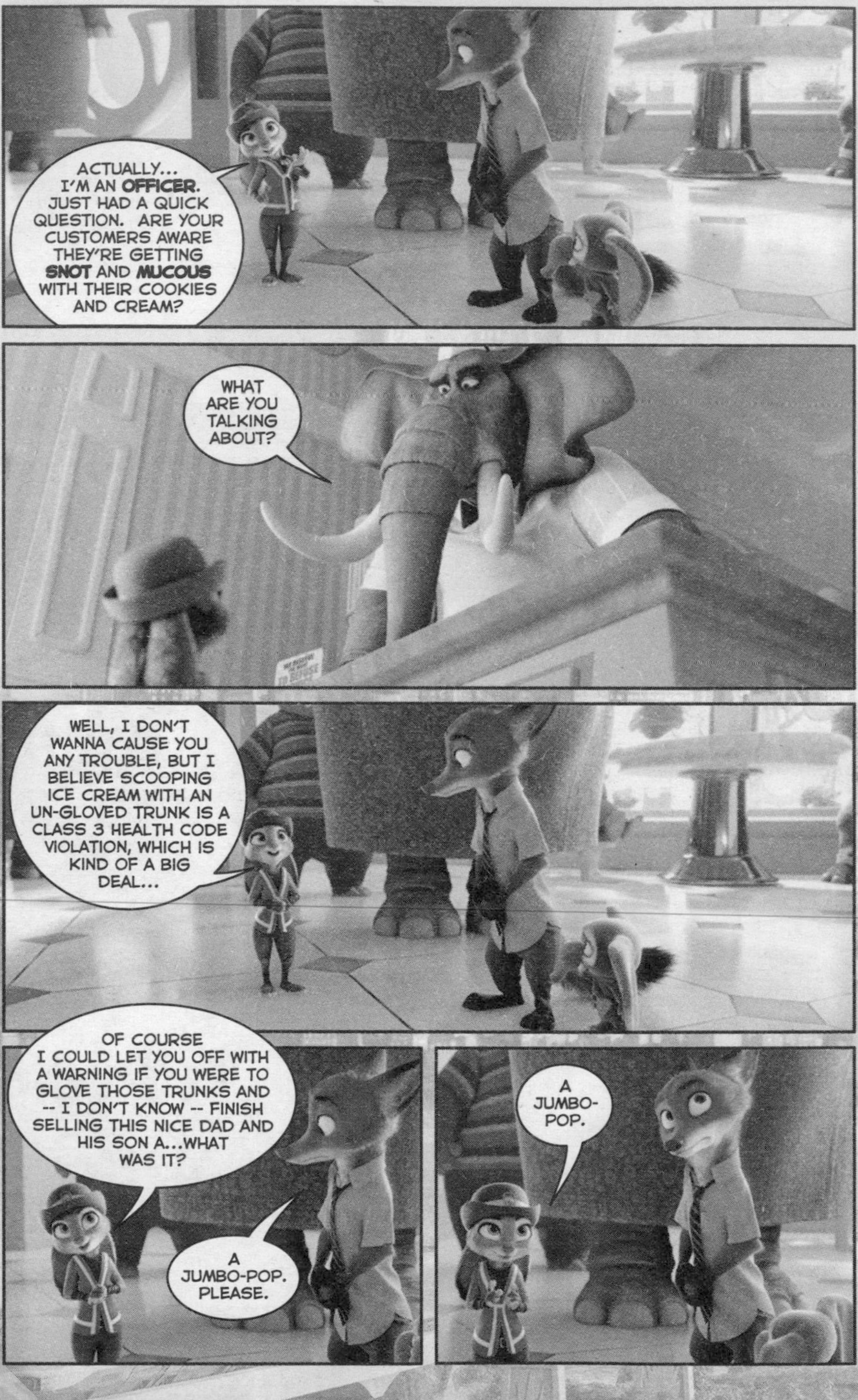
ACTUALLY... I'M AN **OFFICER**. JUST HAD A QUICK QUESTION. ARE YOUR CUSTOMERS AWARE THEY'RE GETTING **SNOT** AND **MUCOUS** WITH THEIR COOKIES AND CREAM?
WHAT ARE YOU TALKING ABOUT?
WELL, I DON'T WANNA CAUSE YOU ANY TROUBLE, BUT I BELIEVE SCOOPING ICE CREAM WITH AN UN-GLOVED TRUNK IS A CLASS 3 HEALTH CODE VIOLATION, WHICH IS KIND OF A BIG DEAL...
OF COURSE I COULD LET YOU OFF WITH A WARNING IF YOU WERE TO GLOVE THOSE TRUNKS AND -- I DON'T KNOW -- FINISH SELLING THIS NICE DAD AND HIS SON A...WHAT WAS IT?
A JUMBO-POP. PLEASE.
A JUMBO-POP.

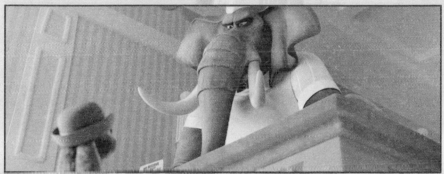

FIFTEEN DOLLARS.

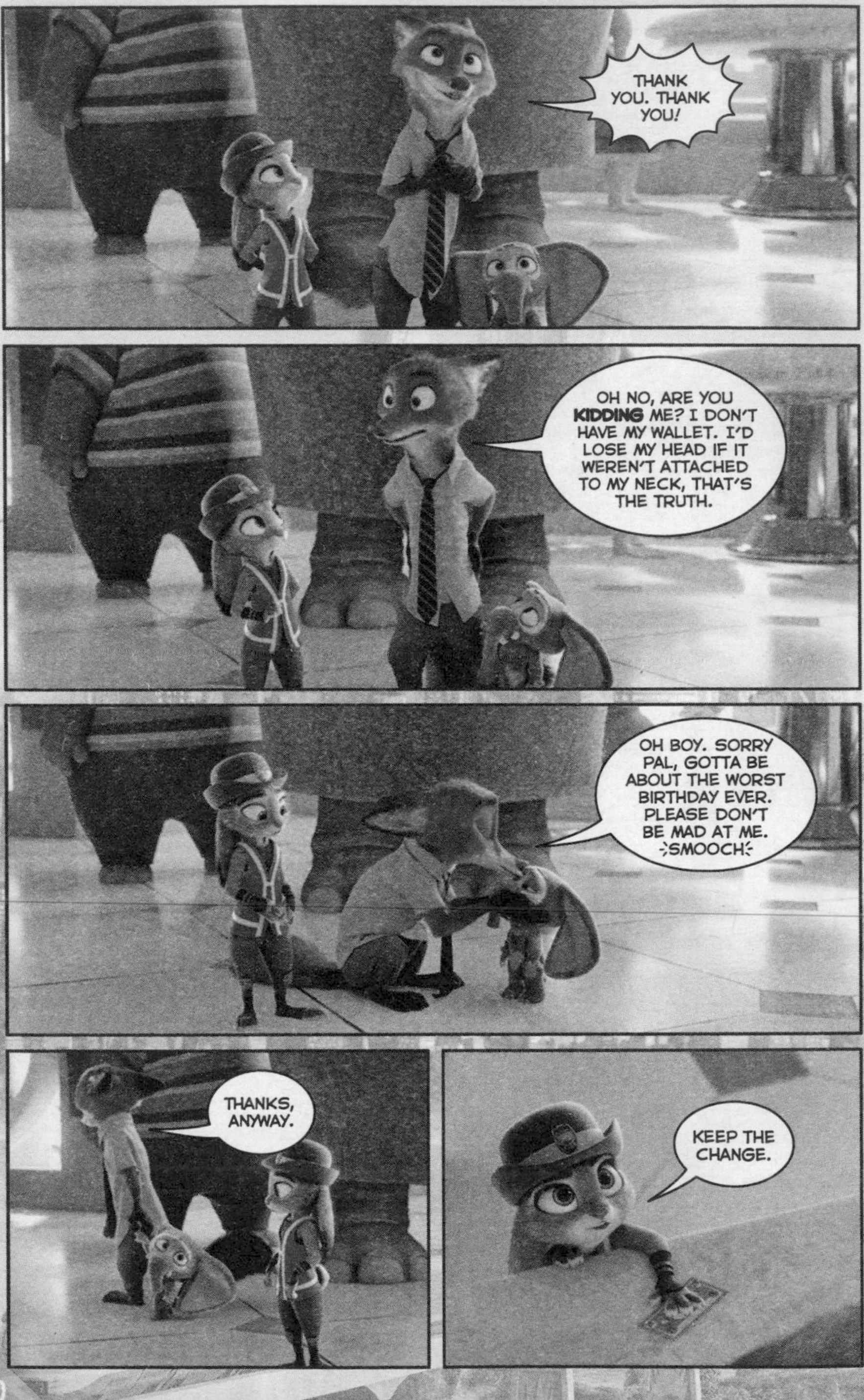
THANK YOU. THANK YOU!
OH NO, ARE YOU **KIDDING** ME? I DON'T HAVE MY WALLET. I'D LOSE MY HEAD IF IT WEREN'T ATTACHED TO MY NECK, THAT'S THE TRUTH.
OH BOY. SORRY PAL, GOTTA BE ABOUT THE WORST BIRTHDAY EVER. PLEASE DON'T BE MAD AT ME. SMOOCH
THANKS, ANYWAY.
KEEP THE CHANGE.

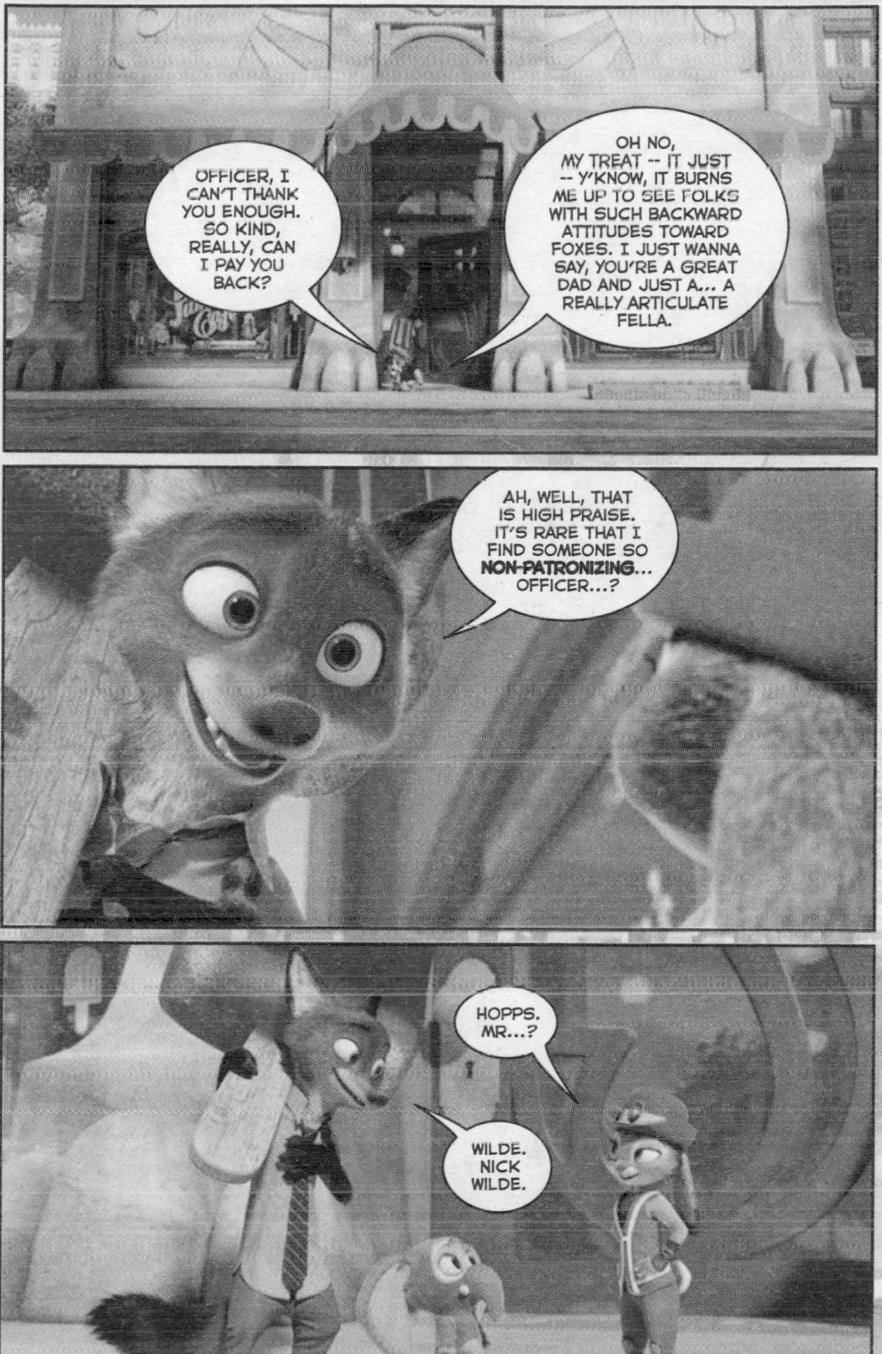
OFFICER, I CAN'T THANK YOU ENOUGH. SO KIND, REALLY, CAN I PAY YOU BACK?
OH NO, MY TREAT -- IT JUST -- Y'KNOW, IT BURNS ME UP TO SEE FOLKS WITH SUCH BACKWARD ATTITUDES TOWARD FOXES. I JUST WANNA SAY, YOU'RE A GREAT DAD AND JUST A... A REALLY ARTICULATE FELLA.
AH, WELL, THAT IS HIGH PRAISE. IT'S RARE THAT I FIND SOMEONE SO **NON-PATRONIZING**... OFFICER...?
HOPPS. MR...?
WILDE. NICK WILDE.

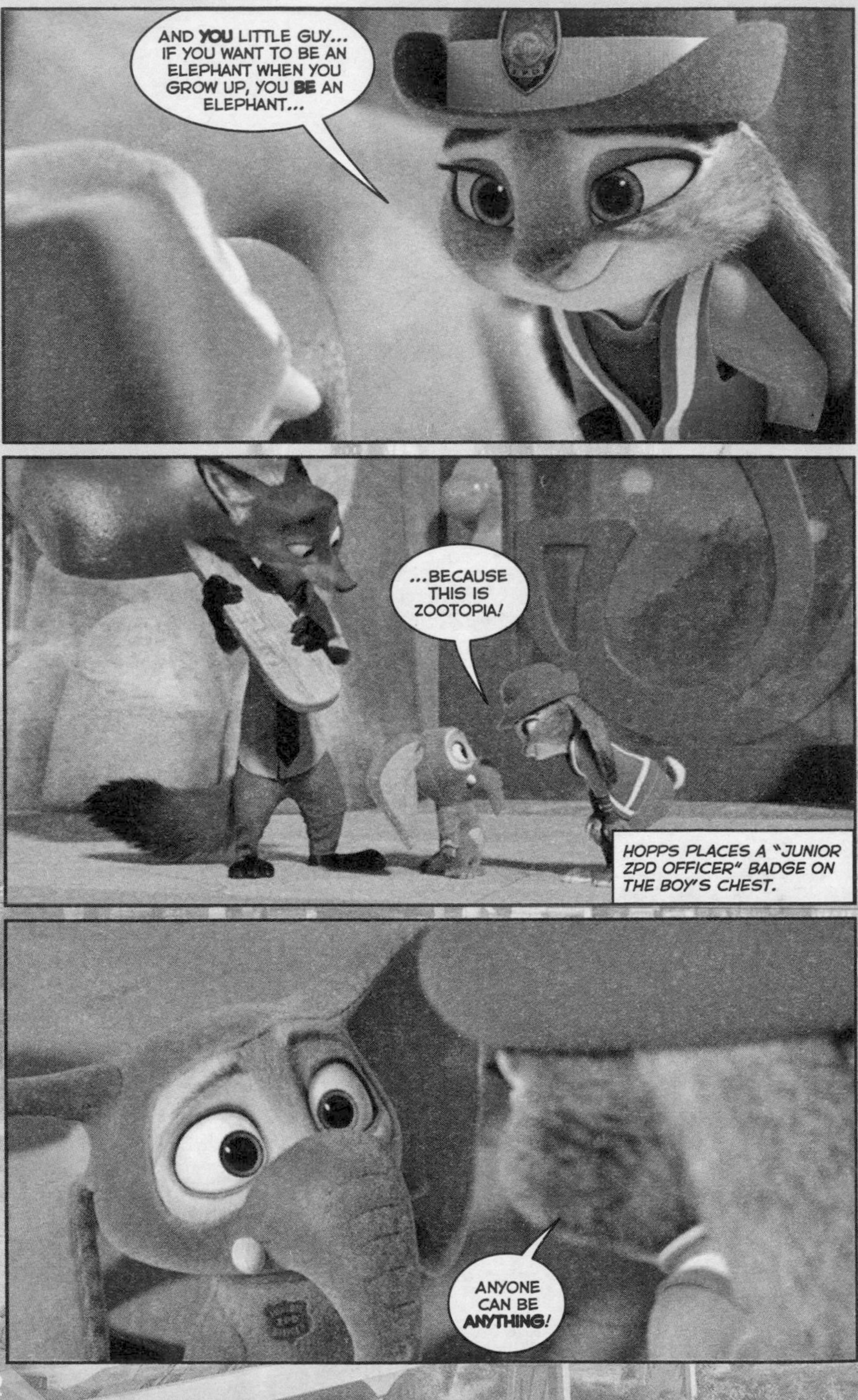

AND YOU LITTLE GUY... IF YOU WANT TO BE AN ELEPHANT WHEN YOU GROW UP, YOU BE AN ELEPHANT...
...BECAUSE THIS IS ZOOTOPIA!
HOPPS PLACES A "JUNIOR ZPD OFFICER" BADGE ON THE BOY'S CHEST.
ANYONE CAN BE ANYTHING!

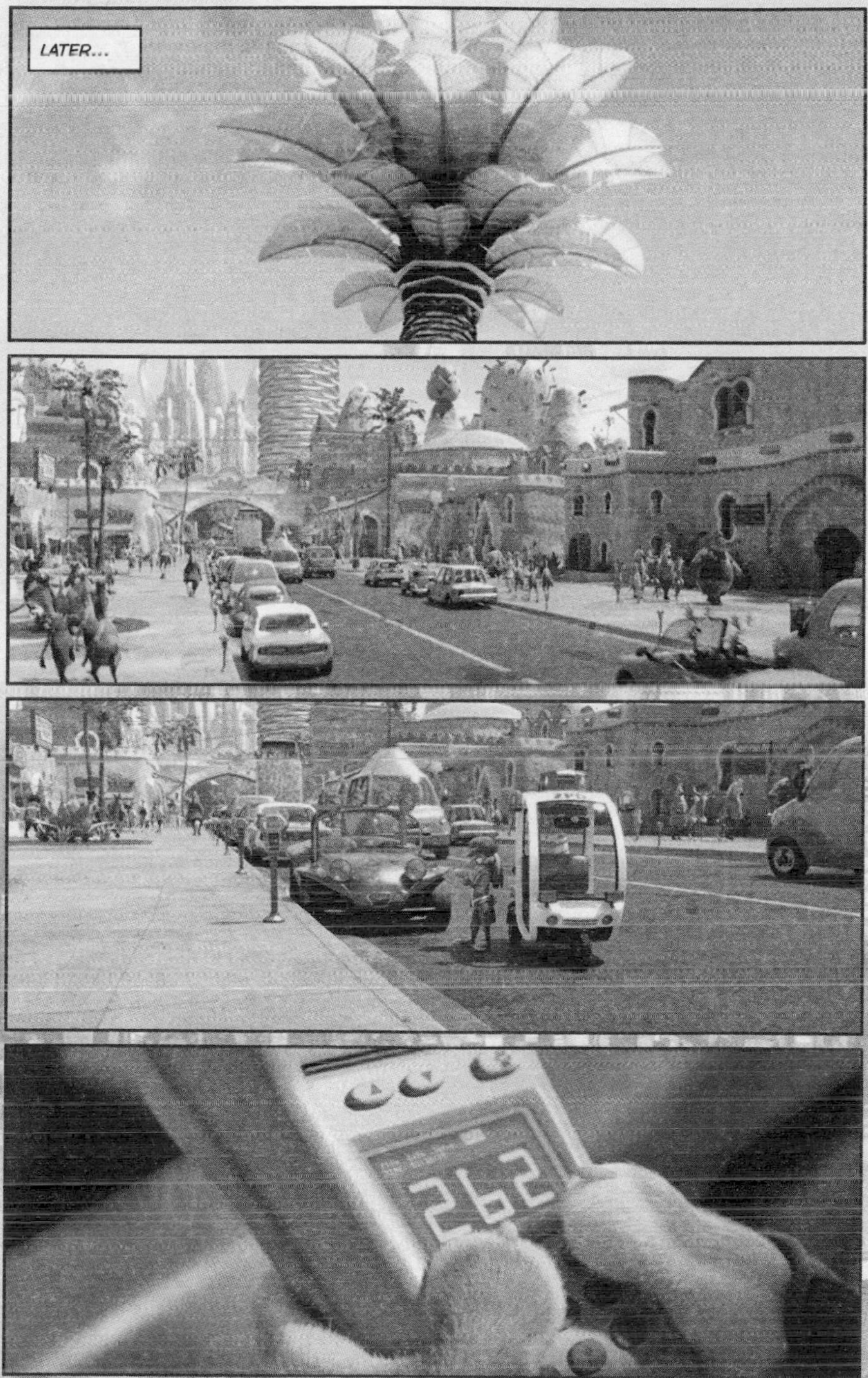
LATER...
262

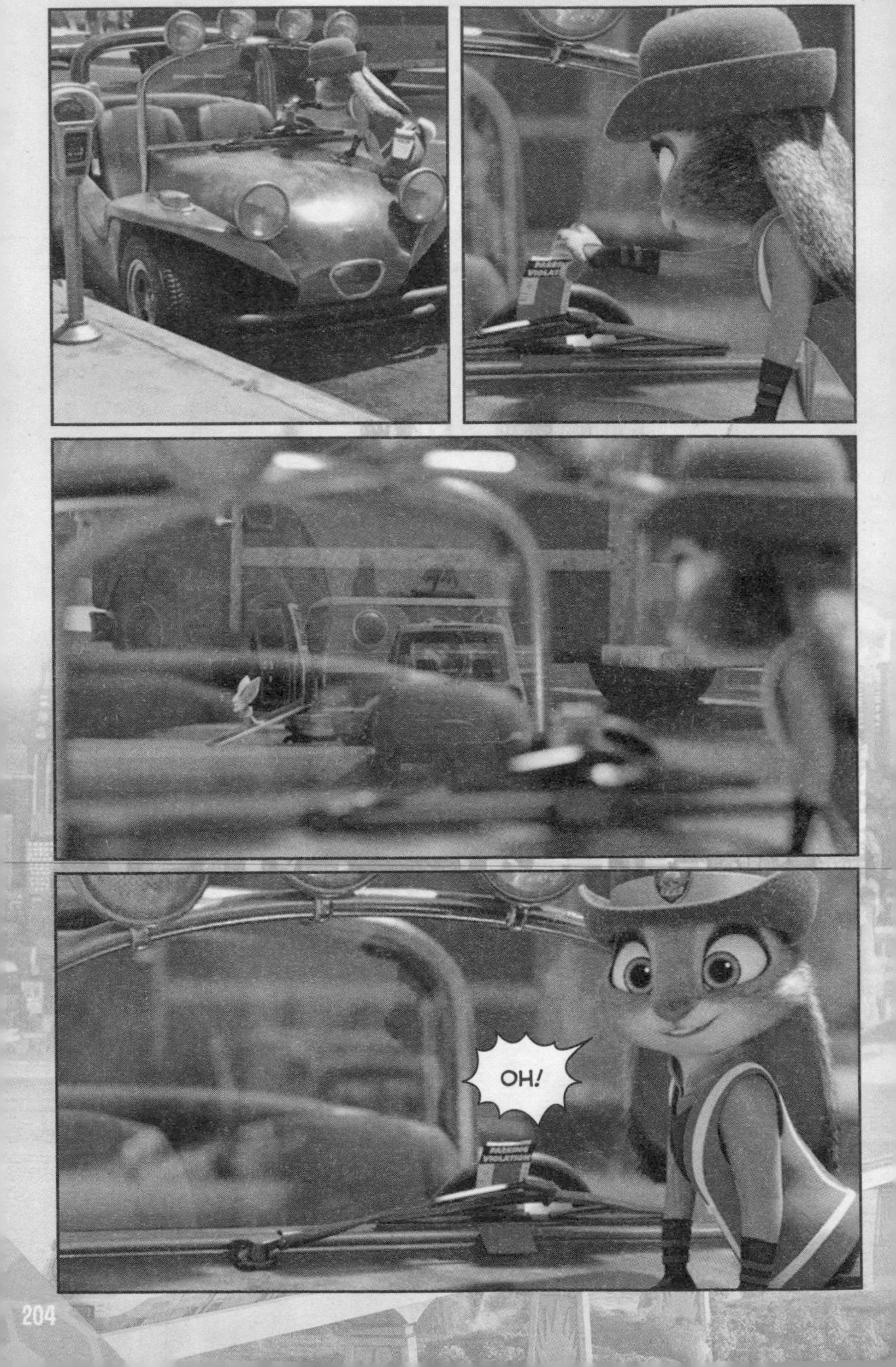
OH!

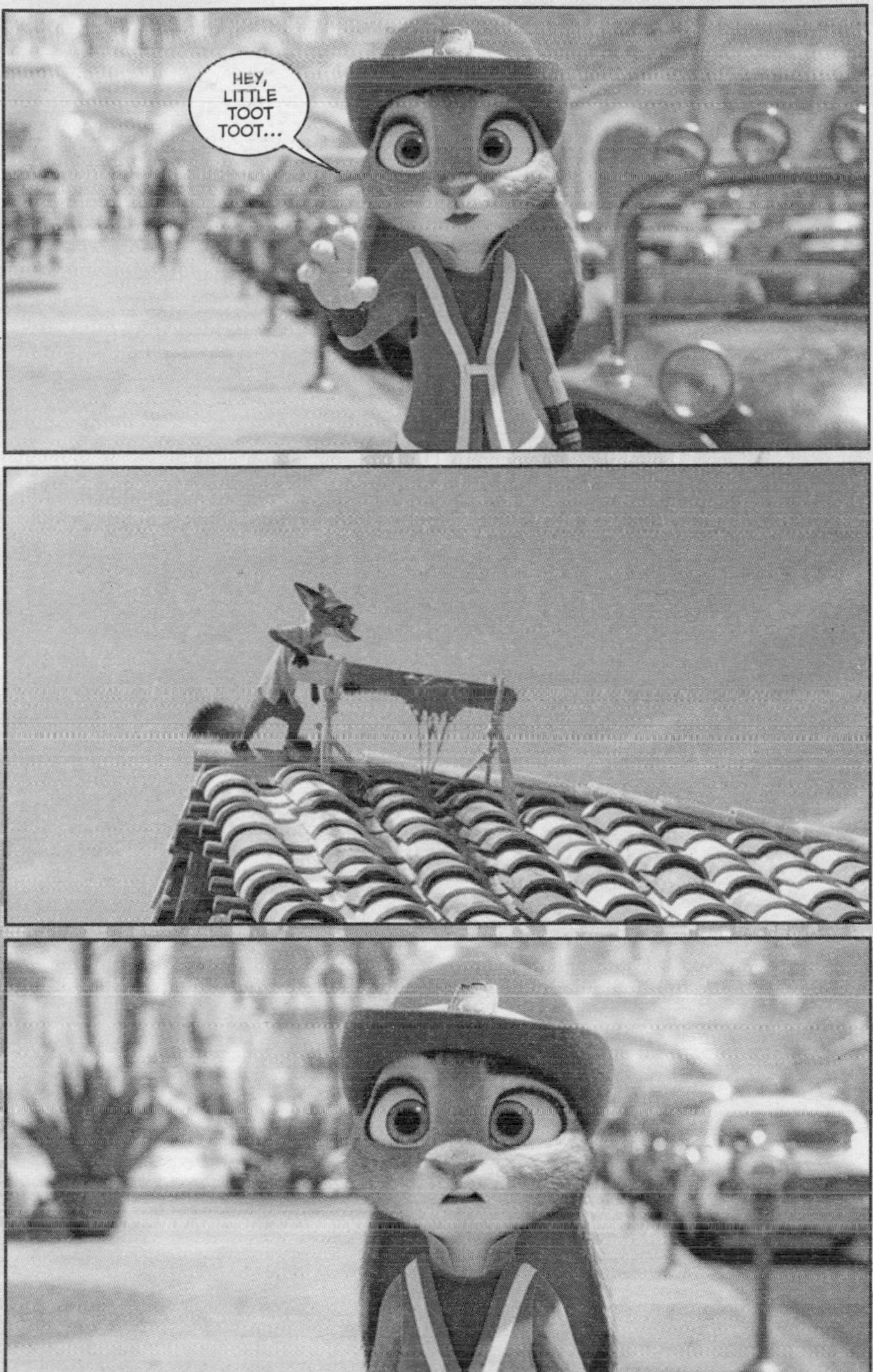
HEY, LITTLE TOOT TOOT...

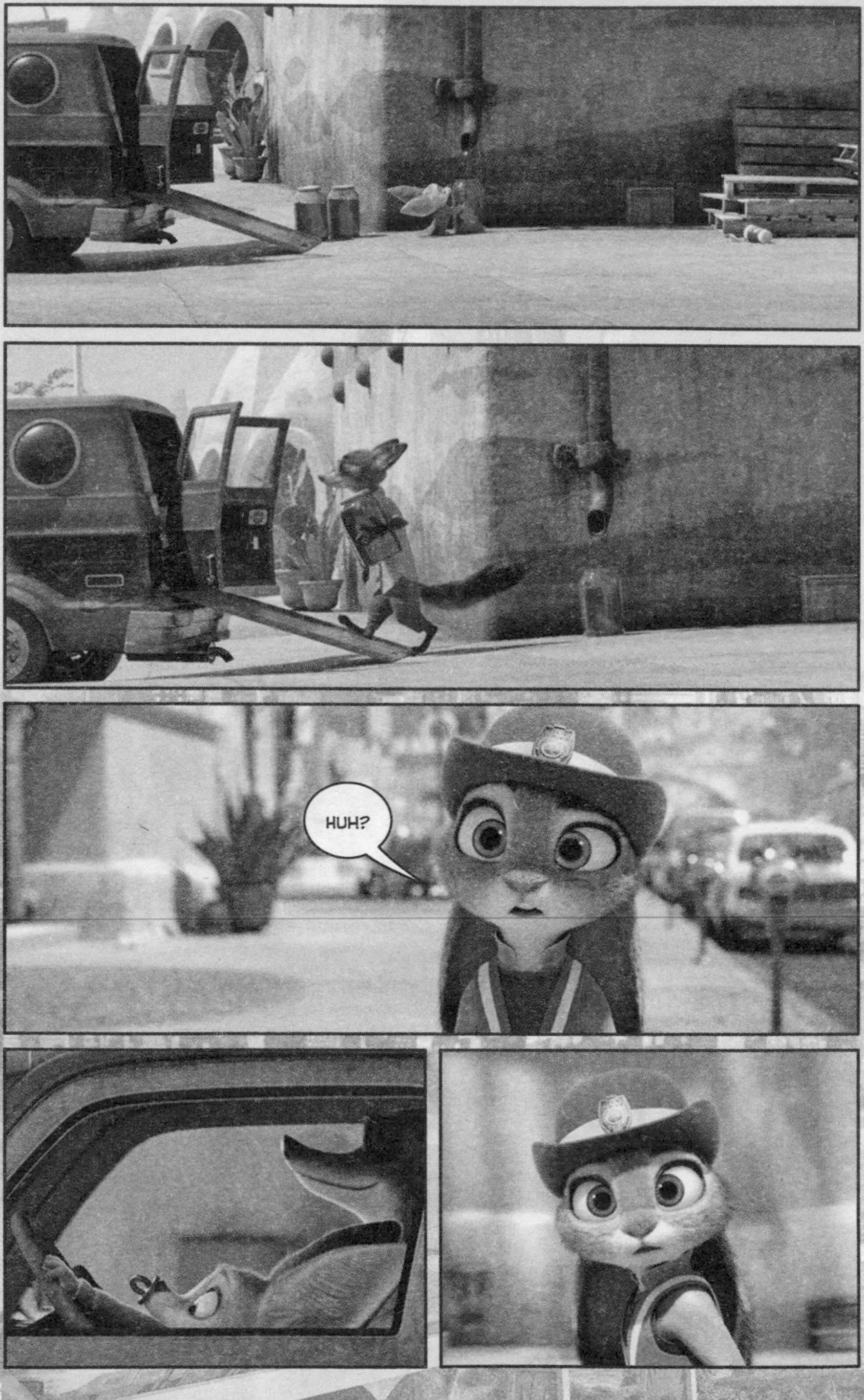
HUH?

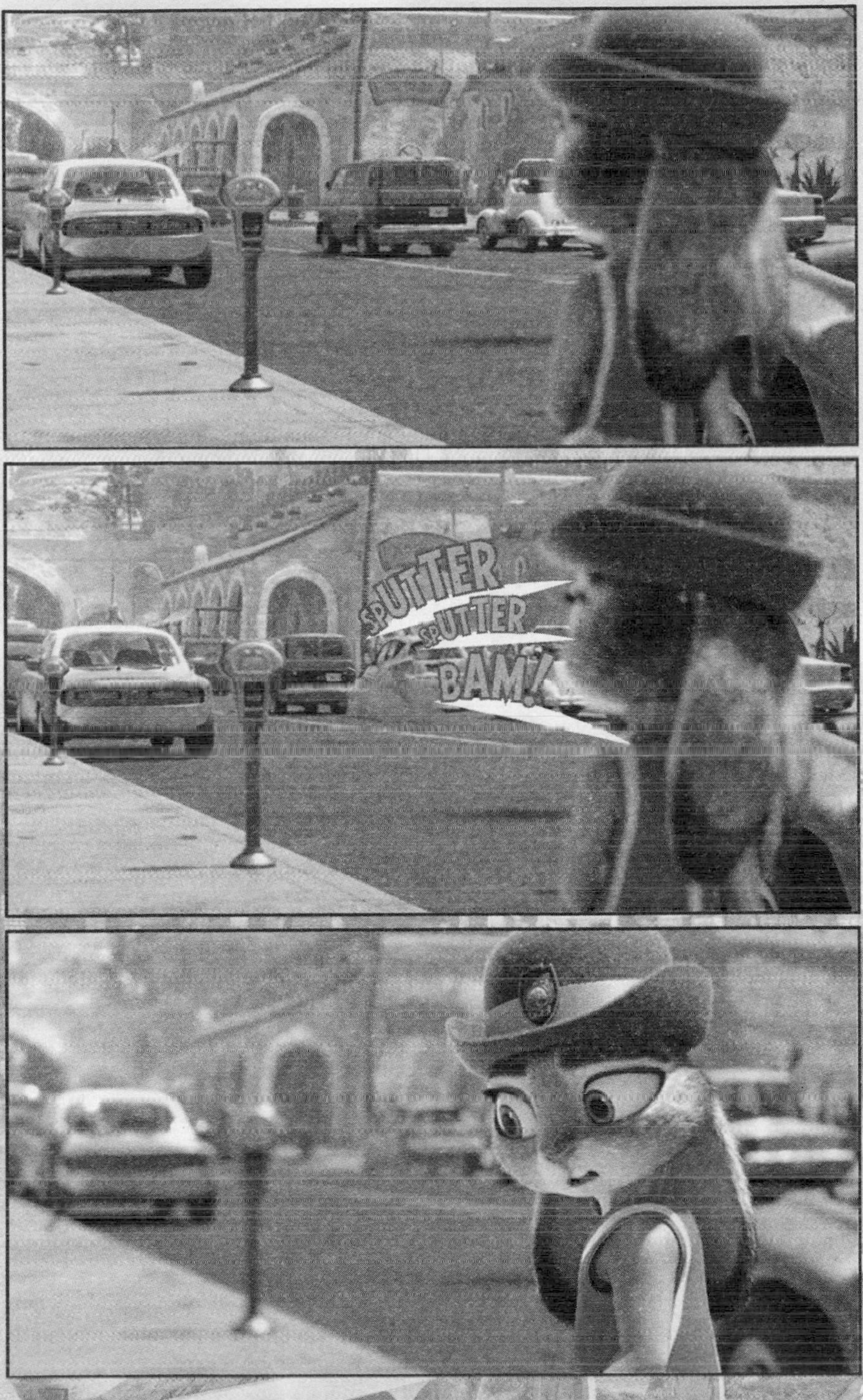
SPUTTER
SPUTTER
BAM!

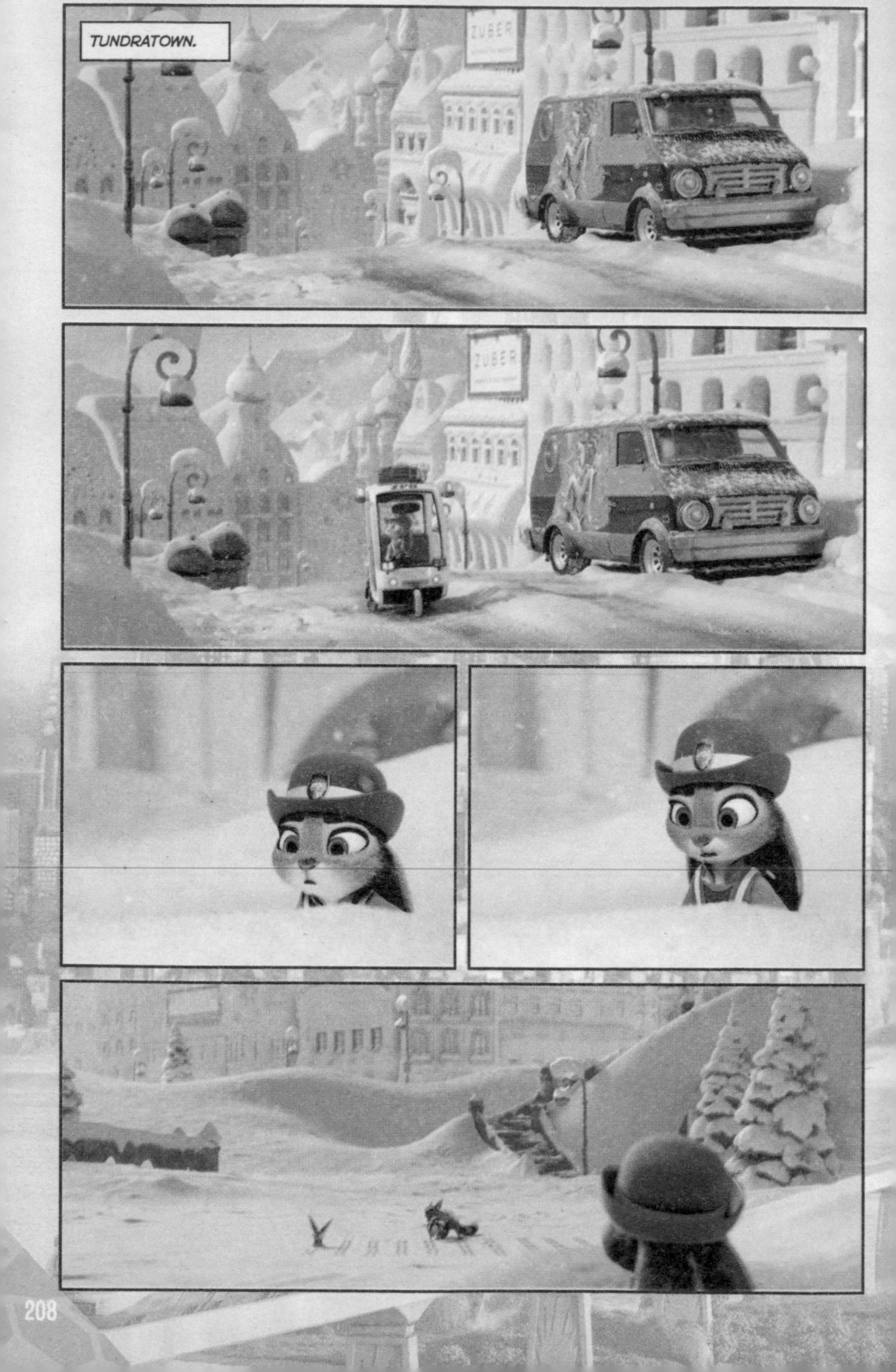
TUNDRATOWN.
ZUBER

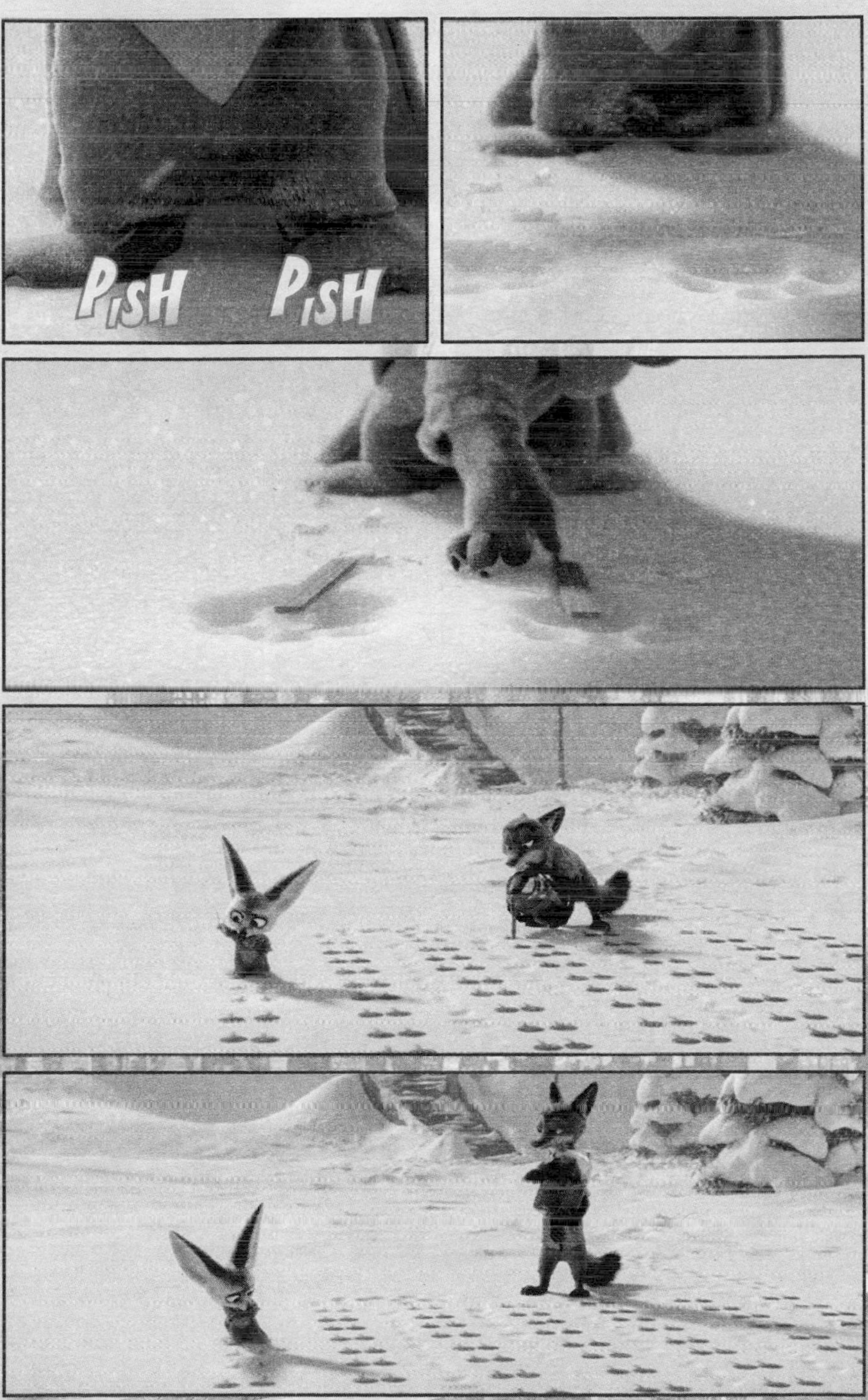
PISH
PISH

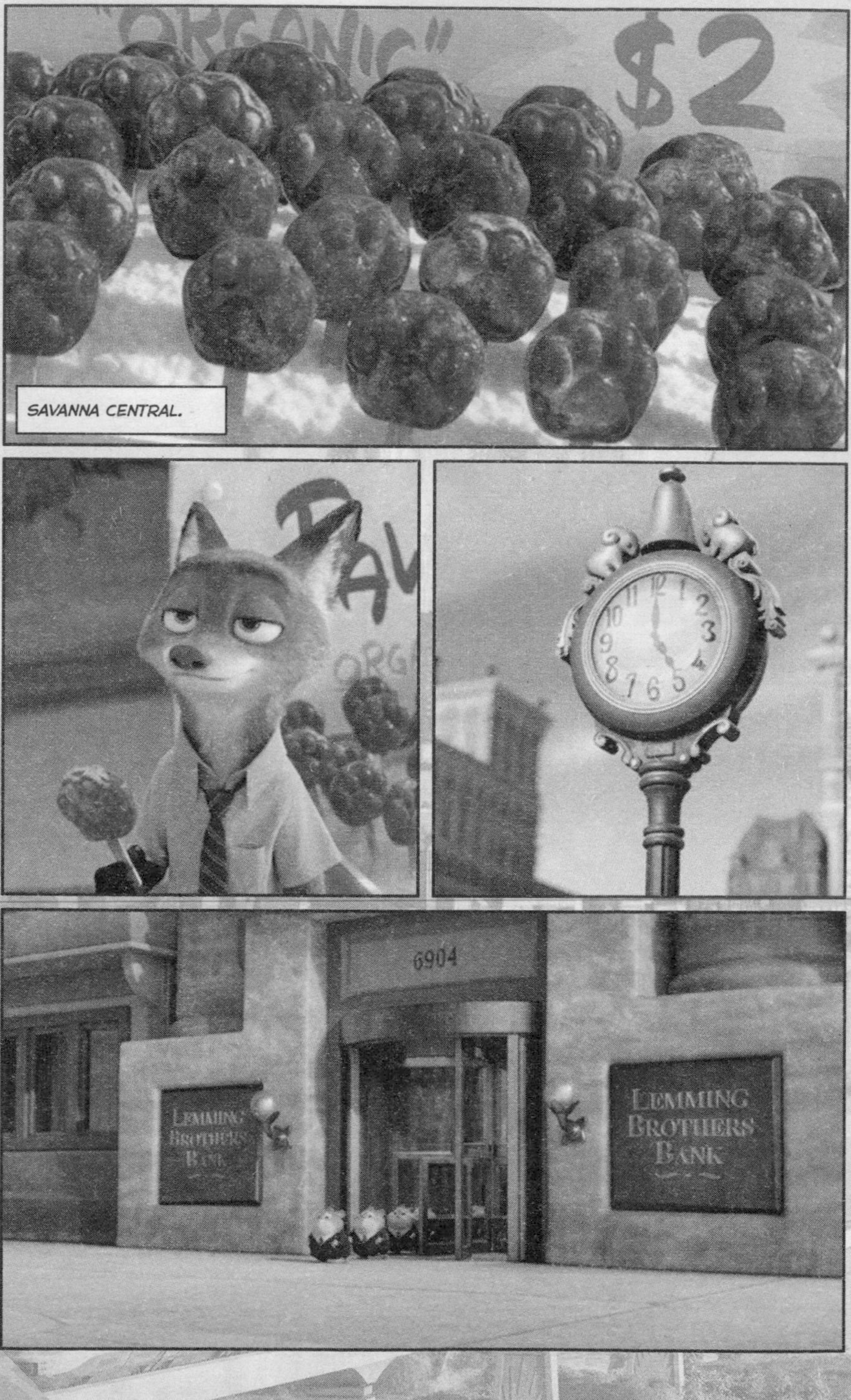
"ORGANIC"
$2
SAVANNA CENTRAL.
6904
LEMMING BROTHERS BANK
LEMMING BROTHERS BANK

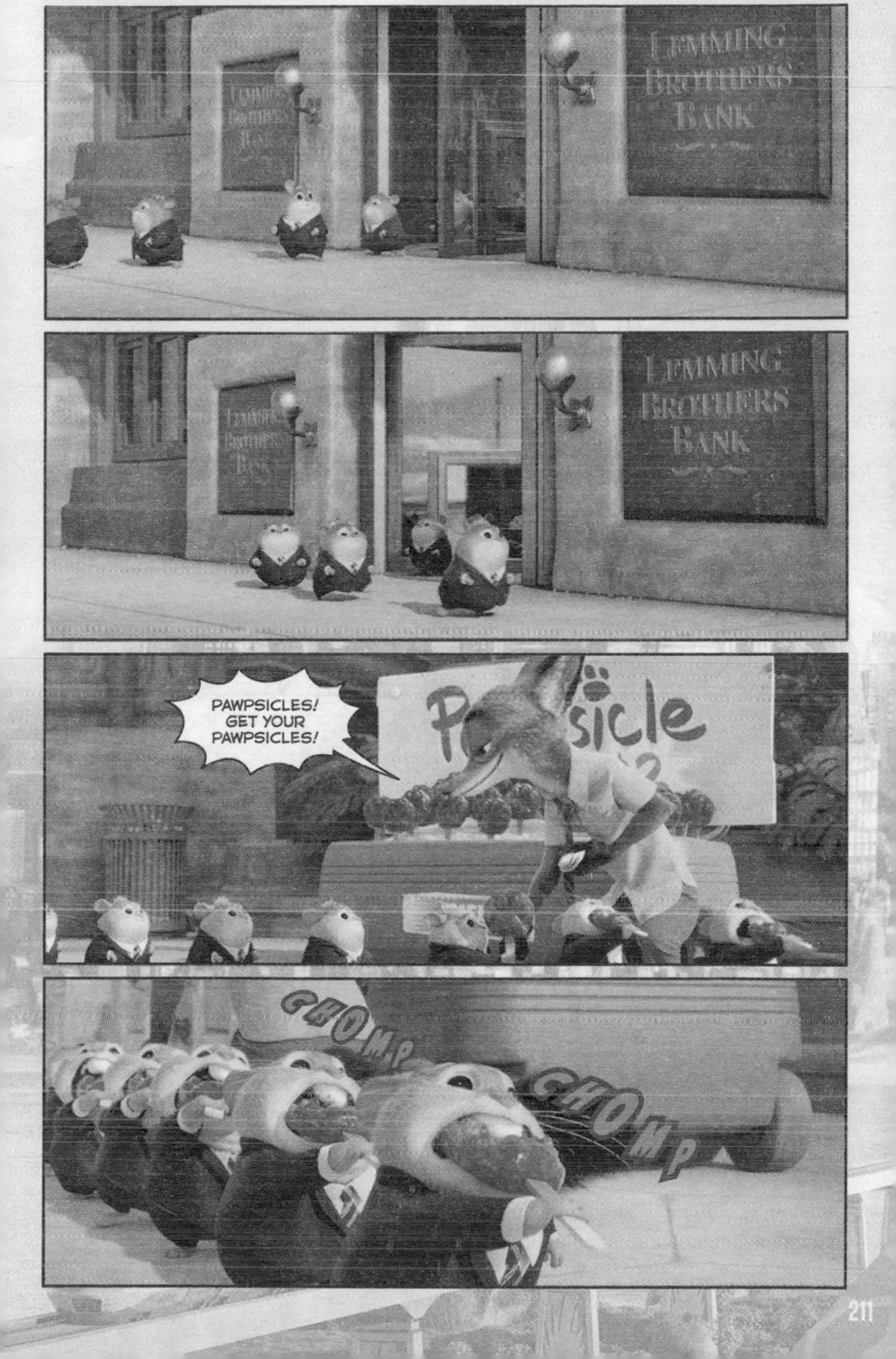
LEMMING BROTHERS BANK
LEMMING BROTHERS BANK
PAWPSICLES! GET YOUR PAWPSICLES!
CHOMP
CHOMP

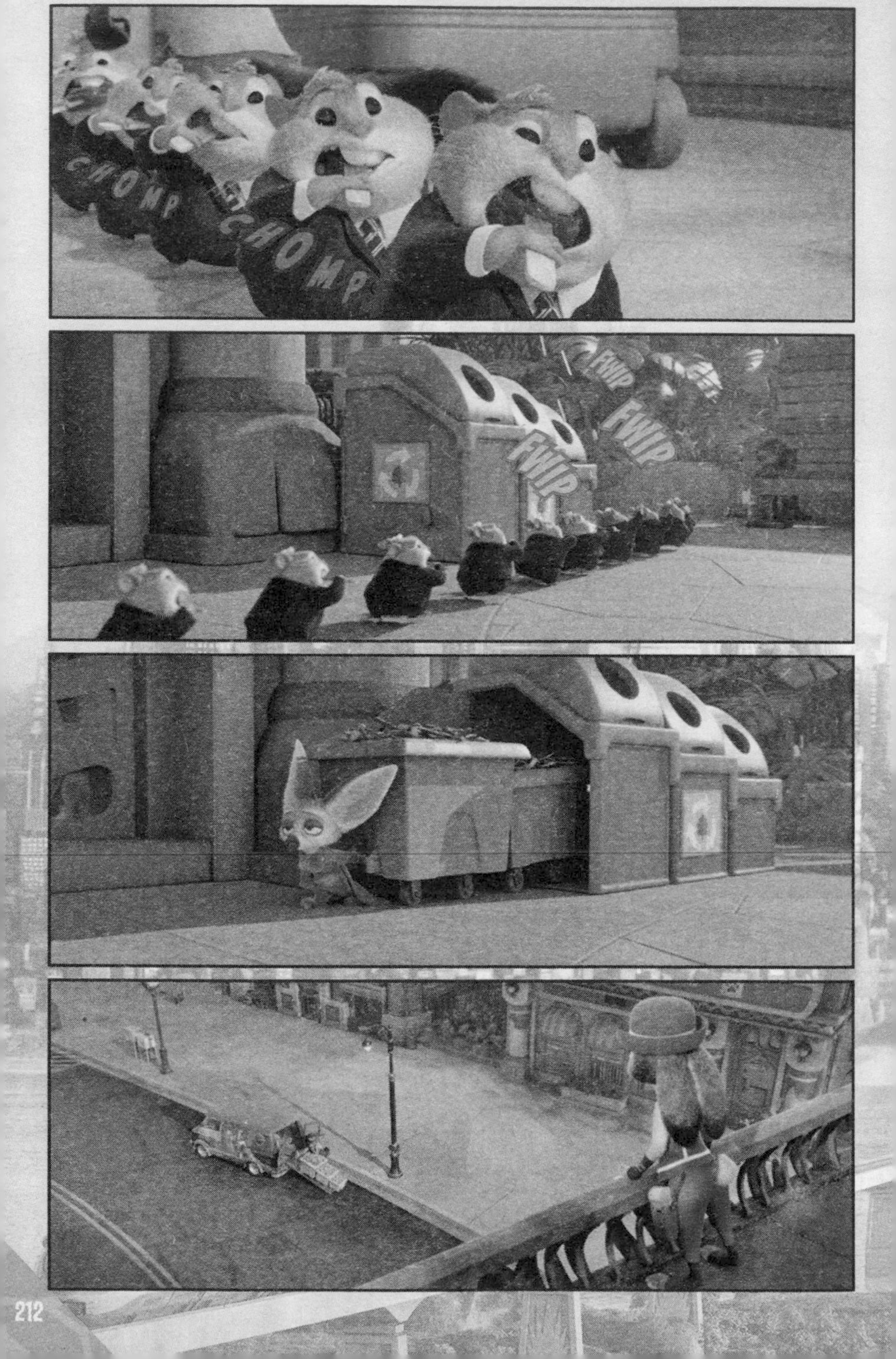
CHOMP
CHOMP
CHOMP
CHOMP
FWIP
FWIP
FWIP
FWIP

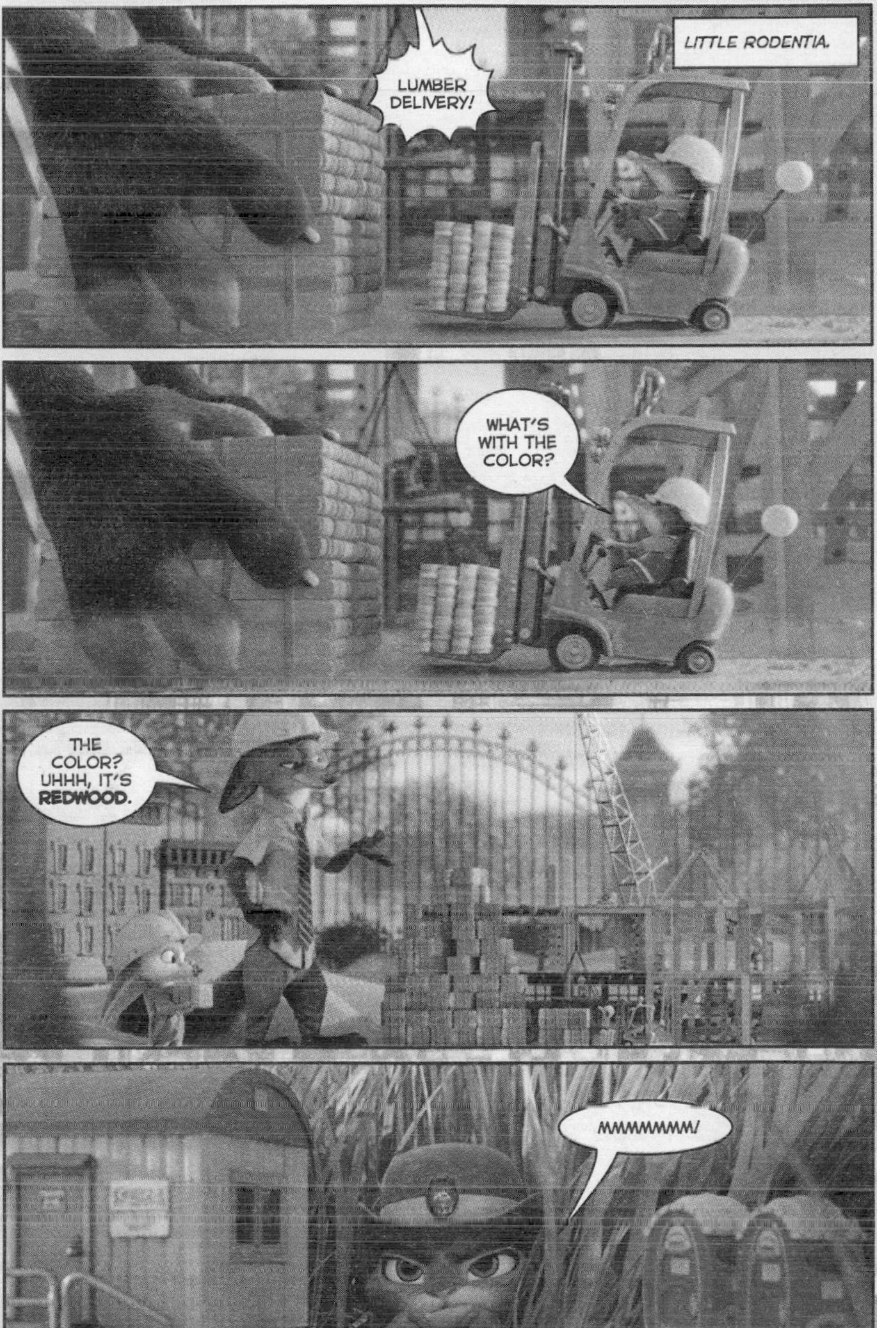

LITTLE RODENTIA.
LUMBER DELIVERY!
WHAT'S WITH THE COLOR?
THE COLOR? UHHH, IT'S REDWOOD.
MMMMMMMM!

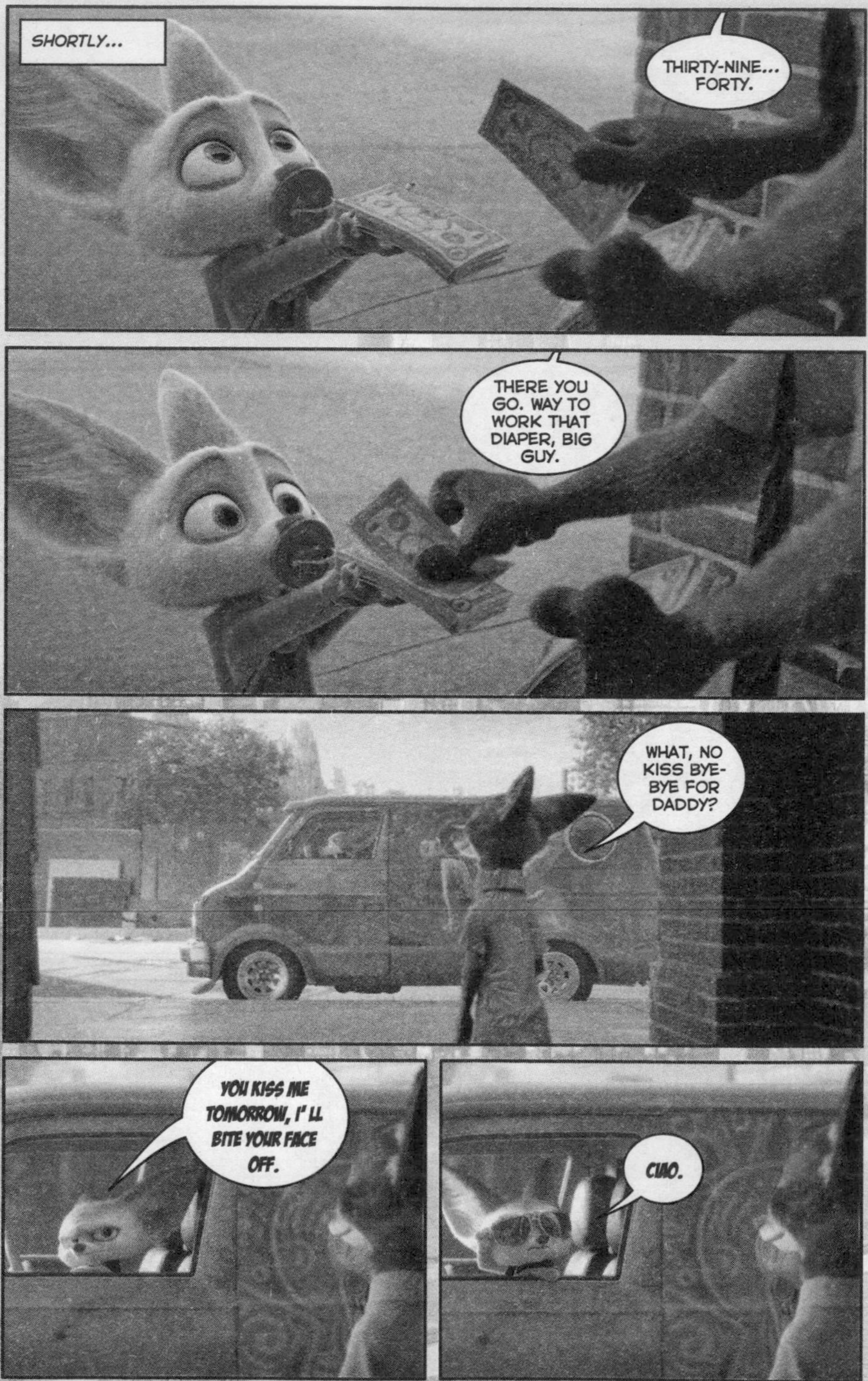
SHORTLY...
THIRTY-NINE... FORTY.
THERE YOU GO. WAY TO WORK THAT DIAPER, BIG GUY.
WHAT, NO KISS BYE-BYE FOR DADDY?
YOU KISS ME TOMORROW, I'LL BITE YOUR FACE OFF.
CIAO.

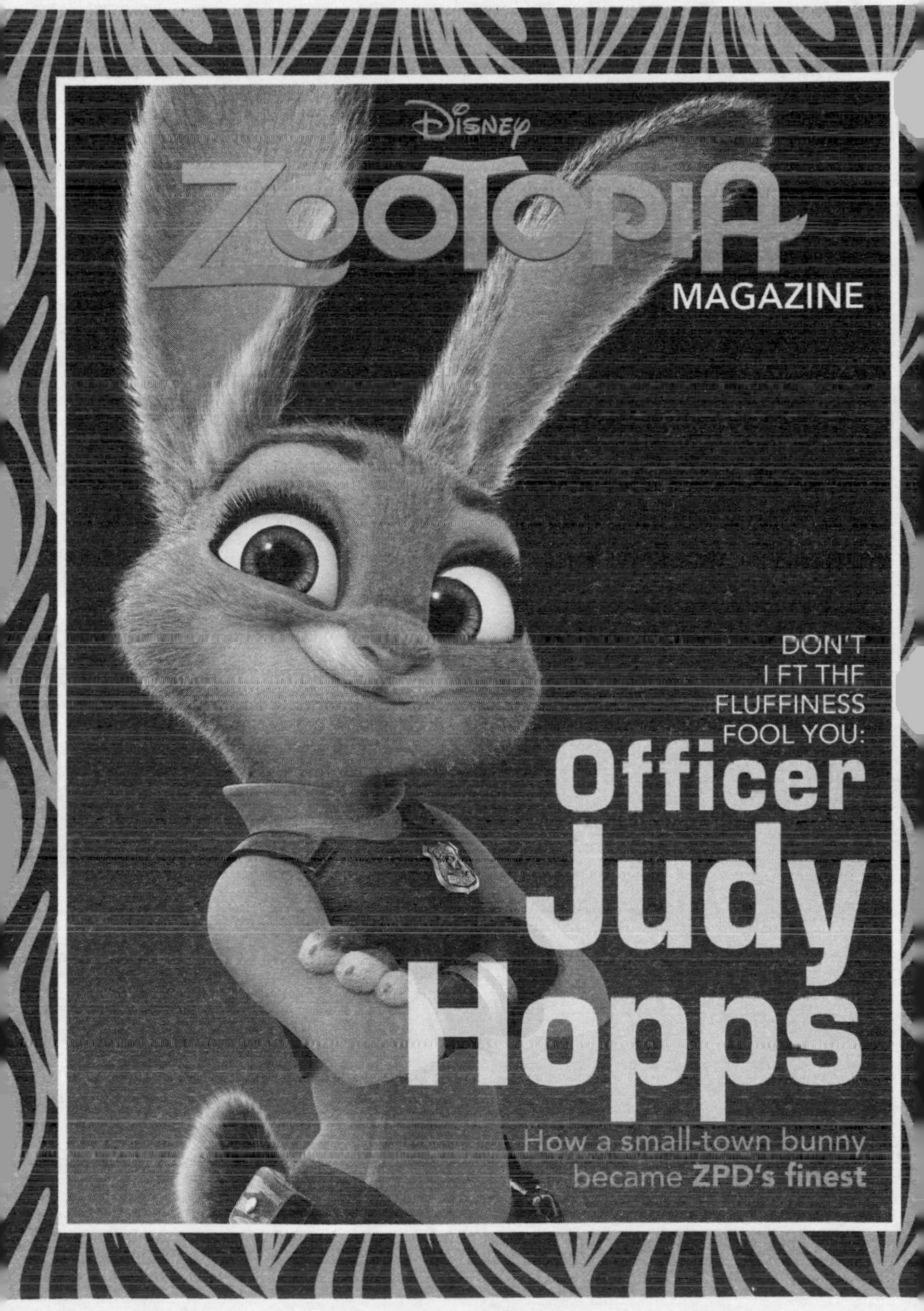
ZOOTOPIA
MAGAZINE
DON'T
LET THE
FLUFFINESS
FOOL YOU:
Officer
Judy
Hopps
How a small-town bunny
became ZPD's finest

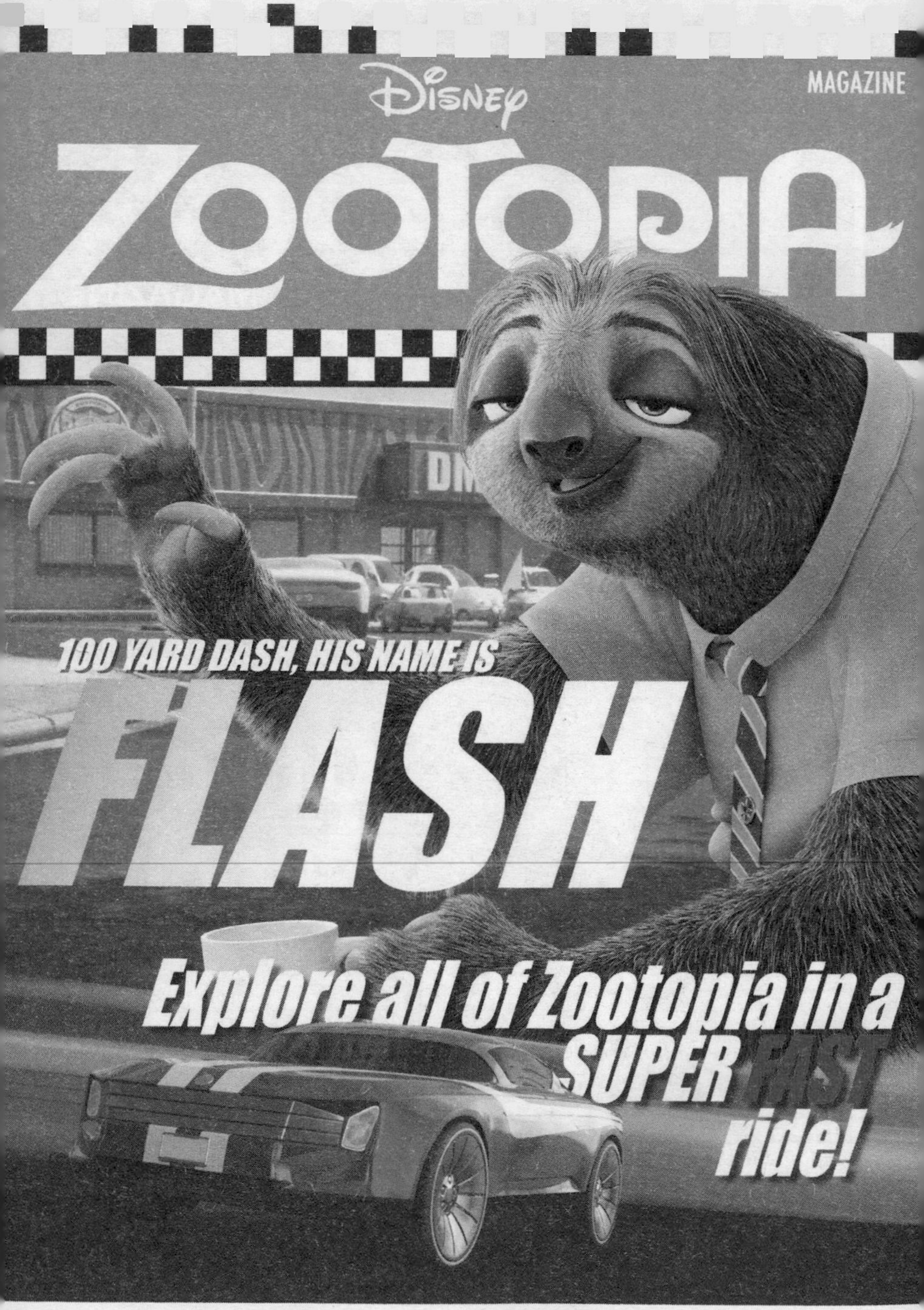
DISNEY
MAGAZINE
ZOOTOPIA
100 YARD DASH, HIS NAME IS
FLASH
Explore all of Zootopia in a
SUPER FAST
ride!